Secret Spaces of Childhood

"The Woods in Autumn," *The Changing Year,* 1884

Secret Spaces of Childhood

ELIZABETH GOODENOUGH, EDITOR

The University of Michigan Press   Ann Arbor

Copyright © by the University of Michigan 2003
All rights reserved
Published in the United States of America by
The University of Michigan Press
Manufactured in the United States of America
♾ Printed on acid-free paper

2012   2011 2010   2009   5   4   3   2

A CIP catalog record for this book is available from the British Library.

Library of Congress Cataloging-in-Publication Data applied for

ISBN 0-472-09845-4 (cloth)
ISBN 0-472-06845-8 (paper)

ISBN 978-0-472-09845-3 (cloth)
ISBN 978-0-472-06845-6 (paper)

Acknowledgments

I began work on this project after moving from Boston to California sixteen years ago. Children's sense of place, this transition made me understand, does not rely on historical monuments. Gertrude Stein said she found "no there there" in Oakland, California, but shortly after moving to the West Coast I learned about bodily place-making. From a warm tub, my son Jamie, then three, announced nakedly, "I like California." Later he affirmed this preference for the state before a hot mound of mashed potatoes. My curiosity about how children shape their worlds recurred in my personal and professional life when Roger Hart, professor of environmental psychology at CUNY, gave a lecture at Pitzer College in 1990 that inspired me to consider literary works from the vantage point of Edith Cobb's *The Ecology of Imagination in Childhood*.

Since that time creating *Secret Spaces of Childhood* has become a collective effort which has drawn on the talents of many people. I would like to acknowledge my students and colleagues at the Residential College, especially Carolyn Balducci, David Burkam, Larry Cressman, Fred Peters, Cindy Sowers, Tom Weisskopf, and Sheila Wilder, who lent their insight, artistry, and encouragement. I am also indebted to the following individuals who provided critical assistance at various stages: Susan Ager, Barbara Bach, Leslie Becker, Kathleen Canning, Brian Carter, Nels Christensen, Liz Elling, Susan Glass, Fred Goodman, Deborah Greene, Robert Grese, Mark Heberle, David Hill, Anne Percy Knott, Lois R. Kuznets, Esther Lamb, Rebecca McGowan, Marianetta Porter, Katherine Rines, Sue Roe, Inger Schultz, David Scobey, Mark Stranahan, and Sandy Wiener. Doris Knight, *MQR* administrative assistant, offered hard work and good cheer. John Woodford lent time and space in *Michigan Today* to consider a proposal for children's studies.

I'm enormously grateful to the community partners that enabled this project to grow outside the university: Child Care Network, Conservation Committee of the Garden Club of Michigan, DD Wood Productions, DTE Energy Detroit BLOOMFEST, Edsel & Eleanor Ford House, Emerson School, the Greening of Detroit, and the Young Actors Guild of Ann Arbor. Gifts in kind came from Delancey Design, Foto I, and Nicola's Books and Little Professor. I also want to thank artists who contributed exhibits in Grosse Pointe Shores and Detroit: Tina Gram, Pamela J. Guenzel, Dan Hoffman, Helen Homer, Balthazar Korab, Duncan Laurie, Gary Rieveschl, and Mary Brecht Stephenson.

Earlier research on this topic was enabled by faculty grants from Claremont McKenna College and its Gould Center for the Humanities, and the University of Michigan's Center for Research on Learning and Teaching. The 1998 University of Michigan Residential College exhibition and symposium, designed in collaboration with Nichols Arboretum, the International Institute, the School of Education, and the College of Architecture and Urban Planning, was funded by the Arts of Citizenship, the Barbara Isenberg Fund, the Center for European Studies, the Dean of the College of Literature, Science, and the Arts, the Elling Family, the Institute for the Humanities, the Office of the Vice President for Research, and the Undergraduate Research Opportunity Program. Publication and layout of the color portfolio was made possible by the generosity of Brett Ashley and Kathy Krick, as well as Nancy Cantor, Provost, and Glenna Schweitzer, Director, Office of Budget and Planning.

For the opportunity to develop this project into a documentary for public television, I owe much to filmmakers Katherine Weider, Christopher M. Cook, and Mark Jonathan Harris and to Jay Nelson of Michigan Public Media. Interim President B. Joseph White provided critical funding for the first phase of this initiative.

I am especially grateful to Lester Monts, Senior Vice Provost for Academic Affairs, who provided a subvention to support the publication of this volume. LeAnn Fields, acquisitions editor at University of Michigan Press, provided guidance and enthusiasm. Finally I wish to thank Larry Goldstein for his editorial expertise and belief in this project. He enabled there to be a double issue of the *Michigan Quarterly Review* on Secret Spaces of Childhood and encouraged me at every step. This book is dedicated to my husband, Gil Leaf, who has given me unstinting support, stories to tell, and reassurance that all will be well.

Contents

From *The Life of Charlotte Brontë* by Mrs. Gaskell
J. M. Dent & Sons, 1971

Introduction

Well I wot that heaven and earth and all that is made is great and large, fair and good, yet all that is made is a little thing, the size of a hazel nut, held in the palm of my hand.
Julian of Norwich, *Revelations of Divine Love*, 1373

Where, after all, do universal human rights begin? In small places, close to home—so close and so small that they cannot be seen on any maps of the world.
Eleanor Roosevelt, address to the United Nations, 1958

I was lolling with my six-year-old son Will on a small beach near a rented house at Pocono Lake. Silent woods surrounded us, and we were alone this afternoon, without toys, electronic devices, or other children around to occupy us. I poked some ferns into the sand and formed a little circle of towering fronds, then carpeted the fern palace with emerald moss. Will and I hunted for strips of bark to construct a roof; balancing rough pieces unevenly, we formed an entrance at one corner, making a kind of square-roofed woodcutter's cottage. To this we added a loose teepee made from sapling branches woven together and then fashioned an adobe hut with a smooth dome formed with wet hands over a fist-sized interior. When it collapsed, we used latticed twigs to prop up the round dark space from within. It was an immensely satisfying afternoon for us both.

Later that afternoon I was alone, rocking in a chair on our screened porch. Forest and ferns encircled the cottage, and conifers rose above the wooden eaves. While I gazed at the lofty space above, something strange occurred. Suddenly my senses of large and small, inner and outer merged, and I experienced myself both magically recessed on the porch and yet transported to the dark interior of our tiny fern palace by the lake.

Driving away from the cottage at the end of that vacation, Will and I wondered aloud if any vestige of our structures

1

would survive the winter. When we returned the next summer, we could find nothing in the sand. But as if a door had fallen open that day, I began to ponder questions about the mystery of these secret spaces of childhood and how they linger in the memory long after time and tide have caused them seemingly to vanish. I wanted as an adult to be able to access the world of a child in play, to reenter that secret space in an attempt to answer some of the questions.

When adults read fairy tales, where do they see themselves? In dying or neglectful parents, cruel stepmothers, and feckless fathers? Or in canny orphans bound for the woods and trials that will transform them into glittering selves? Following breadcrumbs or the possibilities of fiction often means keeping grown-up eyes shut. The microscopic lettering of Charlotte Brontë's juvenilia kept her secrets safe. At thirteen, she invented an empire, what child psychologists call a paracosm, with a distinctive language, history, and geography. Over fifteen months in a remote Yorkshire parsonage, her massive output—twenty-two volumes, sixty to one hundred pages each—is magnified by the minute scale of her act of primal imagination. Possessing secret space—in a locked diary or cardboard fort—requires stealth and ingenuity. "Given a cardboard box of the right dimensions, a child will always try to climb inside," says Olivier Marc in *Psychology of the House.* Yet there are times when everyone needs a box retreat—to crawl out the other side or to live out of the box forever after.

Why do babies play peekaboo? Or children hang by their knees and capture insects in small, cupped hands? Reframing the universe teases their brains to claim their true dimensions. Schools exhort pupils to seek, but children know the importance of hiding out, of finding the "just for me" place where they can't be seen. Without a corner to build a world apart, they can't plant what Diane Ackerman calls "the small crop of self." Without freedom to play, they can't be King of the Castle or shout "I win!" because no one found them. Without time to incubate, they can't find their niche. Secret spaces may be found inside, outdoors, or in the middle of nowhere—in a tree fort, snow igloo, or beneath the stairs. But seeking getaways, like Crusoe's bower or the bridge to Terabithia, is essential to putting things together for themselves and becoming who they are.

The various and universal quest to construct secret space is considered by Edward O. Wilson a "fundamental trait of human nature" of "ultimate value to survival." Although architects, city planners, sociologists, and urban historians research adult behaviors in public and private spaces, much less is known about how children explore the outdoors, make imaginary friends, or find havens from violence. What causes them to gravitate to certain locales in quest of comfort, excitement, self-awareness, or beauty and avoid other areas? Conceptions of childhood past, present, and future have been organized around such issues as innocence and deviance, safety and abuse, contemporary kinderculture or the "disappearance" of childhood. But understanding how collective experience, animism, or a child's sense of injustice yields empowerment or liberation, in what D. W. Winnicott calls "transitional spaces," is a far more complex endeavor.

The diverse contributors to this volume build on child-development research on cognitive, linguistic, and spatial skills. But because physical, psychological, cultural, and social processes combine elusively in the volatile domain of play, this collection also enhances our understanding of the enchanted language of interiority, as it is experienced from place to place. Although many writers take us to rather far-flung places—whether it's a squatter camp in South Africa or a Victorian dollhouse museum in Los Angeles, cyberspace or the open road—the lure of secret spaces finds its first fulfillment in the local, somewhere within or just outside the safe matrix of home. Locating a place under the bed, the bedcovers, or the dining-room table is the primal discovery of self-ish space, a site detached from the ongoing, intimate relation with siblings, parents, or other adults. However humble the container, this site endures in memory as a receptacle of the growing imagination, which needs to feel protected as it expands within safe boundaries.

Just as the secret of childhood lives "in nobody's story," as Nancy Willard's poem suggests, the range of responses in this anthology underscores the fact that childhood is everybody's kingdom, regardless of nationality, religion, age, gender, race, class, or sexual orientation. Whether they look to the past, inside themselves, or closely at actual children, all the contributors gesture toward a fleeting domain expressive of emotional paths trodden throughout life. Although the hearts and minds gathered here approach the same topic from entirely different directions—some standing on the outside, clarifying and surveying complex issues; some from the inside, probing and inventing intricate metaphors—all the voices speak of an unseen site from which every attempt to make sense of the world derives. Together they demonstrate that children aren't the only ones who need secret spaces. Humans of all ages must reenter this gnomic, elusive ground if they want to nurture real children or escape role and rote existence for the voyage of self-discovery.

The six parts of this volume show that, however humble, our first getaways and solo vantage points live on in memory and imagination. The vignettes, poetry, fiction, essays, and visual art collected here urge us to preserve sanctuaries for free play and to consider issues of environmental justice. How societies use land and create spaces for children—day-care centers, schools, theme parks, video games—determines how the next generation will see reality. Those who design software for kids or play areas at fast-food restaurants replicate some mental picture of users' joy. Yet in our highly programmed, commercial world, downtime and away space are elusive. Children need the space and time every day to do nothing, so that who they are can grow. Riddle poems ask "Who am I?" Before they can reply in language, the young must take possession of a circle where they are at the center. Then, when a song steals into being, the smell of sweet fern is savored, or a doll's bed is built, a ritual of desire commences, and life gets propelled forward like a canoe.

When this place of discovery is outdoors, Americans like to imagine that kids still find that the best things in life are free: sand, air, trees, animals, water. Too many of our assumptions about childhood reflect romantic ideas of the past, not the white noise of today's advertising and mass media, which assault children with labels and "lifestyles." Fewer than 2 percent of this nation now grow up in the country. The highrise housing projects of the 1950s offered playscapes of asphalt, metal jungle gyms, and concrete towers. Today the relentless destruction of vegetation and the malling of recreational spaces indicate how little adults sincerely care about children's contact with living things or the social isolation of the very poor. Land use attracts public interest and debate. Yet architects, real-estate developers, and city planners remain half-blind to the ways the young relate to their physical surroundings in less structured settings. Rarely do they consider the needs of low-caste children or of those for whom home is not safe. Assumptions made often run counter to the actual needs of kids growing up on a scary street, without a backyard, bike path, congregation, or community barbecue. Researchers have found that in the last twenty years, the "average home range" for American suburban children has shriveled from a radius of one mile to as little as 550 yards. As vicarious pursuits, virtual pets, and synthetic playgrounds take over, should we worry that a world where children have minimal engagement with plants and animals might be threatening to nature itself?

As our sense of endangered survival on this shrinking planet becomes acute, children are our last frontier. They represent 20 percent of our population, but 100 percent of our future. Carl Jung wrote that "the child is on the one hand delivered helpless into the power of terrible enemies and in continual danger of extinction while on the other he possesses powers far exceeding those of ordinary humanity." To the degree that we can envision children as triumphant go-betweens or heroic survivors, they shelter the imagination and sustain the hope of adults. Childhood is thus both a chronological stage and a mental construct, an existential fact and a locus of desire, a mythical country continually mapped by adults in search of their own subjectivity in another time and place.

Since I conceived this project in 1997, much has happened to make secret spaces of childhood an urgent and timely subject. Inner cities have become increasingly rundown and poor, while the ever-expanding ring of suburbs has resulted in more isolated homes, schools, and businesses. One-third of children are now overweight. Cuts in public funding and welfare, called by journalist Mickey Kaus the "umbilical cord through which the mainstream society sustains the isolated ghetto society," have altered lives. Scientists, surprised by the rate of growth in the brain tissue of infants and toddlers, have found evidence of new cells developing later in life, where memories are first formed. In this era of global terrorism, busy adults can't be blind to emotional wiring, bottled-up rage, and scarring events that sink the self. While fifteen children in the United States are killed daily by firearms, juvenile violence jarringly refracts the lesson learned early that, as Brad Davis puts it in these pages, "to kill well is to win big."

Historians on the Learning Channel voted a diary written from the Secret Annex one of the "One Hundred Most Important Achievements of the Twentieth Century." Because it "personalized the Holocaust," the handwritten narrative of a thirteen-year-old girl is itemized on a list that includes the discovery of antibiotics, the exploration of space, and women's rights. Zlata Filipovic, "Bosnia's Anne Frank," on the cover of *Newsweek* (February 28, 1994), alerts us, as does Karein K. Goertz in this volume, of the enduring influence of this hidden writer whose construction of a moral vision gives shape to the problematic face of hope.

Although Anglo-American notions of childhood are still linked to secret gardens and fresh-air funds, the Kaiser Family Foundation's Kids & Media @ the New Millennium reports that children constitute the fastest-growing consumer market in the United States and "influence half a *trillion* dollars in consumer spending a year." Children's museums and after-school programs and child-centered narratives, animations, and film classics attract audiences around the world. As games once played outside increasingly move indoors, on-screen, into commercial and corporate realms, schools are built without playgrounds and with recess cut from the curriculum. Only one-third of children are bused to school; 10 percent walk or ride their bicycle, and the rest are driven. Because other families, "stranger danger," and our own yards are perceived as more menacing, children in the United States have less privacy and freedom of movement, yet paradoxically more unrestricted access to adult media.

"Childhood is not another country," writes anthropologist Pamela Reynolds, adding that "relationships between adults and children are entwined and children are participants in the social, economic, political and moral conditions of the moment. . . . [B]ecause children move through childhood, its constituents alter: the passage can seem swift and can be foreshortened, for example, through poverty, loss, exploitation or war." Bonded labor enslaves millions of young children who have never seen the inside of a classroom. As childhood is perceived as increasingly threatened and polluted, or as "stolen" by adults, vagrant minors around the world search for hide-aways, and street children from Cairo and Bogota to Seoul are seen but not heard. Anthropologist Sharon Stephens points out how easily "at risk" and "out of place" children—at work, in war zones and refugee camps, in prisons and the media—become problematic "risky children" who need to be "eliminated . . . controlled, reshaped, and harnessed" in a rapidly changing global order.

In the academy, research and new books scrutinize the changing face of childhood. Undergraduates focus on the "vast excluded" by connecting dots among courses in anthropology, history, sociology, public policy, and law, while scholars in diverse fields explore the complex web of representations that constitute social constructions of childhood. Symposia focus on children in armed conflict, genetic engineering, juvenile justice, the medicalization of childhood, and the relation between "kinderculture" and youth subcultures. Brooklyn College and Harvard University have framed a nontraditional field that "looks at children as an entire class." Divisions and special sessions—on children's authors, children's studies, children's cinema, autoecologies, neuroscience, and cognitive psychology—proliferate at Modern Language Association conventions. Multidisciplinary units at Michigan State and the University of Florida, rare-book archives at Princeton and UCLA, child- and family-serving institutes like Merrill Palmer and the Skillman Center at Wayne State University, and faculty seminars like that convened by Pamela Reynolds on "Contested Childhoods" at the University of Michigan's International Institute look for fresh ways to integrate research, outreach, and policy engagement. Scholars of children's literature, after decades of being marginalized within departments, library programs, and schools of education, now see their journals and books approached with waves of sudden interest. Mitzi Myers and U. C. Knoepflmacher, whose memoir is included here, coined the term *cross-writing* in 1997 to reconceptualize children's literary studies, calling attention to the "colloquy between past and present selves" in "texts too often read as univocal."

This term heralds the eclectic, even eccentric forms risked here in the symposium, poetry, portfolio and review essay, essays, memoir, and fiction. Where stories take root and childhood shuts down provides a critical crossover for Adrienne Kertzer, who navigates from "kiddibookland" to a review of *Life Is Beautiful* and the works of Anita Lobel. Interrogating the relevance of secret space to a Johannesburg squatter camp, Louise Chawla uses artwork from Canaansland to show that children's freedom to create places of their own presumes the luxury of "a safe center to move out from." Out of Africa, where the small stand with swollen bellies and die en masse, comes Wole Soyinka's poem "The Children of This Land." The manifestos of radical feminist playwright Carolyn Gage, Broadway lyricist Nan Knighton, and poet Thylias Moss prove how one can scavenge a self from environments of terror. A recent spate of childhood memoirs by literary scholars like Edward Said and Jane Tompkins is joined here by the work of Wayne Booth, Jerry Herron, Joyce Carol Oates, Tobin Siebers, and Marina Warner, who dramatize the genius of beginners' eyes and language learners to spill the beans.

The French word *enfant,* and its Latin cognate *infans,* define the essential nature of childhood as unspeaking. Adults assume inevitable author-ity in rendering the literary speech or consciousness of children. But what is the language of a child? And why, if children so rarely have become authors, have fiction writers over the last two hundred years chosen to include their speech and secret escapes—from Huck Finn's raft to Denver's boxwood retreat in *Beloved*? Exploring how language serves humans between the ages of one and eight, Susan Engel opens a window between these related questions. By making sense of the narratives children tell, she illuminates a largely unregarded area where the young cultivate a hedge between inner and outer, both in language and in space. The stories children tell demonstrate that "the line between secret inner stories and shared public stories is a moveable one." Holding back information or dressing up fiction as fact, editing or covering up the unruly, young vocalists rehearse, first inaudibly with themselves, then aloud with others, the lifelong process of negotiating boundaries between what is real inside themselves and the world outside.

The improbable stories of the very young also suggest what motivates children to seek secret spaces. By assembling words—much like balancing twigs or arranging "loose parts" for a little house—they perform an engrossing fictive process that brings inner and outer spheres into synchrony. The semi-transparent curtains of their narratives function like the moveable boundaries, permeable walls, and guarded entries featured in the Residential College Art Gallery's exhibition of remembered hideouts. As Margaret Price recalls, controlling access is critical, for it allows children to show off or share private spaces on their own terms. Insisting on the logic of an area that is "all for me," children script what they look for and become. Like narratives that put a structure onto life, getting into this "child-sized cave" made everything right, "like the shape and redness of an apple, where we belonged like the tiny hard seeds at the core." In the practice of such hand-shaping and story-making, children hone the two survival skills of their species.

Nourishing these small heroics of being human also sustains vital energy in maturity. But as we age, it gets harder to see what lies close by. Although Ellen Wilt built a tent-cave in her Pittsburgh apartment living room, and Gerald McDermott's stairway is familiar to the public at the Detroit Institute of Arts, to the child's-eye view these domains are far from ordinary. Rather, these clandestine observation points function like outposts that offer adventure in the wilds. Many adults overlook the intense significance that secretive dens hold for the fragile unfolding of the child, though artists and writers remain attuned to the need for secluding the symbolism of their inner lives. They still enjoy harmonizing things in smaller, manageable worlds of their own. Like children they find a taproot to the imagination close to home, in the secret spaces of childhood. The images, stories, and poems they create from this ever-replenishing source serve as vast ecosystems, which in turn nourish others to see how individuals grow, expand, and fit themselves into—or sometimes rend—the fabric of society. Stories then go on to multiply, spawn variations, and recombine in new versions that sustain the psychic life of cultures. But no time-lapse study can explore the process by which humans extend their neurology outside themselves and over generations. Stories are secreted slowly, shrouded in the past. In each person they spring from a hidden life that exists well beyond words. And adults are often loath to listen to the nascent narratives of actual children.

Even clinicians like Robert Coles, Kathleen Coulborn Faller, and Susan Engel, who systematically probe their secrets and record their speech, convey the inscrutability of children, so prescient are their revelations.

Though children, like poets, might be called professors of the five senses, their research is silent and invisible. The complex and ambiguous nature of early existence must be reconstructed by others, through memory and from distant points of exile. Coleridge laments in *Biographia Literaria* that growing up is like being dipped in Lethe, the river of Oblivion. Adults can never reclaim the intimate spaces of their first instincts and impressions. Before an "I" emerges, eyes open once upon a given time and place. Tasting, watching, bonding with symbols and songs of myself, infants invest their energies and orient themselves according to what Lore Segal calls "the secret of our ur-geographies." To recover this time when "six months is half a lifetime," Diane Ackerman underwent hypnosis, revisiting the blond varnish of a crib known "like a birthmark." By such personal images, rhythms, and objective correlatives, artists seek to regain a primal connection to their "lost kingdoms." The "Door," in Julie Jordan Hanson's poem, remains ajar each day, though largely ignored. Something as simple as "a tiny line of mouse droppings" can magically open a path to underground history.

Literary sleights of hand that retrieve the past enhance scientific research, which provides little evidence of how the young actually process their own ecology. The secret growth of imaginative powers—called Intercourse by Wordsworth, Moments of Being by Virginia Woolf, Union and Communion by Molly McQuade—is a cosmic force defying definition. Interchange between self and world is both temporal and timeless, a nonlinear accretion like rings in a tree or snow covering the ground. Once children express themselves by the system of verbal signs belonging to the adult world, the isolate integrity of infancy has been shattered. Learning to read and write may be a solitary pleasure, as in Cathy Song's "Book of Hours" when "sky poured in." But to "selve" a beginning—to use Hopkins's verb—is an immense act of specialization. Human offspring need years of nurturing outside the womb, and their psychic survival demands a view of their situation in life. As Tom Pohrt shows, a nest found in natural surroundings provides some evidence and suggests "the satisfaction of becoming more concentrated" on oneself. Birds carry twigs to weave snug hollows, just as authors scan the universe and children scavenge a beach. Finding a talisman or muse enables human consciousness to crystallize sensations, to fuse inner energies into images, which shelter identity and generate "arpeggios."

The social construction of a voice, the discovery of a way to be "Me," thus requires a complex bridging such as words and objects perform, locating a middle ground of experimentation and expression. In this protean spot a personal aesthetic forms. Molly McQuade, in the eerie lines of "Mouse History," recalls a "wild mildness of the skin" at ten, quickened by pulling on a cardigan. Or geography may be absorbed uneventfully, like slivers in flesh. "The pier had a way of working its way inside of you," April Newlin recalls of being eight. Waiting for crabs to bite, building narratives in three dimensions, boys and girls graft old on new, search for what's hidden in plain sight, and like Ann Savageau are intent on "Making Something Out of Nothing."

Sometimes to reconjure the fleeting process of becoming requires inner dialogue: Laurence Goldstein's "Let's say" enacts fantasies from "A Room in California, 1954." Sometimes others are warned to keep their distance, as diaries fend off intruders—"PRIVAT (sic) KEEP OUT!" in Joan W. Blos's essay. But in liminal spaces between past and present—rereading a first journal like Wayne Booth, watching children draw like Paul Karlstrom—adults can envision new pictures of themselves or balance in unfamiliar territories. We routinely underestimate the secret powers of childhood. Ilan Stavans, formulating an urban pastoral of boyhood amid factory ruins in Copilco, sketched "unreachable plants" from the backseat of an abandoned bus. Secret spaces born of boredom, explosive anger, sibling rivalry, or sexual dream can also spawn rich countercultures like those depicted by Karen Heuler and Catherine Ryan Hyde.

The powerful meanings that children embody in any culture have distinct histories. Just as the rebel crusade against Myanmar's military led by twelve-year-old twin "holy warriors" is rooted in the superstitions, fused religions, and mystic traditions of Southeast Asia, the valuation of childhood as a precious preserve of creative storytelling, utopian dreams, and erotic longing developed over centuries in Anglo-American discourse. The separate domain children inhabit was called Innocence by William Blake, the first picture-book poet and artist. He mapped a pastoral world of reckless imagination where children with nurses nearby play joyously into the dusk. But he also illuminated a dark compressed space of psychic violation where children of the underclass comply with an establishment that alienates and exploits them. For industrialized England the bodies of street urchins and offspring of the poor conveniently fit into mine shafts and chimneys. Idyllic retreats in children's literature emerged as legislation restricted child labor in factories and enforced education in schools. Victorian pantomime, with its passion for cross-dressing, forbidden mutation, and little actors, encouraged a prudish culture to clap the femme fatale Tinker Bell back to life. In juvenile texts one could laugh at oversized girls fallen into rabbit holes and perform metafictional games with boys transgressing Arcadia.

Fantasy inspires hideaways, whether an imaginary otherworld like Oz or the so-called "ordinary" neighborhood of Pooh Corner. The place may be literary or psychic, local or exotic, but every children's book provides a lens to a world apart. Yet artists, even those who aim to entertain children, have not always produced hospitable environments for the developing play of the bodies and minds closest to them. Peter Llewellyn Davies, "the real Peter Pan," as he loathed being called, suffered shell shock at the Battle of the Somme. Throughout middle age, until he committed suicide, Davies was haunted by James Barrie's "terrible masterpiece." And Christopher Milne's two autobiographies indicate how deeply he resented the mass production of his Christopher Robin persona.

In our more brazen culture of lost-boy gangs and Lolitas in Calvin Klein jeans, the links between neverland and wasteland, romantic ideals of childhood and modernist despair, rise in retrospect. The green worlds of juvenile pastorals may be dying after two centuries, but the black-and-white photographs of Sally Mann's own children make us consider the complex ways in which childhood radically mutates through history and can be contested in single generations. For example, after 1830 in the United States the Calvinist notion of infant damnation was discarded and gentler discipline was advocated in child-rearing manuals, now addressed to mothers. Ralph Waldo Emerson quoted a "witty physician" who lamented that "it was a misfortune to have been born when children were nothing and to live until men were nothing."

The gender bias in negotiating one's own space is exemplified by the Rossetti siblings: Dante Gabriel founded the Pre-Raphaelite Brotherhood and painted voluptuous beauties with bee-stung lips. Christina, excluded from the Brotherhood, modeled for these artists yet lived like an Anglo-Catholic nun, working with fallen women at St. Mary Magdalene Home. Her poetry proclaims that her secrets saved her. The seductive nursery lyric "Goblin Market" warns the sisterhood of toxic passion fruit hawked by goblin men. Such secret fairylore invented for and about "little people," from the adult fairy tales of George MacDonald to the flagrant cross-writings of Oscar Wilde, endures as tales of transformation in mainstream churches, gender politics, and New Age therapies. The sentimental, voyeuristic lens of Lewis Carroll remains popular because it focused the absurdity and monstrousness of grown-ups. As U. C. Knoepflmacher's *Ventures into Childland* points out, carnal dreamworlds for those presumed innocent expressed the flirtations, fear, anger, and craving of male and female Victorians with uncensored originality.

In 1886 J. E. Millais's "Bubbles" tapped the potential of round little bodies to sell products from Pears Soap to Coppertone, while his "Cherry Ripe" suggests the bizarre weight that prepubescence still carries in our culture as enigmatic eye candy, exemplars of trauma, or victims of what Marina Warner calls "the Oxfam syndrome," which makes the oppression of children "look like endemic perennial hopelessness." The power of photographic images to take us back and forth in time, not always to comfortable spaces, problematizes the supposed objectivity of viewers. Inviting us to ponder the disconcerting work of Sally Mann, James Christen Steward opens a window on the interplay between children and adults in the act of composing images "as art directors do." He expresses the view of many critics that Mann's children arouse attention as potential objects of desire (even as the mother artist hotly denies the erotic in her children). That these images elicit jolting responses, not confined to the Christian right, sparks ongoing debates regarding childhood and sexuality.

How will childhood be contested in the future? Children's books provide clues to unforgettable landscapes and ways the young relate to the physical world. Citing the lack of theoretical frameworks to address this issue, Louise Chawla remarks: "Our society has not been structured to admit that nature may provide more than material necessities. . . . What does it mean to say that a place is felt to be alive? What happens when a natural habitat is loved?" Laura Ingalls Wilder said that she framed her autobiography as juvenile literature because she found her own early life as a pioneer "much richer and more interesting than that of children" in the 1930s, "even with all the modern inventions and improvements." Like Tarbeach and the Secret Garden, the Little House icon, identified by Lois Kuznets as "a focal point for developmental gender issues within Anglo-European patriarchal society," reflects the empathy children have for their surroundings. It validates George Eliot's claim that "we could never have loved the earth so well if we had had no childhood in it."

Children's books, an impossible luxury for many parents, provide essential havens for kids growing up in the middle class. Their presence in the home is considered by educators to be a critical index of future academic success and upward mobility for boys and girls of any race and ethnic background. These literary constructs help forge the self, apart from adults, and as filmmaker Mark Harris indicates, can camouflage inchoate alienation and foster survivalist resistance for children hiding from mass murder. Narrative tradition makes clear that establishing such private worlds is a prerequisite for carving out a place in community or lighting out for the territory.

Ritualistic spaces in narratives, like handmade refuges, also tell us much about the power relations between children and adults. Faller's six-year-old Anna uses the Sunshine Family to closet and disclose the source of her venereal disease. The private parts and psyches of long-silenced children—the very spaces they inhabit—are invaded by people they trust. The violation of their open minds and bodies has a profound but unwritten effect on the next generation. The majority of teen mothers have experienced rape or other sexual abuse.

Through TV, comic books, graffiti, and word-of-mouth slogans, young people hunger for a social universe that allows for happy endings. In a global village where the fierce devour the small, what role awaits those now shunted aside without adequate prenatal or nutritional care, housing or family support? The 1996 budget of the Children's Defense Fund, the leading national lobby for children, was $15 million. The American Association of Retired People in the same year spent $449 million. Marian Wright Edelman cites "a new American apartheid between rich and poor, white and black, old and young" that Detroit would seem to epitomize: 37 percent of children live in poverty, the highest youth-poverty rate for any city in the nation; 40 percent of these households are headed by single women; 18 percent subsist in homes that report income 50 percent beneath the poverty level; 68 percent of those born in Detroit in 1999 had unwed parents.

Organizations like International Childwatch and the Convention on the Rights of the Child (an internatonal treaty signed by all countries in the United Nations except Somalia and the United States) testify to the worldwide attention that child-centered issues and stories have captured in recent years. Yet our society has failed to address the suffering of impoverished children in a holistic manner or to embrace a nuanced understanding of what "impoverished" means in the complex ecology of growing up today. Finding a safe space for reconstructions of childhood—imaginatively, institutionally, and internationally—in legal as well as academic and poetic discourse has motivated this project. In the spirit of the playground, where—as Vivian Paley's book proclaims, *You Can't Say You Can't Play*—this volume has evolved as an experimental endeavor drawing on a wide range of talented people and diverse disciplines—from social work, anthropology, sociology, and history to education, economics, architecture, and urban planning; from pediatrics, human development, and literature to fine arts and religion. These writers provide theoretical and autobiographical reflections, case studies and cultural analyses, that hold a mirror up to us, the people who form a child's human and material environment.

Breaking expectations, children trespass to get closer to something inside themselves. Or they settle slowly on some unexpected border. Robin C. Moore wonders what is going on when a small child fondles the fringe of a rug. What happens when a tiny hand pulls a blade of grass from a shadowy lawn? Would that life be different if the rug had no fringe or the lawn were replaced by asphalt? City parks, an alcove by the furnace, or a piece of derelict fabric may provide uncrowded vestibules, secret spaces in unlikely places we need to honor. Before we manicure the grounds of real-estate developments, cut funding for children's art programs, or allow excessive concerns about safety to cheat children of taking all risks, we need to engender our own participatory learning. The writers in these pages help us come alive to how children, who own nothing, possess places. They make us see how up close, low down, at the pith of life, we must tease the imaginations of the young into hoping for their futures as they extend themselves into landscapes of tomorrow.

Symposium

You can make your own miniatures so easily: just use bathtub caulk,
spackle, wheatena sprinkled on clear glue, broom straws, bleached chicken
bones, broken jewelry, film canisters, grape stems, and above all,
the oval caps from underarm deodorant.
Bebe Harrison, addressing the Chappaqua Garden Club, 2000

Glen Michaels, *Birchbark Duplex,* 2002

A SYMPOSIUM ON SECRET SPACES

As part of *Secret Spaces of Childhood*, a letter went out to authors inviting them to contribute a brief commentary to a forum on the general topic. Along with the memoirs, essays, fiction, poetry, graphic artwork, and book reviews, this symposium is intended to help provide an iconography or conceptual map of the regions of childhood. The general commission posed to authors was the following:

> **Please undertake an autobiographical exercise, at least as an opening into the subject, "Secret Spaces of Childhood." Describe a significant private realm of your own early life that has left vivid images in your memory. Feel free to speculate on why this space or place was so meaningful to you, and whether it has resonated in your later life. Feel free, also, to extend your speculations to the subject in general and speak about one or more "secret spaces" that provoke or engage your imagination, from the experience of other children, or from the arts, and why you find these sites so compelling.**

The commission was not meant to be prescriptive, but suggestive, and what follows provides a striking variety of places and behaviors, in a variety of prose styles, all of the commentaries sharing the condition of being intensely memorable vignettes. From them readers can make some conclusions about the situations and spaces that need preserving and extending because of the salutary influence they exert upon the human imagination and the human spirit.

WAYNE BOOTH

A Rhetoric of Fiction
George M. Pullman Professor of English Emeritus, University
of Chicago

I can remember so many secret spaces, starting about age
four, that it's hard to resist doing a whole book on them. When
I was six, my father died suddenly of Addison's disease, and
memory says that life with my mother and my two-year-old
sister was overturned in ways that no written record could reveal. Somehow from then on I led what seems to me now not
just a double but a multiple life:

> —the perpetual weeper teased as a "sissy" by all the non-
> weepers vs. the "man of the family" that my devastated
> mother nagged me to be;
> —the mean, teasing brother and cantankerous son vs. the
> smiling, loving, helpful "young man" whom my grandpar-
> ents observed—most of the time;
> —the thief stealing notebooks and pencils and even an occa-
> sional book vs. the pious Mormon boy heading already to-
> ward not just a spot in Heaven but, as a male rising rank
> by rank in the priesthood, achieving ultimate Godhood of
> another "world."

And so on.

When I turn from memory to my early diaries, begun at age
fourteen, I don't find anything about the weeping sissy or my
mother's nagging or my occasional thievery. Rather I find three
sharply contrasting "Wayne C.'s" (my official name had been
"Clayson" until my father, Wayne C., died). Perhaps most prominent is the would-be hero, the egoist aspiring to be honored as
"at the top," in every direction. He's the one who proudly
records, a year or so later, "Have been accepted for membership
in the Book of the Month Club." Then there is the poverty-dri-
ven pursuer of cash, willing to work hard delivering and selling
newspapers, or working for twenty-five cents an hour on a farm,
proud about being able to save money by gluing rubber soles to
worn-out shoes; his mother takes in less than $100 a month as
an overworked elementary school teacher, and she is always
short of cash (I wonder why the diary never records that he

would occasionally pick her purse). Often overridding these two and all the others, there is the self revealed in frequent expressions of anguished guilt: the would-be saint, a pious, devout Mormon, struggling with an insurmountable awareness of character flaws, including self-reproach about pride and ambition (and implicit awareness of more serious misdeeds).

The most striking—and most secret—moment of conflict among the diverse "Wayne C.'s" is only half-revealed in separate diary entries. The conflict was discovered, accidentally, by only two people: his mother and his newspaper boss. He began delivering newspapers shortly before starting the diary, and he soon found his boss insisting that he sell subscriptions.

For quite a while he failed to sell any subscriptions at all, and he never became very good at it. Yet the diary makes him sound successful from the beginning, and often boasts about increasing sales totals. What he is willing to boast about is amusingly revealed by the following entry, written after selling "extras" on the main street of a town with 3000 inhabitants.

> Aug 16, 1935 – Friday
> Had pancakes for break-
> fast. Mr. Peterson came and
> told me that there were some
> extras coming out because
> of Will Rogers, the movie comed-
> ian and Wiley Post, the air
> pilot being killed. He has
> previously put me in charge
> whenever extras came out and
> he did so this morning. Lucille,
> Myself and six other boys sold
> 83 papers. Mr. Peterson paid
> me $1.00 in subscriptions and
> I earned .37 by selling.

That inept salesman soon got captured by the excitement of sales contests. The egoist wanted to win, to be "honored" as number one, honor being seen as reducible to whatever prize was offered.

The company gave every delivery boy a small cash gift for each subscription sold. Naturally the money-grubber self wanted to earn a lot of money, while the honors-seeker figured out that since the cash gift for each subscription was almost large enough to pay for a full month of deliveries, he could chalk up a fake subscription at very small cost. So his divided selves faced a dilemma: if he entered fake subscriptions, his chance of winning the contest went up fast, while his income went down only a small amount for each subscription. Which was more important, fame or cash income? The egoist won, hands down, and his subscription rate went up and up, finally leading to his winning a contest.

No hint there of any guilt about cheating. A few pages later he boasts that he has been chosen by the bishop (the head of the congregation) to become "the supervisor of one of the Deacon's quorums. I consider this quite an honor." Again there's no hint of any conflict between that pious achievement and what he is doing each month as he records fake subscriptions.

Suddenly the whole episode, with its fame-winning facade, crashes: he contracts Bright's disease and hears a doctor speculate about possible death. He has to turn over his routes and records to the boss, and they reveal a total jumble of dishonest subscriptions and careless juggling of data: a huge cash debt (actually quite small, as I consider it now), and incontrovertible evidence of non-existent subscriptions.

His boss turns out to be a generous man: he waits until the boy is back on his feet and attending school again, after two months at home, before he shocks the mother by revealing his discoveries. He did not turn Wayne C. in to any authorities; all he insisted on was some more work, without pay, until the losses had been paid off.

Does the diary reveal the truth of any of this? Not at all. It talks as if Wayne C. were now simply working a few hours again for his old boss but in a different job. Does it confess to any guilt about it? Not at all. While confessing guilt about masturbating and about being egotistical and about being "too critical" and about "boasting too much," it never acknowledges that the crazy desire to be number one had produced an atrocious hypocrite reveling in being a winner.

earn $44.00 a month.
Usual things done during
day. Tonight floyd Peterson
came down and talked over
the motorcycle problem
with Mother.
—March 6—Went with Alpine
Carrier again. At 3:00 played
tennis with Earl Kelly. Mother
told me I could get a motorcycle. Tonight I got a haircut
and went to the game. It
was with Provo and they beat
36-35. To bed 9:50
—March 7—Saturday
Collected and loafed. Went
with Alpine carrier. Delivered
papers at 4:00 P.M. At 7:00 went
To Grant Hotel where we
had the banquet to close
the contest. I got a special
prize for getting the most
orders and I 7:00 also.

Occasionally the later entries do, like this report, reproach the boy strongly for his ego-driven aspirations. But they seldom reveal openly what memory records: many other moments when the would-be saint conceals his struggle with desire for fame and desire for money.

I'm naturally tempted to conclude by boasting a bit (oh, yes, I still have to deal with such temptations: I hope, for example, that this account will appeal to many readers) by celebrating the boy's grappling with the very theme of this collection: secrecy, and its limits. Aware that he has many faults, and that he has revealed many faults in his diary entries, he wonders about just who should read what. In the middle of his sixteenth year, he concludes his first volume with a twelve-page confessional about his many faults, including the "sinful" fact of having "periodical sexual excretions," some of them by "violent physical agitation producing the flow of liquid." (He apparently does not yet know the word "semen.") Then he says, "I still don't know whether I should write this or not. I wish that I had a more adequate brain to be able to know what to do. . . . I cannot blame this sin on not knowing of its being a sin, because I knew it was so. . . . I have heartily repented and have tried & succeeded to keep from repeating." Which of course could not have been true.

But then, still to my astonishment, he addresses directly—and in a sense honestly—the question of silence. He turns to the frontispiece of what he labels Volume I, and writes the following:

So the sixteen-year old has decided that at least one of his secret spaces should no longer be kept secret—provided readers are at least six months older than he is as he writes!

PAUL BRODEUR

The Stunt Man
Staff writer, *The New Yorker*, 1958–1996

It was the summer of 1942, and our family had made its annual migration from Boston to a rented cottage on Duxbury Beach, some forty miles south of the city. My father came down on weekends; my mother spent her days at the cottage tending my infant sister; and my brother and I, clad in bathing suits that had faded and dwindled into ragged loincloths, roamed freely from morning until night. The beach was a sandbar peninsula seven miles long, with the ocean on one side and Duxbury Bay on the other, and, except for a few summer people like us, who lived in cottages near the mainland, and some Coast Guardsmen out at Gurnet Point, it was uninhabited. A dirt road that ended at the cottage colony and a wooden bridge that rambled across the bay on piles, a mile farther along the peninsula, were the only routes of access. On Saturdays and Sundays picnickers came over the bridge and spread themselves upon the sand, but during the week the beach was deserted.

Like all boys at the seashore, my brother and I were beachcombers. We poached quahogs, collected driftwood, captured minnows trapped in tidal pools, and filled gunny sacks with pop bottles left behind by picnickers. But, above all else, we considered ourselves patriots. We salvaged tinfoil for the war effort from discarded cigarette packages, helped local residents dry sea moss to collect nitrates for munitions makers, and used the pop-bottle refunds to buy Victory stamps at the Post Office.

The war affected us in many ways that summer. There was a strict blackout every night, and when we went outside before bedtime, the unaccustomed darkness and the profound sea made us feel close and vulnerable to the conflict. Wreckage washed ashore from ships sunk by U-boats, and each day we poked through fresh piles of debris, vaguely aware that we were examining the flotsam of catastrophe. The grownups talked incessantly of a submarine that had surfaced off the shore during World War I and lobbed a few shells into the marshland behind the beach. Had the Germans been aiming at the old Cable Station? Would they try again? The speculation of our elders filled us with delicious tension. The tin cans my brother and I were forever tossing into the waves became submarines, and the rocks we threw at them depth charges, and the constant vigil we maintained for flotsam, pop bottles, and marine life took on a new dimension. For now we were patrolling a stretch of the coast—a strategic flank of the republic.

As it happened, our favorite place to play—indeed, our secret position of defense—was an abandoned duck-hunting camp that lay hidden in the dunes several miles beyond the old bridge and almost halfway out to Gurnet Point. The camp was a rambling frame-and-tarpaper affair, upon which time and the elements had wrought a deceptive camouflage. Winds and winter storms had so shifted the dunes that it was nearly buried. Foxtail and beach-plum bushes had taken root in sand covering the rooftop, and only in a hollow on the leeward side was any part of the building visible. Here my brother and I had torn away some rotted boards and fashioned an entrance.

The interior of the camp was cavernous and dank. It consisted of four rooms, three of which were half-filled with sand that had sifted down through cracks in the roof. In the largest room, there were several bunks with mildewed mattresses, a rusted iron stove, some overturned chairs, and a long table. For us, these were the furnishings of a bunker from which we operated against the foe.

A typical day found us lying on the summit of a nearby dune, waiting to ambush enemy saboteurs who were disembarking from their rubber boats. When they came into range, we unleashed a volley of shots at them from toy wooden rifles. Then we retreated to the invisible fastness of our fort and hid until they stumbled, with Teutonic stupidity, into our line of fire, giving us an opportunity to decimate them with additional volleys fired through apertures in the rotting planks. Fierce struggles took place as the last fanatic attackers breached our bastion. It was hand-to-hand for more than an hour, as we backed slowly into a corner, each forefinger a revolver that barked incessantly, firing at Nazis who were climbing through holes in the roof and dropping grotesquely dead at our feet.

On one of these days, reality intruded upon our game in the form of an explosion that sent a shower of sand upon us from the sagging roof above our heads. The beach, it turned out, was being bombed and mock-strafed by low-flying Army airplanes taking part in a training exercise being conducted by a National Guard regiment that had rumbled out across the planks of the old bridge that connected the peninsula to the mainland. The officers whom we encountered as we tried to run home seemed almost as badly frightened as we when they realized that they had failed to clear the beach properly, which is how (after being sworn to secrecy) my brother and I came to be adopted for one whole week as regimental mascots, and, to the envy of all our friends, were allowed to eat with the soldiers in their mess tent, help them dig foxholes, wave signal flags, stand inspections, and walk guard.

The saddest day of my life till then was the day my brother and I stood at attention, after the last tents had been struck and a long line of soldiers had given the beach a final policing, and watched a column of trucks and jeeps rattle back over the old wooden bridge and on to God only knows how many other beaches.

Seventeen years later, not long after I began what would become a thirty-eight-year career as a staff writer at *The New Yorker,* the magazine published a short story of mine entitled "A War Story." It was a first-person account of the events of the summer I have just described, and it began with a sentence that reads, "This is one of those stories that, for reasons of honor, have had to be suppressed."

That wasn't true, of course, but merely a literary conceit to explain tongue in cheek why I hadn't written the story before. At the time—it was 1959—I had no idea that I would spend most of my tenure at *The New Yorker* unraveling the dark secrets of the manufacturers of asbestos products, and those of other captains of industry, who were inflicting disease upon their workers and poisoning the land, as well as those of government officials, who fostered the climate of secrecy that cloaked so much of our national life during the Cold War.

It may be revealing that in a 1997 memoir, *Secrets: A Writer in the Cold War*, which gives an account of my experiences as an investigative journalist, I include a few sentences about the adventure that befell my brother and me on Duxbury Beach in the summer of 1942, and a longer section about a family secret that my parents kept from me. Having been sworn to secrecy about what had happened on the beach by officers of the National Guard regiment, we never breathed a word of it to our parents. Nor did they ever tell me about my father's previous marriage and a half brother to whom I had been given almost the same name, even though I must have suspected something about it and him at an early age.

Like everyone else, I have been touched as a child by secrets.

Today, a pair of carved decoys from the old duck hunting camp sit on a shelf in the living room of my home on Cape Cod. They remind me of the secret place in which my brother and I waged our fantasy war, of how lucky we were to have been so young, and of the power of secrets kept and those revealed.

FREDERICK BUECHNER

A Long Day's Dying
The Eyes of the Heart: *A Memoir of the Lost and Found*

I can think of two "secret spaces" which, looking back, I recognize were really one and the same. When I was a small child my family spent summers in Quogue, Long Island, and on the beach there; especially toward the end of the afternoon when the sun was starting to think about setting, I would lay a beach umbrella down on its side and lie curled up in the shelter of it with a wonderful feeling of snugness, safety, warmth, as the chill sea breeze whipped the sand around the edges of the ribbed canvas. After my father's death in 1936, when I was ten, we lived for a couple of years in Bermuda, where our pink house, The Moorings, was directly on the harbor across from Hamilton. When it rained, I loved to sit outside on the lawn in a canvas deck chair with a blanket of some sort draped over the sunshade to keep me snug, safe, dry, as I watched the downpour advance in sheets across the grey water and listened to its drumming above my head. To this day, age seventy-three, I can still conjure up in much of its original richness—especially at night in bed—what it felt like to experience both the wildness, wetness, windiness of things, and at the same time my utter protection from it.

PEGGY ELLSBERG

The Language of Gerard Manley Hopkins
Senior Lecturer in English, Barnard College

> "The dollhouse is a materialized secret"
> Susan Stewart (*On Longing: Narratives of the Minia-*
> *ture, the Gigantic, the Souvenir, the Collection*, 1993)

In the final daylight hours of the last century, with no particular plans for celebrating New Year's Eve, I went to a Victorian dollhouse museum in Santa Monica called Angels' Attic. I brought with me my daughters, Catherine and Nini, ages seven and five, dressed in matching red pinafores. The two other people in the museum mistook them for twins. I have grown accustomed to the pleasure observers take in spotting twins, like the brief thrill of sighting a rare bird. "Yes, twins," I lied, not wanting to disappoint anyone.

Like a snow owl or a set of small twins, a scale model or even something simply small—an electric locomotive train, a mocked-up cathedral, a hummingbird's tiny nest, a marshmallow peep yellow chicken in a basket—all rehearse for some grander but somehow diminished version of themselves. And replicas of homes, in particular, are especially pleasing. Creating altars dedicated to food and eating and coziness and sleeping in dollhouses strangely affirms what we do in our real homes. Entering the metonymic world of the dollhouse, we sense ourselves hidden and protected, empowered with a control that in real life escapes us. The message the miniature delivers contains both depth and delight.

Released into the exhibit at Angels' Attic, Catherine pressed herself close to the plexiglass covering an ingenious curiosity, a larger-than-a-seven-year-old-child-sized model of the Woman with So Many Children Who Lived in a Shoe. Frozen in time and receptive to poetic projection, like the figures on John Keats's Grecian urn, doll children spilled out of every room and over the thumb-sized furniture. Catherine wanted no one to bother her. She whispered to the harried mini-mother who, surrounded by a handful of doll children, slaved over a cook stove. Nini meanwhile stepped up on a bench and studied an exceptionally intricate workshop and dormitory for thimble-sized Christmas elves, themselves miniatures within the miniature. Nini, too, her cheek pressed to the plexiglass, began to whisper, answering secret questions. Immersed in their identical experiences of deep looking, I too stood there, gazing at them gazing at interior versions of interiors. Like receding mirrors or Chinese boxes, the miniature students of miniatures in the little Victorian museum absorbed by even littler museums embodied for me the muse of museums.

When I was six, I received a pink and grey tin dollhouse. It was nothing like a museum-quality dollhouse, Queen Mary's electrified plaything at Windsor Court, for example, not like the opulent mimicries of the haute bourgeois domestic environments available on E-bay or in the *Nutshell News*. Mine was an undecorated bread-box of a house, a 1950s Sears prefab. One just like it, plain as a potato, recently appeared on the Antiques Road Show with a price tag of $2000. In 1956, I furnished my tin house with pinecones and round stones and tables made of bottle caps and bobbie pins. I built altars into every room; some cotton batting served as bedding for a capped acorn, my she-baby. I was practicing for something. Kneeling in front of it, I entered a secret museum.

Plato says in his *Laws* that "the man who is to make a good builder must play at building toy houses, and to make a good farmer, he must play at tilling land." I realized, as Angels' Attic was closing, that my children were entering the psychic homes, practicing for a future of indwelling. But the museum really was closing. In a few hours it would be Y2K and outside the twilit streets were filling up with noise and adult visions of glitter and champagne.

"Are you sure they're twins?" asked the kindly lady, eager to lock up and go home. "What a question!" I answered, stalling. Persuading the girls to leave took some strategy, but actually, there was also a twin wonder outside, a double rainbow arching into the blue-grey sky. And as the girls looked up their faces were lit from within by a secret. One for each.

NOËL RILEY FITCH

Biographies of Sylvia Beach, Julia Child, Anaïs Nin
Teaches at USC and American University of Paris

A formal prayer, its denouement always blessing "the hands" that had prepared the overdone roast beef, was followed by formal conversation at our Sunday afternoon dinners. Social decorum reigned for the three Riley girls. When for once no one was looking in my direction and the family discussion picked up at the end of the meal, I would slide silently off the front edge of the chair, pass carefully under the tablecloth without disturbing it, and settle beneath the center of the family dining-room table. The conversation continued up there, but I knew I was safely on my "Moonie."

The legs of my two sisters and parents, and occasionally those of visiting dignitaries, were draped with the generous linen tablecloth and surrounded my secret space—protecting me. I was in a private and magical spot. No eyes. No prayers, challenges, or decisions. In charge of my own domain. Sitting with a grin on my face, I was secure in my cave, imaginatively holding my secret surprise.

A Moonie was what those couples went on after my father, The Right Reverend Dr. John Riley, married them and they walked up the aisle and out of the church. We had heard whispered talk of "honeymoons" for years and understood them to be secret and private places. No prying eyes. My innocent imagination wanted such a space for myself.

When I was older and had stopped my flights underground, my little sister began taking her own Moonie. Now we would playfully call out "where is Gail?" "Where has Gail gone?" But, unlike me, she could not contain her giggles and crawled out to confess that she had been on her Moonie. She never could keep a secret, never seemed to need one. By then I had accepted the truth that my secret place had been discovered. My escapes had always been observed. At any time my cave could have been invaded, though it never was.

Today, placemats have replaced long linen tablecloths, and there are few secrets. I have been married twice, and after each ceremony I did not, for one reason or another, take a honeymoon. But I remember the innocence and excitement, the warm semi-darkness of my childhood Moonies. What has remained of my childhood Moonie is a sense of being in control of my own privacy and a need for having a room of my own. I grasped this truth under the family table long before reading Virginia Woolf. Montaigne was right in comparing life to a shop, in which the keeper needs a "back room."

I need my own study and, preferably, my own toilet. My husband, who stirs humor into every secret place of my life, likes to raise my toilet seat to show he has invaded my space.

More important than this exaggerated sense of space is another lesson I learned in the public scrutiny of busy parsonage life: I learned to savor the pleasure of my own company. As a biographer I spend months, indeed years, at the table of communal history, interviewing persons and travelling to distant libraries. But when the full-time writing begins, I slip under the public cloth to give myself over to my own company and the solitary battle with facts and words. Indeed, I spend my time invading other peoples' secret places.

MARK JONATHAN HARRIS

Academy Award-winning filmmaker
Professor of Cinema-Television, University of Southern
   California

When I was a child novels gave me the chance to participate in a wider, less circumscribed world than my own, one in which others shared my own fears and resentments, my desires and my unhappiness. I could cry over the death of Dora in *David Copperfield*, exult in the rebellion of Tom Sawyer and Huck Finn, relish the revenge of the Count of Monte

Cristo. Reading helped assuage the loneliness I felt growing up, reassured me that I was not as strange or bad a person as I secretly feared.

By high school the authors I read had completely changed—Twain giving way to Salinger, Dickens to Lawrence, Dumas to Hemingway—but books continued to be a refuge for me, a place where I felt safe to explore roles and emotions I wouldn't consider elsewhere. When I got to Harvard, it seemed natural to major in English, but after only a few months of Humanities 6, I developed a fierce and implacable hatred for the so-called New Criticism. I didn't want to deconstruct the imaginary worlds in which I had spent so much of my emotional energy. I wanted to believe in their reality. Like certain emotions in my family, novels were best left unexamined. I still read them as religiously as before—I discovered Russian literature at Harvard—but most of the fiction I read was for myself rather than for classes. Books were still a private retreat, a hideaway I could visit whenever I needed, where I could respond more freely and openly than I often did with other people.

Perhaps because so much of my emotional experience came from books, after college I sought a job that would provide me more direct contact with life. I found one as a crime reporter for the City News Bureau in Chicago. The South Side police beat, from five in the evening until two in the morning, was a different world from any I had ever encountered. All the passions that were repressed or hidden in the sheltered community in which I had been raised exploded every night on the South Side. I would read the crimes on the teletype, diligently gather the facts from the police who investigated them, but found it very difficult to understand or identify with the stories I was reporting. After the first few weeks of hanging out at South Side police stations, I started bringing a book to work each night. For months I carried *Crime and Punishment* around with me the way the cops carried their riot gear, as a shield against the violence, the brutality, the senselessness I was encountering. For a long time Raskolnikov was far more real than any of the people I wrote about.

Daily immersion in violence cannot help but alter you. Often it hardens people, but in my case it pierced the bookish armor I had used to defend myself against the harsher emotions of life. After several months I was transferred to days and assigned to Family Court. I found the stories I covered—most of which never made the papers—heartbreaking. Day after day I watched children brutalized by poverty, neglect, abuse. Their pain and anguish began to affect me as strongly as the characters I read about.

In time print journalism led me to documentary filmmaking. In retrospect it's easy to see the unconscious attractions of this medium. The camera served as my new *Crime and Punishment*, providing me both access to strong emotional experiences and distance from them. As a filmmaker I could participate directly rather than vicariously in important social and political events, but, at the same time, I had the luxury of the editing room to process and interpret my experiences and to form judgments about them.

In my late thirties, although I continued making documentary films, I also started writing children's books—for some of the same reasons I think parents have children—to get a second chance to experience what I had missed in childhood (like throwing a full-blown, dish-breaking tantrum) or to redeem earlier failures and humiliations (finally standing up to the school bully). Writing books from a child's perspective gave me the opportunity to explore the world in a way I had been too emotionally constrained and restricted to do when I was young.

In the last year my work as a filmmaker, my interest in children, and my own history have all converged in a documentary I have written and directed about the *Kindertransports*. In the nine months from December 1938 until Hitler invaded Poland in September 1939, Britain rescued over 10,000 children, 90% of them Jewish, from Germany, Austria, and Czechoslovakia. *Into the Arms of Strangers* (Fall 2000) chronicles the dramatic stories of these children, who were forced to give up their families, homes, even language, as they fled Nazi persecution to England.

Although the pains of my childhood do not begin to approach the traumas these children faced, I strongly identified with them—particularly the loneliness of these refugees living in other people's houses, in a foreign land where they did not speak the language and whose country was at war with their own. In researching and filming their story, I have been asking the *Kinder,* as they call themselves, a question central to my own childhood: In your unhappiness, where did you turn for solace? To my surprise, for many it was books.

One man, who came to England from Vienna as a seven-year-old, and who constantly feared being sent back if he upset his foster parents, remembers two favorite places in their home—one under the grand piano and the other in front of the open hearth coal fire, where he could spread out his books and comics and read "for hours on end." Always on his guard, desperate not to offend, he loved adventure stories most of all, stories where heroes could act boldly and decisively and never worry about the consequences.

Another woman, an avid reader as a young girl, turned to books for relief from the isolation and segregation she suffered as a Jew in Nazi Germany. When her parents decided to send her to England at the age of fifteen, what grieved her most was abandoning her collection of books. "I couldn't bear to leave them behind," she remembers. "I just burned them in the oven. It was wintertime. We had an old-fashioned oven that you fed with coal, and I fed my books into it, one by one."

When she arrived at the foster family in Coventry that offered her a home, her first shock was the absence of books. "It was absolutely traumatic. Can you imagine a house without one book in it? Nothing. Nothing to read. Nothing to learn English from." Her second shock was that the family had taken her in to be a maid for them and wouldn't allow her to continue school.

In making this film, I have been touched by the often desperate loneliness of these refugee children but also by the resilience and courage that sustained them through their trials in Britain, where, as Eva Figes writes, "the fact that I had arrived as a foreign child was never forgotten or forgiven, and with the rise of anti-German feeling after the outbreak of war my nationality was always good for abuse."

For Figes, too, books played a critical role in her ability to survive her uprooting. "Real books, that was perhaps the most important of many discoveries," she writes in *Little Eden*, a wonderful memoir about her wartime sojourn at an unconventional boarding school in a country town in Gloucester. A corollary of this discovery was the realization of her need for separateness, a place where she could be alone—to read, to think: "Perhaps it was because, even as a very small child, I had been conscious of a secret, solitary nucleus inside which nobody could reach. It held pain, but also dreams, and I needed to be withdrawn to allow it to grow."

The hiding place she chose for retreat, "where I would bolt myself in when I wanted to get away from everybody and everything," was the basement lavatory, cold and damp on winter mornings, but the one place she could brood undisturbed, work through her miseries and loneliness, let slip the mask she wore with other children. "By now I had begun to understand that my life involved playing a role, in the dormitory, in the classroom, even at play. It was necessary to appear happy, cheerful and integrated within the group, and in a situation where one was eating, sleeping, working and playing together it was necessary to find a bolt hole in order to give way to one's inner feelings."

For many children books continue to provide this bolt hole, allowing them to shut the door, however briefly, on the pain and confusion of their lives, and open a window into a world of dreams, of fantasy, of hope. If books can sustain children during the upheavals of wartime, as they did me under different circumstances, surely they can still be meaningful, even to today's Nintendo generation. Television, movies, internet chat rooms also offer children a chance to explore other roles and lifestyles, to expand their vision of themselves, but the experiences these media provide are essentially communal, rather than private. Books provide a private psychic space—the core of any secret hideaway—a haven where you are free to feel, to think, to imagine, and to dream.

JIM HARRISON

The Road Home
Just Before Dark: Collected Nonfiction

As a poet and novelist I've grown rather inured to my own peculiarities but have long openly accepted my penchant for secret places, mostly thickets, that I depend on almost daily for solace. I can think of specific locations in Michigan, including the Upper Peninsula, but also in Arizona and New Mexico, a single place in New York City, one in Paris, and another near a friend's house down in western Burgundy.

The original, the ur-thicket, was near the porch of our childhood home in a dense collection of shrubs. I often retreated there for hours with my dog after I was blinded in one eye by a playmate. Soon after this accident (intentional) I also lost the dog because she was over-defensive but kept the thicket for years.

The prerequisite of a first-rate thicket is that you can see out but it is unlikely indeed that you'll be noticed by others. It is helpful to have a dog with me, even if it is a friend's dog, which is the case in Burgundy. Birds often visit. Once in a prized thicket in Arizona during a violent rainsquall I shared my thicket with dozens of rare vermilion flycatchers. They treated me as an equal.

I don't care for the idea of bullfighting but there is a Spanish word, "querencia," which refers to the place in the ring a particular bull feels the strongest, most at home, most able to deal with his impending doom. I'm sure that my thickets offer me peace in a life that is permanently inconsolable but reasonably vital and productive. Thickets quickly draw off the poison. After a few minutes of sitting you hear your own tentative heartbeat. What people clumsily call the "inner child" gracefully rises to the surface without much coaxing. Your normally watchful dog takes a snooze and occasionally you doze off yourself within these few yards of earth where you feel no dislocation and are totally at home.

JERRY HERRON

AfterCulture: Detroit and the Humiliation of History
Professor of English, Wayne State University

I used to think about the room where I learned to read, for no better reason than it seemed to belong just to me, the way childhood things always do, when we grow up, with the portrait of George Washington, and the cheap, nylon flag, "I pledge allegiance . . ." each morning first thing, hand over heart, staring at the alphabet taped across the top of the

blackboard (that really *was* black not green). And the radia-
tors that when you'd put a Crayola on them, the hot wax
would melt down and pool on the hard wood floor that creaked
each step you took across it, and how that smell became the
smell I always thought about first when I thought about the
first day of school with the scents of pencil shavings and
paper and paste made of wheat that if you wanted to you
could eat it. (Bobbie Bentley did.)

And the cloak room in back, with doors you could close from
inside, so all you could see were the patterns of light across
your shoes that came through the air holes at the bottom, and
how that's where the teacher would find William, balled up in
a nest of coats, his face smeared with tears because he always
got upset when we practiced writing in our Big Chief tablets
with the cigar-fat pencils and he would make mistakes and
when he tried to erase he would tear the page and start to cry
with snot running down his lip and when his parents came
home from their trip they found out his grandmother who
they had left in charge had just gotten tired of him one day
and decided she'd enroll him in first grade even though he
was only three and a half, big for his age probably, so they
came to take him home. And we all felt sad not because we
would miss William, since none of us had really talked to him,
but because we knew that nobody was going to find out a secret about us that would set us free.

I decided to look for the room where I learned to read, back
for a visit, when I was forty and got stopped by a guard who
made me wait until a teacher could come and hear what I
wanted who was—the teacher—young enough to be my daughter, if I had one, but not beautiful like Miss Creer, my teacher,
had been when I learned to read, in the Bluebird group (we
were the best), and the young woman listened almost patiently
and said sure take a look around, which I did, not being certain what room it was, but pretending I knew, they all looked
the same now so what difference did it make, with the giant
windows blocked out except for little gun slits at the bottom,
and the ceiling dropped, with fluorescent lights and the cloak
rooms gone where nobody would ever get to see how Kathy Mc-
Naren didn't have a belly button because it had been surgically
removed and she would show you if you asked (even if you
didn't). I wish I'd asked her why. And a little boy was sitting in

the dark with the lights turned off so he could see the computer screen better and he looked up at me with the blue glow reflecting off his glasses so his eyes disappeared, like I was an intruder, which I was, bothering him while he was working, after school. Learning to read. Will he remember this room as if it had belonged just to him? I hope not.

PAUL KARLSTROM

On the Edge of America: California Modernist Art, 1900–1920
West Coast Regional Director of the Smithsonian Institution's
 Archives of American Art

Image-making is fundamental to the journey of self-discovery. Writing and illustrating my own stories played an important role in my childhood. Having an imaginary world that I could populate and control as I wished was reassuring and helped me better understand the larger world in which I was obliged to operate. No doubt my own professional life, including studying and writing about images as cultural documents, began then. Art and image-making arise out of a fundamental human need to bring order to a difficult and often unpredictable reality. Recently I was inspired to look again at these childhood creative efforts carefully preserved by my mother. And as I studied them I understood for perhaps the first time their true meaning in my life: the creation of a world that helped me find personal continuity in a somewhat dislocated childhood characterized by the insecurity of frequent moves. Art provided a means, one that I deployed constantly (as evidenced by the number of early picture stories that remain), to enter a refuge of my own imaginative devising, a place to repair to after experiencing rebuffs (actual or perceived) in my efforts to make friends in a series of new neighborhoods and schools. It even provided an outlet for early teenage fantasies associated with the discomforting but thoroughly irresistible stirrings of sexual awareness. I learned at an early age that you could have at least some of what you long for by creating images with pencil, pen, and watercolor.

California Living Histories, a project of Washington School's

Two self-portraits created in the California Living Histories project. (Top) Antonio Turijan, age 7. (Bottom) Paul J. Karlstrom. Project directors: Elizabeth Converse, Brad MacNeil. Project sponsors: California Council for the Humanities and the LightBringer Project.

Learning Center, instigated this retrospective look. This inno-
vative program in Pasadena, California, is designed to provide
the means and the environment for young students, aged five
to twelve, to discover themselves within the context of family,
neighborhood, and community. The curriculum includes a
field trip to the Autry Museum of Western Heritage which allows students to see how family histories can be captured
using art and artifacts. But what really distinguishes the project is its methodology, the use of oral history and the visual
arts as means to create and communicate to others verbal and
pictorial images of the self as an individual within a particular community. Ultimately such images serve as cultural
markers describing a specific position within the multiethnic
richness that defines contemporary American life. The majority of the students are Latino and African-American, and
many of their families have come to California within the last
twenty-five years. Parents are invited into class to share their
family stories, including the hardships faced and the courage
needed to start over in a new land. Being asked to serve as
academic advisor and curator provided a rare opportunity for
someone in my position to interact directly with students in
primary and middle school.

The thinking and understanding that goes into creating pictures may well provide a sense of at least a degree of control
(the term "agency" is often used to describe this phenomenon)
of one's world. As I drew my own self-portrait with my young
colleagues at the Learning Center, I realized the advantage
they had in being less self-conscious about art than adults are.
The process that the children have embarked upon at the
Learning Center is something akin to discovering oneself in an
invented "secret space" and drawing from it the courage to step
out and engage the world as more self-aware individuals. My
own practice continues in the personal realm as I craft collages
that are basically visual manifestations of my interior life.
Slowly these personal and frequently quite revealing images
are entering into a more public realm, either as gifts to friends
and sympathetic associates or, more recently, in artist-orga-
nized "underground" exhibitions. It occurs to me that as I share
these small pictorial "confessions" with an audience, however
limited, I am acknowledging who I am as an individual or at
least how I understand myself.

As a grownup I find myself an employee of the Smithsonian Institution, directing the West Coast activities of the Archives of American Art. In that capacity it has been my charge to locate and acquire for the national collections letters, photographs, diaries, and related historical documents. The focus of the Archives has been preservation of historic records for use by scholars and writers, a "high end" educational constituency. However, the official Smithsonian motto is the "increase and diffusion of knowledge." Broadly interpreted, this would seem to encompass the purposes and goals of the California Living Histories project. And it seems most appropriate for us to pay attention to the young people who may well grow up to use our scholarly collections. But far more important, it seems to me, is to be involved in the seeking of (self) knowledge, the ultimate humanist goal and reason for studying history in the first place. And it further occurs to me that many of the more personal documents (the intimate letter or personal sketchbook, for example) I collect for study by historians are, when all is said and done, nothing other than adult versions of what children—myself or those at the Leaning Center—have carried back from individual "secret spaces." I suspect that we never outgrow the need for and ability to learn from these comforting and refreshing alternative worlds of our own imaginative invention.

Nan Knighton

Book and lyrics for the musical *The Scarlet Pimpernel*
   (Tony nomination)
Stage adaptation for *Saturday Night Fever*

I suppose I was afraid all the time. I remember living in a constantly vibrant state, jangling inside, ever-vigilant, looking over my shoulder. I didn't talk about my fears to anyone— children usually don't. I lived in a leafy neighborhood in Baltimore, Maryland, and my life, by any standards, was idyllic. From ages five to nine, I appear in each photograph as a smiling child with golden curls. But I look back on these years and see quite clearly that the pulse of my every day was fear.

Fear of *what?* Well, you could make your list. Here's a partial list of mine: 1) Mrs. Bellows, across the street, was referred to as "the crazy woman" and my friends and I would dare each other to run up on her lawn. Invariably, she came hurtling out of the house in a nightgown, screaming at us that we were terrible children and were going straight to Hell. We'd tear away, breathless, just as her nurse emerged to yank her back inside. 2) A friend of my brother's died when his sled hit a metal pole sticking out of the snow. 3) My friend Sally drowned at age seven when her parents were foolish enough to go boating on the Chesapeake Bay during a storm. 4) Catherine, the lady who lived next door and was a surrogate grandmother to me, had a husband who was a doctor, a man with no patience for children. One day when I was touching some of his prized glass figurines, the doctor slapped me across the face. In order to retain diplomatic relations with the neighbors, my parents did not confront the doctor about this incident—it was glossed over and dropped. 5) Catherine died a year later. She drowned in the bathtub. People said it was an accident. I overheard my parents whisper that it might be "suicide." (When I was a teenager, my father confided his belief that the doctor had murdered Catherine.) 6) My brother told me he belonged to a club of eagles. He hinted they might let me join the club. The eagles would come to my window every night, he said, and watch me. If I moved even an inch, they would fly in and kill me. I was five years old. How many nights did I lie paralyzed, sweating and terrified? 7) When my brother was eleven and I was eight, he suffered an anomalous stroke and lay in a coma for two days. For me, the worst part was being alone in the house with him when he first collapsed, stumbling through the neighborhood to get help, hearing the howl of the ambulance. And then my mother came home and shook my shoulders, screaming at me, "What happened? What happened?!"

Those were some of my terrors, but every child has them—bedtime illusions of creatures perched in the dark on that corner chair, nightmares of monsters, fears of kidnapping, abandonment, or that great mystery—death. And, of course, the unluckiest children deal directly with abuse. In a way, fear is the biggest revelation of childhood, the worst surprise: "Oh. Bad things *do* happen." And yet somehow it's kept secret. It's all held tight to the chest. Why don't children talk about it?

Wouldn't it be infinitely logical for a child to go to her parents and say, "I'm a wreck. I think eagles are going to peck my eyes out and the crazy lady across the street is going to eat me alive and how the hell could you let that doctor slap me?" Why do children keep their fears secret? Are they trying to be little adults, imitating their apparently stoic parents? Are they doubly afraid to disclose the horror lest somehow they are at fault? One thing I do know is that children have an amazing ability to dissociate, to simply block it all out. ("Hmm. My friend just drowned. Guess I'll go out and jump rope. Now I'm jumping rope. I'm fine.") Maybe the only way a child can cope with the newly discovered terrors of the world is simply to disable them and substitute a preferred reality. In my case, I wrote. I taught myself to read and write at the kitchen table. I did it regularly and assiduously, with a child's picture dictionary beside me, copying words, sounding them out. I think when I wrote, I must have entered a safe zone.

Following is a poem I wrote at age eight:

The Poor Boy's Dreams   a rhimed story

Poor little boy, I shed tears for thee
your mother sick, Your father dead
Be careful Boy, and cautious
were the last words his father said.

the boy he dreamed of riches
He dreamed of his poor mother well
Soon she passed away, and the Boy,
his house he had to sell.

He worked an honest living, but
he dreamed most all the time
of kings and knights and princesses
and costly cups of wine.

He dreamed of birds that sang sweetly
and of Birds that went coo coo
and one day it Happened, Yes!
His dreams, they did come true

The End

In this poem, life's about as rotten as it gets, but there's that happy ending. As I read through the folders of my old stories and poems, over and over the little girls or boys I created were surrounded with horrendous dangers and sorrows, but I always made them end up "happily ever after." I suppose part of this may have been a by-product of growing up in the 50s, but my gut feeling is that happy endings simply quelled my fears. If I wrote them, then, on *some* level of reality, they existed. Following is something I wrote at age nine. I have no idea what it is, but I copy it here exactly:

> a gun came through the door, she saw it. She stood motion-list, sacred to breath. Suddenly the door opened. She was frantic, she didn't know what to do. There, at the door stood a, why, it was her dog Bingo, with her little boy Bill and his play gun.

> It was dark as he walked down the street. He heard a noise, It was a sort of a cracky noise. He tried not to scare himself, but all he could think of was ghosts, and robbers, and witches, suddenly he saw it. It was a begger. He gave him a dollar and went home.

And terrors dissolve, over and over. Perhaps the core of fear is helplessness: something awful stands in my doorway and I can't do a damn thing about it. A child *has* to do something about it, and I think writing made me strong, gave me armor. As a little girl, I would acknowledge that scary, jangling world out there and then proceed to surmount it. With a pencil and paper, I could call the shots, I could *make* justice prevail. Fear may be a secret space where children dwell, but in order to survive, don't all children create an ancillary secret space for *mastering* that fear? Lord, there are a million scary things out there, all quite real—a child could spend 24 hours a day trembling with that discovery. Or he could find a safe zone, a space where he's got the power. It's like a key clicking in a lock, a silent voice whispering, "This is you. This is your territory. This is how you take command." I found it with writing. Other children build complex Legos, or play basketball or paint or ice skate, tell jokes, play the piano. (And, of course, today there are the inevitable computer games, where God knows it's easy enough to pulverize the bad guys). Ideally, though, a child finds a space where his or her unique gift reigns and empowers: suddenly your head's high, you've found your niche, that thing that makes you the cowboy on his horse, the soldier planting his flag at the top of the hill. The happy secret space is the one where you're in charge.

Today I write for a living. *The Scarlet Pimpernel,* a musical for which I wrote book and lyrics, opened on Broadway in the Fall of 1997. And, oh yes, *The Scarlet Pimpernel* has a classic happy ending where good triumphs, the villain is foiled, and the hero and heroine quite literally sail off into the sunset. Am I still then just a child smacking back the danger? Recently I was sent a copy of a letter from the *Scarlet Pimpernel* website. The letter was from one *Pimpernel* fan to another, and the last line read, "Remember—the good guy always wins in the end!" Not only am I still insisting on the happy endings, but apparently lots of other adults out there are still needing them. Those secret spaces of childhood never really go away. We just tend to tackle them with a bit more sophistication.

As I write this, I'm in Arizona on a ranch. There is much about this place that is "a secret space." I came here by myself for a week's vacation. I'm about to go into a dining room full of families and couples where I won't know a soul. I ride horses every day. Their hooves stumble on the rocks, and the wranglers warn us how easily a horse can spook and buck. When I lope, it's a challenge to stay in the saddle. I've now heard several anecdotes about the bite of the Black Widow spider, and how you should shake your boots out each morning. Believe me, in the mornings I am shaking out every stitch of clothing I own. I also listen carefully to the snake instructions, "Ya meet a rattlesnake on the path, ya just back up, reeeal slow. . . ." All of this is very very very very scary. And I sit here, looking out on the desert, writing.

PHILIP LEVINE

The Simple Truth (Pulitzer Prize, 1995)
Professor of English, New York University

Rafael Alberti, for me the greatest living poet,* tells us in his memoir of a secret grove in which he could with perfect ease become the person no one else saw, the amazingly imaginative child we now know as Rafael Alberti. No Jesuit priest ever entered the grove, nor did those pious aunts and uncles who savaged his childhood, nor did his parents or his brothers and sisters, nor even the "real authority figure in those days," the family servant, Paca Moy. He calls it his "lost grove" because when he was fifteen he left it behind forever, along with his dog Centella with whom he had shared those childhood years and those places of refuge. For financial reasons the family was forced to leave the small town of Puerto de Santa Maria at the mouth of "the River of Forgetfulness" overlooking the Gulf of Cadiz and move to a small, dark apartment near the Atocha station in Madrid. When I was thirteen my family also made a dramatic move. We had been living in the center of Detroit—then a city of two million souls, as Alberti would put it; my mother, who had for years harbored the desire to own her own home, seized the opportunity to purchase an inexpensive house on the still undeveloped outskirts of the city. Within a few months I too found a secret grove which soon became the heart of my childhood. It was, of course, not Alberti's grove, and yet in one central way it was, for like his grove it represented peace and gave me the privacy I needed to conduct my secret conversations with the known and unknown worlds and with myself. If I were this moment suddenly transported to Detroit I could lead you to the very spot, but I would not. I am sure the gigantic copper beech that was its exact center is no longer there, nor are the clustered maples and elms, nor is the thick underbrush, the heaped leaves, and the gnarled fallen trunks of dead trees. I'm sure everything has been replaced by a row of small, modest, lower-middle class homes with tended lawns and fenced yards, homes very much like ours. Could a living child find his or her secret heart in what is there now? Perhaps in an attic room or behind the furnace in the basement or in a dry fruit cellar, its windows papered over. Children are both resourceful and driven, and each requires a secret place of contemplation and invention. I tried those places before I found my grove, before it became the site of my first poems and largely the subject of those poems. Although I'm known largely as an urban poet, one obsessed with the cities I've called home—Detroit, Barcelona, New York—in my early poems I addressed the natural world certain that the natural world was waiting to hear me. At thirteen I sang to the listening stars, the unseen wind, the trees that caught the wind and turned it to music, the rain, and especially the rich perfumes of the earth that received the rain. There in the secret heart of childhood—seemingly isolated and lonely—my words commanded the largest and most extraordinary audience they would ever delight: the whole of creation.

*Alberti died shortly after this commentary was composed—Ed.

WILLIAM MEEZAN

Marion Elizabeth Blue Professor of Children and Families,
    University of Michigan School of Social Work
Outstanding Research Award, Society for Social Work and
    Research

Most people think of children's secret spaces as safe sanctuaries—places to get away from the stress of childhood. But for some children, being alone in a secluded space is lonely, scary and unsafe. They are gay and lesbian children who are confused and feel isolated. They are children who have been abused or demeaned in other ways by their parents, and have had their sense of self scarred. They are children of color or of unusual heritages who have not been taught pride. Because they have internalized negative images, these children don't like themselves and are therefore denied the ability to enjoy solitude.

I was such a child. Being alone, even for short periods of time, was frightening. Being alone meant living with my demons that told me I didn't belong, that I was less worthy, and that I was damaged. It was not just that I was different— that could be celebrated. It was that I was bad, or at least that's what I thought then. My demons made me agitated and hyperactive, secretive in the presence of adults for fear of being "discovered," hypersensitive, and easily brought to tears when criticized for the most minimal indiscretions. They made me afraid of being alone.

And so, safe places—my secret places during childhood—were public spaces. They were places where demons could not come out, or at least where I could control them. They were places where activities were organized and supervised, environments where group activities were structured, where I could be engaged with others and not with myself—Scouts, summer camp, and Hebrew day school—places where I could fit in, or at least pretend to fit in. Because they provided a sense of normalcy, I remained in the Scouts until the troop dissolved, attended day school until after my Bar Mitzvah, and went to summer camp, in one role or another, until I began graduate school.

High school—a "special" public school in Manhattan called the High School of Music and Art—gave me ways not just to contain the demons but to accept them, which was a first step toward conquering them. I got to go there not because I was a brilliant musician but because I was born with a musical ear. Going to M&A meant I had to leave the Bronx, which opened new geographic, experiential, and interpersonal vistas. My classmates were rich and poor, white and non-white, worldly and sheltered, conservative and radical, troubled and undisturbed, fun and somber. Each was unique, and what bound us together were our various talents and shared interests, not our backgrounds. And, because we were talented, we were respected by our teachers and treated with dignity. We were told we were worthy, and because I began to feel worthy being alone became less frightening.

In high school I also discovered that I could be protected by music, and learned that I could be happy and alone simultaneously. I realized this when, as part of an assignment, I had to listen to the Bach *Mass in B minor*. When I put it on my phonograph, my parents were appalled—nice Jewish boys didn't listen to church music or for that matter any choral music written in Latin or German. I was told to close the door to my room so the "noise" wouldn't penetrate the house. At that moment, something amazing happened. The great choruses of Bach simultaneously enthralled and protected me. From that day on, when I needed to feel safe, I shut myself away with Bach or Haydn or Handel or Mozart or Beethoven or Wagner—not their symphonies (unless they had choral movements) but their masses and their oratorios, their requiems and their cantatas, and later, their operas. And just to make sure I would be safe, I developed a love of Gregorian chant.

In college I learned to combine my two secret places. The fraternity house, the public space, meant I did not have to be alone when I did not want to be, and music (some of which I now owned) kept people out of my room when I wanted to be alone. I didn't study much, for that meant being alone and vulnerable. But it was here that I decided, very late in my college career (and having almost flunked out), that my calling was to work with troubled children, something that I knew I could be good at because of my various experiences. As I entered Social Work graduate school, learning became meaningful for the first time, for I had no wish to do harm to those I wanted to help. Not surprisingly, I started to do well academically.

My first job after graduate school was in a residential treatment center for emotionally disturbed latency-aged boys. I loved that work until the system got in the way. It all happened around a child named Luis, an eight-year-old who had been abandoned to the streets of New York at the age of six and had managed to live on his own for a year before coming to the treatment center. A charming child, he had survival skills but little educational or emotional resources. His projective tests said he was deeply troubled.

Over the next eighteen months his progress was nothing short of amazing. He endeared himself to a volunteer who applied to become his foster parent. While his discharge at this point may have been slightly premature, I pushed for it fearing he was becoming "institutionalized." The cottage parents were against it because he was not yet "neat" and the psychiatrist speculated that he still needed structure. So, despite what his teacher, the psychologist, the consultant, and I said, they decided that he should stay another year. I knew this was a disastrous decision (I learned after leaving that within five months he had been psychiatrically hospitalized after being physically and sexually brutalized by older children in the institution; Lord knows what happened to him after that), and vowed that I was going to work to change systems that destroyed children like him.

Wounded and battered by an uncaring bureaucracy, and feeling helpless again, I turned to the one place that gave me solace and rewards. Doctoral education allowed me to concentrate on learning what had become my passion—damaged children and what it takes to make them whole. The freedom of doctoral education gave me another truly private, secret space, where I felt complete and competent: a cubicle (now an office) where all of my energies could be devoted to learning and writing about kids and their families and what we need to do to support them.

And so, I have come to consider academic institutions my "secret space." So watch out for college professors wearing maroon and baby-blue sweat shirts, who have spent 21 years partnered to a church musician, walk on campus singing Handel oratorios, and stop to smile at children who don't seem to belong. They may be in a space as private as a tree house or a fort made out of an old cardboard box. And be equally aware of those who write in silence about something they are passionate about, for their offices may hold secrets few people understand.

VALERIE MINER

Rumors from the Cauldron: Selected Essays, Reviews, and Reportage
Professor of English, University of Minnesota

1955/New Jersey
She is gone. Off with Lily or Gerry or someone who has a car. Grandma is taking care of us, or we are taking care of her. It's fine. I am eight years old already and I understand.

My brothers watch cartoons. Grandma is cooking. I am playing dress-up in Mom's bedroom. It's really my parents' bedroom, but when Daddy is at sea, it becomes her bedroom. A big, light, airy place at the back of the house, separated by a floor from the upstairs bedrooms. It's not a very private room and I feel easy about entering while she's gone. I do close the door because I'll be changing clothes.

First I try on the hats, those close-fitting, feathered hats. Mom has two—yellow and green. The green looks better with my eyes and skin. Then I put on one of her fancy slips and suddenly I am draped in a luxurious ballgown. These satin and lace slips are so pretty, I wish my mother would wear them out—to the theatre or a night club—but Mom doesn't go out. And in the bottom drawer, that fabric Dad sent from Argentina, as if he forgot she couldn't sew. The bright blue and red and green—same color as the hat—material is a little scratchy, but it will work handsomely as a shawl. Now a pair of red shoes from the closet.

There, I stand admiring myself in her mirror and seeing—as I look closely—myself reflected a hundred times (although I stop counting after five) in my father's mirror on the taller bureau across the room. This double reflection is dizzying, so I try to ignore it, concentrating on the angle of my hat and a detail in the lace bodice. Closer, I lean into her mirror.

Minutes pass. I must wait for the right moment. Finally, the cameras start rolling. Local stations across the country have tuned in and I modestly introduce myself. Valerie Miner, child star, here to testify to the beauty aid of Ivory Soap. It really is 99 and 44/100 percent pure. So pure it floats.

On Tuesdays I endorse Pond's Cold Cream.

JOHN HANSON MITCHELL

Trespassing
The 2000 New England Booksellers' Association Award for a
    body of work

The place, even at this distance in time, looms as a metaphor, a half-remembered country of ruined estates, with canted terraces, broken balustrades and toppled pillars, and the whole of it overgrown with greeny, twisting vines.

There was once money in the town in which I grew up, but by my time all the old families had grown eccentric and were living out their days on dwindling trust funds. Some became collectors of birds' eggs, some kept donkeys in the old estate carriage houses and quoted Spencerian couplets to them at night. Some were totally undone by the Depression and walked off the cliffs that ran along the west bank of the Hudson River. The land here was in decline, it was a nation of decaying gardens, huge trees, brick walls, horse barns, and carriage houses, which by my time were deserted and accessible by means of broken windows and crooked backdoors and cellars.

High above the town, overlooking the Hudson River, corporate magnates of the nineteen twenties had constructed larger estates, most of which had been torn down or deserted after the Crash. Here you could find the overgrown ruins of formal Italian gardens, collapsed pergolas, fallen pillars, and cracked swimming pools half filled with green waters and golden-eyed frogs who eyed you from the detritus of sodden leaves and then ducked into the obscurity of the depths when you went to grab them.

Here, amidst the ruins, in the six miles of second-growth woods that ran along the cliff there was rich picking for the adventurous youths who lived otherwise normal lives in the lower sections of the town. And to this spot on any given Saturday morning in warm weather, we, the nomadic tribes of our neighborhood, would ascend to fight. We recapitulated history in this mythic landscape. From the battlements of the terrace balconies we defended our land against the attacking hordes of imaginary enemies with sticks and showers of stones and great clods of mud. We fought day-long battles here and only at the requisite hour—sundown—would we give up and return to our boring, albeit safe homes.

There was only one estate in the entire six mile stretch of woodland that had yet to be conquered by nature, let alone by our militant armies. The house was owned by a man we used to call Old King Cole and was a vast brownstone place with spired turrets and a mean-looking iron fence surrounding it, the type of fence with spear-pointed tips. The grounds, which purportedly had been laid out by the firm of Frederick Law Olmstead, were extensive and unmanaged, with two immense copper beech trees framing a briar-strewn entrance, a small orchard just west of the house, a sunken garden with a frog pond, and many species of exotic trees, including, I was later told, a rare Franklinia.

Of all the properties in the community, of all the woodlots, overgrown backyards, gardens, and frog-haunted swimming pools, King Cole's place held the greatest attraction. For one thing there was a deserted carriage house at the back of the grounds to which we had gained access and used as a hide-out. But the other thing is that, unlike other landholders in the community, Old King Cole did not seem to appreciate tres-passers, even though his property was at a remove from the other holdings in the town. Periodically, sensing an invasion, Old King Cole would emerge from the darkened interior of his house to reprimand us—a tottering old man with an ebony cane and a palsied hand. We were too fast for him. We always broke through various escape routes we had established and headed for other territory. Once or twice he called the police, but they too were disinclined to leave their vehicles and scramble through the tangle of briar and bittersweet and ivy strewn pillars to catch us.

One afternoon Old King Cole surprised two of us and drove us into a walled corner of his sunken garden. Once we were trapped, he approached us, shuffling, his cane raised omi-nously above his head, his green eyes burning under his brushsmoke eyebrows. We thought we were done for. We would be thrashed, perhaps murdered, at very least bloodied from the full strike of his cane. But instead the old man halted in front of us, and there, amidst the wild briars and ivies, delivered a resounding lecture on the nature of title.

"My property," he intoned, "My holdings. My kingdom. My nation." Then, advancing a few steps he pointed southwards with his cane to the town below the cliffs. "Your property, your nation. Return to your country. Respect the national bound-aries."

It was a good lecture, but it had the wrong effect. Up to that time, I had no concept of the nature of trespass. Forbidden passage consisted of Old King Cole's land, and an even more ominous place in the south of the town called the Baron's that was surrounded with a high stucco wall and reportedly guarded by Great Danes. With King Cole's proclamation, the world, which up to that time had seemed to me a wide collec-tive space that invited exploration, was divided and quartered, and guarded by owners of private property. But on the heels of this revelation there came an epiphany. I understood then the lure of trespass, the freedom of open space, and the sublime possibility inherent in wilderness.

KATHLEEN DEAN MOORE

Riverwalking: *Reflections on Moving Water*
Chair, Department of Philosophy at Oregon State University

Do you remember the sound a mother makes, knocking on the door of a damp cardboard box in the morning? She sticks her finger in the hole that serves as a doorknob and pulls. The cut edge of cardboard sticks to the box, so when she tugs hard, the door pops open all at once, and the box sways. All the squares turn to parallelograms and the window-shutters flap open, swinging out over the crayoned window boxes, the red and purple daisies, the pasted-on picket fence, the twining vines. She reaches in the door and leaves three hard-boiled eggs.

The box has grown weak-kneed and mottled overnight, wicking moisture from the lawn. By the mail slot, smooth paper has begun to curl away from the corrugation. But with morning sun shining through gaps along the front door, the air in the box is warm and smells like new books. My sisters and I sit cross-legged, nightgowns taut across our knees, and eat the eggs for breakfast. We call ourselves The Three Flowers, and this is our clubhouse.

It takes a lot of sawing with a steak knife to make a refrigerator carton into a house. The first cut is the dangerous one, stabbing the blade through the cardboard thickness. But once the knife is embedded in the box, you can saw out a window or a door or an escape hatch or a chimney hole. Then you can color the curtains with crayons and paste pictures on the walls.

We didn't use sleeping bags back in those days. We slept on rugs woven from old fabric—every outgrown dress and stained tablecloth torn into inch-wide strips, then the strips sewn end-to-end and woven into rugs by a neighbor who wore house-slippers all day. If we used blankets, I don't remember them. We probably had no use for blankets during Ohio summer nights, nights so hot that we would lie on our backs, spit in the air, and let the spray settle cool on our faces.

This time, I have my goose-down sleeping bag and a high-tech foam pad. The weather has changed in the fifty years since I was a child; it's the difference between Ohio and Oregon, where a sea-wind slides between the mountains at dusk and the temperature drops twenty degrees. Refrigerator cartons don't seem to have changed though, and after the workers dollied our new refrigerator into place, they left the box unceremoniously by the street for the trash-men, just the way I remember. Back then, we would roll boxes home, end over end over end, sometimes for blocks. Today, I hauled the box up the driveway in my Suburban.

I'm embarrassed to be stabbing a good Sheffield steak knife into this cardboard box, sawing windows and doors, and my husband doesn't even ask. But I know that memories live in specific places, and sometimes you can find the entrance to the past, if you can just find the right place. This has happened to me: I will walk into an opening in a juniper hedge, or onto a landing where a stairway turns toward the attic, and it's as if I had dropped down a dark tunnel that opens into light-flooded childhood memories. So I wonder if this cardboard box will take me back to a particular kind of joy I haven't felt for a long, long time. There's nothing wrong with trying, I tell my husband, but he says, hey, nobody's arguing with you.

He and I share a silent beer, watching the moon speckle the lawn under the Douglas firs, until it's time for bed. Then he gives me a quick hug, and I climb into the box to spend the night alone. In the past, my sisters and I worried about neighborhood boys, skinny scab-kneed buzz-headed boys who lied to their mothers and snuck out barefoot at night to kick the box over and run away snickering. Better to stay awake all night than to have your world convulse and turn on its side, spilling you into the laughing dark. There are no boys to worry about now, but I lie awake anyway, shifting in my sleeping bag, wondering how three little girls ever fit in one box. A car door slams. The neighbor's clothes-dryer shuffles and clinks. I hear a slurry whistle from the barn owl that nests in the cedars at the end of the street. Then the neighborhood grows quiet.

I wake up suddenly in darkness so engulfing I don't know if my eyes are open or shut. When I raise a hand to touch my eyes, my fingers collide with the top of the box, only a few inches from my face. The lid is soft and sagging. I reach out for my husband, but my hands touch cold walls instead. Why am I alone? The air is dank, damper than a cardboard box should be on its first night in the backyard. I can't hear anything at all. And never have I felt such darkness—not just the absence of light, but a darkness thick and real and smelling of turned earth.

If this box is a tunnel through time, it's taking me in altogether the wrong direction. In one movement, I lift both legs and batter them through the door, roll onto my knees, and crawl out of the sleeping bag and the box. Climbing to my feet, I kick the box until it collapses on one side and sinks flat on the lawn. Suddenly out of breath, I find myself standing in the backyard, in a long nightgown, in darkly falling rain. The rain has plastered oak leaves against the white siding of the house and knocked the last petals from the wind anemones, scattering them across the grass. As I walk into the porch light, petals stick to my feet.

ROBIN C. MOORE

Childhood's Domain: Play and Place in Child Development
Professor of Landscape Architecture, North Carolina State
   University

What is going on when a small child fondles the fringe on the edge of a rug? What is happening when a tiny hand pulls a blade of grass from a shadowy lawn? Would the life of the child be different if the rug had no fringe, if the lawn were replaced by asphalt? The natural world offers a special place for children to discover themselves, to learn to distinguish "me" from "not me." I grew up on the edge of a small town south of London's greenbelt. From an early age we roamed freely, except when Battle of Britain dogfights raged overhead.

A track made long ago by wheeled vehicles ran along one side of the bracken places in Britains Woods. Just off the track grew a sweet chestnut tree, medium age with branches close to the ground, great for climbing. A stand of foxgloves in late spring thrust pink, chest-high columns through the bracken. The fresh flowerlets open sequentially as the top of the column continues to grow. We used to pick flowerlets, examine their delicate interior markings, sucking the ends to taste nectar, gently holding them between pursed lips, pretending they were fairy trumpets. Note: this plant now routinely appears on lists of "toxic" or "poisonous plants" because of the heart-stimulating chemistry of digitalis. Maybe if we had boiled pounds of the plant to drink, some harm would have resulted. Fortunately there were no adults around to intervene and no paranoia about child safety and this "potentially" hazardous plant. I live as proof, along with surely thousands of kids, that this potential has not been realized!

"Secret" is the special meaning children give to a place when they possess it deeply. Possession, which persists like love in long-term memory, comes from the hands—from interaction or a kind of making, or the creaturely ways animals define territorial boundaries. Nature is really the only medium that allows repeatable rewriting or remarking by the same children over time as they elaborate the place-relationship. Such informal, natural spaces are rapidly disappearing by the blade and under the rationally directed bulldozers of our technologically driven political economy. "We have to teach people to be more flexible," the radio commentator suggests, "in order to be able to change careers and jobs as globalization grows." But can you teach flexibility? Play gives a child a sense of a natural relationship that has no particular limits.

For a group of children playing together, nature is a unique medium that can be continuously and instantaneously used for an infinite range of expression. We must have been around thirteen when we started to spend most of our free time in the small wood next to Hugh's house. There Hugh and I found an old electric motor which we took back to his Dad's garage workbench, hooked it up to a main power supply, and got it to work—a secret fragment of a secret place.

Our visits to the wood then led to imagining other ways it could be used. We needed a place to ride our bikes. No longer satisfied with racing around and around the landscaped island at the bottom of Croft Way, we wanted a more challenging track. Over several weeks we built with pickaxe and shovel a ride twisting and turning around the trees in a circular loop 100 feet across.

One day we had the idea of building an underground "camp," the final adventure of our neighborhood childhood. We had the tools to dig the hole, and our ambition was limitless. One of us brought a bow saw from home to cut down a tall slender tree, which we cut into logs to span the hole as a roof. With four or five of us sharing a saw that had not been sharpened in years, it took many hours of very hard work. I can't recall if there was an image or story that motivated our energy. I think it was just the idea of living underground—secretly.

All the camp lacked was heat. Hence, the "stove adventure." Our plan was to move one of the cast-iron wood-burning stoves from an abandoned row of Nissen huts, where barrage balloon crews had been billeted during the war, two miles to our camp in the woods. The stove must have weighed at least 100 pounds. How to move it? About that time, I had constructed a wooden cart with two old bicycle wheels that could be towed behind my bicycle. Unhitched, it became the stove transport: somehow we managed to trundle uphill and down, yard by yard, on the public roads between the RAF camp and our underground hideaway. The last thirty yards we had to drag the stove through the woods to its final location. We lowered it into place with a rope, added a length of metal stovepipe, completed the roof around it and lit it up. It worked! Soon our earthy abode was deliciously warm and comfortable. I still recall sitting on "benches" fashioned out of the solid earth around the base of the excavations, the mixed aroma of freshly exposed dirt and woodsmoke in the air.

In following the streams, watching the seasons, and crossing the woods, we found both autonomy and adventure, discovery and invention. We learned about cooperation, as well as skills necessary to solve practical problems—skills that have been valuable all my life. For me the meaning of *secret* is deeply linked with sharing among trustworthy friends. Thus a secret place is discovered as the first opening to a delicious mix of predictable, anticipated change and spontaneous, surprise events, continually influenced by the perceptions, interpretations, and creative imaginations of child explorers. The process usually cannot be shared with adults, unless they can recapture the slow temporal and intimate physical scale of childhood exploration. For most adults, perceptually conditioned by clock time and automobile space, this is behaviorally impossible.

As semi-wild landscapes become transformed into suburb and city, the possibility of secondary transformation into children's wild and secret gardens must be ensured through policy development and professional intervention. Burnett's Secret Garden in many ways is a universal garden that all children need to play in, work in, and explore to discover the magic of nature and to nurture their own quality of life, health, and human wholeness. This year I met with a photographer from SPACE magazine covering a story on a recently completed child development center play garden. It was late fall, midmorning, the sun trying hard to assert itself through a high cloud cover. Both of us were focused on the visual scene, taking in the fine detail of the processes of nature as we hunted for "photo-ops." I commented on the fragrance of fall that permeated the yard, that subtle smell of damp decomposition underway on the surface of the soil, an indicator of energy transformation in readiness for the next growing season. "Isn't it incredible to think this is the first time in their lives these kids have experienced the natural cycle of this place where they spend so many hours each day?" His observation illuminated the essence of why this effort to reintroduce the natural world matters. The current generation will spend 5/7 of their childhood in experientially deprived spaces. As fewer and fewer children have access to open space, fewer and fewer attach value to nature's richness. Deprived of this experience, they may see no reason, as adults, to ensure its provision for their own children, and so on, until the opportunity to explore the world of nature is itself lost. No well-established tradition of natural learning exists in the childcare profession even though most of the progressive thinkers in early childhood education (Froebel, Montessori, Pestalozzi) have emphasized the natural world as a critical setting for learning. There children can make do with very little.

Secret can be anywhere where children possess their environment by making places, by the way those places offer the twofold gifts of adventure and sensory identity. Small size and muscular development limit children's ability physically to manipulate their surroundings. What must be "designed in" are ways in which infants and toddlers can possess the Earth in the first steps of childhood within a limited physical range and level of effort. Nature must be very close at hand, instantly reachable, graspable, with the whole body immersed. By "design" I mean the act of designing the possibility for action, not the actions themselves. The design of a place that affords as many actions as possible—this is the bounty of nature for children.

APRIL NEWLIN

Writes a nature column for *The Walton Sun* (Florida)
Practices clinical psychology in New Orleans

I was eight years old, waiting for the crabs to bite, tracing cracks in the old worn planks of the pier. Already the wood cooked in the morning sun, drying and shredding in splinters as long and sharp as the spines of an urchin. The pier had a way of working its way inside of you. At the end of a summer, I would bring home two or three barbs wedged in the palm of my hand or the ball of my foot. I could swear to this day that they never came out, that they were absorbed into the fabric of my being as if they belonged.

Waveland, Mississippi, was a quiet respite from the hot haze of New Orleans. One month each summer, my family settled into my grandmother's cottage on Bay St. Louis, but for my sister, her best friend Carol, and I, the pier was the place, the center, the whole reason for being there at all. Within minutes, we would cross the beach road, shimmy over the stone sea wall, and climb on board. The slats sloped up to a gate and extended into the water for half a city block. Just past midway, the pier widened with benches and an enclosed bathhouse beneath a roof. Steps led down to a lower deck which hovered inches above the water. At the end, a ladder etched with barnacles dropped into the bay and disappeared. By the time I was born, hurricanes had whittled the pier down to a gray skeleton on tall spindly pilings that swayed in the wind as if shifting from one tired leg to another. A sudden jump or dash down the steps could send the whole platform into a wobble and the railings only magnified the effect by bending if you leaned on them. Yet, the wharf had all the grace of an old sage. From the time we could tread water, the pier became a privilege, a ritual of independence renewed each year, every summer building on the one before.

It was a tree house on pilings, a club house over water, a hide-out without walls. Home was too far for help with most situations. Usually we secured not only the pier but the bay for ourselves. From morning until lunch and then again in the afternoon, we lived over the water, watching waves, catching crabs, hunting gars with scoop nets, and playing games on deck. The bay had to be watched, patrolled and scanned. Some days the bay darkened like a good roux and anything could hide in that opaque soup. Below the water line, the pier grew hairy green patches as if underneath it all the thing was alive, growing up out of the sandy silt bottom. We never swam without sounding the alarm, a few hardy and robust kicks off the slimy steps to send the sting rays flying.

Mostly, we spent our time crabbing. I got to know crabs intimately during those years, the way they bubbled and chattered when they needed water, the advantage of separating the violent testy ones from the others, and the sponge of eggs that earned a female another season. We cared for them all day, watering and shading, dipping the wooden hamper just far enough into the bay to let them taste their cool home again and again. We came to love what we hunted.

The crabs occupied brief spikes of activity in an otherwise slow and uneventful day. The wait, the empty space between the pulls of the nets, challenged our patience and taxed the rule of the half hour delay between net checks. We had counting rituals and songs. We watched thunderheads swell over the bay and shivered in the cold pelting of a summer shower. The bay boiled with whitecaps, the wind whipped salt spray like wet towels at our backs and we wondered if the pier would make it, if the old dock would succumb then and there, toppling into the murky bay with a tired sigh. Occasionally something big happened, out of the ordinary, and we forgot about the rules and the routine.

The space capsule remains a mystery to this day. From our high perch, we followed the curious speck on the horizon. At first we identified it as a raft, then a skiff, or perhaps a buoy. The object inched closer and our ideas grew more elaborate. Carol suggested a huge inflated sombrero. We waited, watched, and tracked it down the sea wall at least a mile beyond the pier. As it bobbed within yards of our grasp, a truck arrived, proclaimed the trophy a weather balloon and departed with the prize. It was a deflating moment and we returned to the pier both stunned at our discovery and angry that we had been cheated. We had reeled that catch in with our eyes, slowly, coaxing it until we realized finally that this was no sodden driftwood or lost beach toy but a finely designed and engineered aircraft.

The alligator, on the other hand, slipped under the pier and over the crab nets without notice. When we spotted the eyes, riding the surface of the water with a robber's mask of brown water, we manned the decks of the pier as if under attack. Alligators didn't belong in the brackish bay. We doubted our eyes and yet we knew the telltale markers—the brow, the snout, and the occasional flash of a serpentine tail. No one swam for days until the old lizard finally appeared belly up at the sea wall. Anything could happen out there or so it seemed. The pier had risks and since I was the youngest I took more chances, not out of choice but by being chosen. I can still remember the time that we forgot the key to the gate, how I scrambled over the railing, teetered on a rotted two by four, and swung out over the water twenty-five feet in the air like the boom on a sailboat. As I swooped to a landing on the other side, I saw the stiffened smiles of my sister and Carol, and in their nervous laughter I sensed their disbelief that the pier held.

The absence of adults for long periods of time allowed us to be daring, but also offered us time to explore and master on our own terms. We found our own rhythm, designed our own rules, and immersed ourselves in the patterns of the bay. The mood of the water changed daily and sometimes by the hour—

clear or cloudy, salty or brackish, high or low tide, benevolent green or menacing umber. Every nuance affected the fish, the crabs, the sea nettles, and our relationship to them. We smelled a storm coming and heard it in the water before we felt it in the wind. The three of us became as weathered, toughened, and callused as that wizened pier, and as it swayed in the gusts of an August squall we heaved with it, anchored in the wonder of it all.

When my grandmother died, my parents sold the cottage. A year later, Hurricane Camille took the house and the pier. Not a splinter left. Thirty years later, I stand on the deck of my summer place, tweezers in hand, pulling wood fragments out of my son's soft foot. The house sits on stilts, high on a sand dune, and I know of no better place on earth. I tally the days until I visit again, until I find myself in the counting of crabs and the cry of osprey. "I can't grip the tiny pieces with the tweezers," I tell my son, "but don't worry, they build character," and he dashes off in his sweet bare feet unawares.

JOYCE CAROL OATES

Blonde
Roger S. Berlind Distinguished Professor in the Humanities,
    Princeton University

Spying on *the new baby*, from my secret hiding place.

Spying on those who'd betrayed me. Never would I forgive them!

In hot May in a long-ago time lying on the filthy plank floor of the upstairs of the old barn. Lying on my stomach in the pain of humiliation and hurt sharp as sunburn. Amid clumps of dust and straw, the body husks of dead insects that, living, would have made me scream.

I was peering through the slats of the weatherworn boards at the figures on the grass below. My mother I adored, my grandmother, and *the new baby*. My infant brother who was *the new baby*, five months old and beginning to crawl. I was peering at them, invisible to them. My astonished and outraged and unwavering eyes. *The baby* was no longer me, but another!

Your first lesson: the world betrays.

There I was breathless in hiding, upstairs in the barn. In a forbidden place, for the floorboards were rotted and loose and might collapse beneath my feet; except I knew, from my father, how to walk on the crossbeams. Crawling then behind old farming implements, unused for years, festooned in cobwebs and turned to rust. This was my favorite secret space. Hidden there, beneath a window and able to peer out through slats in the boards, knowing no one could see me. Shimmering light, and I was in shadow. What made this space special was, it wasn't in the pear orchard, or in the fields, or down by the creek, or beneath the bridge, or in a deep cattail-choked drainage ditch at the edge of our property; it wasn't a long hike away, but close by the house. I could lie there calmly observing my mother, my grandmother, *the new baby*. Unseen by them as if I didn't exist.

Did I know I was inventing myself? I did not know and could not have guessed. Beginning the lifelong process of invention that is *self*. Hiding from adults. Saying *no!* to adults.

For when they'd called to me, bringing the baby outside onto the lawn, my mother's voice lifting—"Joyce? Joyce?"—it gave me a spiteful pleasure, a stab of pleasure indistinguishable from pain, not to answer.

No, I wouldn't answer!

Where is Joyce, Joyce is *gone*.

Oh where is Joyce, Joyce has *run away*.

What luxuriant fantasies of revenge, in childhood's secret spaces. Not-seen by those you are eagerly, avidly watching.

I would be six years old in another few weeks. My infant brother Robin, one day to be Fred, Jr., had been born on Christmas Day.

What is a new baby, to the first-born, but the very embodiment of mystery? Mystery-that-wounds?

My earliest memory of *the new baby* was confusion and excitement, an upset in the routine of our lives. *Something is going to happen but what?* In this era, children weren't informed—at least, I had not been—of impending births. The words *pregnant, pregnancy* would not have been freely uttered. If I'd noticed anything unusual about my young mother's body, and I doubt that I did, I would not have known to ask about it, nor had anyone offered an explanation. Up to the very eve of my mother's labor I knew no more of the imminent arrival of *the new baby* than I would have known of death and oblivion and the end of time.

I'd wakened on Christmas morning to hear voices, excited voices, and these voices my parents' voices yet they seemed not to be speaking to me, or of me. I did not hear the magical name *Joyce*. My mother's and my father's voices for the first time—or so in my total self-absorption I would think—not centered upon *Joyce*.

For five and a half years I had been *the baby*. For this unquestioned eternity I had been *the baby*. When visitors came, when my mother's numerous sisters and cousins came, I was *the baby*, much admired, fussed over and hugged, how could I have comprehended the possibility of a day, an hour, when I was no longer *the baby*?

Christmas Day, a special day, yet my father took my mother away, I was left behind. I was baffled, hurt, frightened. Left behind! My father had driven my mother to the Lockport hospital seven miles away, but I wouldn't know that at the time. What I knew was: my mother can vanish, even on Christmas Day.

What I knew was: *Joyce* wasn't so important after all.

Almost, I'd come to think (I'd been encouraged to think?) that the very word *Joyce!* means *special*. One-of-a-kind. Baby. To be the much-anticipated first-born of young, romantically-in-love parents, what a privilege! And for five and a half years to bask in that privilege, that unalloyed love, as an infant basks in its mother's womb, utterly protected, and blind.

A theory: all of metaphysics, the anxious attempt of positioning human consciousness in an unknown and unknowable exterior space, arises from our expulsion from that centeredness.

When at last they'd brought *the new baby* home from the hospital, Joyce was summoned, and, aghast, told to look: your little baby brother, his name is Robin! Look at his blue eyes, look at his tiny fingers, his tiny curling toes! When I shied away, jamming my fingers into my mouth, when I shook my head no, they said teasing *You'll be sorry if you don't.*

Sorry if you don't, well I did not. Not at that moment, at any rate. Though later of course, of course later, fascinated too, and proud, yes but sullen, tearful, hurt. Was I a spoiled child, had I been a spoiled only-child, never would I forgive this shock! this insult! Running away to hide in the chicken coop, in the shed beside the barn, in the barn, upstairs where it's forbidden, running away to hide my hurt, a child's lacerated heart, you can't anticipate how swiftly such wounds mend, how quick a child's tears come, scalding, spilling down her cheeks, and wiped away, and again spilling, and again wiped away, in the tumult of emotions that is childhood.

Always they could find me, if they made a game of it, my young parents, and seriously looked. *Joyce? Where are you?* Hide-and-seek. Our earliest, ecstatic game.

Where's a child so young to *go*?

Later there would be the orchard, the fields. In the country, all of the outdoors is a possibility to hide in. Like time, going on forever. Yet our most prized secret spaces tend to be close to home, and safety.

Secret spaces of childhood: the very words are poetry. Evoking the lost landscapes of the past. When even hurt was precious. Those secret spaces we discover when the open, public spaces of childhood—the family, the household—aren't sufficient any longer to define us.

When our child's pride is hurt. When we believe ourselves betrayed. When we learn by instinct the necessity, and the cunning, of separating ourselves from adults. When, for once, our small stature is an advantage, for once!

Crawling away to hide. Hiding in plain sight. What bliss!

One day soon, it might have been that very day, I would be playing with *the new baby* like everyone else. Or maybe more avidly, with more excited fascination, than others. For *the new baby* was myself, wasn't he?—or, somehow, Joyce was herself *the new baby*, again an infant just learning to crawl on hands and knees, trying to talk, making absurd gurgling squealing sounds, flailing and pumping his arms. It was too difficult to comprehend. No, it couldn't be comprehended. But there was so much not to be comprehended. Staring in amazement at this hot-skinned baby with the startling blue eyes, named

Robin, told repeatedly *Your brother! you have a baby brother! look how he's looking at you,* this mysterious baby one day to be Fred, Jr.; in the five-month infant what yearning, what hunger, that quivering, that need to crawl, to sit up, try to balance himself, pushing his clumsy little boneless-seeming body into contortions new to it, comical but heroic acrobatics that left him baffled, lying on the carpet on his side, baby-limbs pumping. . . . How we laughed! How we adored him! Those moist rounded eyes darting swiftly from face to face, what was he seeing? how did he comprehend us? alert and excited and squealing as if a game were being played, yes certainly a game of incalculable complexity was being played, we were all playing it and the point of the game was *the new baby* at its center. And not me. Not Joyce. But Joyce was encouraged to stroke Robin's fine, soft hair, to play with him on the carpet, and hold him, and help bathe and diaper him, and talk with him, as one day how many decades later, across what dizzying chasm of Time, Fred and I would confer on the phone, earnestly, worriedly, trying not to be anxious, our voices unconsciously lowered as if—but this was absurd—our parents might somehow hear us, groping for words and flailing about in this new bewilderment at being no longer children, but adults of advancing middle age presented with the great riddle of our lives: how to help our aging, ailing parents, still living on that same rural property in a much-changed Millersport, New York, how to help them in what we all must know is the final stage of their life together, without hurting their pride and their wish—a fairy tale wish!—for continued independence. One day Fred and I would so confer, often. But not for a long time.

Secret spaces of childhood. That cryptic little poem of Emily Dickinson's that haunts me, as if, perversely, it were an utterance out of my own quite happy and ordinary childhood:

> They shut me up in Prose—
> As when a little Girl
> They put me in the Closet—
> Because they liked me "still"—
>
> Still! Could themselves have peeped—
> And seen my Brain—go round—
> They might as wise have lodged a Bird
> For Treason—in the Pound—

Out of the secret spaces of childhood we invent ourselves. We begin the lifelong process of invention that is self. But we see, for the first time, irrevocably, wonderfully, how the world continues without us, even as it calls our name.

ZIBBY ONEAL

The Language of Goldfish
American Library Association Best Book for Young Adults,
   1980, 1982, 1985

Madeleine is sprawled upside-down in a chair, book held at arms' length above her head. She is reading. I know she won't hear me when I tell her lunch is ready. I will need to tell her several times before, vague-eyed, she turns to look at me. So compelling, apparently, is this book about trolls.

She has read the book at least three times, but, clearly, she still finds it engrossing. In my grandmotherly way I wonder what there could be about this book to merit so many rereadings. And yet, almost as I am asking myself the question, I think of *Rackety-Packety House* and the number of times I read it the winter I was eight.

That winter I no sooner finished the book than I began to read it again. Its story of a dollhouse family coming secretly to life whenever humans left the room enthralled me. It was not the magic, itself, that I found so fascinating. It was the idea that one could have a secret life. I deeply desired a secret life of my own, but I was encountering difficulties.

Chief among these was the fact that I lived with a mind-reader. My mother was able to take one look at me and know in an instant what I was thinking. Or so it seemed. I believed that she could read my thoughts as easily as if they were printed across my forehead—a circumstance that made a secret life difficult to sustain. As I saw it, my only hope of privacy was distance.

There was a lilac bush in our backyard that made a fairly good refuge in the summertime. I could, and often did, retreat there to crouch beneath its branches, screened by leaves, and think my thoughts in peace. But this was a temporary solution. When autumn came and the leaves fell, I was visible from the house again and no longer sole owner of my secrets.

The autumn I was eight the leaves began to fall as usual and I, as usual, began to anticipate another transparent winter, thoughts as exposed as fish in a bowl. But, as it happened, this was the winter I made a discovery that solved the problem. One day it occurred to me that I had been reading *Rackety-Packety House* for over an hour without a single question or comment directed my way. At first I credited the book, itself, with mysterious powers to ward off intrusion, but soon I saw that any book would do. In a reading family a reader is respected. Pick up a book and you're left alone.

This discovery led to another. Gradually I realized that it was the *appearance* of reading that mattered. So long as I held an open book, as long as my eyes were on the page, I could count on being left to myself to explore my thoughts in private. There was some dishonesty in this. I saw that. When I heard my mother proudly telling friends that I had become a real reader, my conscience troubled me a little, but only a little. A twinge of conscience seemed a small price to pay for the luxury of being left alone.

All winter I gazed blankly, blissfully at printed pages. Words scattered and drifted on the white paper, meaningless as Chinese characters to me, absorbed in my own world. I suppose that sometimes I must have done a little real reading but, if so, I don't recall it. What I remember about that winter is drifting print and solitude.

Oddly, I have no memory now of the thoughts I was so determined to protect. Possibly it was never their content that mattered. Perhaps their real importance was simply that they belonged to me. They were part of a new and shaky sense of myself, proof of an independent existence.

It may be that all hide-outs serve a similar purpose. They are places to try out being separate, spaces in which to contrive a self distinct from others. In the beginning this project of self-definition is a fragile undertaking, requiring courage and determination. But perhaps as much as either of these it requires a private place where a child can safely practice being somebody different from anyone else.

I think this, looking at Madeleine who is dangling from the chair now, anchored by her knees. Her book is lying on the rug a bare two inches from her nose. Is it really possible to read a book two inches from your nose? Is she actually reading? I don't ask. Suddenly I am reluctant to disturb her. Instead I go back into the kitchen where the lunch is waiting and decide that it can wait for a while.

EUGENE F. PROVENZO, JR.

Video Kids: Making Sense of Nintendo
Professor of Education, University of Miami

My brother Nicholas set the curtains on fire the day I was born. I quickly learned to play by myself. My parents never quite learned how to deal with him. He set the tone for our household—making life unpredictable and sometimes violent.

When she was seven, my younger sister Ann moved in with her friend Lindy. Her mailing address didn't change, but her inner self moved across the street and three doors down. She had her own room at her friend's house. We would see her during the week and as part of holidays, but essentially she was gone.

Left alone with Nicholas and my parents, I became a lonely child. I sought solace in books. In books I found a geography that I could shape and explore at my leisure. It was, in many regards, like the space I found to play in under the dining room table—a place where the world could not intrude.

The books I loved most were the ones with grand adventures and secret worlds. My clearest memory from when I was eight was a day when, from early morning until late into the afternoon, I was cocooned in a canvas hammock in our backyard reading *The Swiss Family Robinson*. This was not the celluloid drama created by Disney, but the masterwork by the eighteenth-century Swiss cleric Johann David Wyss. I was transported to an unpopulated tropical island with caves and coves and all manner of adventures.

That same year I read Jules Verne's *Twenty Thousand Leagues under the Sea*. With its hidden spaces beneath the ocean and its submarine the Nautilus, the book captured my thoughts and imagination. I quickly moved on to other Verne novels like *The Mysterious Island* and *Journey to the Center of the Earth*.

I often wonder what secret spaces I would escape to if I were a child today. Would I read a book or would I enter cyberspace instead? I suspect the latter.

In cyberspace I could interact freely with adults or more interesting children than those who occupied my day-to-day life. In a chat room, or in a role-playing game like a MOO (Object Oriented Multi User Dungeon), I could reinvent my life and my self.

Online participatory games like MOOs are places where children and adolescents can assume whatever character or personality they want. This is done through an "Avatar," a term from Hindu mythology which refers to an incarnation of a god. In an online gaming context, an Avatar is a character you create and define for yourself (literally an alter ego or second self) that you can insert into the action and play of a game.

When I was a child, I became characters in the novels I was reading: the tragic and lonely figure of Captain Nemo searching the seas for justice, or one of the boys (Hans or Fritz) in *The Swiss Family Robinson*. As I grew older and my reading became more sophisticated, I assumed (in my mind) the role of characters like the sorcerer Gandalf in J. R. R. Tolkien's *Lord of the Rings*. In my books, I was protected from others— and yet engaged in a society. When I read *The Swiss Family Robinson*, I was the secret son who watched, and looked, and learned throughout all of the adventures. When entering cyberspace and constructions like MOOs, I enter a region that is secret and isolated from the physical and social world that I occupy. In the secret spaces of cyberspace there are distinct dangers, problems, and rules quite different from those encountered in books.

In cyberspace you can participate in violence that is limited only by your imagination. Power has almost no restraints. Magic is very real. Spells can be cast and opponents vanquished. In a book, the author can set limits to the secret space the child enters. Librarians, teachers, and parents can determine whether or not certain books and the fantasy realms they provide are suitable. Materials deemed inappropriate can be kept out of the hands of the child reader.

Somehow the secret space provided by the book seems much

safer and much more appropriate to the experience of childhood. The dynamic of cyberspace is significantly different
than the dynamic of the book. It is clear that we have entered
a brave new world whose secret spaces are more like the
seemingly infinite black holes found in outer space than the
comforting spaces found in books. One cannot help but wonder
what we might be losing, and just how concerned we should
be for our children.

PAUL ROAZEN

Erik H. Erikson: The Power and Limits of a Free Vision
Professor Emeritus of Social and Political Science, York
    University

Memory is notoriously tricky, and I think formal autobiography only justified by the most talented, but I would like to
venture to recreate what has always seemed to me a paradise
from my early childhood—a little beach which was part of the
small town at the beginning of Cape Cod where we used to go
summers during World War II. I cannot remember ever discussing this place before, and I have never checked my version of things with any surviving relatives; so it remains a
personal realm even as I am writing about it now.

Since I was born in 1936, I am thinking of the years when I
was, let us say, four to six or seven years old. I have looked at
some photo albums, and there are shots of me at this beach in
those years. (The photos were almost certainly taken by our
long-standing housekeeper.) What strikes me now as most
memorable about that time is just how unprepossessing the
beach can look from adult eyes. I happened to go back there a
few years ago, and I can testify to how utterly lacking in
glamour it now is. Yet it is very much today as it was then: a
smallish stretch of sand adjoining a good-sized body of water
ultimately connected to Buzzards Bay. There was no surf, just
the changing of tides; on exceptionally windy days there
might be whitecaps, but it was so tranquil that there was
never a lifeguard.

I can still vividly remember exhilaratingly setting off alone, barefoot, in the early morning with my pail and shovel heading for a wonderful day at the beach. I would most likely have known whether it was going to be high tide or low tide, or in which direction in between the water was moving. Probably it was a weekday. Our house was so close to the beach, and the traffic so minimal, that even on Saturdays and Sundays traffic would not have been any problem. The street I have in mind lacked a sidewalk, but there were some sidewalks in our section of town. The cottages were all set close together, but at the start of the day everything was quiet.

The beach itself was wholly transformed as the hours passed, and on weekends people came who would never visit in the normal course of events; on holidays it could be crowded. (The absence of a parking lot meant that it was restricted to the local people who got there almost entirely by foot.) It was possible to go and come from it all on one's own; I am presuming it was a nice day, and therefore I could expect my older brother and younger sister to come along at some time during the morning. One of my cousins, who lived nearby, was also a reliable playmate, and we had a fun live-in grandmother. But I could get intensely absorbed with building and digging in the sand; castles with moats were designed to withstand for at least a while the ravages of water. If the tide were coming in, then my objective would be to make constructions far enough back so that they would withstand the oncoming water. The low tide (at which the beach was technically at its most expanded) seemed to last awhile, and would not be the time of greatest excitement. The day's work would be interrupted at least once daily by the ice-cream truck, and small change would enable one to join in the lineup. A simple popsicle, a "push-up," or the more expensive ice-cream sandwiches, tasted perfect in hot weather.

Talk at the beach was more significant to me than the swimming; but the water was warmer when the tide was not at its highest. At the lowest tide the sand was unattractively squishy under foot, and one seemed almost to sink in. Special excursions were possible, such as walking a bit along the edges of the bay; the shells of dead horseshoe crabs seemed reminders of dangerous possibilities which had been miraculously rendered safe. The agony of stepping on the upright tail of such a creature seemed too dreadful to contemplate. There would be occasional dinghies sitting in the sand; getting in and out of them was an adventure in itself. Late in the war we had the use of a small war-surplus inflatable raft, but I don't remember our ever paddling very far. Sometimes we had the inner tubing of tires for swimming, but that pail and shovel were the main essentials of my beach life.

The excitement came from the small beach itself, all the daily changes that took place in it, and the shifting sets of people who arrived. There seemed an almost endless variety of things going on. For special occasions like birthdays we would get taken by car to Silver Beach near Falmouth, and although that always seemed an unusual treat, our own little beach never lost its special allure. In hindsight, it was such a humdrum dull-seeming place that older children would have been bored by it, and so it was frequented mainly by small children and their caretakers.

Although the sand and the water were both perfectly clean, it was, in retrospect, one of the worst beaches I ever saw; when I think of the world-class beaches on Martha's Vineyard, for example, that I later took my own children to, it scarcely seems possible that I was ever once so content with the space given to me. But I don't think that as a parent I ever looked back on beaches with the eyes of a small child. Spectacular expanses of sand or broad vistas were not what attracted me as a youngster; waves are of course only for older children. I suppose, now that I have spent so much of my time writing, that I have continued to live in my imagination; but the reality of that beach, and how it could ever have so entranced me, brings back how much I lived largely on my own resources. The stability and predictability of the outside world then made possible my happiness; but how busy I kept, and how entirely content I was, is testimony to the different perspective a child brings to things. The relative autonomy of my existence at that beach lends a special glow to my whole childhood. The fact that a world war was going on only entered our lives in the form of special costumes worn for dancing occasions. The main part of town had places which were part of the world of soldiers, but they only bore on our lives in the most distant way.

Rainy days did happen, but then there would be movie houses which would open up for the occasion. One could walk (a long way) to a couple of them too, but in the rain that would not have been likely. A whole separate set of memories would be associated with the break in our normal schedule involved in going to movies in bad weather. But I am writing now to commemorate how absolutely magical and joyous was the social entity associated with that one small beach. At the time it seemed completely fulfilling, and one of the highlights of a city kid's whole year. However claustrophobic and secure my extended family life, that beach provided an escape hatch from the outside world. No matter how crowded the life we led, with schools, lessons, hobbies, and religious routines, the beach remained a symbol of how the external world was beckoning.

ROBYN SARAH

Promise of Shelter (stories)
The Touchstone: Poems New and Selected

At the bottom of the slatted iron fire-escape there was a place where we used to play, not together but singly and at different times, because it was a secret and hidden place, enclosed on three sides by the back of our house and the house adjacent. Hardly any sun ever reached this place, and when it did it was like a pale finger that crept down between the buildings to touch a spot on the ground without warming it. No grass grew here. The earth was hard-packed and damp, and it had a smell like potatoes going to sprout. In places it was dusted with a thin fuzz of yellow-green moss that you could scrape away with the edge of last year's popsicle stick stained grey from winter. Here and there were tall spindly weeds with a rank smell, and tiny white specks, with tinier yellow centers, for flowers. The only other thing that grew here was camomile.

You were alone and secret in this place, even if it was blazing noon out in the street. Above you, washing flapped in the breeze, and sometimes something wet and clammy came tumbling down through tree branches to land beside you on the muddy ground—a pair of white cotton panties you might lift gingerly on the end of a stick and heave aside. Sometimes a woman came out to bang a mop against a railing, and down floated dust bunnies, dreamy as snow. Out of open kitchen

windows came the sounds and smells of other people's houses:
a baby crying, a radio playing, the whine of a vacuum cleaner,
a mother singing or scolding, clatter of cutlery, smell of
tomato soup, smell of floorwax.

Sometimes I think my love of cities is actually the love of
such small, enclosed spaces, glimpsed from bus windows, from
other people's balconies, through dusty screen doors: spaces
that breathe a promise which has no words but can be heard in
the wind that rises before the first summer thunderstorm, or in
the first night rains of early spring. Spaces that make a har-
mony out of an old tree trunk, grey wooden sheds and stair-
ways slanting between walls of buildings, a balcony rail graced
with geraniums, a line of washing, a black iron spiral of fire escape, the dance of leaf shadows on a red brick wall. Sometimes
a squirrel, a cat—the ambiance of cats, their musk in the
sparse weeds at the base of the presiding tree. These spaces are
cool and dank, they are shafts, well-like, in which—one can
sense—the pull of generations has been caught forever in an
eddy, to swirl there like a movement of air, like a silent chord,
born again and again out of its own echo.

One glimpses these spaces in passing but does not enter
them. Only a child, alone, may play there, singing a private
song, squatting under the fire escape and scraping at the dirt
with half of a broken clothes-peg to uncover sacred relics: a
blackened penny; a scratched marble; pieces of blue glass, of
green glass; a rubber wheel off a Dinky toy, or maybe the hollow body of the truck itself, packed tight with claylike mud;
Coke bottle caps, caked with the same mud; a large button, a
small button, their holes mud-plugged; an orphaned earring; a
key that will open nothing.

LORE SEGAL

Other People's Houses
Professor of English, Ohio State University

The secret I want to talk about is the geography of my first
bedroom.

My first bedroom coincided with the *Herrenzimmer*, the

"gentlemen's room" as the family living room used to be called in prewar Vienna. Here, come nighttime, my mother opened my little bed and she and my father retired through the door located at the foot of the bed into the dining room behind the right wall. I could hear the mumble of the conversation grownups have, after the children are got out of the way, about things grown-up people know.

In May 1938 the Nazis requisitioned our Vienna apartment. The most interesting thing, sometimes, about a memory is the stubborn impossibility of filling in the holes in it: I can see the alien uniforms standing around our *Herrenzimmer*. I know there were more than one but not how many, nor do I see myself, or where I stood, though I sense my father like the unseen dream presence behind a dreamer's back. I do see my mother. She is standing to my left. I was ten years old. The time had come for me to learn that what the grownups didn't know was how to save me, that they didn't know how to save themselves.

My parents and I took the train to the village of Fischamend and went to live with my grandparents. In August, the Nazis requisitioned my grandparents' Fischamend house, and my grandparents, my parents, and I got back on the train to Vienna. We lived with aunts, cousins, and friends—whoever had room—until we were able to leave Vienna on our thirteen-year migration via England and the Dominican Republic to New York. I put it all down in a novel I called *Other People's Houses*. I wonder if the Ancient Mariner in his latter days got really tired of rehearsing his old trauma. Every story I tell starts, willy-nilly, with this ur-story.

I returned in 1968 with my American husband. The stairs of a Viennese prewar apartment building spiral round the central elevator in its wrought-iron cage. On the second floor I said, "There: Number 9. That's our door. Number 10 was Xaverl. At least my mother called him Xaverl. He had sinus trouble and my mother said you could set your clock by Xaverl's early morning coughing, honking, and spitting."

"What are you going to do?" asked my husband uncomfortably.

I rang the bell of Number 9: the sound of a Vienna door bell.

"What are you going to say?" asked my husband.

"Boring!" I remember thinking of Alain Robbe-Grillet's new wave novel because instead of using metaphors and similes to describe a habitation in colors, shapes, smells, and histories, he related the front porch in measurements, width by length, and the plantation of trees visible from the porch in terms of metric distances and compass directions.

I've come to think Robbe-Grillet was on to something. What do we bring away from our nostalgic—our so curiously, so helplessly urgent pilgrimages to a past long since refurnished with the colors, shapes, and smells of the histories of the new people living in our old childhoods? We confirm the blueprint plus elevation of our first geographies. And what if they've removed the walls? In an essay called "The Mural" I've described how my husband and I rented a car to Fischamend and crossed the village square toward the oversized father/mother/child painted on the building that housed the new police station which replaces my grandparents' house. "What puzzles the imagination," I wrote, "is the inability to reconstruct the spaces in which we had moved: I can't position the window that overlooked the square in the wall at the right distance from the angle of the door there used to be on the left." They had removed the floor I stood on.

With my ear inches from the door of our Vienna apartment, I was intensely excited to discover I knew that when the door opened I would see, directly across the foyer, the door to the little toilet I refused to go into, nights, when it was infested with ordinary robbers. To the left, I told my husband, is the kitchen and beyond the kitchen the miserably narrow maid's room my mother had regretted in her refugee days when she was maid and cook in an English household. Listen: the slippers slurping across the parquet floor toward us from the night are coming out of my parents' bedroom, past the bathroom door and along the wall where the little wardrobe with my clothes used to stand. They're turning the L of the foyer past the door with the glass inset that leads into the *Herrenzimmer*. I mapped the *Herrenzimmer* in the air. Here's the window. Here are the three leather armchairs around the round table, here's the glass-fronted bookcase, the tile stove, door into the foyer, door into the dining room. My bed stood right here.

The chain on the inside stopped the door from opening. In my mind's hindsight it is Hansel and Gretel's crooked, beak-nosed witch peering through the crack. She asked me what I wanted and I asked for my father. She said there was nobody by that name living there. I knew that. My father had died a quarter of a century before during the week that ended the European war. The elderly witch who was living in my Vienna apartment suggested I go and talk to the concierge and then she shut the door.

I have polled my friends. Put yourself back into your first bedroom. Lie down on the bed: You know which way your feet point and the position of the window in relation to the door in relation to the chest of drawers, and the direction of the room in which your parents are asleep. Did you know that you have this map in your head? My friends are surprised, but not overly interested. Boring. We're not excited by the elemental fact that we carry our heads north of our feet, yet this is our basic orientation: it determines what we call up and down, what we experience as right and left. It's not something, when we're talking together, that we mention to ourselves or to each other. We take it, or would take it, if it so much as occurred to us, that this is what we have in common. But neither do we account to ourselves or to each other for the place in which we stand—the standpoint—from which we do our talking.

The kids have a bit of slang that gets near to what I mean. "I know where you're coming from," they say. Or "You see where I'm coming from?"

No, I don't know. I don't see, and neither do you, and that's why the things we tell each other seldom achieve direct hits. What we mean is likely to land, if it lands at all, to the right or left or aslant of what we intended. Ask someone to quote back to you what you just said. Do you recognize yourself? Proust put it best. He said when A and B talk there are four conversations—what A says and what B hears and what B says and what A hears.

It's the secret of our ur-geographies that poets and people of that sort never stop trying to give away; it's into each other's earliest space that lovers, in their first weeks, believe they are going to be able to enter.

DAVID SHIELDS

Dead Languages
Professor of English, University of Washington

I recently went by myself to ring the doorbell of my childhood home in the Griffith Park section of Los Angeles, and no one answered, so I looked around a little outside. The brick wall was gone, the garage was replaced by a deck out back, and the living room appeared to have been turned into a wet bar. Incense burned out open windows. What was once a white and lower-middle class neighborhood was now integrated and middle class. I could remember only a few things about the house in which I lived the first six years of my life: between the front lawn and the front porch, the brick wall which served as an ideal backstop for whiffleball games; an extraordinarily cozy living-room couch on which I would lie and watch *Lassie* and apply a heating pad to relieve my thunderous earaches; the red record player in my sister Sarah's room; and the wooden rocking horse in mine. . . .

I'd hold the strap attached to his ears and mouth, lifting myself onto the leather saddle. One glass eye shone out of the right side of his head; its mouth, once bright-red and smiling, had chipped away to an unpainted pout. His nose, too, was bruised, with gashes for nostrils. He had a brown mane which, extending from the crown of his head nearly to its waist, was made up of my grandmother's discarded wigs glued to the wood. Wrapping the reins around my fist, I'd slip my feet into the stirrups that hung from his waist. I'd bounce up and down to set the runner skidding across the floor. Then I'd sit up, lean forward, press my lips to the back of his neck, and exhort him. Infantile, naive, I thought I could talk to wooden animals. I'd wrap my arms around his neck and kick my legs back and forth in the stirrups. I'd lay my cheek against the side of his head, press myself to his curves. When he pitched forward, I'd scoot up toward the base of his spine, and when he swung back I'd let go of his leather strap and lean back as far as I could, so I was causing his motions at the same time as I was trying to get in rhythm with them. I'd clutch him, make him lurch crazily toward the far wall, jerking my body forward, squeezing my knees into wood. Then I'd twist my hips and bounce until it felt warm up under me, bump up against the smooth surface of the seat until my whole body tingled. I'd buck back and forth until it hurt, in a way, and I could ride no longer. Who would have guessed? My very first memory is of myself, in my own room, surrounded by sunlight, trying to get off.

TOBIN SIEBERS

Among Men
Professor of English, University of Michigan

I owe to the army shovel an intimacy with red clay. Designed small enough to be packed by a GI, it was still big for a boy to carry any distance, though lighter than the garden spade. But it was perfect for the close work of tunneling, and so in the summer of my fifth-grade year my little brother and I equipped ourselves at the local army surplus store and set to work on the cliff of red clay overlooking the Fox River behind our house in Wisconsin.

"It's just like the modeling clay at home," Robby said, "only dried up."

"Only dried up," I agreed, forcing the edge of my shovel into the ridge of red clay.

We carved a hidden fort in the hillside, burrowing deep into the ground, chipping out the brittle clay—rubble of red cubes—until we found ourselves in complete shadow on a sunny day. We washed down the walls of the cave with water from the Fox, until the clay grew slick and smooth, and when it hardened we took up residence inside a secret organ of the earth. Dark and warm and red, it was our shelter from grown-ups and a treasure trove of mud—the "Clay Mine," we called it.

Over the next weeks we snaked deeper and more danger- ously into the hillside, conversing with glee about cave-ins, avalanches, and tremblings of the earth. I sank an air shaft down from above, three feet in length, and carved a hearth at its base, where tiny bodies huddled around a fire big enough to bring a solitary can of chicken noodle soup to a boil. My brother had his first cigarette in the Clay Mine—Camel unfiltered—pilfered from our father's supplies. On the package, behind the golden camel, was the great pyramid of Egypt—grander, I felt, but not more ingenious than our own digging.

Our success with the Clay Mine sparked an enthusiasm for building, and we moved into the open where the adults might catch us. We crawled up the hillside, rose out of the shadow of sumac and wild grape vines, and laid claim to the glorious hilltop. We axed young birch trees, five inches in diameter, spent an hour strapping them together, and launched a footbridge across the drainage creek at the base of the ravine. Another set of logs, laced together with pink plastic clothesline rope, was to be our raft, but the rope unraveled and the logs broke apart the instant we hit the water. We nailed up a platform between the three trunks of an old basswood tree and strung a network of flashlight bulbs sparked by a dry-cell battery through the upper limbs as if it were Christmas.

Then one day we found ourselves up the tree and face to face with old man Sager—a hermit, miser, and notorious grouch who owned all the land stretching from our street to the river and screamed at any child who dared step foot on his property. He looked at us hard, smiled crookedly, and disappeared over the hill.

"Guess we're pretty lucky," I said.

Robby climbed down the tree and ran home in a hurry.

The next day I could see right away that things were bad in the woods. The tree house was gone. Someone had attacked it under cover of darkness, snapping each little light bulb with his fingers and flinging the timber down the hill onto the railroad tracks. Then he had chopped the footbridge in two with a hatchet. The logs rotted in the creek for years until they finally dislodged and floated away. We ran up the crest of the hill and down to the Clay Mine, but when we arrived, its roof was caved in, the opening rim broken in an arc, as if it were the Coliseum tipped on its side.

That night we told our father what old man Sager had done. Dad asked again about the light bulbs.

"Not him," he said. "Other boys."

The next morning as we were riding our bikes up and down the street, Scotty, a neighbor boy, yelled out, "Sorry about the Clay Mine," and ran back into his house. Robby turned his bike around and stared at me. I stared back. So Dad was right.

Children hide themselves instinctively from adults, as if from a natural enemy, but they need to hide themselves equally from other children who turn adult-like in their envy when confronted by the small things their friends have made. The Clay Mine fell to this envy of secrets, and we didn't have the heart to remake it because we knew, somehow, we could never keep it safe from the other children.

DAVID SMALL

Imogene's Antlers (among 26 picture books)
Illustrator, *The New Yorker*

I came in through a narrow hall with two U-turns in it; at each turn the light diminished sharply. Rounding the second turn, like entering a cave, I stepped into total blackness. The dark was filled with the sound of gushing, gurgling water, also slammings, thumpings, and other noises hard to identify.

Gradually my eyes adjusted and forms began to appear, everything lit with a ruby glow. To my left were stainless steel tanks of water, a bubbling black bath whose rippled surface writhed with snakes of red light. Tall figures toiled along the long counter beneath the red-tinted safety bulbs. X-ray films were removed from their metal cases, developed, rinsed, and transferred to drying racks. The technicians who worked in there—because I was a doctor's son—welcomed me in to this dark interior world. With their military buzz-cuts and strong arms they looked to me like the capable, squared-off young men shown in magazine ads for the Bright and Shining Future coming soon to everybody in America. Feeling invisible in the dark, I eavesdropped on their banter and, from them, caught on to the rough camaraderie between men. This was 1951. I was six.

Listening, I dangled my hands in the water, watching the red serpents coil around my wrists, feeling a delicious deadly chill creep all the way up to my elbows.

Perhaps I decided then and there to try fearlessly to enter the realm where forms develop from nothingness, as images come up gradually of film, or, as water calms, fractured vi-

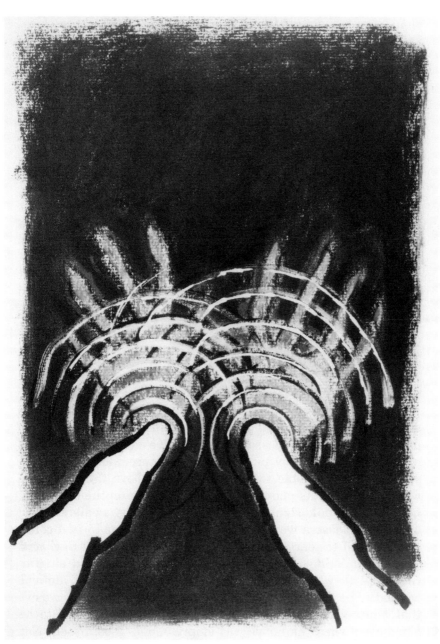

David Small, *Ripples*, 1999
Brush and Ink

sions regain their readability on its elastic, reflective surface. In this same way pictures develop from the awesome nothingness of the blank sheet of paper. [*see artwork*]

CATHY SONG

School Figures
Picture Bride (Yale Younger Poet Award)

I was born to sing. This fact had less to do with gift or talent than simply being a birthright I exercised early on despite having been born without the necessary physical apparatus required of even halfway decent singers. Had I been blessed with exceptional equipment I may have chosen to enter the entertainment business, and in doing so, forgotten my birthright. I may have ended up an entertainer, singing background music for others to dine by. The shadow world abounds in talented entertainers.

In the company of others I was too shy to sing; no one had heard my true voice. In the company of others I remained for the most part quiet, quiescent, as if waiting to sing to life.

I was born to sing despite a lung capacity that was never strong, even before years of bad habits like smoking ruined it forever. And though I possessed a sensitive ear (my voice recognition is uncanny), my pitch like my balance was wobbly, unsure, never quite able to hover precisely above the notes the way a dancer floats above her feet by focusing on the abdomen, her center. I would struggle, slide up to the notes, swallow a few, and then release a warble. Oh, but my heart was in it! I could move myself to tears at my own rendition of "Danny Boy" and "Red River Valley," the beloved ballads my untrained singing retreated to when I wanted to be alone. Just how alone I wanted to be became more apparent the older I grew. It wasn't that I just wanted everyone out of the house; I wanted to be alone even when the house was empty. Alone to be myself. Not the self who had to negotiate her way through the daily ritual of social interaction and responsibility appropriate to her everyday reality, which as an adolescent meant adhering to authority, teachers and parents, as well as conformity, the changing whims of frivolous friendships. That self came away exhausted, pummeled by the forces that conspired to keep me from myself. I suppose I longed to be task-less. I longed to simply be.

Perhaps in another life I had been a monk who sat for eternity and chanted, shrouded in a halo of sound, pure sound where the text is secondary to the sacred vibrations spinning within every cell, every cell waiting to hum its part in the intricate workings of the universe. So my ancestors did not come from Ireland or the American West. This fact had everything to do with these two songs. They served as templates for my humble voice to reproduce for my own benefit sounds as sacred as any sutra.

When my own children were young, I used to dream of a break in the tedious hours devoted to their care, as if praying for a break in the weather, the long still afternoons when only flies answered at the screen door. Frequent naps were a requirement in our household during the years before the arrival of school relieved me so I could catch up, not on much needed sleep or long neglected housework, but rather so I could catch up on myself. A habit begun long before I had my own children, when I was still a child myself yet old enough to stay home without supervision. How introverted and uncooperative I must have appeared to my parents, who set out on countless family expeditions without me, asking one last time as they pulled out of the driveway, "Sure you don't want to come along?"

I did not want to come along; so much of living as I saw it meant keeping occupied, filling in the gaps between the major events of eating and sleeping. Already then I feared time was being gobbled up and frittered away by amusements invented by someone else. I did not want to tag along. How could I tell them gently in a way they could understand that I preferred my own company, that I enjoyed being alone? I tried not to appear too gleeful, solemnly pronouncing I had work to do— work, a word my parents approved of, bought me liberation. Of course, if I had work to do I was allowed to stay behind. Indeed, it was work that required my fullest attention. Once they drove off, I would race back into the house, not a minute to spare, sit in the middle of the blessedly empty house and sing. "Danny Boy" and "Red River Valley," my two standbys, served as warm-up, preludes to some new song I wanted to practice, the choice often depending upon finding to my delight one with a suitable range. Around the age of thirteen I discovered the epiphanies of Joan Baez's hymnal interpretation of Bob Dylan's "I Shall be Released," Judy Collins's cold spring surges of "My Father," and Joni Mitchell's sad inflections on "Both Sides Now." I heard in their voices courage, each breath a commitment to give each moment fullest attention, and I responded, something within me unfurling, lifting, turning toward the light.

In singing I found my true voice, a resonance that began deep within my body, and once engaged, encouraged my entire being to expand beyond the confines of my limitations. I found true power residing there, the pouring in of something larger than my own breath and the resultant sound, a boundlessness, reverberating, radiating, shining forth. It was like dipping into an ongoing eternal river and emerging anew, revived. My entire being would heat up as the conscious production of sound began to accelerate an awareness of my own body, not the boundaries of the subservient one fulfilling the necessities of utilitarian existence, but the other body, the secret one whose skin is composed of light.

Sometimes the singing stopped, sometimes for years, and I would return to it from a long absence, hesitantly, afraid I might find I had lost my way. Though at first my voice would be rusty from disuse, it would, with a little coaxing, respond with such forgiveness that I would be moved to believe in the generosity of this gift that required no talent, that needed no explanation for my lapses, as if it knew only too well about those things, those obstacles and distractions that tie us down, keep us from ourselves, making us so busy, too busy to sing.

ELLEN HANDLER SPITZ

Inside Picture Books
Lecturer, Department of Art and Art History, Stanford
  University

Words shaped the secret spaces of my childhood. From the start they mattered—even before I knew what they meant.

My mother made certain of that. Our family legend has it that frosty mornings on New York's Upper West Side in Riverside Park a bundled-up baby girl in fur-trimmed hood, harnessed to an oversized perambulator, astonished passers-by with impromptu renditions of the Preamble to the United States Constitution. At bedtime, my mother sat close to me on a satin coverlet and read aloud. Poetry often, not just stories, and I waited for the effect of her voice. Modulated and mellifluous, it filled me with sounds, images, and wistful longings. It made me sad and happy all at once. Even now, reading stories to young children makes me cry. My daughter, when she was small, cast furtive glances at me during especially long pauses in my reading—the silences that gave me away.

Lying perfectly still beside my mother with her voice in my ears, I floated off to lands where pastel-colored gumdrops cascaded from silvery trees, and turreted stone castles rose out of landscapes carpeted in the deepest of green. Witches cackled and grimaced; shy boys gave knitted caps to princesses. Ogres menaced me with gaping mouths and guttural roars; stalwart toy soldiers perished, their paper hats askew. Flowers with human faces erupted into bursts of tinkling laughter; rocking horses teased their riders; a delicate lady in black rescued an elephant who had lost its mother. Rhinoceroses on the banks of gray-green greasy rivers unbuttoned their heavy skins; a woman gave birth to a mouse. I shivered when Carrabbas the uninvited fairy cast her hundred-year spell and tasted the drops of blood that fell from Sleeping Beauty's finger. Envious and lonely, I longed to be cared for, like the Darling children, by a furry Nana or to have a fairy godmother or a turbaned genie of my own.

Speak clearly and distinctly, my mother repeated, as we grew taller and began to play with other children who didn't. Whenever you open your mouth, the world is waiting to judge you. Never be imprecise. In our house, some words were strictly forbidden. "Thing," for example. If my sister or I forgot and carelessly resorted to it, Mother would stare at the offender and shake her head slowly, knitting her brows in pretend confusion: "*What* did I hear? You must say exactly what you mean." One day my mouth opened, and an unknown word flew out, syllables I had heard uttered by another child. Her edict came swiftly: were I ever to use that word again, my mouth would be washed out with soap. Looking back, I cannot remember what word it was or whether the threat was actually carried out, but a bitter taste remains, a gagging sensation, a feeling of rage at being held down, a profound sense of humiliation.

At eight years of age, I was sent off to summer camp in the Berkshires, where all the other girls in my bunk gathered in clusters, their hands cupped, whispering a word I did not know. Desperately, I tried to decipher its meaning from context but couldn't. All summer long, the hovering presence of this word oppressed me; I felt miserably left out, too ashamed to reveal my ignorance. Colorful, wild fantasies haunted my imagination until, back in New York, I began to circle my mother. Waiting for just the right moment to ask her, my heart beat loudly, but in the end my courage failed. The word I hadn't known was "Kotex."

Words determined my childhood loves. Nathan, for example, was my father's oldest brother and my favorite uncle. I begged to be allowed to sit next to him because of his prodigious vocabulary. He specialized in arcane polysyllabic words and was fond of quoting world literature as he launched into complex stories with Homeric flourishes. He never talked down to me. After dinner, he indulged himself with aromatic cigars, and traces of their scent clung to his scratchy tweeds. When my direct gaze met his, he responded with a knowing twinkle. Seated beside him, I felt enveloped not only by his wonderful words but by his bulk, his aroma, and my primitive realization that he was, because of his linguistic gifts, a font of limitless mental adventure.

My second favorite was Uncle Phil, born in England. He had an oddly sharp way of pronouncing words that delighted me. Taking my beribboned sister on one of his knees and myself on the other, he regaled us after dinner with cunningly crafted renditions of the great European fairy tales. Especially thrilling was his telling of "Rumpelstiltskin." Astonishingly inventive, he could make the terrified queen guess dozens of names, each more exotic than the last. Streams of names seemed to pour effortlessly from his lips until finally in the end when the dwarf simply has to be recognized by the queen, he would pronounce "RUMPELSTILTSKIN" in stentorian tones and let go suddenly, dropping us two small girls from his knees to the floor below, where we collapsed in a heap only to plead for a repeat performance.

Occasionally our parents went out in the evening, and just after they left, I would run to my room. Creeping under my bed with a cache of picture books, I would try to remain there for as long as I could, stretched out in my secret hiding place. Inevitably, the irregular tapping of our sitter's footsteps disrupted my solitude, warning me that my sanctuary was about to be invaded.

Not long afterwards, I developed the habit of running away. From home, from school, and eventually from summer camp. When interrogated and punished, I was unable to explain myself. The best I could do was try to refrain from using another word Mother had prohibited, namely, *hate*. "I hate you" was what I longed to say—to teachers, to counselors, and even to her. She did not allow this because, as she explained, the world was still recovering from a war in which hate had caused the murder of millions of innocent victims. To me, however, a child whose hands and face never came perfectly clean, whose long tangled hair resisted brushing, whose demeanor was insufficiently sedate and mood inexplicably sullen, the word *hate* made sense. So sometimes I transgressed and did utter the terrible word. It seethed on my lips, and afterwards produced shame and a renewed impulse to run away.

At eleven, I was terrifed of the male gym teacher at Murray Avenue School in Larchmont, where, just before his presence in my life became a reason for escape, my parents had purchased a Tudor-style manor house with leaded windows, majestic twin fir trees under which I could hide, and five lovely bathrooms including one I did not have to share with my sister. The move disoriented me. After apartment living, the new house seemed overwhelming. I fantasized secret passages and was afraid of getting lost. School intimidated me as well. Especially the other girls. Whereas Mother dressed me in plaid pinafores and jumpers with knee socks and matching ribbons for my braids, the Larchmont girls wore nylon stockings, shoes they called "flats," slips they called "crinolines," "cinch belts" for their waists, and dresses more grown-up than anything that hung in my closet. With his megaphone to his mouth, surly Mr. Smith dominated the school playing field in a ranting voice that blended with the guttural harangues of my childhood ogres ("fee-fi-fo-fum . . ."). Anything I could do to avoid him was acceptable to me. Small and new in sixth grade, the year when everyone's body is changing at a different rate, I felt ashamed to be scrutinized in my regulation green gym suit, ashamed to be chosen last for every sports team, ashamed above all to be bellowed at. Thus, a pattern developed.

Each day of gym class, I descended to the breakfast room for my bowl of hot cereal and then dashed off to school. But instead of going to school, I doubled back. Gingerly and furtively, I climbed down into one of those leaf-filled wells that surround the windows of basements. Fortunately, our maid had the habit of leaving at least one window ajar to air out the laundry, and reaching with my small fingers I could unlatch the bar and squeeze myself through. Tiptoeing to the tiny bathroom on that floor, I silently slipped the bolt and locked myself in. It was cold enough for me to keep my coat on. Curling into a ball between the toilet bowl and sink, I pulled out a book from my bag and settled down to read. Magical hours passed as I flew off to other times and spaces.

Mother however still thought me too young for a wristwatch, and so my anxiety over whether the maid might divulge my secret was trumped by a more urgent concern—namely that, lost in a book I might fail to reappear at just the right time for lunch. Knowing when to stop reading and retrace my steps—when to climb back out of the window and pretend to come home from school—was an insoluble problem. Eventually, I was caught and chastised. "Dire consequences," as Mother put it, were the fruits of misbehavior.

One other scene of clandestine activity took place that year in a turreted house that belonged to my friend Mary Lennon's family. A trapdoor to their attic was located in Mary's own bedroom. In addition, she and her siblings were the possessors of massive stacks of comic books, including the so-called classic comics which I adored but was forbidden to read. Mary herself, moreover, had vowed to protect me, even if it meant lying occasionally on my behalf. For Mother despised comic books; whereas other children spent their weekly allowances on them, my sister and I had none.

Rebelliously, I marched weekdays to the Lennons' imposing house. Mary and I, our hair done in braids for school, would smile knowingly as the heavy oaken doors opened and closed. Once upstairs in her bedroom, we silently released the folding stair that led to a dark attic and then, equipped with flashlights and laden with our comic book treasure, we ascended. How delicious it was there amidst the dank odors and eerie shadows we cast! Never will I forget my terror when Milady, in the classic comics version of Dumas's *Three Musketeers*, was to be beheaded. The silhouette of her hooded executioner still haunts my dreams, for I felt myself to be guilty, like her, of wrongdoing.

Mother died before my sister and I had fully grown up. It has been decades since we've heard her voice. She died too young to read anything I ever published, too young to grasp the immense expanding impact of her words. But one granddaughter of hers teaches English now in China and carries on the family tradition of surrendering to words and to all the faraway places, real and fantasized, to which they lead. This granddaughter has a way too of glancing at me when I fall silent. Ever watchful, she still expects, perhaps, to detect a tear.

ILAN STAVANS

The Hispanic Condition
Professor of Spanish, Amherst College

Not far from my house in Copilco, the southern neighborhood in Mexico's capital where I grew up, there was a factory in ruins—its name, La Curtidora, still decipherable on top of its entry door. It was a roofless structure with decrepit walls that invoked London after World War II but far more humid. It was magical, full of secret alleyways, treacherous dead-ends, and undiscovered chambers. Heavy rain multiplied its ubiquitous puddles. It is those puddles that I first think of when La Curtidora comes to mind because my brother and I enjoyed catching tadpoles and frogs, which we would bring home in old marmalade bottles with tops full of holes for the tadpoles to breathe. The puddles, and the factory as a whole, seemed like a Darwinian wonderland to me: micro-organisms reproducing at amazing speed and rivalries between breeds playing themselves in front of my eyes. In spite of it being in urban surroundings, I sensed I was in an alternative reality: a rustic, unfinished site suspended in Time.

My all-time favorite place within it was an abandoned school bus—flat tires, broken seats, rusted roof, wild plants growing through the windows, but with its windshield intact. When my brother wasn't around, I usually ended up in one of its back seats, making sketches of unreachable planets in a notebook. Later on, in my adolescence, it was in the bus that a friend and I meticulously studied wrinkled copies of *Playboy*, but those images are less meaningful to me than the comforting solitude I found before, when I sat undisturbed in it. What made the bus so attractive, so stimulating? I often envisioned the children that used it decades ago—their faces, their words, their aura was vivid to me. I felt them around, like ghosts, speaking to one another, exchanging cards or sharing lunch items while navigating the daily route. Did anyone ever kiss for the first time in the site I was? Did any one of these children imagine it to be a spaceship too? Around then my mother got me a book called *Un automóvil llamado Julia*, written originally in German—in Spanish, the title means *An Automobile Called Julia*—, about a pair of children that find a *chatarra*, a useless motorcar left untouched in a barn. They clean it, fix the engine, remodel its interior, and little by little transform it into a brand new vehicle. (It was exactly the premise of the musical film *Chitty Chitty Bang Bang*, which I saw many times.)

The plot enthralled and inspired me. What if I too transformed the school bus into an appetizing item? I went to a hardware store and with the few pesos I had in my piggy bank bought brushes and paint and decided to make the effort. While doing so, I thought that perhaps, after I finished with the bus, my next project could involve asking a few neighbors to help me rebuild one of the chambers of La Curtidora—plaster the walls, rebuild the roof, set new floor tiles. But first I had to finish with *el autobús llamado*. . . . Halfway through the job, though, the results already quite inviting, I was overwhelmed by second thoughts. Why should I turn my favorite site into a place others would want for themselves? What I most liked about the bus, about the factory, was precisely their "unappetizing" quality, the fact that they were mine alone. Why make my private hide-out public? So I stopped *in medias res*.

La Curtidora became a casualty of the voracious modernity of the mid-1970s, a decade in which Mexico City, like an octopus, extended its tentacles far and wide to devour everything around it. In its stead a huge building complex was erected. The last recollection I nurture of the bus is of its interior half painted in an emphatic yellow.

JOHN R. STILGOE

Outside Lies Magic: *Regaining History and Awareness in Everyday Places*
Orchard Professor in the History of Landscape, Harvard University

Just south of the hen house, the gravel bank tumbled down toward the logged-over maple swamp and the lone white pine at its edge. Thousands of maple saplings stymied any casual exploration of Valley Swamp and while I could walk barefoot and soaked to Jacobs Pond, Third Herring Brook, and salt water, I never did. The saplings blocked any long-distance views from the bulldozer-sculpted gravel bank too, making the swamp visually opaque, mysterious. I liked to look at the swamp, even if I could not look far into it.

Before age ten I had a sort of observation spot on the bank, an oval of bare gravel surrounded by sweet fern and bayberry and sheltered from the northeast wind by the hen house. Active play happened just to the east in a zone of toy soldiers, steel Tonka trucks, and Michigan cranes, even an eight-foot-diameter concrete pond my parents built for toy boats. Small white pines and cedars punctuated that end of the bank and long before any high school teacher explained ecological succession I knew it firsthand. Year after year the bank greenery grew more dense, and by the time I reached my teens only the sweet-fern-encircled gravel spot remained bare. I spent a lot of time in it, but always in brief fragments, sitting or sprawled, watching the swamp or gazing at the sky, gauging the weather, then heading elsewhere. Never did I read in it.

Instead I sort of floated my senses, filament-like, always in part because the sweet fern smelled.

Sweet fern (*Comptonia peregrina*) is not a fern, but one of the bayberry family, and its lustrous fernlike leaves prove wonderfully aromatic, especially on a hot day. The smell floats several feet from the plants, and crushing the leaves between the fingers means scenting them for hours. I put a few sweet fern leaves in my elementary-school pencil box, and sometimes in my windbreaker pockets. Some school years I shoved one or two leaves into the back corner of my desk, so I could touch them, pull out my hand, and smell the smell of home. I did not hate school, but I disliked its indoor regimen, its emphasis on knowing by seeing and listening only. Never did I buy a school lunch. My lunchbox tastes connected me with home at midday, but sometimes as the hours dragged I needed the faint odor of sweet fern too, to remind me of the gravel bank, the swamp, the joyousness of nothing to do. When I happened on the idea of putting the leaves in books I cannot recall, but I remember inserting sweet fern leaves in junior-high-school math books. Smelling the leaves made me glimpse the swamp, put me back in my spot for an instant, rescued me momentarily from Modern Math.

In cold weather or warm, the spot focused my senses, indeed reassured me of their value. In mid-spring and mid-autumn I heard migrating birds, the rush of wind through the maples, the slicing of rain. Mid-summer meant smelling the swamp as it dried, meant measuring the dusky odor of hot maples underlying the scent of sweet fern or noting the smells that presaged a thunderstorm. Hot days meant grading the different consistencies of gravel under my bare back or between my fingers. Any season, even winter, rewarded any visual scrutiny of the swamp, or the sweet fern leaves curled up, withered and russet brown, mere shadows against the cold, the snow. What I learned surrounded by sweet fern is only the old rural Yankee way of meditating, the quiet time everyone once valued. On the gravel bank I discovered the inestimable value of down time, of just being, of the way particular aromas waft through all sorts of mental jumble, the moments that make one distinguish between busyness and business, school and education.

STEPHEN TRIMBLE

The Geography of Childhood: Why Children Need Wild Places
  (with Gary Nabhan)
The Sagebrush Ocean: A Natural History of the Great Basin

When I was boy, and Ike was president, Little America meant
freedom. It wasn't Richard Byrd's Little America, the polar ex-
plorer's 1929 Antarctic outpost. My Little America was
Covey's Little America, the world's largest gas station, hun-
kered low against windscour and winterblast on the rim of an
eroding Wyoming mesa.

These summers of my childhood reeled out as adventures,
their rhythms dictated by my father's fieldwork as a geologist.
When school ended each spring, we left our home in Denver
and drove west through Wyoming to Oregon or Idaho. In these
outposts of home—home because we were together—we
rented a house in the town closest to my father's mapping
area.

This run of the open-space West stretched as wide as the
Cinerama screens in its cities, out to the limits of peripheral
vision, where it kept going. When something happened in that
emptiness—a dust storm, a rainbow, a fleet of pronghorn
dashing across the road so close I always imagined them actually leaping over the hood—it made my day. My mother and I
joked about the emptiness. We would croon, "Why-O-Why,
Wyoming," and dissolve in giggles. A city girl, she was fond of
the place name that epitomized Hicksville for her: Tie Siding,
Wyoming.

We began to see signs along U.S. 30 outside of Laramie.
"Little America." "World's Largest Gas Station." "65 pumps."
"Nickel ice cream cones." Black-and-white cartoon penguins
and Fifties signboard cursive led us to the faux-colonial buildings topping a rise west of Rock Springs. Here, one day's comfortable travel northwest of Denver, we stopped for the night
at the motel and truck stop punctuating the windy middle of
nowhere.

Covey was the founder of the place, a visionary whose story
was printed on every placemat in the restaurant. *"Away back
in the Nineties, when I was a youngster herding sheep in this
dreary section of Wyoming, I was forced to lie out in a raging*

blizzard. . . ." On that stormy night, Covey dreamed of surviving to build a haven for travelers in the remote spot. When he heard about Admiral Byrd's base in Antarctica, he knew what he would call his traveler's rest.

His dream—Little America, Wyoming—opened for business in 1934. On these long-ago evenings at Little America, we gratefully took our key to one of the modest red brick units. When we pushed open the door, I was gleeful to be out of the car and in this room with chenille-covered beds set close enough for a boy to somersault across the gap between them. We showered off the sweat that came from driving before air conditioning, with the windows open and my parents still smoking. We walked to the dining room where smiling, elderly Alice Hand played bouncy tunes on an electric organ. With a switch, she flipped on a fake drum accompaniment, beaming with pleasure at this whiz-bang technology.

We rejoiced in our family intimacy. Surely no one understood as we did the humor in Covey's self-conscious "Legend of Little America" printed on the placemats. We smirked at each other when Alice Hand played her un-hip music, just as we joked about Lawrence Welk, my grandmother's equally un-hip hero. But, the truth is, I didn't have to look up Alice's name to write this. I remember it, and I remember her benign smile, a benediction bestowed on anyone with the means to sit in those brass-studded leatherette armchairs and pay for their spaghetti with its slightly acidic sauce, for their hamburgers and steak and fried shrimp and soft dinner rolls.

While my parents stopped at the bar for their before-dinner gin and tonics, and again, the next morning, as they lingered over coffee, they freed me to wander around Little America, exploring. Everything about the place seemed a little askew: a gleaming shield of tile in the restaurant bathroom, otherworldly green; in the gift shop, a stuffed penguin in a glass case. The penguin stood sentry over bins of knick-knacks. Rabbit's-foot keychains. Ceramic jackalopes. Pastel felt fedoras with "Little America" stitched on the brims. I coveted them, every one.

There were fireworks, too—illegal at home, but legal in Wyoming, and therefore mesmerizing. Cracker balls were my weapons of choice, the little wads of brightly colored paper and gunpowder you winged at the pavement for a satisfying explosion. I used up my allowance on the cracker balls and used up the balls one by one on the oil-stained cement curbs.

I counted the gas pumps, wondering if this really was the world's largest service station. For my tally of license plates from different states, I censused the parking lot, pen and notebook in hand. I remember wrestling with a minor moral dilemma: could I check off more than one state for a single vehicle, using the semi-trucks registered in several places?

Most of all, I remember walking to the edge of the vast parking pads, where cement ended abruptly at the brink of what the awestruck ranchers in western movies of the time called "Big Country." From this frontier of the mid-twentieth century, I stared into the empty red-desert scrubland, into the tantalizing space of Wyoming, squinting up Black's Fork toward Fort Bridger, shrinking under too much sky, dreaming of mountain men.

These dreams stay with me. In the time-travel parlor game, where you pick any time and place to visit, I choose the West of my imagination, the West of Crow and Ute and Pueblo, of Indian America. The West of those exquisite, terrifying Blackfoot warriors and worthy Mandan holy men in Karl Bodmer's watercolors from 1833. The West that Lewis and Clark and the trappers saw, with no roads, no towns, no resorts in the Shining Mountains. No dams on the desert rivers, no polluting roar from internal combustion engines.

Just as the mountain men escaped from the civilized East, my father's field seasons for the U.S. Geological Survey furnished an escape for the three of us. From the sorrow of the family tragedy—my retarded older brother, swept away by schizophrenia at puberty, institutionalized, and lost to us. Escape from the taunting of my classmates, who hazed me each school year for my bookishness and ineptitude at sports. Escape from my mother's needy sister and dismissive brother-in-law, toxic to her peace of mind. Little America was our gateway to three months of freedom.

These summers had the open-ended allure of a summer vacation heightened by the dare of being on the road. My father had been driving the West for twenty years already, and he plotted his route from mountain to mountain and restaurant to restaurant. He loved the cool rise of the peaks as much as he loved the flake and fruit of homemade berry pies. Fort

Collins: Iverson's Dairy for chicken sandwiches and ice cream made from milk from cows we could see out the window. Laramie: windy, railroad-dingy, a line of motor courts with cowboy neon. Branding iron, bucking bronco, buckaroo.

And on across Wyoming, with broken-down gas stations constituting most of the towns, Red Desert, Wamsutter, Point of Rocks, Medicine Bow. Hamburgers in Sarasota, or lunch in Rawlins, at the Adams Restaurant with its special salad dressing or the steamy Willow Café, where descendants of the Chinese who followed the railroad made spaghetti for me ninety years later.

The map. A provocative array of "Points of Interest," the red squares that told me that Wyoming mattered to history, some-how. "Site of Fort Fred Steele" (who was Fred?). "Dinosaur Graveyard" (were there gravestones?). "Remains of Old Almond Stage" (why almond?).

When I turned sixteen, I ferried my mother to Little America in our 1962 Dodge Dart, an ugly pinkish-tan one-of-a-kind confrontation of curves and angles. I was determined to drive every mile of the open highway, following my father as he drove the government Jeep. I remember getting dangerously tired on those ups and downs of central Wyoming, but I sure wasn't going to yield the wheel to my mother.

When adolescence flooded me with hormones, I lay in my bed at Little America on hot summer nights obsessed with a wakening sexuality that the freedom of that first day on the road enflamed. I fantasized about being taken, ravished, by one of those businesslike waitresses, off-shift, in her cottage at the back of the parking lot. Somebody, please, somebody, take me by the hand and lead me to bed and show me how to make love.

In 1999, I again drive the familiar road across Wyoming, this time reversing the direction of my childhood venture into the freedom of summer. I journey through a February snowstorm— toward Denver, not away from it, to move my aging parents from our family home to a retirement apartment. I will gather up my rock and postcard collections and my newspaper clip-pings from the Sixties and drive back to my home in Salt Lake City with my childhood in boxes in the back of my truck.

And so I return to sit in the dining room at Little America

for the first time in years. There is a new, gleaming, too-brilliant building next door, with fast food and high-tech gas pumps. But the old motel and its lobby and restaurant remain as I remember, unrenovated. Instead of Alice Hand at the organ, inoffensive selections of classical music play for me and for the Wyoming ranch families out for Saturday night supper on this frigid February night.

Edward Curtis prints hang in sepia on the walls—the classic romantic image of the West. Here is another dream, Indians as we want them to be, noble profiles and tragic mourners, frozen in 1880 before vanishing with the buffalo. I'm sure few travelers stopping here at Little America think of the real Shoshone and Arapahoe people of Wyoming, not exactly flourishing but proudly surviving still, struggling to keep their families intact and make a living up north on the Wind River Reservation.

I sit in the same high-backed chairs I sat in at five, at ten, at sixteen. It's disorienting to be here in this museum diorama of my childhood, writing in my journal about memories thirty and forty years old now.

It's ironic, too, that the very reason for my trip lies waiting in Denver—where I will encounter my childhood when I sift through the closets and shelves of my family home. In those boxes lie forgotten Little America post cards and keychains, snapshots of my mother and father standing on the curb here, younger than I am now.

My parents saved these things without making a judgment about their worth. They were mine. They once mattered to me. And so I'll have to be the one to decide to keep them or dump them. Many times in the decades since, I would have tossed them all. Now, I save the funkiest trinkets, some for my own children, a few to connect me to my past when I encounter them on my desk.

The storm sifts snow across the parking lot to drift against the windbreak of blue spruce. Fuchsia neon reflects from a molded green Sinclair Oil dinosaur grazing on the front lawn. Darkness settles, the ground blizzard grows more daunting. Back on the road, the semis barreling over the black ice and through the wind-driven blind of snow threaten me, a roaring force at odds with my fragile memories. I drive east, into my future and back to my childhood.

MARINA WARNER

*From the Beast to the Blonde: On Fairy Tales and Their
   Tellers*
Visiting Fellow Commoner, Trinity College, Cambridge
   University

Before I was sent to boarding school in England, across the
Channel from my parents in Brussels, I didn't have any secrets, except the precious hoard I accumulated in my treasure
drawer, which nobody else was allowed to open without my
being there: a set of tiny white porcelain Chinese horses in
different poses (most fascinating the one rolling on its back); a
filigree brooch in the shape of a tennis racket with a pearl attached for the ball; some shiny studio portraits of stars (Leslie
Caron, Howard Keel, Mel Ferrer) cut from my mother's
monthly magazine from London; miniature detergent packets,
plaster-of-Paris painted vegetables, and tiny scales and
weights for playing toy shop; the pink frou-frou hat, complete
with hat-pin, worn by my doll Jennifer, who had been given to
me in a wonderful box rustling with tissue paper by my
mother, in Rome when we went back to her home country for
the first time; some numbers of the weekly comic *Girl*, and a
few feathers, relics of my pet birds, bought in the Grand Place
at the Sunday market. They always died because their feet
fell off. (Since then, I've learned that fowlers trapped them
with lime or nets that damaged their legs.)

My treasure drawer doesn't point forward to what I have
become—I never liked riding or tennis. However, *Girl* did run
on its back page a series on *Heroines of History*, and I've since
studied and even written about several of them (Joan of Arc,
Emmeline Pankhurst). But later, posted to the huge, imposing
convent of St Mary's with its cobwebby pine copses and bleak
playing fields, I developed a far deeper secret life. I was en-
gulfed by a sense of being severed from everything familiar—
from family and, in my case, even language; at home, in the
kitchen, we spoke Italian when my father was at work, and
with my friends in Belgium I spoke French, so when I first arrived at St. Mary's I appalled my new schoolfriends with my
curious, unchildlike English, acquired from books and adults
only. The food was strange to me as well; I couldn't penetrate

the barter economy of toffee and fudge and gobstoppers and liquorice bootlaces and humbugs because I didn't know what any of these things were, as I'd never eaten English sweets. In the drab Belgium of the 1950s, children's treats were limited to marzipan sabots (clogs) on December 6, St. Nicholas's day, and bunches of lily of the valley at the beginning of May—to mention "les muguets de mai" would have set my English classmates hooting with derision.

So I built ramparts and defenses around enclaves that nobody could spoil by sarcastic mockery. These secret places hold in kernel far more of my future than the contents of my treasure drawer and yet, at the same time, the normal banality of that little girl's accumulation doesn't feel as alien to me now as the private world I fervently made up as a refuge from England.

The school day followed a rhythm set by monasticism: chapel, breakfast, study punctuated by prayers at noon (the Angelus bell sounding); lunch in the refectory, followed by a period of "recreation"; then more schoolwork (prep. for the next day's lessons); supper; more chapel (every other day); games and dancing to 45s in the school hall (this was the era of Cliff Richard's hit, "Livin' Doll"); followed by bedtime, and, if we were lucky, "My Curly-headed Baby," sung in her thrillingly big soprano voice by Mother Barbara in the dormitory. This timetable, with its long stretches of imposed tedium, its structured contrasts of activity and quiet, its punctuating rest bars and pauses, now strikes me as a genuine achievement of the Catholic faith, and its disappearance from the crammed schedules of children today a profound mistake. As Adam Phillips observes, "It is one of the most oppressive demands of adults that the child should be interested, rather than take time to find what interests him. Boredom is integral to the process of taking one's time." There was nothing to do during that empty, "boring" time of afternoon "recreation," for that very reason, fantasy flowed in to fill it.

The Lower School where I arrived aged nine occupied a large suburban house and garden that bordered on the purpose-built convent; a grass path led through sandy soil, where azaleas flourished; beyond these flowerbeds dark and dusty rhododendron bushes spread their angular limbs; I learned how to pull off the flowerheads, split the petals and put the tip of my tongue into the groove, like the philtrum of the upper lip, and lick the drop of nectar collected there. There were some small headstones in the bare soil under the bushes, where pets were buried—they had belonged to the house's former owners. But these discreet graves were few and gathered in one spot near the garden wall, and they didn't lead on from one part of the grounds to another, as did the images of the crucifixion and the statues of Mary that were placed at strategic moments in the garden—at the corner of the hockey field, at a meeting of two paths in the pine woods, or in the Lourdes grotto where we prayed on special feast days.

I would stare and stare into the mild, blank face of the Madonna, and will her to speak to me; with the full force of my concentration I defied her to remain an inert, wooden, painted thing. The visions of Bernadette and the children of Fatima were mixed up in my mind with the statues that replicated the very young girl who'd appeared, with roses between her toes, in the Massabielle grotto, and the radiant, floating queen who'd spoken to the three seers at Fatima and given them secrets, which, we were told conspiratorially, only the Pope had seen and wouldn't be opened for fifty years. The inert statues in the convent grounds might start vibrating with visionary light if I fixed them, like Max and the Wild Things, with my special, intense, commanding stare. I beseeched Our Lady, I implored her, I searched for her tears, her smile; I'd look away, and quickly look back to see if I could catch her moving, as in a game of Grandmother's Footsteps. She was the biggest of all possible dolls; if I could have reached to take her down from her pedestal I would have shaken her to life, like Alice and the Kitten. She wasn't a kitten, and she wasn't a doll, and up there, carved taller than any mortal woman, she was literally out of reach. But she took the leading role in my games of make-believe, and Rilke is so deep and right when, in his essay "Some Reflections on Dolls," he says, "the doll was the first to inflict on us that tremendous silence (larger than life) which was later to come to us repeatedly out of space, whenever we approached the frontiers of our existence at any point. . . . Are we not strange creatures to let ourselves go and be induced to place our earliest affections where they remain hopeless?"

Underneath the rhododendron bushes were crawl spaces,

and I found one that was roomy enough to kneel in; it must have been summer, for the ground was warm and dry, I remember. I broke off twigs from other, lesser bushes than my chosen shrine, and bent them into the tracery of the rhododendron branches in the manner of a wattle fence; I didn't have any twine and the long grasses I tried to use to tie them in place quickly dried and frayed and broke; so the walls of my hiding-place were ramshackle. But I continued to work on weaving a secure perimeter, and I felt a huge happiness and pride in the private grotto I was making—that rush of excitement that accompanies a secret.

I used to pray there fervently, that summer of my tenth or eleventh year, for the Virgin Mary to appear to me. I don't remember how I lost interest or when I gave up; a certain relief followed, as only one part of me wanted to be a saint.

PAUL WEST

The Tent of Orange Mist
Chevalier of the Order of Arts and Letters

Childhood is work, requiring not only exact reporting but a willingness to discern its effects: woof and afterlife, so to speak. The first, I think, is easier in that the images have sunk in and become permanent, if remembered at all, whereas the second is open to self-persuasion and deceit, lending itself to adult embellishment and mature hyperbole. If you ponder childhood at all, you end up with an album and something like King René's Very Rich Hours, in which childhood figures as almost a character in a narrative, tilted this way and that.

I never live a minute of my adult life without thinking of my childhood. My grown-upness is drenched in childhood. The child, as Wordsworth says, is father to the man, but also the man's overseer, wizard, and catalyst. I first discovered the ambivalence of childhood when I began writing (poems) at seventeen, suddenly recognizing how the cast-iron fact could melt and redeploy itself once in the presence of willing words. There is what you mean when you say "It was like this," and what you intend when you say "It meant this to me." The two are hard to separate, but I somehow manage to do so because I have, on the one hand, a near-photographic record of what happened, and, on the other, an only too acute sense of what the imagination can do once provoked. Proust is instructive here because he stresses the way memory does not oblige. There is the voluntary memory, which can be schooled and made to serve, and there is the involuntary memory that pleases itself, goes its own way, and cannot be harnessed, only awaited, depended upon, for whatever it tosses up. I myself find this reassuring because it almost corresponds to my initial distinction between fact and embellishment; the voluntary memory will dish up whole gamuts of material, whereas the involuntary one obligates you at once to the quirkiest mystery there is—you are lucky if you have this at all, or at least some awareness of it. There are those with albums, and those with radiographic plates of a haunting. I hope to do justice to both. Suffice to say, when I reached seventeen I was much aware of recalling my childhood as something "over," done with, complete, like the literature of a dead language, but also of childhood as a gift, a fuel to the ego, a mass of mystery and joy that would somehow ballast and fortify the incipient adult. So there occurs a natural pause at that point as the mind tries to stabilize itself before delving beyond.

Meeting the Sitwells

It was rumored that if any of us in our uncouth way, presented himself at the doors of the Sitwells' Renishaw Hall, begging a penny for the Guy (effigy of the Gunpowder Plotter Guy Fawkes) or simply pleading for a leftover crust or two, or even "a drink of water, Mester," Sir Osbert or his minions would send us away calling us all *Mellors*, after the plebeian upstart of D. H. Lawrence's novel *Lady Chatterley's Lover*, set in this very village (and one other). When I myself showed up hoping for her and not him (Dame Edith rather than Sir Osbert, the poet rather than the autobiographer), he never said *Mellors* at all.

"So you write, young feller-me-lad."

"Yes sir, I do. Stories."

"Ah, but not often."

"From time to time, sir."

"Thank God for that. How may I disappoint you?"

"Well, sir, I wondered—"

"I never help, I never advise, boy. Are you Jewish?"

I told him no, but I would have answered no to anything. Was I an Assyrian, Kurdish, Cypriot? I had little idea of what he meant.

"Well, good, that's a blessing. So you write. Well, don't. Whatever form the disease takes with you, resist it and get a decent job mining coal."

He hadn't even asked to see the sheaf of twaddle I'd brought with me, rolled up like certificates. He hadn't identified me as the genius I hoped I was. His own prose, like his speech, was spattered with single dashes—not dashes in pairs—and, although I thought his *Left Hand, Right Hand* a plausible theory of personality (the left's palmistry is the givens, the right's what you've made of them), I had never thought him a convincing theorist. I just wanted a sign from above that all was going well. I was sixteen and rather helpless. Who on earth, what prankster, had put me up to this, fessing my fetish at the portals of well-to-do aristos?

His sister's response, when I showed up a year later to ask her to judge a poetry contest (she agreed), was entirely different. At once she engaged the future for me, spelling out answers to questions I had never intended asking. She read my superego like a book, insisting that of course I should try for Oxford, where they trained prime ministers and taught you how to drink brandy and get plump, whereas Cambridge was for those awful scientists or boffins, back-room boys, who wanted to blow the world up. She mentioned *The Shadow of Cain*, which I had actually read. "Oxford," she said mesmerizingly, "will make you reach beyond yourself and *be* something in this world, the other place will stand you, dear boy, at a microscope and send you blind. I never attended a University myself. My nose was so hideous they decided to keep me out of sight in the hall cupboard. At least until some doctor, not a Nazi, made me presentable and straightened my dear old Plantagenet schnoz straight. You take those exams, and don't let me catch you not doing well.

Tell them you know me and that I have taught you to appreciate poetry."

"Well, you have, Miss." I had read her extraordinary patient look at the texture of Alexander Pope, a most unusual book for its period, with all the virtues of F. R. Leavis's close reading without his moral bigotry.

She was shocked, yet stubbornly gratified.

"No science, young you."

"No, Ma'am. I promise. I can't count anyway."

"Oxford."

"Oxford, Ma'am, if I can."

"Of course you can. If you don't, they'll hear from me. There are some awfully nasty people in the literary profession, young you, and they are going to hear from *me*, vulgarly known as getting it in the neck."

I don't know about Mellors, but if it were true it was more likely to have been Maynard Hollingsworth the estate agent who swept through the village in gaiters, braying and barking, his demeanor one of irascible gentility. When he bowed, some internal mercury tilted free of its meniscus and silvered his track behind him. A loose god had walked among us, urgent and aloof. Would even he have said *Mellors* except as a curse under his beery breath?

Perhaps the most incongruous part of my childhood and adolescence was the way in which, unnoticed by me, various creative and cultural worthies—icons even—sauntered with the Sitwells through the village streets of Eckington, stopping at this or that pub for a drink. Here came Alec and Merula Guinness, the painter John Piper, the composer William Walton, the poet Dylan Thomas (virtually adopted and protected by Edith), and several others, an aesthetic invasion unidentified by locals who regarded them as mere "nobs" come slumming. With them, I vaguely recall, came Osbert's constant friend Captain Stanier, one of those who held on to and exploited his rank after the First War. The teenager who saw them without heeding them was planning his exit into, he hoped, their company, faintly marveling at the facile way the Sitwells arranged for a couple of railway companies (the London-Midland-Scottish mainly) to put on a special train to whisk these luminaries from London up to the Renishaw halt. Money, plus grace and favor, swung that, I imagine; after all, the world was the Sitwells' oyster, they who spent much of the year in a castle in Italy, or in a mansion on the east coast at Scarborough. I imagine now that W. H. Auden and Aldous Huxley used to put in an appearance in Lady Chatterley's village until they lit out for the United States.

Had I realized, what on earth would I have said, butting in with my "I toos" in the village street, chronically unaware that the world I longed to join had several times strolled past the aspidistra in our music-room window. I should have been more alert to the way these unself-conscious artists argued in the street, heedless of traffic or villagers, almost a grown-up version of the schoolboys from Spinkhill College, the Catholic establishment high on a hill not far away, whose boys trickled into our streets on Saturday afternoons to buy candies and cookies. I think I once saw Dylan Thomas, untidy moppet, pausing in front of the tripe shop, afflicted with a complex rune the Brit reviewers would scold him for. But I was only just waking up, so to speak, coming to ambitious life, after a long and fruitful sleep in which, I distinctly recall, I had a recurring dream of reading, yet reading too slowly for all I wanted it to do for me, and therefore in a preparatory panic. How ironic to have had such illustrious visitations while gestating, pecking through the shell with my literary beak. First the Romans, so long ago, then the Norse and the French, and then the illuminati of London lent invisibly to that village of fact and fable.

EDWARD O. WILSON

Consilience
University Research Professor and Honorary Curator in
   Entomology of the Museum of Comparative Zoology,
   Harvard University

For a long time I have considered children's secret hideaways to be a fundamental trait of human nature. The tendency to build them is, I believe, one of the epigenetic rules that compose human nature—a hereditary regularity in mental development that predisposes us to acquire certain preferences and to undertake practices of ultimate value in survival. From the secret places come an identification with place, a nourishing of individuality and self-esteem, and an enhanced joy in the construction of habitation. They also bring us close to the Earth and nature, in ways that can ensure a lifelong love of both. Such was my experience as a boy during the ages of eleven to fifteen, when I sought little Edens in the forests of Alabama and northern Florida. On one occasion I built a small hut of saplings in a remote off-trail spot. Unfortunately, I didn't notice that some of the saplings were poison oak! That was the last of my secret-house constructions, but my love of the natural world waxed ever more strongly.

Poetry

There was a child went forth everyday,
And the first object he looked upon, that object he became. . . .
Walt Whitman

There was a time when consciousness did not yet think, but perceived.
Carl Jung

"The Woods in Autumn," *The Changing Year,* 1884

NANCY WILLARD

THE SECRET SPEAKS

"Childhood is the kingdom where nobody dies."
Edna St. Vincent Millay

I am not under the table tented with blankets,
or under the attic stairs,
or in the cellar where jars of tomatoes and pears
sleep pickled in shadows, like leaves bruised
black by six months of snow. Don't look
in the clubhouse shanty lodged in the maple tree,

from which you see
your future: men mowing, women digging out
dandelions—little space pilgrims
globed in light. I am not the oak
from which the soldier spoke

to three dogs guarding the chests of copper,
silver, gold, and the tinderbox in the story.
I live in nobody's story,
not even the mirror's comfortable rooms
booklined like yours, but only the mirror reads
its own writing. Apparition? Dream?

I live in the seam
of sleep and waking and leave my fingerprints
on time. What did you hope to keep?
In me nothing of childhood is lost,
not even our holy game of hide and seek.

JULIE JORDAN HANSON

DOOR

I'd found a tiny line of mouse droppings
behind the silverware tray in my kitchen drawer,
and so my peripheral vision was on the alert
when a quick flat shadow along the mopboard
zipped into the cupboard where I found the farther hole
it must have vanished through. Then it came—
unasked and plain, without reason or meaning
or comment, without event—the outside entryway
to my grandparents' basement. And inside it was light,
like a porch. So light, I remember thinking,
it should have been done in rattan and white.
And then I remembered it was.
Even though this was a storage basement
and no one, I was sure, ever sat in the chair,
feet on the oval of rug, reading a book,
it was pleasant enough down there to do that.
Open shelves ran low around the walls—
the floor was dirt—who'd thought to paint the shelves?
Grandmother? Fussier than I'd supposed?
Or had it been the aviator uncle
I never knew, who was never anything
but young and handsome, whose face in every
photograph was the face of his father, younger?
Eulogies collapsed and billowed about him
like parachute silk. But these were brought to mind
mostly in the attic three flights up,
where once we slept with our cousins in cots
and an iron double bed and where his remaining
uniform was hung in a cardboard wardrobe
we'd punctured with a sword that must have been a relic
from another war. A gun stood by,

and striped hat boxes, the heaviest full of letters,
the lightest given to a hat kept centered
with crisp tissue. Not all of the attic concerned him.
It might have been the basement he'd remember.
Or that low room of cans of halfgone paint
might have been no more to him
than a place run down to for lightbulbs or lubricant
or screens. When a basement opens in
from out of doors through a hollyhocked wall,
the white shelves get flecked with points of dust
you'd never otherwise notice.
Stacked neat were the clean and multicolored rags
and, spaced apart from all I don't remember,
the two wood and gray wire traps
not at the time in use, neither set nor sprung.

ROALD HOFFMANN

FIELDS OF VISION

From the attic the boy
watched children playing, but

they were always running
out of the window frame.

And the weathered shutters
divided up space, so

that he couldn't often tell
where the ball Igor kicked

(he heard the children call
Igor's name) would end up.

The boy was always moving,
one slat to another,

trying to make the world
come out. He saw Teacher

Dyuk's wife with a basket,
then he saw her come back

with eggs; he could smell them.
Once he saw a fat goose,

escaped from her pen, saved
from slaughter, he thought. Once

he saw a girl, in her
embroidered Carpathian

vest. He couldn't see the sky,
the slats pointed down; he

saw the field by the school,
always the same field, only

snow turned into mud into
grass into snow. Later

the boy grew up, came
to America, where he

was a good student, praised
for his attention to facts;

he taught people to look
at every distortion

of a molecule, why
ethylene on iron

turned this way, not another.
In this world, he thought, there

must be reasons. His poems
were not dreamy, but full

of exasperating
facts. Still later, he watched

his mother, whose eyes were
failing, move her head,

the way he did, to catch
oh a glimpse, the smallest

reflecting shard of light
of our world, confined.

MOLLY McQUADE

MOUSE HISTORY

They are winging over me
so politely,
this interested, separate species.
Unction ghosts their feet
with possibility
and spreads to me
with divine weight, a bobbing might
as they run this fine,
fine course
of curiosity
treading an unseen, airy loop of light.
No problem. Union. Communion. A rout
by mouse of human
willing, like a tale of what can be:
they peel forward on their feet
up my arm to the shoulder,
roost at the neck,
and breathe delirious, dainty puffs
at the ear,
alarming and fortuitous flower.
Their floss is my might
or could it be?
My cardigan loses their delicate steps, a rival
in subtlety.
This is legal, isn't it?
Mice all over me,
a royal family of souls
gone far,
gone right,
so slight on their feet,
their thinking feet,

pausing only to skid and restore,
angels at the shrinking edge and unafraid,
whirling down,
kneading a forearm's puny hairs
and doing everything again.
They're maestros
of what is modest and certain,
and I'm claiming kin,
feeling quibbles, purges, and such swift lulls
of temperature
and intelligence.
This is species mingling,
though who would believe it?
Well, I'm ten
and I can
and I also can believe
that mice are writing their lives
lightly on my shoulder, on my forehead
with such decorum,
in the slippery pores of sweater, in the little learning
that embalms me,
in my wild mildness of skin.

BRAD DAVIS

ON LITTLE BOYS AND THEIR GUNS

One new video game engages four players
cradling their joysticks and staring into
separate monitors in separate time zones—
teams two pairs of combatants, each pitted
against the other in a maze of courtyards
and passageways until one pair is terminated,
dispatched by handgun, assault rifle, missile
launcher. Could it be our best and safest
domestic strategy is to permit them their
virtual death matches, their take-no-prisoner
human targeting games, and thereby keep
the short-fused deficients off the streets,
out of the mainstream and honing those
feather-touch motor skills required to pilot
a fighter or drive a tank? Haven't recent studies
confirmed that nature, by denying some
their full hormonal birthright, supplies us
with warriors, the tightly-wound, aggressive
type the rest of us know to steer clear of,
trusting in God and a fragile rule of law?
Understatement be damned, these players
are out to win, and to kill well is to win big.
A far cry from shivering alone beneath
the Brinkers' rhododendron, rain dripping
from the rim of a camouflaged bike helmet,
and out there an unseen enemy patrol fearing
my smooth, triggerless oak branch, the pine
cone grenades crammed in my pockets.

LAURENCE GOLDSTEIN

A ROOM IN CALIFORNIA, 1954

Let's say

I spent my boyhood in the Rhineland,
one of the blond Wandervögel, drifting downriver
past the Lorelei, under the steep towers of Cologne,
outwardly a pagan, muscular, Aryan,
inwardly a partisan for the Spartakus Jugend
spying for my father's trade-union cell in Mainz.
Prisoner of the Death Head Guard, he smuggled
from Gestapo headquarters coded messages:
    THE QUIET SHALLOWS YEARN FOR THE SHARK
    EVIL TURNS ITS OPPOSITE TO ITSELF
After he tunneled under a wall we strangled a guard,
torched a munitions factory, laid plans
to stalk the beast to Berchtesgaden, and
with a carbine and silver bullet turn the Third Reich into

what? Some languid commune near the Pacific,
way down the western coast, ur-hispanic,
sun-burnished, retro-spective, live-and-let-live;
some sleepy spot like the allergy-inducing
only used bookstore in Culver City, Stanley Brile's,
my summer asylum and back-street agora
more overflowing of fantasy, more steeped in dreams
than the series of studio films set anywhere but there:
Mogambo Stalag 17 Shane The Robe Ivanhoe Moulin Rouge

In the closet-like sweatbox behind the children's books
beside the true crime and girlie mags, every *Life* lay in wait.

I put down my lemonade, turn on the news from Kosovo
and leaf through one survivor: September 18, 1944.
"Let's all back the attack," says Cadillac:
"Victory is our business." Farnsworth engineers
promise, "Eventually, after the war, you'll have
home television . . . in cabinets of your choice."
GIs march down the Champs Élysées. Joseph Auslander
pens a "New Iliad" below classic photos of the Normandy boats:
>"When Homer called the roll and read the names
>Of the tall heroes plumed for war's wild courses,
>Their splendid spears a forest of bright flames,
>The frantic trumpets and the frenzied horses,—
>He sang his litany of names and places,
>Even as I, who am no Homer, sing
>Our lads, with light of battle in their faces,
>Who stormed a deadlier Troy one night in spring."
A glorious birthright for war babies like myself, a diction
one hungered to deserve, a nourishing speech of the gods

but let's say

I chose to stand my ground at Mons, a *tall hero*,
tall for my age, following my gun-toting dad as he led
the American armored division to the Nazi flank;
"a deathtrap" he chuckled. "Watch the infantry
close its iron jaws." I reveled in the great game;
I manned a machine-gun. I took prisoners.
I was worthy of Homer's and Auslander's praise.

I looked up *simile*:
"Hektor came on against them, as a murderous lion on cattle."
I looked up *pentameter*:
"Who stormed a deadlier Troy one night in spring."

I watch my son watch the refugees in Kosovo.
They are war's real thing, not chess pieces, not lambs,
simply what shuffles ingloriously because it must.
The Unknowable. The stuff of next week's *Life*.
And when he returns to cyberspace, the reborn site
of Stanley Brile's vanished emporium, I shut off the screen
and open the memory stored on shelves, back issues
of occult childhood: June 19, 1944, July 2, 1945 . . .

Realms pressed together, glossy, akinetic.
Debutante balls at the Hunt Club; wildcat strikes at Ford;
backyard cooking; Swedish glass; lithium;
Dumbarton Oaks and Trader Vic's; Fala; four seasons
on a Nebraska farm; the all-American art of Grant Wood;
We Want Willkie; magic acts; Hollywood pinups—
I was the heir of all culture; I bought and brought home
bound pictographs from that airless cave, the past.
All the visuals of *Life*   All the reportage
The splendid spears   The frantic trumpets
the habit of saying to myself

Let's say

Tactics dancing in his head, the son poles his craft
under the guns of Düsseldorf, biding his time
as he spells out mile by mile   his self-definition:
archivist, scribe, witness, antitype of psalmist and bard.
The river is broad and swift, flows near squatters' houses
in which the fate of nations is plotted by restless kids,
Kommandants of the twentieth century's happier half,
in free verse, free as the prose of personal histories
shelved alphabetically, renewable till death:
*Not So Wild a Dream   Only the Stars are Neutral   Out of the
    Night*

WOLE SOYINKA

THE CHILDREN OF THIS LAND

The children of this land are old.
Their eyes are fixed on maps in place of land.
Their feet must learn to follow
Distant contours traced by alien minds.
Their present sense has faded into past.

The children of this land are proud
But only seeming so. They tread on air but—
Note—the land it was that first withdrew
From touch of love their bare feet offered. Once,
It was the earth of their belonging.
Their pointed chins are aimed,
Proud seeming, at horizons filled with crows.
The clouds are swarms of locusts.

The children of this land grow the largest eyes
Within head sockets. Their heads are crowns
On neat fish spines, whose meat has passed
Through swing doors to the chill of conversation
And chilled wine. But the eyes stare dead.
They pierce beyond the present through dim passages
Across the world of living.

These are the offspring of the dispossessed,
The hope and land deprived. Contempt replaces
Filial bonds. The children of this land
Are castaways in holed crafts, all tortoise skin
And scales—the callus of their afterbirth.
Their hands are clawed for rooting, their tongues
Propagate new social codes, and laws.
A new race will supersede the present—

Where love is banished stranger, lonely
Wanderer in forests prowled by lust
On feral pads of power,
Where love is a hidden, ancient ruin, crushed
By memory, in this present
Robbed of presence.

But the children of this land embrace the void
As lovers. The spores of their conjunction move
To people once human spaces, stepping nimbly
Over ghosts of parenthood. The children of this land
Are robed as judges, their gaze rejects
All measures of the past. A gleam
Invades their dead eyes briefly, lacerates the air
But with one sole demand:
Who sold our youth?

CATHY SONG

BOOK OF HOURS

What led you to the book
and kept you there
was pleasure, a simple
stirring—unconditional.

The function of spelling,
the mechanics of handwriting
fed an orderly compulsion, repetitive
acts as tight as stitches—
a balm for inner disruption.

Pure to the task of setting
letters in a row, filigreed nonsense
curved extravagant and slow.
Intent on making O just so,
sound connected on air's blue note.
Meaning broke, lifted: sky poured in.
The hand's enactment of the mind's enchantment.
The letters illuminated—glowed.

Hours spent in odd posture,
girl with head bent, her hair a scrawl.
Who knows where she went,
hanging letters on pale blue lines—
hook of star,
tiny magnificent clothes,
adornments to an original country.

ALLISON EIR JENKS

BOY OF SEA

The boy lost himself in the woods for days
until he was found drifting peacefully,
fearlessly as a blanket of firelight
atop the swamp water, alive.
Hungry, but alive and unharmed.
This God of sea, a child
who we claimed had a lesser sense,
who went about life at a slower pace than us,
managed to turn his body-water into sea,
and cross hordes of snakes, wasps,
alligators, sharks and other sea urchins
without provoking or frightening them.
The sea-life treaded through their routines,
and the boy drifted alongside them gracefully.

Something in the human body, its godlessness
perhaps, or the way we disguise ourselves
from the animals and from our own latitude,
but still hunt against the hunters
and prowl among the prowlers,
keeps us earthbound, apprehensive, dishonest,
maintaining the dying things, the hunger, and the land,
with no Gods in the sea and no angels or miracles in our way.
Drawn from the embryo toward everything perishable,
we want only to believe in our own magic,
and when one of us understands the instincts
of the larger beasts and answers to the invisible
we still let the dogs smell our fear,
and can barely hear them coming.

JAMES NOLAN

JAPANESE PLUMS

When they chopped them down
something unraveled
like the catcher's mitt
of a ten year-old's heart.
Didn't they see the stone circles
I'd built around the trees?
Then I kept so many secrets
with the earth, names of plants
and African countries, clay castles
in crawfish holes, continents
in live oak roots.

                      By the time
I got home they had chain-sawed
the trees, flat-topped the yard
with cement: "better for basketball,"
they joked. We battled
the landlord; next month,
the moving van. And I . . .
this was the moment it
dawned: the world outside
exists more than I do.
A war. Ever since
I've camouflaged myself
among lost Japanese plums
as I sign treaties
with concrete.

                      And suddenly
in Spain, on the terrace
of this house I happen

to be living in, a Japanese
plum tree in a tin washtub
leaps out like a burning bush,
yellow, gnarled. I reach
to pluck the sweet, spitting
slippery pits in arches
into the street:

                        victory
of Biblical patience
and an impossible love.

VIRGIL SUAREZ

LA ISLA DE LOS MONSTROS

for Jarret Keene

In Los Angeles I grew up watching *The Three Stooges,*
The Little Rascals, Speed Racer, and the Godzilla movies,

those my mother called *"Los Monstros,"* and though I didn't
yet speak English, I understood why such a creature would,

upon being woken up from its centuries-long slumber, rise
and destroy Tokyo's buildings, cars, people—I understood

by the age of twelve what it meant to be unwanted, exiled,
how you move from one country to another where nobody

wants you, nobody knows you, and I sat in front of the TV,
transfixed by the snow-fizz on our old black and white,

and when Godzilla screamed his eardrum-crushing screech,
I screamed back, this victory-holler from one so rejected

and cursed to another. When the monster whipped its tail
and destroyed, I threw a pillow across my room, each time

my mother stormed into the room and asked me *what,*
what I thought I was doing throwing things at the walls.

"Ese monstro, esa isla!" she'd say. That monster, that island,
and I knew she wasn't talking about the movie. She meant

her country, mine, that island in the Caribbean we left behind,
itself a reptile-looking mass on each map, on my globe,

a crocodile-like creature rising again, eating us so completely.

Portfolio

*My recollection of the first bird's nest that I found all by myself
has remained more deeply engraved in my memory than that of the
first prize I won in grammar school for a Latin version.*
A. Toussenel, *Le monde des oiseaux,* 1853

Tom Pohrt, *Untitled,* 1998

MARGARET PRICE

NEGOTIATING BOUNDARIES, REGENERATING RUINS: THE "SECRET SPACES OF CHILDHOOD" EXHIBITION

Secrets on Display

In the Benzinger Library of the University of Michigan's Residential College, near the entrance to the gallery containing "Secret Spaces of Childhood: An Exhibition of Remembered Hide-Outs," stood a dollhouse-sized diorama representing a one-room cabin. The cabin's floor and roof were of balsa wood. Inside stood a bed, table, and cradle, as well as tinier pieces including a lamp, coal scuttle, and tablecloth fashioned from a lace doily. Affixed to the front of this work was a note in the hand of the child artist:

> *Colonial cabin you can touch*
> *if you have to but Do not take!*
> > *By Maris.*

Maris's cabin and accompanying note were from another part of the two-day symposium centering around the theme "Secret Spaces of Childhood." But her piece introduced me, even before I entered the gallery, to the spirit and substance of the exhibit I was about to view. Standing in front of her diorama, I was reminded of what it felt like to have a secret space as a child. I remembered the charm and power of creating a world of my own. I remembered, also, the intense need for privacy and the desire to create my own boundaries, rules, aesthetic. And I remembered the accompanying wish to show off and share my created spaces—but only on my own terms. I appreciated Maris's intelligent acknowledgement that sometimes you "have to" touch things in order to understand them—after all, when a child says "Can I see that?" he is usually asking to hold something in his hands. Finally, I was reminded of the childhood fear that our secret spaces, created with such dedicated attention to detail, may be invaded, co-opted, even stolen by others: "Do not take!"

"Secret Spaces of Childhood," mounted in the gallery adjoining the library, contained professional artists' works that recalled and interpreted childhood secret spaces. These spaces were rendered in materials including paint, ceramic, textiles, found objects, metal, plastic, and wood, and varied dramatically in their approaches, tones, and levels of accessibility. Some took up common childhood activities, like Ellen Wilt's "A Tent-Cave," a series of sketches, photos, and models depicting the building of a fort from household furniture. Some were highly individual in import, like Gerald McDermott's black-and-white drawing of a spiral staircase carved in stone, called simply "Stone Spiral." Colors tended to be bright, or starkly contrastive, and textures intently noticed.

Although there were fewer than twenty works in the exhibit altogether, as I moved past and through the succession of hideouts I became more and more overloaded with images and textures. My factual notes began to be interspersed with fervent questions and personal recollections. Being plunged into one of these spaces after another left me drained, a feeling familiar to anyone who has spent an afternoon in a museum. But this relatively small exhibit had an effect on me I would have expected from a larger exhibit, and there was more to it than simple sensory overload.

Part of it was the unstated but constantly present tension of viewing works that depicted *secrets*. Behind each artwork was a child, real or imagined, who had once developed this space for his or her use only. The decision by the artists to unveil two creations at once—the work of art itself, and also the remembered world it represented—resulted in a doubled sense of risk around each piece.

When I walked out of the gallery and back into the quotidian halls of the Residential College, which smelled vaguely of dorm food and echoed with the shouts of students, I felt much the way I used to as a child when I had to leave a secret space I had been creating. I was a little sore in the shoulders and knees, blinking at the changed light, and mildly vertiginous from the transition from one land to another. I didn't know how much time had passed.

Inside the Hideouts

Each of the fourteen works in the art gallery was accompanied by a short text written by the artist. I began my tour of the exhibit with Mark Nielson's "Gathering Apples" (Fig. 1). The photographic reproduction that forms the basis for this piece is blandly idyllic, like a picture out of a 1950s reader. It shows an enormous apple tree under which stands a girl with long blond braids. In the tree's branches a boy, smiling, tosses apples from his perch into the girl's outheld apron. In the middle distance stand a stone bridge and a white-spired church. Nielson's alterations include a number of small black creatures that look like the offspring of a devil and a bat. (These bat-beings, as I think of them, are a recurring motif in Nielson's work with photographic reproductions.) One of the bat-beings reclines against the apple tree's trunk, another cavorts in the branches of a more distant tree, and a third fishes casually in the brook running past. Along with the bat-beings, four cupids in paper cutout are added to the original reproduction. From their postures, the cupids could be seen as either flying or falling.

Nielson's accompanying text explains that the painting reminds him of "a hiding place I shared with a friend named Kay," a hollow-trunked apple tree into which they would wriggle and hide. "In this child-sized cave," Nielson recalls, "[e]verything seemed right." And yet the presence of the bat-beings and of the half-falling cupids reminds us that children, even those whose lives are comparatively idyllic, live with a daily awareness of the sudden malevolence that can crop up from any corner. Nielson's language parallels the pre-fall/post-fall tone of the work: "[O]ur real interest was the magnetism of the beast's absent core. . . . Once inside we were in darkness punctuated by three torn circles of sky." Perhaps one reason that nature is so important to many of the secret spaces of childhood shown in this exhibit is that nature, to children, is no more or less mysterious than the way all the world works: beautiful, unpredictable, demanding constant adjustment of response, and at times, pointlessly cruel.

Moving counterclockwise from Nielson's work I encountered Ann Savageau's "Making Something Out of Nothing" (Fig. 2). This piece recalls the sense of power children derive from their secret spaces, the joy (or relief) of being creator and sovereign. The work also emphasizes the intense precision of aesthetic that so often characterizes children's secret spaces. "Making Something Out of Nothing" is a collection of treasures, each item alone only mildly remarkable, but together creating an arresting window into one person's view of what should be saved. Gathered together in a wooden box lie fragile skeletons of cottonwood leaves, brown and green beach glass, a piece of quartz as round and regular as a Chips Ahoy cookie, and a shining peeled horse chestnut. Among these lie more spectacular finds: a section of delicate vertebrae, a turtle shell, a piece of jawbone, half a small skull. A dried snakeskin, rippled with ghost-scales and wider than a child's hand, stretches across the inside of the box's lid. Savageau's box of treasures lies open in the gallery, unprotected by glass or even a written admonishment not to pick the items up.

I almost did. I wanted just to stroke the perfect surface of the quartz, or to see if any of the teeth in the jaw fragment would wiggle. But I didn't. I was controlled partly by my adult sensibility, which has spent thirty years learning not to touch other people's belongings. I was more strongly controlled, though, by the precision of the items' arrangement, by their fragility, and by how fiercely evident was the vision behind their presence together in that box. On its own each item was fairly ordinary, even ugly. But together they sketched the longitude and latitude of one person's sense of value. Savageau's text reads in part, "I was a collector of rocks, bones and junk. The things that other people threw away I saw as treasure." This is power, too—the alchemic transformation of *not-valuable* into *valuable*, simply by the way one sees. Children learn early to collect power where they can, and the spaces they create and govern are not only physical areas, but also the secret spaces of their private visions.

After the complexity and precision of Savageau's box of treasures, the blunt directness of Gerald McDermott's "Stone Spiral" (Fig. 3) comes as a shock. This drawing, in oil crayon and india ink on charcoal paper, shows an old-fashioned stone archway leading to a set of stairs that curve upward and out of the viewer's sight. The walls of the staircase are also stone blocks. Although the picture is apparently roughly drawn, upon closer inspection the space's particularity becomes evident: the stone arch is meticulously constructed, with a keystone at its highest reach, and the stones in the stairway's wall curve as the stairs curve, indicating the tunnel-like stretch beyond. McDermott writes:

> From the age of four onward, I spent ten years of Saturdays in the galleries of the Detroit Institute of Arts. . . . The most mysterious and alluring space I found in the museum was a medieval spiral stairway. Ascending and descending the stone steps, I felt sure it was a passageway between magical realms. Without [my] being conscious of it, this became my Axis Mundi, spiraling to the center, connecting me with secret wonders.

McDermott's drawing highlights one of the most important features of a child's secret space—the point of access. Almost always the entrance to a secret space is guarded, to protect the privacy and sometimes the fragility of what lies inside. In Frances Hodgson Burnett's *The Secret Garden* (1911), for instance, not only is the garden's door overgrown and locked, but the protagonist Mary must undergo a series of tests in order to find the door and obtain the key. In Katherine Paterson's *Bridge to Terabithia* (1977), the secret space is accessed by a rope swing over a gully, a "doorway" so important it eventually changes the course of both protagonists' lives. Sometimes the point of access to a secret space is magical, as in McDermott's stone-spiral vision or in C. S. Lewis's *The Lion, the Witch and the Wardrobe* (1950). Moving through the doorway into the space itself is a rite of passage, and often the point of access is the most highly charged area of the whole secret space: usually elusive, always exciting, and sometimes dangerous.

Like "Stone Spiral," Susan Glass's painting "Cottage Garden" (Fig. 4) is concerned with the question of access but, in contrast to the former work, shows what lies beyond the portal: in this case, color. "Cottage Garden" is a wooden window frame with glass intact; painted in oils on the glass panes are yellow lilies, blue delphinium, white daisies, and silver licorice leaves. According to the painting's perspective, the viewer is only inches from the garden that lies on the other side of the window, yet remains held back from it. Still, the closeness of the oil colors and the flowers' abundance give the piece an overall tone of eagerness and invitation. This sense of openness continues in the painting's background, which shows a porch door left ajar.

Jaye Schlesinger's painting "Walls and Windows" (Fig. 5) continues the theme of access, and through its title refers directly to the concern of negotiating a secret space's boundaries. Schlesinger's accompanying text develops her work's interest in this theme further. Describing her childhood in 1950s suburban Chicago, she writes of the ways that she created imagined worlds from everyday spaces such as basements and closets: "Mostly I remember walls and windows. Walls were always made of bricks. They had many possibilities . . . [and] were the starting point from which many games evolved." Windows, on the other hand, Schlesinger writes, "extended space. They were a way out of a space that I didn't want to be in."

The painting is a close study of a house's pink brick exterior wall. The edges of "Walls and Windows" delimit a section about eight feet square. Set into the wall so that half of it disappears at the painting's edge is a plain sashed window. A vivid green lawn, painted with attention to individual blades, stretches cleanly to the edge of the house. In the painting's foreground— truncated, like the window, by the piece's edge—a red toy fire engine sits parked.

In keeping with Schlesinger's description of suburban 1950s Chicago, the tone of "Walls and Windows" is quiet, precise, and tidy. The colors of the gouache-on-paper medium are crisp and opaque, and each section of color—pink wall, white window frame and drainpipe, green lawn, red car—contrasts dramatically with the others. There is no obvious movement in the painting—no thrown apples, not even the subtle waving of flowers we might imagine in Glass's "Cottage Garden." As in McDermott's "Stone Spiral," the action of this secret space is implied by the artist's concern with the space's visual geography. The viewer cannot share directly, but must imagine, the exact worlds that a child might create if given that brick wall, that gaping window.

Continuing to travel counterclockwise around the gallery, I came to one of the most visually surprising works in the exhibit, Susan Crowell's "Excavation" (Fig. 6). This installation was mounted in a corner, and used the walls of the gallery themselves in its construction. Ranged along two walls that met at right angles were a series of dark-colored shelves shaped like the large fungi that grow on trees. Some shelves were as low as my knees and some almost as high as the ceiling. Among the shelves protruded what appeared to be wires, each about as thick as a pencil and slightly wavery, extending from the wall like large bristles from a chin. Upon each shelf stood an arrangement of one, two, or three plastic model horses. There were twenty horses in all, and their groupings seemed to have required considerable care. A mother and foal stood together, touching noses; a trio all pricked their ears toward the same invisible stimulus; and a large stallion reared on his own shelf, alone. To the left of this surprising arrangement was a ladder, fastened vertically to the wall and also reaching higher than my head.

It wasn't until I read Crowell's text that I realized where I was. Each summer, according to her written piece, she and her sisters used to excavate an underground room large enough to occupy. They would dig shelves into the walls, cover the floor with leaves and needles, and bring in furnishings such as chairs, rugs, and candles. (The horses, however, were a fantasy within a memory; although Crowell as a child wished to bring their collections of horses into the space, she writes, "my sisters wouldn't let me. They reasoned it was dangerous to leave them there overnight.") In "Excavation," the viewer is inside the hideout, underground, before he knows it.

"Excavation" elides the importance of a secret space's point of access, since the viewer is always already inside the space. Its interest seems to lie instead in a different question of geography—size. By placing the viewer at the bottom of her excavation and forcing him to peer upward, Crowell reminds us that one of a child's ongoing preoccupations is his or her own size. Children live in a world of pants legs and belt buckles, something that is easy to forget if you spend most of your time able to see faces easily. Yet this challenge becomes an advantage in many childhood secret spaces: often they, or their entrances, are small. A fence under which you can wriggle; an upper shelf that will support your weight; a cupboard into which you can squeeze yourself and close the door—in such settings, being small of stature confers the privilege of access. A hideout cannot function for a person too large to fit into it. On the other hand, a child's small size is a passing attribute, and children know it. Nielson's text accompanying "Gathering Apples" comments specifically on this temporality: "We knew we'd soon be too big to wiggle through."

Beside "Excavation," one of the most concretely representative pieces in the exhibit, appear two of the most abstract, "Cushion Window" and "Cedar Spot" by Ben Upton (Figs. 7 & 8). Both woodcuts on paper, the two works emphasize the importance of color and texture. "Cushion Window" displays a large white expanse cracked with ocher and brown. The work's title suggests that the cracks of color may represent light glimpsed between pillows, which in turn are represented by the broad stretches of white. In this work, what would ordinarily appear as negative space—the cracks seen through the pillows—becomes positive. "Cedar Spot," more dynamic, uses light green, yellow, steel blue, black, and white in streaks and bursts of patterns and textures. The two pieces are very different in tone and approach: "Through the Pillows," with its extensive stretches of blank space, confers a sense of calm, almost of waiting, while "Cedar Spot" is filled with activity, encouraging the viewer's eye to rove its spaces.

Upton's text develops the viewer's sense that what is primary in these works is the careful consideration of colors and textures and how they interact: "The language for me of 'secret spaces' revolves around words like hidden, partial, covered, and temporary. Dominant thoughts [are] the closeness of light—textures and patterns. Their ins and outs, the there and here, the shadow and light still inform me." This attention to detail resonates with a similar preoccupation in many of the other works in the "Secret Spaces" exhibit. Over and over, the artists remind us, when a child is observing and creating a space, what is important is not just any arrangement but *this* arrangement, *my* arrangement—the mare and her foal just barely touching noses, the individual bricks in the wall, the leaves scattered through the treasure box with fastidious care.

Tom Pohrt's untitled construction (Fig. 9), next after Upton's woodcuts, continues to emphasize precision. Inside a square glass case stands a silver bowl the shape of an egg cup, but large enough to hold an ostrich egg. Cradled in the bowl is a bird's nest. A dried moth and beetle perch on the edge of the nest, and dried leaves of yellow, red, and green adorn it also.

Delicate and deliberate, composed mostly of natural found materials, it seems to be a cousin in sensibility to Savageau's "Making Something Out of Nothing."

The text written by Pohrt refers to the importance of precision and of creating a personal aesthetic: "The entire act of constructing the box reminded me of what I like about packing my bags before travel, the satisfaction of becoming more concentrated on myself. As with my painting, there is a meditative quality to this construction." Like Savageau's, Schlesinger's and others', Pohrt's depiction of a hideout reminds us of the peculiarly intense focus of which many children are capable. When we are creating our spaces, as children, we often fall into a state of mind that is much like meditation: quiet but filled with activity, concentrated, and ungoverned by chronological time. In the novel *A Ring of Endless Light* (1980), Madeline L'Engle's young narrator Vicky describes this state of being as "beyond words . . . out on the other side of myself." Such a state becomes a cherished rarity for most adults, impelling us to take yoga classes, jog, pay for massages, or study formalized meditation techniques in search of a feeling that we used to be able to accomplish with a leaf, a sunny day, and a magnifying glass.

The politics of geography returns in the secret space represented by Jim Cogswell's "Ruins, Tunnels, Walls and Alleys" (Fig. 10). This glazed ceramic, several feet square, is composed almost entirely of curves, passageways, and openings. Glazes applied in patches of colors and textures alternate with unglazed sections on a ridged and cracked surface. As I looked at it, I began to notice that every position I took in relation to the work revealed new passageways, rooms, even tiny "skylights"—and hid others. I began to wish I were small enough to crawl into it and explore.

The expanse of "Ruins, Tunnels, Walls and Alleys" reveals so many entrances and exits, as well as hills and grottoes, that it's hard to tell where the piece itself begins and ends—somewhat like a Klein bottle were someone to flatten it and add extra openings. Cogswell's creation seems to be all about transit. There is no square inch of the ceramic surface that is not subtly, by means of a curve or an opening, on its way somewhere else. This "here/not here" impression is further developed by the artist's text, which explains that he grew up in a family that moved "every few years, back and forth between this country and Japan." Cogswell's text goes on to describe a variety of spaces he occupied as a child: rooms stacked high with boxes between which he "built secret cities"; a traditional Japanese garden filled with twisting paths and sheltered corners; and the narrow, curving streets of postwar Japan. The cracked and ridged ceramic of "Ruins, Tunnels, Walls and Alleys," as well as its seemingly haphazard glazes, reflects Cogswell's description of the empty lots in Japan where he could find "some ruin from the war . . . abandoned buildings, the remnants of some garden." Like his ceramic piece, the secret spaces Cogswell recalls in writing were "spooky . . . [full of] presences I sensed but could not define."

Many of the artists represented in the "Secret Spaces" exhibition write in the first person singular: I collected, I saw, I concealed myself. But several also refer to a "we," sometimes specified and sometimes uncertain, bands of fellow travelers in the secret spaces recollected. Janie Paul's "Kalmia Woods" (Fig. 11) is one of the pieces in the exhibit concerned with—indeed, almost dependent upon—the notion of a secret space created collaboratively by several children.

"Kalmia Woods" is a large hand-bound book with a cover of handmade pinkish-gray paper and gray cloth. Opening it, the reader first encounters the words "For Martha McClintock" and then views pencil sketches of a wood crowded with deciduous trees, dense ferns, and patterns of light and shadow. Between the frontispiece sketch and the closing sketches of stones and flowers, a poem by the artist appears on several pages, also written in pencil. The poem's images are sensual, attentive to odors, shapes, and temperatures.

In her text, Paul describes a wooded area in Concord, Massachusetts, that she explored as a child with ten other girls her age (then about six). Her story of this secret space is inextricable from the story of the other children with whom she shared it: "The land was our territory. . . . We inhabited the enclosed places below the giant ferns which dwarfed our small bodies. Our fern club swore to treasure ferns and never tear their leaves." Interestingly, the pencil sketches in "Kalmia Woods" show no children. The poem, however, is written in the first person plural, thus giving subtle life to the several girls whose secret space was this wood. Its final lines refer most directly not to the space, but to the group:

Forever fascinated by the edge of
that dark pool
our reflection lay on a surface
whose depth we desperately
believed in,
a promise to always earth and unearth
with our long sticks
in mud
delving

After Paul's sensual "Kalmia Woods," Eugene Provenzo's crisp and metallic "Einstein's Brain" (Fig. 12) forces a startling change of perspective. In the artist's own description, "Einstein's Brain" is composed of "[a] broken projector, a piece of crystal, a fan motor, wooden egg, silver balls and mirrors, a radiometer, and pictures of Einstein as a child with his classmates, naked women dancing through his subconscious (or my own) all brought together inside a box." The box is silver-painted, and all the elements named by Provenzo are in tones of gray, clear glass, and chrome.

"Einstein's Brain," like Savageau's and Pohrt's constructions, centers upon found objects. From a short distance it looks like an unusually outfitted medicine cabinet hanging on the gallery wall. Upon closer inspection, its complex layerings of image and metaphor become apparent. First, the work is itself a secret space. Like many (if not all) of the artists represented in the exhibit, Provenzo considers his art a secret space, noting in his text, "I still create secret spaces for myself in my boxes." Second, "Einstein's Brain" is influenced by a secret space that Provenzo occupied as a child, the abandoned barn behind his house. There, he writes, "I discovered all kinds of junk to play with . . . [and built] secret places away from my brother." Third, and moving deeper into its layers of representation, the box is also a visual study of one man's brain—an organ that remains to us part machine, part archive, part mystery. Finally, "Einstein's Brain" and its accompanying text address the secret space within the secret space of the brain: what Freud called the subconscious. Provenzo's text, commenting upon the pictures of naked women that dance subtly along the lower edge of the box, notes that although these women on one level occupy the artist's conception of Einstein's subconscious, they must also inevitably occupy the artist's own mind as well.

Like other artworks in "Secret Spaces," Provenzo's silver box is concerned with geography. Instead of focusing upon physical geography, however, "Einstein's Brain" seems more concerned with mental geography—those particular twists of childhood logic and knowledge that are as temporal as a child's small size.

Jean Magnano Bollinger's "Evidence of a Life" (Fig. 13) takes up some of the same questions, though through very different media. Magnano Bollinger's piece is drawn using graphite on vellum and depicts a complex, abstract system of shapes and shadows. The drawing is about four by five feet, and every inch is taken up with enigmatic negotiations of shapes and shades of gray. Trails of near-white move through the grays in patterns suggesting leaves, insect wings, cathedral windows, and sunbursts. The lines draw the viewer's eye to all corners of the paper, around in swirling paths, and inevitably back to the center. One of the artist's chief concerns, according to the text accompanying "Evidence of a Life," is to demonstrate the complexity present in adult life. "When I was a child," Magnano Bollinger writes, "life was presented in black and white, simple and clear. As an adult this oversimplified frame became insufficient to represent the intricacies of the real world." Her drawings, she writes, are "a process of self-discovery . . . finding a place in the world and perhaps offering something of value to it."

Like Provenzo's, Magnano Bollinger's work is interested not only in visual and other sensory recollections; its concern is also with intellectual geography, and with the particular secret space that is a child's mind. Unlike Provenzo's piece, however, and others in the exhibition, "Evidence of a Life" is less a time capsule from childhood than an exploration of movement beyond childhood frames of reference. Notably, Magnano Bollinger's text refers to the adult world as "real," whereas some other pieces, like Savageau's and Crowell's, indicate that most important—in fact, almost exclusively important—within the artwork's perspective is the child's understanding of reality.

The next-to-last stop on my circuit was Richard Kroeker's two watercolors, "Cold Feet" and "The Apple" (Figs. 14 & 15). In these paintings, particularly after the quiet whites and grays of "Kalmia Woods," "Einstein's Brain," and "Evidence of a Life," the color is almost comic in its intensity. According to Kroeker's text, each is an illustration for a children's book. He painted them, he writes, "during the early 1990s in London, England, when I needed my own children to know about my childhood. I wanted to communicate the fact that I had a history that pre-dated their arrival." These two "hideouts," then, are intended not only to show a child's experience but to be viewed by an audience of children.

In "Cold Feet," a little boy lies in bed under a blue-checked quilt. The bottoms of his feet are in the immediate foreground, and his body stretches away from the viewer, who is thus treated to an uncompromising but cheerful view up his nose. Watching over the sleeping child are two enormous turkeys with large ruffs and gay red combs, their color and shape repeated in the red turkeys printed on the boy's wallpaper. The size of the turkeys and their flamboyant presence in the bedroom announce them as visitors from another world: inhabitants of the boy's dreams, or perhaps escorts between the waking and the sleeping worlds. Kroeker's intention to blur the boundaries between consciousness and dreaming is amplified in his text: "'Cold Feet' is about the connection of tactile and spatial sensation with the imagination, an awareness we hold strongly as children." Although children are usually encouraged to think in terms of easily separable constructs of "real" and "not real" (Magnano Bollinger's "black/white" lesson again), this lesson fights with children's empirical experiences, which teach that in fact between the two is a broad and negotiable path. "Cold Feet" shows one child's traversing of that path.

The second watercolor, "The Apple," according to Kroeker's text, "is about being caught in that space between nature's benign state of grace and the world of external obligations." After studying the painting, I rephrased this in my mind as "being caught between what you want to do and what grownups tell you to do." "The Apple" shows a glum-faced boy, the same child-Kroeker from "Cold Feet," now wearing blue overalls and a red-striped shirt. He is confronted by two women in long skirts with their hair worn in buns (Kroeker grew up in a Mennonite family), one with her hands on her hips, one shaking a forefinger. The point of contention seems to be an apple, bitten into, which is foregrounded so that it appears to be the same size as the boy's head. It floats in front of its tree in a lush green garden. Like Nielson's "Gathering Apples," this painting takes up Edenic imagery and uses it to tell the story of a particular child's fall. The "external obligations" to which the child-Kroeker is being subjected in "The Apple" remind us of one important reason why children's secret spaces *are* secret: they operate according to systems and rules separate from those imposed by adults.

The last piece, Ellen Wilt's "A Tent-Cave" (Fig. 16), uses a combination of sketches, photos, and scale models to create a collage of images. Fixed to the wall with push-pins is a mosaic of tent-cave drawings in pencil, photocopy image, chalk, and crayon. The sketches are done on white paper, vellum, and clear plastic. Scattered among them are Polaroid photos—two of model chairs and two of an actual chair fort. In the center of the collage, which covers about sixteen square feet of wall space, are affixed three cardboard shelves lined up in a row. Each shelf supports a tiny model of a tent-cave constructed from wood, paper, and cloth. The collage as a whole seems to be offering both a record of Wilt's tent-caves and, possibly, comprehensive directions to future architects of such caves. In her text Wilt writes that she created tent-caves because she did not have a room of her own and that the caves "shut out everybody and protected the dolls I revered." Leaning close to the door of one model tent-cave and peering in at a sharp angle, the viewer can glimpse a white paper-doll girl tucked inside the shelter.

Wilt calls this piece an "investigation," a term that reminds us that childhood hideouts can be processes of exploration as well as physical locations. Secret cities built among movers' boxes; a hole excavated and re-excavated each year; a mental progress away from the taught "black/white" lessons of childhood; a fern wood to be discovered; a fort torn down when the grownups need their chairs back, but resurrected the next day—like their creators, the secret spaces of childhood match vulnerability with the power to regenerate.

Loss and Regeneration in Secret Spaces

Few, if any, of the artists represented in the "Secret Spaces" exhibition romanticize the notion of childhood and its secret spaces. Each work seems acutely aware of the hazards of being a child. Sometimes a secret space is a refuge from cruelty or danger. Sometimes it represents a refuge from the danger of becoming an adult oneself, as in Zibby Oneal's *The Language of Goldfish* (1980). Consciousness not only of beauty, joy, and peace, but also of ugliness, cruelty, and danger, are expressed and implied in these works. Some of the pieces in the exhibit acknowledge this directly. Some refer to it more obliquely, as in Schlesinger's description of windows as "a way out of a space that I didn't want to be in." If childhood is an idyll, which it is only under the most privileged of circumstances, even that idyll must include—as Kroeker's and others' pieces indicate—the inevitability of loss.

Attached to that inevitable loss, however, is another corollary: regeneration. Many of the secret spaces depicted in the gallery deal in some way with a cyclical building and rebuilding. Found "junk" is re-conceptualized into treasure by Savageau, Pohrt, and Provenzo; "Cottage Garden" and "Excavation" both depend upon the cycle of the seasons to make their spaces possible; and Paul's "Kalmia Woods" poem offers "a promise to always earth and unearth." This sense of the importance of cycles may be one reason why awareness of and materials from nature play such a central role in many of the exhibit's artworks. In a world where, sometimes, very little reassures, nature may appear to be as close to a constant as a child can find. I would argue that if there is a primary law of childhood secret spaces, it has less to do with a static and romantic state of being than with a dynamic search for constancy.

It is not my experience that children are usually in search of happiness. The memory of childhood as a time that was, or should have been, happy, is a notion we tend to assign to it as adults. More often, the children I've known—in person (including myself) and in literature—have been more interested in something I will call "truth": not *the* truth, but *a* truth, some fixed point by which one might navigate. The secret spaces recalled in the gallery exhibit operate for their creators variously as kingdom, refuge, private gallery, or club headquarters. What they have in common is their representation in each case of a truth that the artist constructed and relied upon as a child. Even the most protected of children leads a life filled with unexplained contradictions and sudden shifts underfoot; conversely, even the most threatened child will find ways to retreat into a place solely his or her own. The secret spaces of childhood are the places we went—perhaps can still go—where, for at least a short time, there is refuge from dangers, and where the ground will hold still.

Secret Spaces of Childhood

An Exhibition of Remembered Hide-Outs

November 13 - December 12, 1998

Residential College Art Gallery
East Quad
University of Michigan

Co-curated by Larry Cressman and Elizabeth Goodenough

[Fig. 1]

Gathering Apples

Mark Erik Nielsen, Ann Arbor, MI

Altered photographic reproduction
14″ x 17″

[Fig. 2]

Making Something Out of Nothing

Ann Savageau, Ann Arbor, MI

Sculpture: pine box with animal bones,
snake skin and shells
10″ x 12″ x 8 $\frac{1}{4}$″

[Fig. 3]

Sketch for Exhibition
Ink and crayon on
charcoal paper   10″ x 8″

Gerald McDermott, Marina Del Ray, CA

Stone Spiral
India ink and gouache on
watercolor paper   18″ x 12″

[Fig. 4]

Cottage Garden

Susan Glass, Detroit, MI

Oil and glass with wood
48″ x 24″

[Fig. 5]

Walls and Windows

Jaye Schlesinger, Ann Arbor, MI

Gouache on paper
7″ x 5½″

[Fig. 6]

Excavation

Susan Crowell, Ann Arbor, MI

Installation
8′ x 6′ x 30″

[Fig. 7]

Cedar Spot
Woodcuts 17″ x 24″

Ben Upton, Saline, MI

[Fig. 8]

Cushion Window

[Fig. 9]

Untitled

Tom Pohrt, Ann Arbor, MI

Pen and ink, watercolor
Drawing of 3-dimensional construction
8″ x 6″ x 5″

[Fig. 10]

Ruins, Tunnels, Walls, and Alleys

Jim Cogswell, Ann Arbor, MI
With the assistance of Melissa Titus

Glazed Ceramic
18″ x 14″ x 8″

[Fig. 11]

Kalmia Woods

Janie Paul, Ann Arbor, MI

Artist's book (detail)
$6^1/_2''$ x $6^1/_2''$

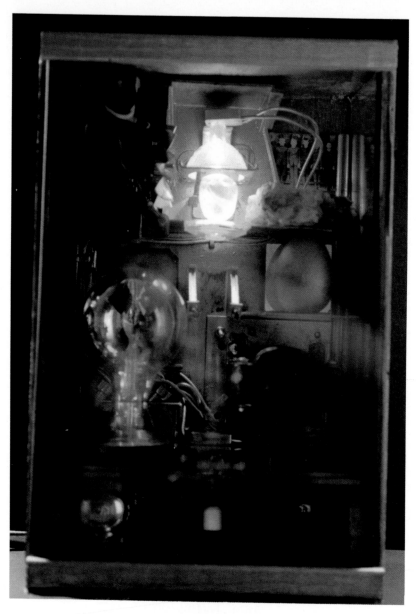

[Fig. 12]

Einstein's Brain

Eugene F. Provenzo, Coral Gables, FL

Construction
13″ x 9″ x 4″

[Fig. 13]

Evidence of a Life

Jean Magnano Bollinger, Ann Arbor, MI

Graphite on vellum
57″ x 45″

[Fig. 14]

Cold Feet
Watercolors 11″ x 10½″

Richard Kroeker, Halifax, Nova Scotia

[Fig. 15]

The Apple

[Fig. 16]

A Tent Cave

Ellen Wilt, Ann Arbor, MI

Multimedia
5′ x 3′

Craig crawled in Cracow.

Anita Lobel's illustration for the letter C in *Away from Home*
(New York: Greenwillow, 1994)

Essays

To protect the nature that is all around us, we must think long and hard about the nature we carry inside our head.
William Cronon, 1996

Ann Mikolowski, *Starville Farm,* 1975

SUSAN ENGEL

PEEKING THROUGH THE CURTAIN: NARRATIVES AS THE BOUNDARY BETWEEN SECRET AND KNOWN

A colleague tells me that as a boy he often told himself stories about playing baseball. In these stories he would begin by describing something that he recalled from an actual Little League game, but at some point the story would begin to change. Fiction would replace remembered events, as he accomplished heroic plays that won the game. He says, "Mostly I told these inside my head. But they were vivid, and I would often repeat the same story several times, sometimes changing certain details. Once in a while I even began saying a certain story out loud to myself. But I don't think I ever told anyone." As his account demonstrates, the line between secret inner stories and shared public stories is a movable one. What begins as a completely silent story may then become spoken, yet still narrated only when one is alone. These types of fluidity reflect the dynamism and psychological power of children's storytelling.

It is hard to say which is more compelling about children's stories—their complexity and idiosyncrasy, or their formal and rule-governed characteristics. In an essay on autobiographical memory, the literary critic Daniel Albright says, "Literature is a wilderness, psychology is a garden" (Albright 1994). He is talking about the disciplines of literary study and psychological research, suggesting that where the literary critic focuses on the unruly, the unique, and the uncertain, psychologists attempt to find or impose order and pattern in human experience. Children's narratives (like adult narratives) are almost always autobiographical at one level or another, and (like adult narratives) they can be treated as both literature and psychological phenomena. It often appears that investigators of children's narratives don't know whether they are contending with gardens or the wilderness; whether to proceed as if they were gardeners or trekkers.

Perhaps this confusion should tell us something. Narratives may form the psychological curtain between what is wild and private and what is orderly and public. Children often use narratives to create a boundary between the two. They also use narratives to cross that boundary. This boundary (the narrative curtain) is particularly potent because it is symbolic. This means that creating stories allows children to manipulate the connections between inner and outer, public and private. The child telling a story can actively negotiate the distinctions between what is revealed and what is concealed, between following the conventions of one's culture and breaking those conventions. A parent gave me one concrete example of this process about her two daughters, one of whom was four and the other six. The four-year-old was going on and on, while they were driving in the car, about the many things that had happened to her in school. The story sounded to the mother as if only some of it was plausible ("They served pizza for lunch, and a huge bear came into the room and grabbed the pizza . . ."). The older daughter ran a quiet steady commentary on her sister's narrative, "True, not true, not true, true." Children use stories (their own and other people's) to differentiate between what they consider to be the domain of fact and the domain of fiction. Narratives allow children to construct domains, and at the same time to create permeable boundaries around those domains.

The Rational View of Children's Narratives

In recent years, psychologists have viewed narrative as the vehicle through which children become socialized. Thus great emphasis has been placed on the ways in which children learn shared habits of mind and interaction through their storytelling. With an increased excitement about what narratives can tell us (and the seeming accessibility of their meanings) has come a gradual shift in focus, from thinking of narratives as a solitary and private activity to one that is visible and apprehensible (Nelson 1985; Engel 1995; Brice-Heath 1985). This mirrors a general trend among developmental psychologists toward the construct of a knowable, rational, and socialized child (Nelson 1998).

Creating a story does many things for a child, just as it does for the storytelling adult. One function storytelling serves for the young child is to create a bridge between the self and important others (friends, teachers, and parents). To some extent the developmental paradigm of storytelling has by and large focused on the ways in which children use stories to become members of their communities. Thus a great deal of psychological research has shown how children acquire the storytelling habits and values of the culture, how they become more able to use stories in social interactions, and how those interactions then shape their representations of experience. Another focus of developmental research has been on the way in which stories become more logical, more thematically organized, more sequential, and more grammatical as children get older. The implication in much of this research is that stories reflect more general changes in the way children think, changes from disorganization to organization, from cryptic to explicit, from idiosyncratic to formal and conventional (Franklin 1999).

The developmental account of narrative processes has yielded important information about the principled or regular changes that most children exhibit as they age, and the relationship between narrative and other aspects of inter- and intra-personal processes. This developmental account is convincing, and enlightening, but only to an extent. With all the clarity and systematism that has emerged from the research, an essential aspect of children's early narratives has been lost. For those of us studying children's narratives from a psychological perspective, it is important to keep in full sight, at all times, the wilderness from which narratives emerge.

The Wild Side of Children's Stories

The unruly and wild nature of children's stories is a vital clue to one of the secret spaces of childhood—the child's inner thoughts and fantasies. Stories do conform to social conventions of storytelling, and they do reflect the inner logic of narrative, something that seems to emerge willy-nilly like other mental shifts (for instance, the understanding that the volume of matter doesn't change even when its appearance changes, the ability to see things and situations from a variety of perspectives, or the ability to understand abstract concepts such as justice). But stories also reflect deeply internal ways of organizing experience. Young children construct stories as a way of wresting meaning from their daily experiences. Often their narratives contain evidence of the emotional and cognitive conundrums they are trying to solve. The form of the narratives often offers clues about the kinds of solutions they have devised.

The following story, written by a first grader, illustrates the principle that many of the most arresting stories constructed by young children do not fulfill formal narrative criteria (or even look like they are the precursors to more mature forms), nor do they seem conventional in any sense of the word.

The Walking Eyeball

The eyeball was a yoyo. He ran, yoyo yoyo. The eyeball was with his little brother. And he did a rolypoly bunk. And he squirted a rock out of the hose. There was a windstorm. They didn't blow over from the windstorm. And they were holding on to their feet-hands. He kicked another eyeball. He thought it was a ball. He was rolling in circles. He went home and he saw the sun.

This story is particularly cryptic and confusing. The status of the eyeball is unclear. Is he a character, human-like, with a brother? Is he a ball? Does he have subjective experience? Identity is a conundrum for this young boy. This is reflected in the content of his story (an eyeball is a yoyo. A yoyo has a brother. Their feet are hands. Another eyeball appears as a ball.) It is also reflected in the form of the story, where each sentence surprises the reader and nothing leads to what you expect (the windstorm didn't knock them over, the yoyo is both noun and verb, a storm is followed by sun).

Boundaries are also a puzzle to this storyteller. Though the story is cryptic, it grabs the listener's attention, and certainly grabbed the attention of the narrator as he told the story.

"The Walking Eyeball" is characteristic of young children's storytelling in that the process of telling was as important to the child as the story itself. In this sense narrating constitutes a form of play for the storyteller. The narrator plays with language, each sentence emerging from the one before, with little if any governing thematic or dramatic structure. The experience of creating scenes and images with words is as satisfying to the young child as making a house with blocks or enacting a fight between two dolls. And as with play, what the story is about and the process of symbolization merge to fulfill the child's impulse to construct and transform reality.

Narratives are the converging points of primary and secondary process thinking. Primary process refers to unconscious thinking that is unhampered by rules of everyday logic, and draws instead on more dynamic modes of symbolization. This kind of thinking is typical in dreaming. Secondary process thinking refers to the more rule-governed and conventionally organized thought processes usually employed in waking, task-oriented daily life, symbolic processes that adhere to constraints of the external and social world. We tend to think of primary process thinking as being id-governed while secondary process thinking is ego-governed. It is often hard, with young children's narratives, to distinguish developmentally immature forms of organization (preconceptual ways of grouping things, for instance) from idiosyncratic ways of structuring experiences that simply express the closeness between the two kinds of thinking (primary and secondary process) in young children.

Clinicians and those within a Freudian framework have long said that children's stories contain meanings the storyteller is unaware of. This assumes that the skilled listener (or analyst) can penetrate the hidden meanings in a story. In this essay, however, I am not talking about unconscious meanings, but about thoughts, feelings, and experiences the child knows about. However, the story form allows her to edit and cover up, so that her thoughts and feelings are communicated with varying degrees of forthrightness.

In the following pages I describe some of the ways in which stories serve as the curtain between private and public realms. Choosing *curtain* as my metaphor suggests that by the time a child is three-years-old, he or she has an emerging though tentative awareness of all kinds of boundaries—what is allowed and what is not allowed, what is real and what is imagined, what belongs in a story and what does not. But these boundaries are permeable and shifting. More specifically, the child can use the narrative as a semi-transparent curtain between what is public and what is private, what is secret and what is known. For instance, a four-year-old comes home from preschool, and her mother asks her how the day went. The little girl answers readily, "It was fun. I don't like Mrs. Poulos. She's mean. She won't let us talk during snack . . . and then we got so mad at her that all the kids tied her up with rope and left her sitting in the middle of the room." In this narrative the child has glided from reality to fantasy, from what was to what she wished had been. The narrative allows her to connect and compare the two types of reality. And it allows internal experience to become external landscape. Her fantasy of revenge on a feared authority becomes an actual scene with actors, props, and gestures.

Spheres of Experience

But children don't simply cross back and forth between reality and fantasy in their stories. More fundamentally, the symbolic process of creating a narrative involves constructing spheres of reality.

Heinz Werner was perhaps one of the first and only developmental theorists to focus on tracing the changing relationships between rational and irrational thinking during childhood (Werner 1980). His work constitutes the one overarching theory of development that points us toward investigating children's experience of themselves and the world, rather than their capacities. Babies and young children initially experience the world globally (self and other, symbol and referent, reality and fantasy are examples of domains that feel merged in the world of the baby and young child). Development entails an increasing differentiation between domains (for instance, the baby begins to realize that he is separate from his mother, that words and the things they name are not the same). As these domains become differentiated they also become more distanced from one another. Specifically, as children become aware of the distinction between what is real and what is imagined, what is playful and what is pragmatic, the boundaries between these types of experience become firmer.

One central tenet of Werner's theory is that people can and do construct a variety of different spheres of reality. Franklin has extended Werner's theory to argue that people use symbols and symbolic activity as a way of constructing these spheres of reality. Thus the act of forming a story allows the storyteller to create worlds that can be fantastical, autobiographical, permeated with aesthetic association, or transparent and utilitarian. Though Margery Franklin's work does not focus specifically on developmental comparisons, her argument has developmental implications. As the young child becomes increasingly aware of the differences between fact and fiction, story teller and story listener, speaking aloud and keeping things quiet, the narrative provides her with a way of constructing spheres of reality. But storytelling also provides her with a way of exploring the relationship between these spheres of reality.

The argument presented here is not the first to propose that stories give children the means to make fundamental distinctions in their organization of reality. In describing the ways in which narratives guide people's formulation of experience, Bruner and Lucariello argued that toddlers use stories to sort out the canonical from the non-canonical, the usual from the unusual. For instance, they provide a classic analysis of a toddler who talked herself to sleep each night in her crib: Emily would often go over the day, talking about what "usually" happens, what might happen, and something special, exciting, or worrisome that had happened. Bruner and Lucariello argued that, by definition, narratives distinguish canonical from non-canonical. In this way, they suggest, the narrative form drives our construction of experience (Bruner and Lucariello 1989).

In the same way, slightly older children use stories to sort out the seen from the hidden. Their concern with these boundaries is evident not only in their stories but also in what they say about stories. The parent of a six-year-old boy named Riley reports that Riley has heard an extremely scary ghost story from his much older brother. That night Riley is afraid to go to sleep. Lying worriedly next to his mother, he keeps saying, "If I go to sleep I might have a nightmare about it and in the middle of the dream I can't tell that it's not real." Riley has to figure out what he already has a glimmer of: that stories you hear can become internalized and reappear as dreams, and that dreams feel, at the moment of occurrence, as if they are actually happening, and that a dream is therefore even scarier than a story told by one person to another. One of the benefits of spoken conscious narratives is that they provide us with the means of putting a fence around scary material. When you tell a story there are all kinds of soothing indications that it is a story, not actual life. For the young storyteller, this is not only a characteristic of stories, but a focal point of the storytelling process.

When adult authors use narratives to create boundaries, they choose rhetorical techniques deliberately. An author such as Philip Roth uses autobiography as a screen or curtain that confuses the reader further about what is fact and what is fiction in his writing (see his autobiography, *The Facts*). But herein lies an important developmental difference. The child uses narrative devices and the narrative form itself to create these spheres of reality for herself. Through her symbolic action she creates spheres that she can reflect on. She can explore the boundaries of those spheres, and vary what she reveals and conceals. When the adult author dissembles and plays with boundaries, he does so for an audience. The young child, on the other hand, does so for herself as much as she does so for a listener.

In the following story, a nine-year-old girl named Ella does a masterful job of both concealing and revealing. Philip Roth or Jamaica Kincaid could not improve on Ella's artful shift between what is real and what is imagined, and between the types of reality she chooses to express and her ability to simultaneously expose her inner thoughts and keep them shrouded.

I am Ella from Vietnam. I am in the war. The Americans are attacking us Vietnamese people. I am spying on my sister who is from the U.S. She is in the army too. Sargent Knuckle is sending me in. Oh I have two Americans on my tail. Good I killed them. Here is the medical doctor taking care of some of our hurt people. It is very dangerous. I just got a foot away from my sister who is known as one of the best fighters in America she is also my evilest sister. I am so glad to be in my tent once again. And to be writing my Mom and Dad a letter. Just so you know my sister would never write a letter to Mom and Dad only I would. Except she would if it was mean.

Dear Mom and Dad,
I miss you very much. And I know that you worry about me but there is nothing to worry about because with Sargent Knuckle by my side I will never even have to worry. I love you.
Signed,
Ella

There goes a gun shot. I better track down my sister. Wake up Knuckle, wake up. But he wasn't there, he left a note saying he was by the pond so I ran over there as fast as I could. And there he was laying down dead. Oh no he couldn't be dead. But he was. It is the army so I have to leave him and track down my sister. O.K. back to my journey. I hear my sister, I will find her. But first write a letter to my Mom and Dad.

Dear Mom and Dad,
Sargent Knuckle died but don't worry, I'll be fine.
I love you.
Love,
Ella

I am tracking my sister down there she is. I am Justine, my sister is Ella and I just shot her now she is dead.

Dear Mom and Dad,
I just killed Ella so too bad. I know when you get this letter you will cry your sorry little butts off but too bad. I hate you.
From Justine.

In this story the author clearly combines fact and fiction. She does have a sister named Justine. She has never been to Vietnam. She has dramatized her view of the family competition for parental love, as all good storytellers do. She is American but chooses to write this from the point of view of a Vietnamese. I have argued elsewhere that children invent and adopt narrative devices (such as perspective, live action narration, switches in tense, and epistolary communication) in order to convey meaning. Thus when the meaning is rich and potent the invention and borrowing of literary device is at its most active. Here I would like to suggest that these devices allow the storyteller to come out from behind the curtain, and then slip back behind it, within the space of two sentences.

Using Narratives to Cool Things Down

One reason the curtain is so visible in Ella's story is because her material is clearly so loaded with personal meaning and affect. In another story by the same young author, written a few years earlier, she shows how the act of storytelling can serve to cool down hot material. The story, written when she was four, recounts a complicated relationship between two friends and a hot dog:

The Hot Dog

Once upon a time there was a hot dog. And that hot dog was a funny kind cause it would talk. And there were only two people who were friends with that hot dog. And their names were Tess and Ella. And they loved it cause they thought it was a HOT DOG! And they just loved it to pieces. And they were best friends. And they loved and loved each other. And one day they wanted to get married. And both the two girls were fighting over which one would want to be married to the hot dog.

And so they both got married to the hot dog. And they had such a great time with the hot dog. This hot dog wasn't like something you eat. It was a real dog. Like fire. Not that hot. Like sweaty. And since they were married they loved playing with each other. But they were only about six years old or seven. But no one knows except the two little girls and the hot dog.

One day someone came along walking down the street. And the two little girls and the hot dog saw the person walking down the street. And they said: "We have a hot dog!" And that's how Ella and Tess made a cold dog. The End. (Engel 1995, 79).

Ella is playing with (and only secondarily expressing) her more forbidden thoughts and impulses about her friendship. She even states quite clearly at the end that this story comes from a private or internal mental space (only Ella and Tess and the Hot Dog knew. . .). Perhaps the most marvelous and for our purposes revealing part comes at the end, when she says, "and that's how Ella and Tess made a cold dog."

Bruner has argued that narratives serve as a cooling vessel for children, allowing them to gain first symbolic, and then emotional and cognitive, distance over the experiences they recount. When feeling (rivalry, love, sexual curiosity) takes shape in a story, the words and narrative form both embody and contain the feelings, thus giving the narrator distance from her own affect. Where Ella might have had inchoate feeling she now has constructed a sphere of reality that she can move in and out of. But as author she also has some freedom over what is explicit and what is not. In recent years several psychologists have noted that the silences and omissions in narratives are as important as what is said. Often provocative clues about a child's thoughts or experiences are followed not by amplification but by silence or a complete switch in topics. In other words, the child has pulled the narrative curtain, obscuring her material. She has used the story to first reveal and then conceal.

Forbidden Fruit: What Children's Stories are About

Ella's story is a vivid example of the kind of hot material children are most drawn to using in their stories. In this way they are not so different from adults. The difference may lie in what constitutes "hot" for the young child.

In his essay "The Interested Party," from his collection *The Beast in the Nursery*, psychoanalyst Adam Phillips argues that Freud believed that curiosity is the natural avenue of sublimation for children's sexual appetite and interest (Phillips 1999). Phillips claims that this condition explains why society, in the guise, say, of school, ends up discouraging and quelling curiosity, because those who function within and on behalf of institutions know, unconsciously, that curiosity is as dangerous as sex. The essay also shows why stories provide children with a perfect vehicle for exploring sex, satisfying their curiosity and seeking pleasure.

The stories themselves are not always about pleasure. But the story form allows children to peek, flirt, imagine, encounter danger, and concretize wishes. Phillips might argue that stories, like play, will often involve the body. However, I would argue that stories represent a first symbolic embodiment of the physical and the sensuous. Telling the story is itself a pleasurable activity. The story may or may not be about the body, but the process of creating events through words and sentences teeters on the boundary between the physical and the mental. Telling the story offers the child a way of experiencing the vacillations of the boundary that separates thought from action.

> My harmless inside heart
> Turned green.
> I stabbed myself by accident
> And my heart rotted
> Because it could no longer
> Live
> Without being
> In me.

A five-year-old boy uttered these lines while looking at a cucumber lying on his kitchen table. It speaks to the fine and shifting line between language play and storytelling for young children. Both play with words and storytelling afford the child endless opportunities for exploring just the themes Phillips speaks of: the body, pain, love, vulnerability, and violence.

It is time now, after more than a decade of rich, expansive, and precise work on children's narratives, to close the gap between the clinician's focus on content and the researcher's focus on form. It is apparent that the form of children's stories reveals much about what concerns them, and that content can reveal much about how they organize the world mentally. The action of telling a story is one way children negotiate the boundaries between inner and outer life. Children express and consider their ideas, experiences, and impulses by embodying them in stories. The process, form, and content of stories allow them to discover the boundaries between what is revealed and what is concealed, and to develop some control over those boundaries.

In this essay I have argued that young children use storytelling as a way of constructing spheres of reality. Part of the time they are simply drawn to what those spheres contain, the worlds described in their stories. But part of the time they are drawn also to the very act of creating and crossing boundaries.

One of those boundaries is the line between what is secret and what is revealed. Much of the time children tell stories in which they shift back and forth between transparency and opacity. They tell something, and then become covert. Stories are on the one hand a means of revealing information to others; on the other hand they offer rich opportunities for dissembling, fabricating, and hiding material. In *China Men*, Maxine Hong Kingston describes a man who comes from China to America with an unbearable secret. Eventually he cannot stand the pressure of keeping this secret to himself, so he walks way into the woods where he first digs a hole, then shouts his secret into the hole in the ground. Stories contain secrets—both in content and through the process by which the narratives are formed and expressed. As children discover the myriad of ways in which a story can contain a secret, they also discover that they can use stories to reveal bits and pieces of a secret. The process of revelation is as variegated as other aspects of the narrative endeavor.

Narratives are rule-governed, and can be used to understand the rational and social aspect of experiences. But they are also meandering, non-linear, cryptic and idiosyncratic, filled with layers of material, as are the minds that create them. The wilderness is worth exploring.

REFERENCES

Albright, D. "Literary and Psychological Models of the Self" in U. Neisser and R. Fivush, eds., *The Remembering Self*. New York: Cambridge University Press, 1994.

Brice-Heath, S. *Ways with Words*. New York: Cambridge University Press, 1983.

Bruner, J. *Actual Minds, Possible Worlds*. Cambridge, MA: Harvard University Press, 1986.

Bruner, J. and J. Lucariello. In K. Nelson, ed., *Narratives from the Crib*. Cambridge, MA: Harvard University Press, 1989.

Engel, S. *The Stories Children Tell: Making Sense of the Narratives of Childhood*. New York: W. H. Freeman and Co., 1995.

Franklin, M., in press, "Considerations for a Psychology of Experience." *Journal of Adult Development*.

Kingston, M. H. *China Men*. New York: Ballantine Books, 1981.

Miller, P. and L. Sperry. "Early Talk about the Past: The Origins of Conversational Stories of Personal Experiences." *Journal of Child Language* 15 (1988): 293–315.

Nelson, K. *Narratives from the Crib*. Cambridge, MA: Harvard University Press, 1989.

Nelson, K, D. Plesa, and S. Henseler. *Children's Theory of Mind: An Experiential Interpretation* 41 (1988): 7–29.

Phillips, A. *The Beast in The Nursery*. New York: Pantheon Books, 1998.

Roth, P. *The Facts*. New York: Vintage Books, 1988.

Werner, H. *The Comparative Psychology of Mental Development: Revised Edition*. New York: International Universities Press, 1980.

ADRIENNE KERTZER

LIKE A FABLE, NOT A PRETTY PICTURE: HOLOCAUST REPRESENTATION IN ROBERTO BENIGNI AND ANITA LOBEL

Why, more than fifty years after the end of the Second World War, are we so fascinated with narratives (memoir, fiction, film) that explore questions of Holocaust survival with child protagonists who are far younger than the adolescent survivors (Elie Wiesel's *Night*) and adolescent victims (Anne Frank, *The Diary of a Young Girl*) whose narratives published closer to the war have become canonical Holocaust texts? Why are we increasingly drawn to stories about much younger survivors even as our historical knowledge about the unlikelihood of such survival makes such narratives less credible? The context for my questions lies in statistics cited by Debórah Dwork's *Children With a Star: Jewish Youth in Nazi Europe*, statistics that tell just how rare young child survival was. Dwork relies on the figures in Jacques Bloch's 1946 report to the Geneva Council of the International Save the Children Union: of the 1.6 million European Jews under age sixteen in 1939, only 175,000 survived. This survival rate of just under 11% is a generalized rate for all the countries that were invaded by the Nazis; thus in some countries the survival rate was much higher, but in others, much lower. Dwork, for example, refers to a study by Lucjan Dobroszycki that concludes that of the close to one million Polish Jewish children age fourteen and under in 1939, approximately 5000 survived, i.e., only .5%.

In her introduction, Dwork argues that the reluctance of historians to examine child life under the Nazis is partly derived from the different way we respond to the murder of children: "Our unwillingness to accept the murder of children is emotionally different from our incomprehension of the genocide of adults." Dwork then positions her research as central to an understanding of the Holocaust. She insists that it is only by confronting the persecution and murder of children that we will be driven to ask the "right" questions about the Holocaust, questions that do not blame the victim and reveal their unfairness as soon as we apply them to infants and young children.[1] Perhaps our increasing fascination with the narratives of young children surviving demonstrates not only a reluctance to ask the "right" questions, but evidence of a deeper resistance. For we seem unable to confront the murder of young children except by celebrating the exceptional—and the more we know, even more incredible—narratives of very young children surviving not just the European scene of war, but the death and slave labor camps. Again, Dwork's analysis illustrates how our desire for such exceptional narratives conflicts with our awareness that nearly all the "children" who were likely to survive were either adolescents or children pretending to be so. Dwork points out that children who survived the initial selection at Auschwitz were in effect no longer children; they were passing as adults: "There were no young children and there was no child life." For such children, death was a matter of time, but through luck, most often just the temporal accident of when the camps were liberated, some of those adult-like children did survive. Dwork cites figures we need to keep in mind: "180 children under the age of fourteen were found alive at the liberation of Auschwitz, about 500 in Bergen-Belsen, 500 in Ravensbrück and 1,000 in Buchenwald."

If so few survived, and if we remember that at least some of these survivors were barely alive at liberation and died soon after, and many of them have died since, is this sufficient to account for our current fascination with the exceptional young child survivor? And are we more willing to listen now not just because there are so few of these child survivors left, but because those few survivors are now elderly? Do we in effect trust and tolerate their voices because they are no longer children, because their postwar survival and lengthy lives provide the safety of distance as well as the authority granted their present age?[2] Or does our eagerness now to imagine such next-to-impossible stories simply reflect the shift to a culture intrigued by narratives of childhood trauma and more accepting of childhood memory, more willing to believe in what children say? In acknowledging how unusual her focus on child survivors is in mainstream Holocaust history, Dwork notes specific cultural reasons for ignoring child survivors immediately after the war, when many people, traumatized by what they learned had occurred in the camps, preferred to forget events that seemed unbelievable, particularly when the survivor was a child. If Holocaust narratives told by adults made us uncomfortable and incredulous, narratives told by children were even more disturbing and unbearable. It was hard to believe that young children could survive, let alone want or be able to narrate their stories. Narratives of young children hidden outside the camps, or fictional accounts that began once the young child was outside the camp (e.g., the excessively vague *I Am David*) seemed barely tolerable. Thus for many years, child survivors of the camps who were compelled to narrate seemingly impossible stories were heard mainly by medical professionals interested in the psychological makeup of children who survive extreme situations; the general North American public remained indifferent, content if they thought about Holocaust survivors at all to imagine such survivors only as broken-down adults.

Three recent and very different works speak to our increasing desire for child survivor narratives that resist Dwork's analysis. Both Roberto Benigni's *Life is Beautiful* (1997), a film about a father's determination to protect his four-year-old son, Giosuè, in a concentration camp, and Binjamin Wilkomirski's *Fragments: Memories of a Wartime Childhood* (1995, English translation 1996), a memoir about a toddler's amazing survival in a series of camps, have received numerous international awards; Anita Lobel's *No Pretty Pictures: A Child of War* (1998) made the *New York Times* Notable Book List and has already appeared on recommended children's booklists, a predictable development given her established reputation as a children's book illustrator. Benigni and Wilkomirski have created works that are highly contentious: Benigni because of his audacious willingness to apply comedy to the Holocaust, Wilkomirski because of an article published in *Die Weltwoche* in late August 1998 by a Swiss journalist, Daniel Ganzfried, who alleges that Wilkomirski is an imposter, and his memoir of Holocaust survival, a complete fabrication.[3] Such controversies indicate not only how the Holocaust continues to be for many the defining trauma of the twentieth century, but also how problematic we still find the question of aesthetic response to historical atrocity, particularly as such atrocity affects young children. So long as we believe in its status as memoir, we are willing to accept that *Fragments* tells an amazing truth; as soon as we regard it as fiction, our response changes as we question fiction's right to construct such an unbelievable story.[4] Similarly the very title of Lobel's memoir, *No Pretty Pictures*, confirms her determination to separate her Holocaust memories from the aesthetic work of her adult life. Whether such separation is possible, Lobel's determination accords with our own desire to protect the child viewer, to construct her as the one who does not know.

But maybe it is adults who do not want to know what some children already know. Although I hesitate to speak about *Life is Beautiful*, so excessive and misplaced is the outrage that I have heard since its appearance—it is genocide that should provoke our outrage surely, not the aesthetic question of the limitations of comedy—the outrage cannot be divorced from this question of the viewer's knowledge. Is the film's viewer constructed as a child, the one who does not know, and therefore believes that what she sees on screen is the historically real, or is the viewer constructed as the adult, the one who already in some sense knows, and can therefore imagine what is not shown? My analysis tends to presume the latter; opponents of the film, I would argue, assume the former. I think that the tension in the film, and over the film, relates to the ambiguity of Benigni's response,[5] and the refusal by critics to even acknowledge the possibilities of a children's literature on the Holocaust, and what such a literature might tell us about aesthetic response to atrocity and the related question of the child's knowledge.

Even though Benigni has himself suggested that one significant impulse behind *Life is Beautiful* is the childhood memory of his father magically transforming war experience into reassuring and comic narrative for his children, reviewers of the film have chosen to disregard both the perspective offered by this particular anecdote and the insights offered if the film is situated in the context of the representational strategies familiar in children's literature. Yet such contexts offer a different way of understanding the limitations and strengths of Benigni's film, i.e., that it makes a difference to our understanding of how the film works if we situate it not beside *Schindler's List*, but in the context of the representational strategies that it openly asserts that it is using. In this context, I similarly set aside the claim that Benigni adapts his title, *Life is Beautiful*, from Trotsky's words just before he was murdered, for I find a different lineage far more provocative and useful. It is one in which the title rewrites a statement that appears in the final chapter of Primo Levi's memoir, *Survival in Auschwitz: The Nazi Assault on Humanity*, a memoir published initially in Italian with the far less hopeful title of *Se questo è un uomo*. In Levi's final chapter, "The Story of Ten Days," Levi describes how, ill with scarlet fever, left behind when the Nazis evacuate Auschwitz in January 1945, he and all the others who have been abandoned to die reach a stage where, despite the armies battling nearby, they are "too tired to be really worried." In this state of exhaustion, Levi makes a surprising statement: "I was thinking that life was beautiful and would be beautiful again, and that it would really be a pity to let ourselves be overcome now." The contrast between Levi's careful use of tenses, "life was beautiful and would be beautiful again," a use that excludes the possibility of beauty in the present time and in the Auschwitz location, and Benigni's insistence on the present tense points to how the practice of a children's literature on the Holocaust is deeply implicated in what is most controversial in the film. Although the second half of Benigni's film ironically repeats incidents from the first half as though to demonstrate how insane and desperate is Guido's attempt to persuade Giosuè that life remains the same even when they are in the camp, Benigni's title insists that the passage of time cannot alter eternal truths. The child who becomes the grown-up narrator of the film may possess a deeper understanding of how his father protected him, but it is one in which the essential loving and trusting relationship to the father remains the same. As in a children's folktale, life *is* beautiful.

The film thus carefully situates its perspective with the opening voiceover spoken by the grown-up Giosuè in which he twice compares his "simple story,"[6] to a fable. At the film's end, still believing in his father's story that the point of their incarceration is to obey the rules, play the game, and win a prize, Giosuè greets the arrival of the American liberators as the evidence that he has indeed won the promised tank. Giosuè's ride in the tank is interrupted by a reunion with his mother, Dora, and immediately afterwards the adult Giosuè in a voiceover provides the fable's requisite and apparently unambiguous lesson, "This is my story. This is the sacrifice my father made for me." This structural dependence on a fable, with its promise of a lesson, like the film's parodic reliance on folk tale elements, games, and riddles, suggests that much of the success of the film (and its controversy) lies in applying to the Holocaust strategies of representation familiar in children's literature but more problematic in adult Holocaust narratives, particularly films, where we assume that documentary realism alone is appropriate to the subject.[7]

It is striking how similar the film's strategies are to those found in Jane Yolen's young adult novel *Briar Rose*: "I know of no woman who escaped from Chelmno alive," Yolen writes after completing a fairy tale novel in which she imagines one such survivor. As in a fairy tale, Dora, the heroine of *Life is Beautiful*, lies in bed like Sleeping Beauty, longing to be rescued by her hero, the man who introduces himself as Prince Guido, and whose last name, Orefice, means goldsmith. Of course, parody demands that this prince does not climb up the tower, but meets his *principessa* when she falls out of a barn silo into his arms. Nevertheless, Guido clearly does rescue Dora from the miseries of a wealthy marriage, as they ride away from the engagement banquet on the horse appropriately named Robin Hood.

What Yolen accomplishes through the contrast produced by her concluding "Author's Note," Benigni achieves through the visualizing of absence, what the screen does and does not show us. The tension of the film lies in its playing between two registers that always threaten to collapse: a children's fable of rescue; an adult narrative of what cannot be said (at one point a character even says that silence is the greatest cry). Certainly existence in the death camps is governed by rules as ludicrous and insane as those involved in the game Guido invents to protect Giosuè from knowledge of the camps, but when Guido tells Giosuè that Schwanz, the other child seen earlier hiding in the sentry box, has been "eliminated," for a second we are not sure which game is being played. Similarly Giosuè tells his father about the other children whose absence no comedy can hide: they took the children to the showers he says; they make buttons and soap from us. Guido mocks his son's gullibility; what kind of game is that? Who can imagine burning people in ovens? But not even Guido, the one who can answer nearly all of the Nazi doctor's riddles (including one about Snow White), can answer the riddle of Nazi categories, the riddle whose answer we know as the Final Solution.

Cautioned by his uncle to heed the warning when Robin Hood is painted with anti-Semitic symbols, Guido jokes that he didn't even know that the horse was Jewish. Like many Italian Jews, Guido is unwilling to imagine himself as vulnerable, and jokes that the worst the Nazis can do is paint him yellow and white.[8] Guido's words are echoed in the unanswered and ultimate riddle that later torments the Nazi doctor and prevents him, a believer in the Final Solution, from seeing Guido as human. The riddle describes something that looks and acts like a duck. If it looks like a duck, maybe it is a duck, but if the riddle's answer is Guido, then the doctor's loyalty to a Nazi ideology that sees Jews as inhuman vermin in need of extermination, prevents him from recognizing the man in front of him. For if many riddles are based on faulty categories,[9] the Nazi desire for a Final Solution demonstrates not only the horrific consequences of riddles based on faulty categories, but also how genocide can be regarded as merely the solution to a challenging riddle. Yet the film has little interest in philosophical analysis. Guido may think himself indebted to Schopenhauer for his belief in will power, but when Guido desperately turns to that will power as a magic spell to prevent the SS dog from discovering his son's hiding place, few adult viewers are likely to forget the Nazi fondness for the rhetoric of will power (a rhetoric inscribed in the title of Leni Riefenstahl's 1936 film, *The Triumph of the Will*), or to accept that Giosuè's subsequent survival is proof of Schopenhauer's theories.

Throughout the film, Benigni draws attention to the difference between what the child sees and what the father/viewer sees: the contrast between the child's joy and belief in his father's explanation of the camp rules and the incredulous faces of the adult prisoners who are never taken in by Guido's jokes. The sleeping Giosuè does not see the mountain of skeletal corpses that Guido and the viewer see when Guido carries the child through the night and fog, a night and fog that is resonant for the viewer familiar with either Alain Resnais's documentary, *Night and Fog*, or with the secret order, *Nacht und*

Giorgio Cantarini (center) and Roberto Benigni (right) enter the concentration camp barracks in *Life Is Beautiful.*

Nebel, that "mandated the arrest of anyone suspected of underground activities against the Reich" (Epstein). Most poignant is the contrast between the child's final view of his father as Guido is marched to execution: in the restricted vision of Giosuè peering from his secret hiding place appears a father still confident and clowning for his son, repeating the mocking gesture he made earlier in the film; in the eyes of the informed adult viewer is a man fully aware that this time he will not return.[10]

Presumably it is Giosuè's adult voice that makes *Life is Beautiful* an adult film. Yet it is worth observing both the abruptness of the film's happy ending and its dependence on an adult voice that is remarkably faithful to the presumed perspective of childhood. Although it is the adult Giosuè who narrates the film, his adult perspective at the film's conclusion is perfectly consistent with the fable that structures his childhood memories, "This is my story. This is the sacrifice my father made for me." Yet this insistence on an unproblematic, coherent narrative is only possible if the film concludes at the moment of liberation, the moment when the fable proves to be both true and impossible to continue. For if the fable is true, and the father saved his life, how does a child live with that knowledge? And does Giosuè really survive because of the father's sacrifice? What then is the sacrifice: Guido's silence about the genocidal purpose of the camps, or Guido's death? Accounting for his survival through the father's sacrificial death seems appropriate to a fairy tale, yet it contradicts the evidence of the film, for it is just as likely that Giosuè might have died because of his ignorance of the camps' purpose, and just as likely that Guido might have survived if he hadn't searched for Dora that final night. The logic that the father sacrificed himself in order that his son might live does not fit the camp universe where if any logic applies, it is the logic of death by which any Jews saved for work have only been given a temporary reprieve. And any logic, let alone the patterns of fairy-tale justice and the good luck of being the special child of the prince and princess, always comes up against the role of accident: the accident that the next morning the camp is liberated; the accident that Dora survives; the accident that riding on the American tank, Giosuè finds his mother. The adult Giosuè's belief in his simple story that begins with his first words as a child, "I lost my tank," and ends with his cry of victory at the film's conclusion, "We won, we won," means that the film must end when it does. It cannot afford to proceed further without confuting its own logic.

A "simple story," *Life is Beautiful* demonstrates that in speaking of the Holocaust it is not just children who long for consolatory fairy tales. Yet the film also illustrates how questions of intended audience in Holocaust representation often blur the distinction we draw between child and adult. For the controversy over the appropriateness of telling a fable about the Holocaust seems directly consequent to a binary view of Holocaust representation in which adult representation of the Holocaust, precisely because it is adult, is to be judged only in terms of a kind of full (meaning realistic) representation. In contrast, we expect Holocaust representation in children's literature to work with limits, by employing narrative structures that protect the child reader even as the narrative instructs that reader about the Holocaust and attempts to make meaning of what is too easily dismissed as incomprehensible. While some might object that these very limits make the idea of any children's literature on the Holocaust itself incomprehensible and trivial, children's books may simply be more honest about their limitations than adult works. For the objection to limits of representation in children's books implies that there may be another kind of literature, i.e., adult literature, that is somehow free of such limits, and can therefore provide the reader with a full knowledge. Such belief in an ideal literature on the Holocaust necessitates setting aside general theoretical objections to the ability of any language to mirror any reality, objections that are further complicated by the oft-cited survivor perspective that whoever was not there cannot know what it was like, that there may well be words to represent this reality but only survivors speaking to other survivors can possess and understand them. And this survivor perspective has been taken even further, by Primo Levi, when he says that those who survived by virtue of their survival, are themselves an exception and cannot tell the stories of the majority who did not survive.

What is even more apparent is that if *Life is Beautiful* is ultimately and paradoxically an adult film that is dependent upon the techniques of children's literature, it is also a film whose foregrounding of Guido's need to protect the child distracts us from its equally urgent need to protect the adult viewer who wants to believe not only that the power of parental love will persist even in the death camps,[11] but more wistfully, that the child survivor recognizes and remains ever grateful to the memory of that love. Those who object to the film's comic approach are understandably reluctant to address this as central to the film's comic vision, and I do not wish to generalize that all child survivors are not eternally grateful. Certainly memoirs by children whose parents were murdered are intensely loyal, guilt-ridden at any lapse in that loyalty, as in *Night* when Elie Wiesel confesses his relief at his father's death. But if the parents survive, the postwar relationship described in the memoirs is often far more troubled, and particularly so if the child survivor was very young.[12]

Guido must die therefore, not to save his son, but to save his son's fabulous memory of him, and the audience's belief in the integrity of parent-child relationships under all circumstances. Listen to the collapse of this belief in *No Pretty Pictures* as

Lobel recalls her feelings regarding her uncle and aunt the night in January 1945 when she and her young brother arrive in "yet another concentration camp": "They didn't matter to me anymore. First they had pretended to take care of us. And then they had lied. They had tried to trick us. The failures of the grown-ups around us had landed us in this place." Lobel will later learn that her uncle and aunt do die before the end of the war, but that night, having lost trust in all adults, she has just refused their well-intended advice to escape during a forced march from Plaszów to Auschwitz. Lobel's "Epilogue" even considers, then dismisses, the question of how her lack of trust may have contributed to her uncle and aunt's death.[13] That Lobel's parents not only survive (the father in Russia, the mother in hiding) but also avoid imprisonment in a camp, makes her memoir far more complex than Benigni's film in its analysis of child-adult relations in the Holocaust and the possibility of happy endings.

For the contrast between Lobel's memoir and Benigni's film lies not in Giosuè's amazing survival, but in the filmic depiction of that survival as the narrative's redemptive ending. Lobel rejects the neatness of Benigni's happy ending, even as she insists in the voice of the American citizen/illustrator/grandmother who writes the memoir that, "My life has been good." The audacity of Guido's hiding Giosuè in the camp barracks seems more credible to those familiar with Lobel's account, which is just as astonishing as Giosuè's, for she and her brother do not have a parent protecting them in the camps even if Lobel does learn years later that the likely reason she was not killed upon arrival in Plaszów was because her uncle pleaded successfully with the Nazi commandant who still needed his services. But no special pleading explains Lobel's survival in the women's camp, Ravensbrück, for several months, when no one cared that a ten-year-old girl was accompanied by an eight-year-old brother, a brother no longer disguised as a girl.

Unlike the triumphant ending of *Life is Beautiful*, therefore, Lobel's liberation from Ravensbrück is a complex moment that represents only one part of her story and one which she misunderstands, not knowing either who her rescuers are or where she is going. Initially "walking in a halo of light," she feels that a miracle has occurred, a miracle she attributes to her wearing of the "holy medals" that her Catholic nanny had given her and that she has managed to retain despite the stripping and shaving that she has been subject to. Yet she also feels shame at being photographed as she steps off the ferry in Sweden wearing the "same layers of rags" that she wore in the camp. Sweden represents a new world; the rags she wears belong to a different world. As a memoirist, Lobel places this photograph of arrival in Sweden on the cover of her book, as if writing the memoir demands confronting that shame, and all the other moments of bodily humiliation that are part of her experience. A reluctant memoirist, Lobel views with suspicion the current fashion for celebrating Holocaust survivors: "it is . . . wearisome as well as dangerous to cloak and sanctify oneself with the pride of victimhood."

In an era so fascinated with trauma narratives, in which we look for stories about younger and younger victims, Lobel is ambivalent about her own claim to trauma, and she refuses our expectations that as a child she suffered more than the adults around her. "Mine is only another story" is the final line in the memoir, a line that occurs immediately after Lobel tries and fails to imagine the feelings her grandmother must have experienced when she was transported. This attempt may be Lobel's adult gesture countering her childhood memory of refusing any recognition to a "large, shapeless woman" thrown in the truck when they are transported. When her brother guesses that the woman is their grandmother, Lobel is terrified that he is right: "'Don't be stupid,' I whispered. 'And keep quiet.'. . . I didn't want us to be connected to a Jewish relative."

The ambivalence that the child feels regarding her parents' behavior (her father's disappearance, her mother's powerlessness) thus produces a memoir in which a child separated from her parents learns to prefer that separation: the parents who find her two years after liberation in a Swedish shelter for Polish refugees embarrass, shame, and anger her. Lobel is outraged when her mother wants immediately to cut her hair as though oblivious to how the trauma of having her head shaved would produce a child unwilling to ever cut her hair again. The memoir structurally enacts Lobel's sense of separation: the years in Poland are but one chapter of her life; "Sweden" follows; and then there are her years in the USA, far longer, she keeps reminding the reader, than she lived as a child in Poland.

If she concludes that hers is a happy story, happiness exists only through her ability to block out a "time from which I have very few pretty pictures to remember."

This principle of separation seems apparent as well if we turn to Lobel's picture books. For much of her career, the biographical notes on the dust jackets of her books are silent about her Holocaust childhood. Lobel is presented as a decorative artist, capable of pretty pictures, but not much else; typical are the notes to her illustrations of *Three Rolls and One Doughnut: Fables from Russia Retold by Mirra Ginsburg*: "Having lived close to peasant art as a child, Mrs. Lobel has always been interested in the decorative arts. She embroiders clothes whenever she can and designs needlepoint tapestries." What is missing in this description is the political aspect to this aesthetic decision, the politics that makes of Lobel not simply a female artist who has time on her hands to do needlepoint, but a child survivor who knows what it is like to live without beauty, and who defies that childhood every time she makes a pretty picture. For just as the powerful effect of *Life is Beautiful* lies in the scenic representation of Giosuè's fabulous survival in the context of the significant absence of the other children, a different story of Lobel's art is told if we position the picture books and what they suppress in the context of the memoir.

Despite the way the title, *No Pretty Pictures*, draws a line between Lobel's later life as an American illustrator and her Polish childhood, the line is not only less solid than Lobel claims, but is itself a marker of the survival strategies she found necessary. What is the relationship, for example, between Niania, Lobel's Polish nanny to whose memory Lobel dedicates her memoir, and the many babushka-wearing women who populate her art? The memoirist concludes that Niania was her "demented angel," undoubtedly anti-Semitic yet just as clearly devoted, loving, and determined to protect her two charges. Lobel begins her memoir with the memory of her five-year-old self watching the arrival of the German soldiers in September 1939; holding tightly to her nanny's hands, she records how Niania categorizes and identifies the world for her, first saying, "'Niemcy, Niemcy' ('Germans, Germans')" and then just as contemptuously muttering whenever she sees the neighbor Hasid "Jews!" In hiding Lobel and her brother, the latter dressed as a girl, and with his curly blond hair more easily disguised as a

Christian than the dark-skinned Lobel, Niania seems to have regarded the children as somehow not quite as Jewish as the Jews she disliked. Gradually Lobel too absorbs Niania's attitudes and sees herself as more Catholic than Jewish. She longs for blond hair, worries that her dark skin betrays her, and shuns association with other Jews. In the Polish village where they first hide, Lobel feels threatened when her own mother comes to visit, yet the Polish countryside is no paradise: exchanging tablecloths for food, Niania and the two children have excrement thrown on them.

Such ambiguous memories of Poland contest the biographical notes in which Lobel admits to only positive images, e.g., "As a little girl in Poland, I remember weaving chains of flowers and wreaths for my hair" (*Alison's Zinnia*). Three picture books that span her career, *Sven's Bridge* (1965), *Potatoes, Potatoes* (1967), and *Away from Home* (1994), further indicate not only that Lobel's separation of her Holocaust childhood from her adult art is less tidy than the memoir claims, but that Lobel's need to separate hints at a more complex narrative about child survivors than the one celebrated by the neat happy ending of Benigni's film. Initially the illustrations seem to exist in isolation from Lobel's wartime memories, as though Lobel with her pictures were returning the beauty that was taken away from her by creating a separate utopian world. This is a relationship of replacement, covering over, like the incident she records in the memoir when the Nazi visit to her parents' apartment is marked by the theft of a beautiful rug. When Lobel later sees her mother crying over the transport of her parents and sister, the first time that she ever sees an adult so vulnerable, she recalls her mother standing "in the middle of the empty spot where the kilim rug had been" (*No Pretty Pictures*). What is covered over in Lobel's first picture book, *Sven's Bridge*, what cannot be said in 1965, is the memory of that humiliation. The biographical notes to *Sven's Bridge* carefully avoid any reference to the Holocaust and we read only that "Anita Lobel was born in Krakow, Poland, where she spent much of her early childhood."

Yet like Benigni's viewer who imagines what is not represented on the screen, the reader of the memoir notices in the utopian world of *Sven's Bridge*, where even kings can be fooled by loyal gatekeepers, that the only colors are yellow and blue, the colors of the Swedish flag, and of the pajamas that Lobel and her brother are given in the Swedish sanatorium when they are rescued from Ravensbrück.[14] Surely the book is a tribute to the land where Lobel first learned to do embroidery and watercolors, the land that returned her to a world of life and color, the land where when a foolish king blows up a bridge, it is replaced with a more beautiful, ornate design. It is not simply a matter of colors. For the narrative itself seems a tribute to Sweden, where Lobel could recover from the terror of sneaking out of the Kraków ghetto by crossing a stone bridge that "felt like a tightrope," aware that any moment Nazi soldiers might turn around and discover her. In order to cross the bridge, Lobel forced herself to remember a painting that hung over her bed before the war of a "beautiful angel . . . [with] giant wings hovering over, almost enveloping two children crossing a bridge over a ravine," a memory with which she controls her fears of Niania's lack of power. Better a utopia in which Sven, the gatekeeper, protects the wooden bridge and all those who need to cross it; in place of Niania with her string bag to fool onlookers into thinking that she is a "lady . . . going to market" (*No Pretty Pictures*), are the men and women whose fishing nets are not disturbed when Sven raises the bridge. In *Sven's Bridge*, bridges are safe places.[15]

In contrast, Poland is the place of death: "In Poland everybody ended up laid out, with noses and feet pointing to the ceiling" (*No Pretty Pictures*). This image of death occurs repeatedly in the memoir, and is established initially when Lobel recounts hiding during a Nazi roundup in the Kraków ghetto. Lying beside her mother, she notes her resemblance to

> the corpse of an old woman we had known in the country. The dead woman had been laid out on a table in her cottage. Her nose, long and thin, reached far away from her face. And her feet were neatly pointing straight up. Mother's big nose and pointing feet looked just like that corpse. (*No Pretty Pictures*)

Given the circumstances, it is not surprising that the child imagines the mother as a corpse, and it is easy to understand why, when Lobel later acknowledges the contribution of her wartime memories to her fable *Potatoes, Potatoes*, she gently belittles reviewers who take the book seriously (Hopkins). Although Lobel resists constructing herself as a child survivor, she nevertheless demonstrates the perspective of a survivor who knows too well the difference between fables and the grim historical reality of Holocaust survival where, as Primo Levi tells us, "it needs more than potatoes to give back strength to a man." By ridiculing reviewers who take the book seriously, Lobel maintains her principle of separation and distances herself from the dust jacket reference to the "timeless lesson" hidden in *Potatoes, Potatoes*. Memoir writers rarely offer such clear lessons, and the dust jacket biography remains silent on her wartime experience.

Yet in *Potatoes, Potatoes*, Lobel does draw on her memory of the mother as corpse. The image of the dead mother becomes the comic turning point of the fable, for the two brothers who left home captivated by the attractive uniforms and swords of the opposing armies have become military leaders battling for the potatoes their mother has hidden behind her walls. When the two armies break through the walls and destroy everything, they discover what appears to be the dead body of the boys' mother, a body that Lobel draws as the image she will describe more than thirty years later in the memoir.[16] Just as Lobel's mother only appeared dead, the brothers' mother is also pretending; a critical difference between the fable and the memoir, however, is that in the world of fables the mother has what all mothers lacked during the Holocaust, the power to teach a lesson, and make a difference.[17] The picture book mother lets everyone cry until the lesson sinks in, and then offers the soldiers potatoes only if they "promise to stop all the fighting / and clean up this mess, / and go home to [their] mothers." Yet a further difference is significant, for the boys' mother is dressed not as the fashionable urban woman who appears in the photographs of Lobel's mother that are included in the memoir, but as Niania, the babushka-wearing nanny whose meals of potatoes come to represent the safety in Polish identity that Lobel longs for and misses as soon as she is separated from her. Niania also resembles the mother in *Potatoes, Potatoes* who learns the impossibility of building "a wall around everything she owned." For like the "woman who did not bother with the war" (*Potatoes, Potatoes*), Niania learns the futility of advising the children to ignore the fights and hide among the potatoes.

Just before Lobel and her brother are captured by the Nazis in the chapel of the Benedictine convent, the two children dis-

"Mother, Mother, this is our fault!" cried the older son.

"What have we done?" cried the younger son.

"Speak to us! Speak to us!" they begged.

Illustration by Anita Lobel from her book, *Potatoes, Potatoes* (Harper & Row, 1967). (c) Anita Lobel and used with her kind permission.

obey Niania by sneaking out of the convent and visiting a local carousel. Although having to cross a small bridge to get to the carousel reminds Lobel of the trauma of crossing the ghetto bridge, for a moment she is distracted from the constant anxiety of hiding, and is able to see what so rarely appears in her memoir, a pretty picture:

> I turned back to look at my Kraków. In the soft layers of air the city looked so like a beautiful painting in the pink and gold of an almost evening sky. I could see the tower of the town square and a little to the side the spire of *kosciól Mariaki*. From where we now were I could no longer see the bridge we had crossed.

Given the representation of Kraków as a "beautiful painting," perhaps it is not surprising to see how the memory of this picture enables Lobel to risk crossing the bridge between her

Holocaust childhood and her pretty pictures. For the memory of "my Kraków" also constitutes the background to the illustration of the letter C in a recent alphabet book, *Away from Home*, and the image shocks, not only because it is so unusual in Lobel's work, but because its aesthetics are so contradictory.

Away from Home is structured (according to the dust jacket) as "a whirlwind tour of some of the world's wonders," in which young boys visit "exotic places in alliterative fashion" (Library of Congress publication data). The dust jacket assures the reader that in the book's pages she can "start with A and go anywhere [she] want[s]!" The book is clearly autobiographical; on the dust jacket, Lobel identifies herself as a woman who travels in three different (and presumably equivalent) ways: "I have been a refugee. I have been an immigrant. I have been a tourist." Dedicated to Lobel's son Adam, the dedication page shows the Lobels receiving a letter from their son, and the text for the letter A says "Adam arrived in Amsterdam."[18] In the background notes for the letter C, we learn that "Cracow is the city in Poland where I was born. This is its central square." What startles me is the illustration's implied narrative, for the letter C shows a child, obviously Jewish since he wears a Jewish star on his cap and presumably a partisan since he carries a rifle, caught in the stage lights. When "Craig crawl[s] in Cracow" and is caught by the stage lights, I cannot help but see a Jewish child caught by other, more terrifying searchlights, and even find myself worrying about the intentions of the two men holding the stage set. (See photo section in this book) The image is so haunted by my reading of the memoir that the stage itself starts to look as narrow as a bridge.

While it may be that Lobel can only incorporate the Holocaust into her pretty pictures by repressing her own memories and replacing them with the imagined heroic resistance of a partisan, I am struck by the contradiction between Lobel's attempt to allude to the Holocaust in a children's travel book, and her insistence in *No Pretty Pictures* of the stark contrast between two kinds of travel: that of a tourist, and her memory of a very different kind of travel: "the furtive ride in a hay wagon, the escape from Niania's village on the old train, and the few steps of a frightening walk across a bridge that then loomed as a dangerous enormous distance." Lobel has refused to return to Poland, to be a tourist in "Auschwitz or Plaszów or Ravensbrück." Her refusal is understandable, far more so than the aesthetics produced by an alliterative alphabet book in which the statement, "Craig crawled in Cracow," is no more frightening or meaningful than "Frederick fiddled in Florence," or "Henry hoped in Hollywood." Lobel ends her biographical statement on the dust jacket with a very clear pedagogical impulse: "I hope this theatrical picture-postcard journey is an invitation to learning more about places far away from home." But how does the invitation to learning work here? Making of the Holocaust an alphabetical entry like any other in a child's tour of the world's wonders, Lobel attempts an aesthetics that is deeply disturbing, one that makes me question the impossible demands we make upon Holocaust representations for and about young children. For what is the point to a Holocaust image that is so determined to give pleasure to young children that it is silent about its own implicit terror? Benigni's fable demands an adult viewer whose aesthetic pleasure is produced and affected by her awareness of a genocide that Benigni refuses to show; thus when Guido is caught in the searchlights, the viewer knows, even if she does not see, what happens next. In contrast, Lobel's pretty picture requires a child reader whose ability to take pleasure in the image of a Jewish child caught in the searchlights is dependent on an ignorance of the history that produces it, and a refusal to imagine what happens next.

NOTES

[1]Dwork is thinking of the absurdity, for example, of asking an infant why she didn't resist being taken to the gas chambers.

[2]A comparable example of the authority and safety provided by age is operative in the Canadian children's book, *Uncle Ronald*, by Brian Doyle. The narrator, Old Mickey, is one hundred and twelve years old, old enough apparently to tell a narrative of child abuse that is both painful and comic.

[3]I refer to this text as a memoir and the author as Wilkomirski since the text's critical success was determined by readers who accepted its presentation as memoir and never questioned the identity of the author. Wilkomirski has given few interviews since the publication of the allegations; in an interview that was part of a *60 Minutes* documentary broadcast February 7, 1999, he still insists that *Fragments* is a true account of his past. See Elena Lappin, "The Man with Two Heads," *Granta* 66 (Summer 1999), 7–65, and Philip Gourevitch, "The Memory Thief," *New Yorker*, 14 June 1999, 48–62 and 64–8, for articles that contest and explore this self-presentation. At the Frankfurt Book Fair, October 1999, Suhrkamp Verlag, Wilkomirski's original publisher, acting on a preliminary report by a Swiss historian that concluded that the

author of *Fragments* was not Binjamin Wilkomirski, a Holocaust survivor, announced that it was withdrawing all hardcover copies of *Fragments*.

[4]For an example of such questioning, see Blake Eskin, "Lawyer Demands Probe of Wilkomirski," *Forward*, 19 November 1999, 15.

[5]Critics of the film seem both inconsistent and indifferent to the question of a child's knowledge; they typically condemn the film because they assume that adult viewers are ignorant of the Holocaust and so will naively believe that what they see on the screen is historically accurate. Yet such critics routinely base this aesthetic objection on their own historical awareness of the Holocaust. And they ignore how the film itself problematizes the child's limited knowledge; i.e., Giosuè hears more than what his father tells him. In addition, such critics do not consider how Holocaust representation in children's literature always works within limits. For example, in David Denby's second and extremely negative review of the film in the *New Yorker*, he concludes that "Benigni protects the audience as much as Guido protects his son; we are all treated like children" (99). In response, Eric McHenry chastises Denby for treating the film's viewers "like children" when he ignores how the film "depends upon the audience's remembrance of the Holocaust" (Letter, *New Yorker*, 10). My attention to the question of the child's knowledge is also indebted to a colleague who concluded his contemptuous dismissal of *Life is Beautiful* by asking me if I knew that the concentration camps were dirty and that people vomited in them. My astonishment about his assumptions regarding my knowledge or lack thereof prompted me to think more clearly about the question of knowledge and the construction of the child.

[6]All quotations from *Life is Beautiful* are from the English version.

[7]This faulty assumption has led some reviewers to praise Benigni's film while advising viewers that if they want the truth of the Holocaust, they turn to Steven Spielberg. It may also account for how some viewers of Claude Lanzmann's *Shoah* celebrate the documentary's "truth" without considering how Lanzmann pushes the survivor, e.g., the barber, to communicate only the traumatic truth that Lanzmann is interested in; Lanzmann is simply not interested in post-Holocaust narratives that tell other kinds of truth.

[8] For an analysis of why Italian Jews generally did not believe that they were threatened by the Nazis, see Susan Zuccotti, *The Italians and the Holocaust: Persecution, Rescue, and Survival*.

[9] When is a door not a door? When it's ajar.

[10]That some adult viewers are shocked when Guido is killed (the hero is not supposed to die) indicates how my analysis presumes an adult viewer, familiar with the history of the death camps and the chances of survival. Like much of the fiction of Aharon Appelfeld, Benigni's ability not to show us atrocities is dependent on our awareness of what is not shown. (See the discussion of Appelfeld in Michael André Bernstein's *Foregone Conclusions: Against Apocalyptic History*.) If the viewer is ignorant of the history of the death camps, then Guido's death works very differently, in fact more like the educational plot of children's narrative, and the viewer is then responding as adults imagine a child would.

[11]I am thinking also of newspaper advertisements for *Life is Beautiful* that tell us that the film demonstrates how love and imagination conquer all.

[12]In children's Holocaust novels such as *Hide and Seek* and *Anna is Still Here*, Ida Vos narrates the postwar trauma of family relations for the child reader.

¹³A question that Dwork might say is another example of the wrong kind of question.

¹⁴In discussing *Sven's Bridge*, I am responding to the original edition, not the revised full color edition published by Greenwillow in 1992. In the revision, the words remain the same. Despite the full color, the flags are still painted in the original yellow and blue. The new edition is larger than the original; what adds to its size is the white space that now frames the illustrations and becomes the new location for the words. Marketed for parents "who loved it when it first appeared," the new edition restricts its dust jacket authorial information to a listing of Lobel's "well-known" books. Since the dust jacket also asserts that Lobel is "well known" to the purchasers who presumably read *Sven's Bridge* when they were children, there is no need to provide any biographical information. Yet it is worth observing that the original dust jacket identity of an artist "born in Krakow, Poland" has been replaced by the less specific identity of the artist as celebrity.

¹⁵In e-mail correspondence, Maria Nikolajeva has pointed out that the illustrations to *Sven's Bridge* combine the colors of the Swedish flag and some aspects of Swedish folk art with other details that seem closer to central European art.

¹⁶The relationship of life and art is unclear here. What comes first, the child's memory of the mother as corpse, or the illustration of the picture book mother as corpse?

¹⁷The most traumatic incident in Lobel's memoir, one that demonstrates the general reality of maternal lack of power, is when a woman whose son has just been shot begins to scream and demands from the guards why they have not shot Lobel's brother who is so much younger. Lobel admits that she is more afraid of the woman than of the Nazis and loses her own ability to speak, for fear that the woman's appeal will be heard.

¹⁸Lobel's notes for the letter A tell the reader that in Amsterdam there are "houses that look like these." That Anne Frank, the most famous Holocaust victim in children's literature, lived and hid in such a house, only comes to mind because of the problematic inscribing and erasing of Holocaust history in the letter C, i.e., the lack of such information is not problematic in the notes to the letter A.

WORKS CITED

Bernstein, Michael André. *Foregone Conclusions: Against Apocalyptic History.* Berkeley: University of California Press, 1994.

Denby, David. "In the Eye of the Beholder: Another Look at Roberto Benigni's Holocaust Fantasy." *New Yorker*, 15 March 1999: 96–9.

Doyle, Brian. *Uncle Ronald.* Vancouver: A Groundwood Book, Douglas and McIntyre, 1996.

Dwork, Debórah. *Children With a Star: Jewish Youth in Nazi Europe.* New Haven: Yale University Press, 1991.

Epstein, Eric Joseph and Philip Rosen. *Dictionary of the Holocaust: Biography, Geography, and Terminology.* Westport, CT: Greenwood Press, 1997.

Eskin, Blake. "Lawyer Demands Probe of Wilkomirski." *Forward*, 19 November 1999: 15.

Frank, Anne. *The Diary of a Young Girl: The Definitive Edition*, ed. Otto H. Frank and Mirjam Pressler. Trans. Susan Massotty. New York: Bantam, 1997.

Ginsburg, Mirra. *Three Rolls and One Doughnut: Fables from Russia Retold by Mirra Ginsburg*. Illus. Anita Lobel. New York: Dial Press, 1970.

Gourevitch, Philip. "The Memory Thief." *New Yorker*, 14 June 1999, 48–62 and 64–8.

Holm, Anne. *I Am David*. Trans. L. W. Kingsland. Harmondsworth: Puffin, 1969.

Hopkins, Lee Bennett. "Anita and Arnold Lobel." *Books are by People: Interviews with 104 Authors and Illustrators of Books for Young Children*. New York: Citation Press, 1969, 156–9.

Lappin, Elena. "The Man with Two Heads." *Granta 66* (Summer 1999): 7–65.

Levi, Primo. *Survival in Auschwitz: The Nazi Assault on Humanity*. Trans. Stuart Woolf. New York: Collier-Macmillan, 1961. Trans. of *Se questo è un uomo* (1958).

Life is Beautiful (La Vita è Bella). Dir. Roberto Benigni. Alliance, Miramax, 1997.

Lobel, Anita. *Alison's Zinnia*. New York: Greenwillow, 1990.

———— *Away from Home*. New York: Greenwillow, 1994.

———— *No Pretty Pictures: A Child of War*. New York: Greenwillow, 1998.

———— *Potatoes, Potatoes*. New York: Harper and Row, 1967.

———— *Sven's Bridge*. New York: Harper and Row, 1965.

———— *Sven's Bridge*. Rev. New York: Greenwillow, 1992.

McHenry, Eric. Letter. *New Yorker,* 29 March 1999: 10.

Nikolajeva, Maria. "Sven's Bridge." E-mail to the author. 11 Aug. 1999.

Vos, Ida. *Anna is Still Here*. Trans. Terese Edelstein and Inez Smidt. Boston: Houghton Mifflin, 1993. Trans. of *Anna is er nog* (1986).

———— *Hide and Seek*. Trans. Terese Edelstein and Inez Smidt. Boston: Houghton Mifflin, 1991. Trans. of *Wie nieht weg is wordt gezien* (1981).

Wiesel, Elie. *Night*. Trans. Stella Rodway. New York: Discus-Avon, 1969. Trans. of *La Nuit* (1958).

Wilkomirski, Binjamin. *Fragments: Memories of a Wartime Childhood*. Trans. Carol Brown Janeway. New York: Schocken, 1996. Trans. of *Bruchstücke* (1995).

Yolen, Jane. *Briar Rose*. The Fairy Tale Series. New York: Tom Doherty, 1992.

Zuccotti, Susan. *The Italians and the Holocaust: Persecution, Rescue, and Survival*. Lincoln: University of Nebraska Press, 1987.

KATHLEEN COULBORN FALLER

CHILDREN WITH A SECRET

Child sexual abuse is taboo behavior, usually shrouded in secrecy. At times in history, the shroud has been lifted and sexual abuse has been recognized, only to be re-enshrouded because sexual abuse of children is too disturbing and disruptive to the social order (Herman 1979; Masson 1984; Rush 1980; Russell 1986). Thus, in the late nineteenth century, Freud described the etiology of hysteria in middle-class, Viennese women he was psychoanalyzing to be grounded in childhood sexual abuse at the hands of their fathers and other important men in their lives (Freud 1896). He was criticized and ostracized by his colleagues in the medical establishment, and in 1905 he retracted his assertion that his patients had experienced actual sexual abuse. He is said to have had a failure of courage (Masson 1984) or perhaps a crisis of belief (Russell 1984). Acceptance of his theory that actual sexual abuse caused hysteria meant that sexual abuse was very widespread indeed and that prominent citizens were perpetrators. Freud recast his theory of the etiology of hysteria to derive from children's fantasies of sexual activities with father figures in their lives (Masson 1984; Russell 1986). Thus, child victims became offenders, and adult offenders became victims of sexualized, lying, and fantasizing children. Sexual abuse of children was thereby re-enshrouded.

The ebb and flow of appreciation of the phenomenon of child sexual abuse continues. Presently, most, but not all, professionals studying and working with sexually abused children and adult survivors believe that Freud erred when he recanted his first theory of the etiology of hysteria in favor of his second, a theory that assumes children wish to have sex with adults (Butler 1985; Faller 1988; Herman 1979; Miller 1986; Rush 1980; Russell 1986). This recent shift in consciousness about sexual abuse began in the late 1970s with the convergence of research on prevalence rates (Finkelhor 1979; Russell 1983), the women's movement, and changes in the Child Protection System to require mandated reporting of child maltreatment, including child sexual abuse (Faller 1993; Finkelhor 1979). Today, accounts of adult survivors of childhood sexual abuse abound and chronicle victims' humiliation, rage, pain, and suffering in secrecy (e.g., Armstrong 1978; Evert & Bijkerk 1987; Fraser 1987; Hill 1985; Kunzman 1990; Montagna 1989; Randall 1987; Sisk & Hoffman 1987; Thomas 1986). In addition, the professional literature includes the pioneering work of Summit (1983) describing the Child Sexual Abuse Accommodation Syndrome, a theory that proposes children's responses to child sexual abuse comprise five stages: 1) secrecy, 2) helplessness, 3) entrapment and accommodation, 4) delayed, unconvincing disclosure, and 5) recantation. Summit's theory of the Child Sexual Abuse Accommodation Syndrome is supported by research findings (Elliot & Briere 1994; Faller 1988; Lawson & Chaffin 1992; Sorenson & Snow 1991).

I began evaluating allegations of sexual abuse, providing treatment to child victims, and training professionals about child sexual abuse in 1978, when belief that the phenomenon existed was re-emerging. Direct social work practice with abused and neglected children has been part of my responsibilities at the University of Michigan since I joined the faculty in 1977. In 1985, with colleagues in the Medical School, the Law School, the School of Social Work, and later the Department of Psychology, we started a clinic, the Family Assessment Clinic, presently a program in the School of Social Work. The Clinic evaluates and treats complex child welfare cases, including those involving sexual abuse claims, and thereby provides a context for knowledge development and teaching about child welfare issues.

The observations and case examples presented in this essay are based upon my work as both a forensic evaluator and a therapist at the Family Assessment Clinic. I will endeavor to fill a gap in the literature by describing children's reactions to their sexual abuse and how they cope with these experiences. First, I will discuss reasons why children keep sexual abuse a secret. Then, using three cases from my clinical experience, I will illustrate different effects the secret of sexual abuse can have on children.[1] I will conclude with brief comments about where we have come from and where we appear to be headed with the secret of child sexual abuse.

Why Children Don't Tell

There is almost nothing so secret as child sexual abuse. There are generally no witnesses because sexual abuse occurs in a very private space, usually involving only the child and the adult. The secrecy is reinforced because for most children sexual abuse is a most unusual activity. They have no experience with an adult behaving sexually toward them. As a consequence, the sexual encounter can be quite bewildering.

Young children have no name for the activity and therefore cannot speak about it. Furthermore, often the names and characterizations the offender provides for the abuse are calculated to normalize the behavior and confuse the child. For example:

1. "It's a game, a special peepee game. Isn't it fun?"
2. "It's part of your education; I have to teach you how to do this. It's my responsibility as a parent."
3. "I need to do this to take care of you. I have to wash you real good down there. I have to use my finger to get the medicine in there."
4. "As your church leader and mentor, I have chosen you to participate in these acts. God will love you for doing these things."

Older children, who understand the meaning and inappropriateness of sexual abuse, may nevertheless keep the secret because of the stigma associated with their participation. They fear that if they tell, they will be marked. Often these victims feel they are in some way responsible for their abuse. Moreover, delay in disclosure reinforces feelings of guilt and responsibility.

Furthermore, the offender may actively encourage the child to keep the secret. Admonitions not to tell are varied and sometimes inventive. They include the following:

1. The offender may trade on his/her relationship with the child, threatening loss of love, loss of material benefits, or loss of privileges. The closer the relationship between child and adult, the more likely the offender will use love to mo-

tivate silence. The more distant the relationship, the more likely he/she will rely on other manipulations. Thus, a seventeen-year-old girl was allowed to use her mother's boyfriend's car, with the understanding she would lose this privilege if she refused him sex or told anyone.

2. The offender may warn that disclosure will result in his/her having to leave the family or the parents' marriage breaking up. Added to this may be a plea that the child must take care of the offending parent sexually because the other parent refuses to. A father told his twelve-year-old daughter that if she didn't keep the secret, he would have to leave the family, and they would be poor. He also warned her that her younger brothers wouldn't have a daddy anymore.

3. Offenders may also try to ensure silence by warning victims of the consequences of disclosure to themselves, such as being sent to foster care or being blamed because they did not resist or agreed to participate in the sexual acts. The husband of a day-care provider took nude photographs of the children his wife looked after. He told the children that they had better not tell or he would show the pictures to the police, and the children would go to jail. They believed him.

4. Offenders without continued access to their victims may try to persuade the children they are omniscient. One offender pointed to a UPS truck and told a preschool victim that the truck belonged to him and his co-offenders. They would be watching her to make sure she didn't tell. Every time the little girl saw a UPS truck, which happened often, she was terrified (Kelley 1994).

5. Some offenders employ threats of bodily harm. Twin five-year-old boys were told by their offender that he was "stronger than the Incredible Hulk, and would break every bone in their bodies if they told." When they finally told, they insisted their mother lock all the doors and windows to protect them, even though it was a sweltering summer. They also begged to be allowed to sleep under their beds so the offender couldn't find them.

6. Finally, offenders may threaten people close to the child, or the child's pets. A very sadistic offender took advantage of his victim's father's illness. This five-year-old boy's father was in the hospital with leukemia. The offender coerced the boy into sexual acts by threatening to follow the

boy's mother to the hospital and kill his father. After several weeks, the father died. The offender then told his victim he had, indeed, killed the father by stabbing him in the heart with a knife. This meant the father would not go to heaven. He warned the boy that if he told, he (the offender) would stab the boy, his mother, and his little sister in the heart, and they, too, would not go to heaven. For more than two years, the boy did not say a word.

The Experience of Sexual Abuse For Three Children

ANNA

Anna was six when I met her. She had a venereal disease, and my job was to try to find out how she got it.

Anna was assumed to have contracted the disease from her father, whom she visited every other weekend. He had a history of sexually transmitted disease and a promiscuous lifestyle. However, Anna loved her father. They did exciting things on visits, like going to the circus and to Chuck E. Cheese's. He let her shoot his rifle. He also bought her toys she loved, but her mother disapproved of. These were Barbie Dolls and water guns. She would have to leave these toys at her father's because her mother would not allow them in the house.

According to her mother, Anna would have nightmares and wet the bed both before and after visits, but she always wanted to go. Her visits with her father were stopped when the venereal disease was diagnosed. Anna was upset. She said she missed her father and complained that it was boring at her mother's.

When I first met with Anna and asked her what had happened that made her need to go to the doctor, she began to whimper. I explained that I needed to know what had happened in order to make her safe. She curled up in a ball in the corner of the room. She asked for her blankie and mother. (Until concerns about sexual abuse emerged, she had only needed her blankie at night. She now was taking it to school and hiding it in her desk.) When I suggested we talk a little, she bolted out of the room and came back with her mother and her blankie. From this first meeting, I learned that Anna couldn't bring herself to talk directly about what had happened.

However, over several sessions, Anna communicated indirectly, letting me learn her secret. She discovered I had Barbie dolls. She would come into the session and immediately go to the closet where the Barbie dolls were kept. She would get them out, and at first, she just engaged them in benign activities. She had the dolls go to a restaurant and go on vacation. Then one day she undressed Barbie and Ken and made them engage in genital intercourse and oral sex. When I asked her what they were doing, she gave me a knowing look but said nothing. Over the next two sessions, she had the Barbie and Ken dolls engage in similar sexual acts and made them say things, such as "I need you to do this for me so I don't go all crazy." "After this, we can go to Chuck E. Cheese's." "Once you get used to this, you'll like it more." However, she still did not respond to questions such as "Who does that?" "How do you know about this?"

Then at the end of a session, Anna asked, "Where's the Sunshine Family? I have a Sunshine Family at my dad's house." I said I didn't have one, and she said, "You need to get one." So I did. When Anna first saw the Sunshine Family, she gave me her knowing look and put them in the closet. She whispered, "They've got a secret." I asked her about the secret, and she said, "Don't bother me. I'm playing." My further questions about the secret and the Sunshine Family were met with silence. Anna turned her back to me and played with spelling cards.

The next session Anna took the Sunshine father and the little girl out of the closet, slowly undressed them, and put the father in an intercourse position with the girl, gave me her knowing look, and then whispered, "They're humping." I pointed to the girl, and asked, "Who's that?" Anna whispered, "Me." I then pointed to the father, and asked, "Who's that?" She again whispered, "You know." I said I didn't, and with her lips close to my ear said softly, "My dad. He likes to hump. I don't."

Bit by bit, additional information came out. Anna's father used trips to Chuck E. Cheese's and a day at the circus as rewards for sexual activity. Anna had been thrilled when her father helped her shoot his rifle, even though it made a big noise. She missed the target, but her dad hit the target twice. Afterward they took the target home. It had two big holes in it. He told her "don't tell" her mother about the humping. Her mother might get mad and then he might have to put a hole in her mother like in the target.

Sometime after this information came out, Anna stopped having nightmares and wetting the bed. She also learned to read and began to do better in school. She still wanted to see her father, but said she wanted him to come to my office.

Anna both loved and feared her offender. These complex emotions made it impossible for her to reveal her secret in response to invitational questions. Instead, over time she was able to reveal her sexual knowledge and experiences using dolls. That she showed rather than said what happened and whispered her verbal responses probably were attempts to literally comply with her father's instruction, "don't tell." Her symptoms of bedwetting and nightmares probably derived from the complex dynamics of being richly rewarded for compliance with an odious activity. Her symptoms eventually ceased after she revealed the secret, but it is not clear whether cessation of sexual abuse or disclosure led to the remission of symptoms.

NATHAN

Nathan was brought to me for treatment. He was sexually abused when he was four, by Jerry, who was a male helper in his day-care center. Nathan was one of about fifteen children who were abused by Jerry. Before the abuse was discovered, Nathan said he didn't like going to day care and he often misbehaved there. His mother thought his resistance came from not wanting to be separated from her because of recent upsets in his life. Nathan's parents had divorced when he was three and shortly thereafter his mother was in a serious automobile accident and hospitalized for several weeks.

Nathan's mother had told him that she liked the people at the day-care center (she was friends with the director), and he should do what they told him to. Later it became clear that in Nathan's young mind, he had told his mother that he was being hurt at the day-care center, and her response was that she approved of how they were treating him.

When I first asked Nathan to tell me about Jerry at day care, he said he couldn't. I asked why, and he said if I tried to make him talk, he would take all his medicine (he was on antibiotics for an ear infection and had his medicine with him). Then he said, "I'd rather jump out the window," walking up to the third story window and trying to open it.

Nathan eventually was able to talk about how Jerry had "touched him" in his "private spots." These were "in the front and in the back," but other children, who had witnessed his abuse, described much more. Specifically, they said, Jerry had "played the Baby Game" with Nathan. The Baby Game involved Jerry cradling the boys in his arms and sucking their penises. Nathan denied even knowing what the Baby Game was. One boy also said that Jerry had "put his dick in Nathan's little butt" when Jerry had taken Nathan to the bathroom.

This boy testified at Jerry's criminal prosecution. Nathan felt guilty that he was too scared to testify. Jerry was sentenced to 25 years in prison, but Nathan was still frightened of him. He thought Jerry would break out of prison. Nathan's mother drove him by the prison to show him how enormous and secure it was, and to convince him that Jerry could not get out. Eventually, Nathan revealed that Jerry had threatened to hurt him and his mother if he told. Although this threat does not seem severe, for a four-year-old with Nathan's background, it led to all sorts of horrible imaginings.

Nathan dreaded coming to see me because he hated talking about his abuse. He would often become sick in his stomach when it was time to come to treatment. During sessions, he would frequently say, "Is it time to go yet?" "Don't you want to talk to my mom now?" Finally his mother and I decided to end treatment. Nathan was getting along well in kindergarten and was able to stay in his bedroom by himself without becoming overwhelmed with fear of being alone.

When Nathan was six, I received an urgent call from his mother. Nathan needed to come back to treatment. Within a matter of a few weeks, he had sucked the penises of six of his friends. This was discovered when one of the boys urinated in Nathan's face, and Nathan ran out of his room, exclaiming, "Sam peed on me!" When Nathan's mother learned what led to the urination episode, she asked Nathan if he had ever done this before. Nathan readily identified five other friends whose penises he had sucked.

When he came back to treatment, he also named these friends to me. I asked Nathan what he was thinking when he did this, and he said, "I was child abused. They weren't. I want them to be child abused, too." This time, when I asked Nathan if he had ever heard of the Baby Game, he said he had. He showed me with anatomical dolls what the Baby Game was. He said Jerry had done the Baby Game to him "lots of times." It made him feel "weird." Nathan was able to understand that what he was doing to his friends was "kinda like the Baby Game" and made his friends feel "weird." He responded very well to a behavioral intervention, which rewarded him for days and weeks without any sexually inappropriate behavior. In fact, there were no further instances of sexual acting out noted by his mother, nor any reports from school or his after-school activities.

Things went well for Nathan until he was nine. Then he was caught on the playground sucking the breasts of a classmate. She was another victim from the day-care center, and had allowed Nathan to do this. Nathan came back to treatment again. He told me, "I get that feeling," which we were able to identify as the fusion of anger and the urge to sexually act out. I again used a behavioral intervention, but this involved self-monitoring. We developed a strategy, other than abusing other children, for him to use when he got "that feeling." At this age, Nathan was much better able to articulate his feelings and urges to abuse others, and to understand their relationship to his abuse. He was also able to discuss in detail and with greater comfort the abusive acts he could remember.

Nathan is now finishing high school and has had no further sexual problems. He is popular among his schoolmates and an accomplished athlete.

Nathan's situation illustrates some of the special difficulties boy victims experience with telling and talking about sexual abuse. Most offenders are male, and thus most boy victims must overcome twin taboos to tell, sex with an adult and a same-sexed encounter. Moreover, male socialization, which implies that being unable to protect oneself from injury and needing to talk about worries are "unmanly," adds to boys' difficulty in telling the secret. In addition, boy victims are prone to act out sexually and aggressively, in response to sexual victimization. In Nathan's case, his inability to use treatment to talk about his sexual abuse and his feelings about it led to acting out against other children. It is significant that an event he could not tell about, the Baby Game, was repeated in his sexual acting out with other children. Finally, like many victims, Nathan needed treatment intermittently, not just at a single time in his life, in order to reveal his abuse and to address its impact.

NANCY

Nancy, her sister Carol, her brother, and her parents came to me for evaluation for possible sexual abuse when Nancy was sixteen.

Nancy's father was an alcoholic with a vicious temper. He was also a batterer. Nancy recalled that when she was about eight, her father became enraged at her mother because she wasn't dressed on time for a party. He dragged her mother by the hair down the stairs and into the car. The babysitter, who was the children's aunt, acted as though this had not happened. Nancy's mother's response was to cut her hair so this wouldn't happen again. She made excuses for her husband, saying he was being treated unfairly at work.

The first time Nancy remembered her father sexually abusing her was when she was six. Her mother was out of town and her father was in charge of her, her younger sister, and younger brother. It was nighttime and she was in bed. She was facing the wall, and her father got in bed behind her. He had been drinking. He fumbled with her pajama bottoms. He put his penis "down there." She didn't know what was happening to her and pretended to be asleep.

Initially, the sexual abuse was infrequent, about once every three months. However, when Nancy was ten, her father lost his job. He begin drinking more and sexually abusing her more. The pattern was almost always the same. Her father would come home from the bar drunk and would come into her room. Her mother would already be in the parents' bedroom. Nancy thought her mother was probably asleep. Her father would try to have rear entry intercourse with her. Because he was drunk he had difficulty achieving and maintaining an erection. His attempts to penetrate her would last "a real long time." Usually he could not ejaculate and would end up leaving the room very disgruntled. Through all his attempts, Nancy would pretend to be asleep. The next day, her father would be in a bad mood and hung over.

Nancy kept her silence. She said she didn't tell because she didn't want her mother to be without a husband. She called her mother "a real sweet lady" and said she didn't think her mother could cope on her own. She also didn't want her sister and brother to be without a father. When Nancy was fifteen and her sister, Carol, was twelve, Nancy learned from Carol that she was also being sexually abused by their father. Nancy felt betrayed. She had assumed that her cooperation was keeping her sister safe. Nancy decided she needed to tell.

Nancy told her secret to her school counselor, who reported the abuse to Child Protective Services. The Child Protection worker interviewed Nancy at school and placed her in a foster home. When the Child Protection worker interviewed her father, he denied abuse and said Nancy was manipulative and a liar. Nancy's mother also doubted the sexual abuse, stating that during the last couple of years, Nancy had become a real disappointment. Although she was very smart, her grades had slipped, and recently she had been caught smoking. Nancy's mother also asked, "Why didn't she tell before? Why would she let this go on so long? It just doesn't make any sense." She wondered if Nancy had made up the sexual abuse to divert attention from her poor grades and smoking.

When Carol was interviewed by Child Protective Services, she denied she was being sexually abused by her father, but said she wanted to go into foster care with Nancy. After two weeks in foster care, Carol admitted she, also, had been sexually abused by their father. Their father insisted that Carol's allegation was untrue and was instigated by Nancy. He described Nancy as lazy and "always sitting on her pity pot" (feeling sorry for herself).

When faced with two daughters making allegations, their mother decided something must have happened but thought it was a result of her husband's alcoholism. The father agreed to a substance abuse assessment and was sent to inpatient treatment for sixty days. Protective Services sent Nancy and Carol home. Nancy, Carol, and their mother went to counseling. When the father got out of substance abuse treatment, he wanted to join them in counseling and said he wanted to work on his problems so he could return home. Other family members were willing to try, but Nancy refused to have anything to do with her father.

Ultimately, Protective Services allowed the father to return home, and Nancy chose to go back to her foster home. She worked hard in school and her grades improved. She went to counseling faithfully. She had one close girlfriend and would have nothing to do with boys. She wanted to become a nurse.

However, then she met a young man who was several years older than her and a high school dropout. He did not work and reportedly dealt and used drugs. He became her boyfriend. Although her foster parents tried to keep him away from Nancy, they were unsuccessful. She became pregnant by him. He beat her up when she refused to have an abortion.

Nancy kept her secret for almost ten years because she naively thought it was in her family's best interest. She finally told for altruistic reasons, to protect her younger sister. Research and practice indicate that maternal support is the key factor to recovery from sexual abuse. Sadly, Nancy and Carol's mother was not strong enough to support her daughters. Thus, initially she doubted the abuse and then excused it as caused by alcoholism. Later, she allowed her husband to resume his control over the family. Because Nancy was not willing to live this way, she was excluded from the family. Nancy's father never acknowledged his wrongdoing, and other family members did not require him to. Despite her efforts, Nancy was not able to overcome the pattern of relationships she had internalized. Thus, she found a boyfriend who like her father was unemployed, a substance abuser, and batterer, and was not able to prevent him from getting her pregnant.

Conclusion

These cases illustrate the dynamics of secrecy related to sexual abuse, how children tell, and what happens when they do tell. Research involving adults with a history of sexual abuse indicates that a substantial proportion of child victims kept the secret into adulthood (Russell 1983). Nevertheless, presently, both professionals and the public have some appreciation of the extent of child sexual abuse. About one in four girls and about one in eight boys are estimated to be sexually abused during childhood (Faller 1993). Approximately one million new cases are identified each year (Gallup 1995). Furthermore, these statistics do not include children who don't tell.

As stated at the beginning of this essay, the recent history of child sexual abuse is that until the mid-seventies it was considered uncommon (Finkelhor 1979; Weinberg 1955). However, with greater awareness has come increased knowledge about the signs and symptoms of sexual abuse. These may be recognized by adults who can protect children. More publicity about child sexual abuse means that victims may understand that there is a name for their experience and that they are not alone. Thus, children are probably more likely to reveal their secret.

These optimistic trends are countered by a new ebb in belief called the Backlash. The Backlash consists of renewed challenges to children who state they have been sexually abused and to institutions and professionals who believe them and act on their behalf. Thus, the history of 100 years ago may be repeating itself.

As a consequence, when children tell the secret, that is the mere beginning of a long journey toward social justice. Many children never get there. They are faced with obstacles placed in their path by their offenders, supporters of and advocates for their offenders, and skeptical professionals. As they encounter these obstacles, children often give up and recant, which may leave them in jeopardy. In addition, their supporters may cut deals with offenders to protect children from the legal process. Finally, a substantial number of children lose in court.

I write this article not only to air the voices of children with the secret of sexual abuse, but also to battle the Backlash. Adults in positions of power must fully understand what the impact of sexual abuse is like for children and support them. Otherwise children's secrets will remain buried or will be retracted when they encounter disbelief by professionals and other adults and retribution by perpetrators and their supporters. The Child Sexual Abuse Accommodation Syndrome will persist.

202 SECRET SPACES OF CHILDHOOD

NOTES

[1]The case examples have been altered somewhat to protect confidentiality and to illustrate salient issues.

REFERENCES

Armstrong, L. *Kiss Daddy Goodnight: A Speakout on Incest.* New York: Simon and Schuster, 1978.

Butler, S. *Conspiracy of Silence: The Trauma of Incest.* San Francisco: Volcano Press, 1985.

Elliot, D. & J. Briere. "Forensic evaluations of older children: disclosures and symptomology." *Behavioral Science and the Law* 12.3 (1994): 261–77.

Evert, K. & I. Bijkerk. *When You're Ready: A Woman's Healing from Childhood Physical and Sexual Abuse by Her Mother.* Walnut Creek, CA: Launch Press, 1987.

Faller, K. C. *Child Sexual Abuse: An Interdisciplinary Manual for Diagnosis, Case Management, and Treatment.* New York: Columbia University Press, 1988.

Faller, K. C. "Criteria for judging the credibility of children's statements about their sexual abuse." *Child Welfare* 67.5 (1988): 389–401.

Faller, K. C. *Child sexual abuse: intervention and treatment issues.* Washington, DC, USDHHS, National Center on Child Abuse and Neglect, 1993.

Finkelhor, D. *Sexually Victimized Children.* New York: The Free Press, 1979.

Fraser, S. *My Father's House: A Memoir of Incest and of Healing.* New York: Harper and Row, 1987.

Freud, S. (1896). "The aetiology of hysteria" (translated by James Strachey) in J. J. Masson, *Assault on the Truth.* New York: Farrar, Straus, & Giroux, 1984.

Gallup Poll. Representative sample of 1,000 parents in the United States. Princeton, NJ: Gallup, 1995.

Herman, J. *Father-Daughter Incest.* Cambridge, MA: Harvard University Press, 1979.

Hill, E. *The Family Secret: A Personal Account of Incest.* New York: Laural, 1985.

Kelley, S. *Ritualistic abuse of children.* Second national colloquium of the American Professional Society on the Abuse of Children, Boston, MA, 1994.

Kunzman, K. *The Healing Way: Adult Recovery from Childhood Sexual Abuse.* New York: Harper/Hazelton, 1990.

Lawson, L., & M. Chaffin. "False negatives in sexual abuse disclosure interviews." *Journal of Interpersonal Violence* 7.4 (1992): 532–42.

Masson, J. J. *Assault on the Truth.* New York: Farrar, Straus, & Giroux, 1984.

Miller, A. *Thou Shalt Not be Aware: Society's Betrayal of the Child.* New York: Meridian, 1986.

Montagna, D. *Prisoner of Innocence.* Walnut Creek, CA: Launch Press, 1989.

Randall, M. *This Is About Incest.* Ithaca, NY: Firebrand Books, 1987.

Rush, F. *The Best Kept Secret: Sexual Abuse of Children.* Englewood Cliffs, NJ: Prentice Hall, 1980.

Russell, D. E. H. "The incidence and prevalence of intrafamilial and extrafamilial sexual abuse of female children." *Child Abuse and Neglect* 7 (1983): 133–46.

Russell, D. E. H. *Sexual Exploitation: Rape, Child Sexual Abuse, and Workplace Harassment*. Newbury Park, CA: Sage, 1984.

Russell, D. E. H. *The Secret Trauma: Incest in the Lives of Girls and Women*. New York: Basic Books, 1986.

Sisk, S. & C. F. Hoffman. *Inside Scars: Incest Recovery*. Gainesville, FL: Pandora Press, 1987.

Sorenson, T., & B. Snow. "How children tell: the process of disclosure in child sexual abuse." *Child Welfare* 70.1 (1991): 3–15.

Summit, R. "The child sexual abuse accommodation syndrome." *Child Abuse and Neglect* 7 (1983): 177–91.

Thomas, E. *Le viol du silence*. Paris: Aubier, 1986.

Ward, E. *Father-Daughter Rape*. New York: Grove Press, 1985.

Weinberg, S. K. *Incest Behavior*. New York: Citadel, 1955.

JAMES CHRISTEN STEWARD

THE CAMERA OF SALLY MANN AND THE SPACES OF CHILDHOOD

While photographer Sally Mann's work covers a wide range of territory, including exquisite and nostalgic landscape photographs taken with a large format nineteenth-century view camera, it is her black-and-white photographs of children—most frequently her own children—that have struck a vein. First exhibited collectively in the exhibition "Immediate Family" that opened at the Houk Friedman Gallery in New York in 1992, these photographs chronicle the growing up of the Mann children, including wet beds, insect bites, nap times, rural escapades, playacting at adulthood and what the *New York Times* writer Richard Woodward has called "their innocent savagery."[1] Most notably the Mann children are commonly photographed nude, in rural idylls and in their beds. While the series found almost immediate commercial success, not all of the scrutiny the photographs have received has been positive; even the most liberal art periodicals in the 1990s have often refused to publish unedited photographs of the nude Mann children. Other photographs, notably one entitled *Damaged Child* of her daughter Jessie with a swollen eye that was the result of an insect bite but somehow suggests battering, or another called *Flour Paste* in which Jessie's legs appear to have been burned (but were not), have led some critics to make accusations of child abuse or of improper intent surrounding the photographs. The *San Diego Tribune*, for example, ran a headline asking, "It May Be Art, But What About the Kids?"[2]

Mann's photographs of the world her children occupy—a territory where Mann has, in the words of Vince Aletti writing for *The Village Voice*, "staked an astonishingly authoritative, intensely personal claim"[3]—have tended to elicit largely unin-

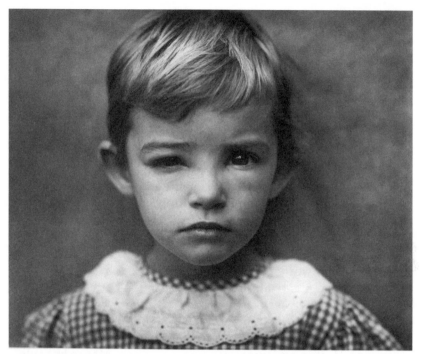

Sally Mann, *Damaged Child*, 1984, gelatin silver print, copyright Sally Mann, courtesy of Edwynn Houk Gallery

Sally Mann, *The Wet Bed*, 1987, gelatin silver print, copyright Sally Mann, courtesy of Edwynn Houk Gallery

formed responses about child pornography and abuse,[4] yet they do raise serious questions about our examination of the world of children. Can a child freely give consent to be photographed, especially in vulnerable positions including nudity, when the photographer is a parent? Do these photographs unintentionally put children at greater risk given the reality of pedophilia in society? Do they unintentionally encourage a sexualized view of childhood? Does such work on any level exploit these actual children?

The photographs are pointedly attached to place, and specifically to the area in and around Lexington, Virginia, where the Mann children have grown up. As Mann herself has said, "Even though I take pictures of my children, they're still about here. It exerts a hold on me that I can't define."[5] The photographs are particularly idyllic for capturing the children in the sticky, moisture-laden world of Virginia in summer, a byproduct of the fact that Mann has traditionally photographed only in the summer, devoting the rest of the year to printing the photographs herself. Mann's photographs are also rooted in her past, for she was herself photographed nude by her father, Robert Munger, a Lexington doctor and amateur photographer. Mann has commented, "I don't remember the things that other people remember from their childhood. Sometimes I think the only memories I have are those that I've created around photographs of me as a child. Maybe I'm creating my own life. I distrust any memories I do have. They may be fictions, too."[6] Mann's own work, including that of children, is frequently tinged with a sense of nostalgia, hints of a separate world of childhood that is long distant and beyond retrieving. Of Mann's more recent return to landscape photography, taken in Mississippi, Georgia, and Virginia, she has written that Southerners "embrace the Proustian concept that the only true paradise is a lost paradise"[7]—a comment that certainly characterizes much of Mann's photography, including the images of her children, who are now, in 2000, no longer children. In all of Mann's work, such effects of nostalgia and ambiguity are often achieved or at least enhanced by light effects, using light as the great Victorian photographers such as Julia Margaret Cameron did to draw our attention to several points at once. The nuances of light—where the slightest shift can turn a sky from promising to threatening—further play on issues of memory, so that the images of children at play look like the dreamlike recall of subjects looking back toward an earlier time.

Most of the photographs of Mann's own children were taken on a 400-acre farm that Mann owns with her brothers, deep in the woods and miles from electricity. Mann cites this setting as evidence that she has merely captured the "Edenic" quality of her children's lives. Indeed, she describes the work of *Immediate Family* as "the story of three remarkably sentient children, very aware and—immodestly—very beautiful children, who have a pretty good life—a very free, very open, very natural life. At least certainly in the summer; the rest of the time they get up and go to school like every other kid. Make their bed, get bad grades, get their allowance. But in the summer they're allowed a measure of freedom that I don't think very many children enjoy."[8]

Mann began photographing her children not long after she began to have children in 1979, with three children coming in five years and thus limiting her ability to work in distant landscape settings. Photographing her own children thus became a part of her active parenting. The family portraits themselves began in 1984 with the photograph *Damaged Child*, showing Jessie with her face swollen from insect bites, an image that in Mann's words "made me aware of the potential right under my nose."[9] From the beginning, the works have combined factual observation and contrived fiction, nature and artifice, putting her in the camp of postmodernist photographers such as Cindy Sherman. Mann admits to the artifice in some photographs; in *Jessie Bites* (1985), the sets of tooth marks on the arm of the adult were made by Mann herself, long after those made by her daughter had faded, while Jessie's face still conveys a sense of anger that seems to authenticate the image. In *Popsicle Drips* (1985), the artifice is art historical, clearly referencing Edward Weston's photograph of his son's prepubescent torso (*Neil*, 1925), but updating Weston's detached formalism with actual childhood in the form of dark popsicle drips on Emmet's groin.[10] Moreover, the image demands examination: what is this liquid that outlines the boy's penis? Is he wounded? Some images are ambiguous on the point of artifice: in *The Wet Bed*, for example, it is not clear whether the young Virginia is asleep or posing, coloring our view of the circles of urine that stain the sheet around her. Many observers of Mann's work feel manipulated

by this sense of artifice, yet Mann argues for its use, stating
that "You learn something about yourself and your own fears.
Everyone surely has all those fears that I have for my children."[11] And again she connects this to her own intent in the
work: " . . . the more I look at the life of the children, the more
enigmatic and fraught with danger and loss their lives become.
That's what taking any picture is about. At some point, you just
weigh the risks."[12] Mann argues that such ambiguity has a further purpose in attempting to broaden the resonance of the images, avoiding specificity of location or of class signifiers in
favor of more metaphorical meanings. The images are thus not
about the "things" of childhood but about, in Mann's words, "the
idea of being a child and a family member, the complexity of
it."[13]

Mann's photographs of her own children are not the only images in her body of work to elicit concerns about the sexuality
of children or their sexualized representation—even though
Mann objects that "childhood sexuality is an oxymoron."[14] Certainly the popularity of Mann's work from the late 1980s and
1990s rests in part on her transgression of taboos concerning
the nudity of young children. Her series published in book form
in 1988 as *At Twelve* examined the world of young girls in and
around Lexington, capturing the sense of confused tension in
their eyes and bodies as they pass from the state of girlhood
into that of womanhood. Even as these images suggest the bur-
geoning of adolescent sexuality, they also imply for some viewers the more forbidden topics of incest and child abuse. For
Anne Bernays, "The photographs seem to out-Freud Freud in
acknowledging the pervasiveness of childhood sexuality."[15]
Bernays argues that the sexuality in these photographs is allowed to operate freely while also being manipulated (even exploited) by the artist. Yet Bernays also suggests—wrongly, I
think—that the point of the photographs is to deny the reality
of childhood innocence as a sham. This innocence is still present in Mann's work—sometimes oddly accentuated by a sense
of unknowing knowingness of the sitters—but it is a more complex issue than has been incorporated into the notion of the
"Romantic" child.

For these photographs and for *Immediate Family*, Mann has
been attacked for approaching the world of child abuse—however unintentionally—with the eye of an aesthete, without im-

posing a political view. As Anne Higonnet writes, "precisely because everyone agrees that Mann is a superb technician and
formalist, her photographs have been perceived as estheticiza-
tions and eroticizations of violence against children."[16] Mann
even plays with the possibility of death, and was for years
moved by a picture she took of Virginia with a black eye because "you couldn't tell if she was living or dead. It looked like
one of those Victorian post-mortem photographs."[17] Even after
Emmet was struck by a car and thrown fifty feet in 1987, Mann
couldn't resist such ambiguous and, at least for many viewers,
troubling images: *Immediate Family* contains a picture of a
nude Virginia in which she appears to have hanged herself by a
rope from a tree. Bernays sees these images, which she compares to corpses, as the "conscious imitation of nineteenth-century photographs taken of dead children for grieving parents
just before the coffins were closed, as mementos of the departed."[18] Often it is the viewer who brings misreadings to the
images, colored by a larger societal paranoia about our conduct
toward our children. In *Last Light* (1990), for example, the
man's fingers rest gently on the side of the child's neck, perhaps
gently testing her pulse and reminding us (like the watchband
on the man's wrist) of the fragility of life, of the preciousness of
all children, especially such an achingly beautiful one. Yet how
often in my own experience have viewers remembered this as a
threatening image of strangulation?[19]

One of the most obvious questions that emerges from examining the photographs themselves is that of the complicity of
the child sitters. Surely these children are cooperating with the
photographer in ways that prevent us from seeing these intru-
sions as unmediated. According to the Mann children themselves, this is often true: they have learned to think as art directors do, and abet their mother in composing images. As
Jessie observed in 1992, "I know what my mom likes sometimes, so I point it out to her."[20] Other images are apparently
the result of pure luck with little artifice at all, as in *The Perfect Tomato*, where we see Jessie tiptoeing across a long outdoor
table as if about to take flight. For this image, Mann reports
that she was in the middle of taking another picture when she
observed her daughter in this posture, "just put the film in and
shot."[21] The children have also commented that they have had
no objections to being photographed—Jessie once observed, "I

have no objections, none. . . . The few times I don't like it is when I have a friend over and I'm just in my room and Mom says, 'Picture time,' and I don't really want to do it."[22] Even so, some objections seem to have been registered from the children, and honored, as in *The Last Time Emmet Modeled Nude* (1987), reflecting the boy's growing discomfort with posing nude for the camera as he approached adolescence. Yet even here there is ambiguity, and the artist has suggested that the title has been traditionally misread. For Mann posed her son waist-deep in the water on seven separate occasions before she got the image she wanted, suggesting that the image is not thus about the onset of adolescent modesty but about a child's growing impatience. Indeed, Mann has joked that she should have called the

Sally Mann, *The Last Time Emmet Modeled Nude*, 1987, gelatin silver print, copyright Sally Mann, courtesy of Edwynn Houk Gallery

image "The Last Time Emmet Would Let Me Take That Picture." It may be useful, finally, to think of these images as Luc Santé has suggested as a kind of improvisatory theater in the tradition of Jerzy Grotowski or Peter Brook, in which the actors are involved in "a process of creation that alternates constantly between spontaneity and instruction, narrative and play, chance and certainty."[23]

Before the works from *Immediate Family* were publicly exhibited, two of the Mann children were sent to a psychologist, who found them to be well-adjusted and self-assured. And the children were each given veto power over specific images which, when exercised, resulted not in the exclusion of nude images but in others that reflected different concerns. As Mann has commented, "They don't want to look like dorks. They don't want to be geeks or dweebs."[24] Yet Mann also, troublingly for

Sally Mann, *Candy Cigarette*, 1989, gelatin silver print, copyright Sally Mann, courtesy of Edwynn Houk Gallery

Sally Mann, *Emmett, Jessie, and Virginia*, 1989, gelatin silver print, copyright Sally Mann, courtesy of Edwynn Houk Gallery

some, commonly takes her children out of the realm of childhood and inserts them into the melodrama of adulthood. It could be argued that the images suggestive of child abuse do this, even if unintentionally or in a sense of complicity with the adult viewer. Intent seems clear, however, in *Candy Cigarette* or in *The New Mothers*, in which Jessie is posed with a candy cigarette and Virginia wears starlet sunglasses, props whose dark associations for adults the children surely do not understand. Such images play with the knowingness of the viewer, and rush the children into the adult world rather than allowing them to enjoy a separate space for childhood. Other images do this less obviously merely by showing Jessie clearly vamping for the camera.

Anne Bernays has pointed to what is perhaps the most telling issue in Mann's photographs of her children: "the pictures' very power works against them by implying a moral connection between the models and their parent. This connection is as false as it is seductive."[25] The false seductiveness of the images is in the viewer's too frequent desire to confuse the artist and the art, when we need to remind ourselves that fundamentally all art is fiction. Even a photograph never says anything unequivocally, even when it most appears to do so. Certainly it can be argued that the most shocking aspect of Mann's photographs of children is the possibility of our own sexual response to them; we see these beautiful children, feel desire, and immediately repress it. Mann's art plays on this tension, between the extremes of childhood and sexuality or childhood and death, and keeps them in extraordinarily skillful balance. This balance and tension in Mann's art seeks to suggest that childhood is a more complicated state than our society has historically accepted. The photographs point to spaces of childhood that are anything but innocent and that many viewers would prefer not to see or talk about—and yet we talk about abuse and molestation almost obsessively, as if these were the only sensory experiences available to children. Mann's images do not corrupt childhood innocence, for it is there as well. But there is something more going on, beyond the romping of sprites in Edenic fields that is gentle and vertiginous and frightening all at once. These children are knowing and wounded as well; childhood is seen both from within and without. Mann's work suggests that a redefinition of the worlds of childhood and adulthood, and the artificial lines drawn between them, is in order, that the much-discussed crisis of the American family is among other things a crisis of representation. And surely all of this is what Mann had in mind. The epigraph for her book *At Twelve* is taken from Anne Frank, age 12: "Who would ever think that so much can go on in the soul of a young girl?"

NOTES

[1]Richard Woodward in *The New York Times*, September 27, 1992, Section 6, 29.

[2]For a useful summary of critical responses to Mann's work, see Janet Malcolm, "The Family of Mann," in *The New York Review of Books*, February 3, 1994. For a larger and richly informed discussion of the problematics of contemporary visual representations of childhood, see Anne Higonnet, *Pic-*

tures of Innocence: *The History and Crisis of Ideal Childhood* (London: Thames & Hudson, 1998).

[3]Vince Aletti, "Child World," in *The Village Voice*, May 26, 1992, Vol. 37, No. 21, 106.

[4]For a useful summary of the Christian Right's crusade against "child pornography" in the visual arts, see Richard Goldstein, "The Eye of the Beholder," in *The Village Voice*, March 10, 1998, Vol. 43, No. 10, 31–6.

[5]Quoted in Woodward, op. cit.

[6]Quoted in Woodward, op. cit.

[7]Quoted in Carol Squiers, "Sally Mann," in *American Photo*, March/April 1998, Vol. 9, No. 2, 70.

[8]Quoted in Aletti, op. cit., 106.

[9]Quoted in Woodward, op. cit.

[10]For a full discussion of Mann's debt to Weston, and to other photographers of children such as Julia Margaret Cameron and Dorothea Lange, see Shannah Ehrhart, "Sally Mann's Looking-Glass House," in *Tracing Cultures: Art History, Criticism, Critical Fiction* (New York: Whitney Museum of American Art, 1994), 52–69.

[11]Quoted in Woodward, op. cit.

[12]Quoted in Woodward, op. cit.

[13]Quoted in Aletti, op. cit., 106.

[14]Quoted in Woodward, op. cit.

[15]Anne Bernays, "Art and the Morality of the Artist," in *The Chronicle of Higher Education*, January 20, 1993, Vol. 39, No. 20, B2.

[16]Higonnet, op. cit., 195.

[17]Quoted in Woodward, op. cit.

[18]Bernays, *The Chronicle of Higher Education*, op. cit., B2.

[19]Higonnet notes the same propensity of viewers to misread this image, op. cit., 202.

[20]Quoted in Woodward, op. cit.

[21]Quoted in Aletti, op. cit., 106.

[22]Quoted in Woodward, op. cit.

[23]Luc Santé in *Katalog*, December 1995, 54.

[24]Quoted in Woodward, op. cit.

[25]Bernays, in *The Chronicle of Higher Education*, op. cit., B2.

LOUISE CHAWLA

SPECIAL PLACE—WHAT IS THAT?

Significant and Secret Spaces in the Lives of
Children in a Johannesburg Squatter Camp

Children Outside Childhood

Imagine that you and your family have moved to the city
from a rural village where you didn't have enough to eat. Imagine that people around you speak many strange tongues. Imagine that, in the beginning, you and your family slept on sidewalks, and still often went hungry, until your parents managed
to find space in a new squatter camp on the edge of downtown,
where more than 1,000 people settled on 1.5 acres of land.
Imagine that there was one water tap for the whole camp, and
no toilets, and that the men often drank and fought with guns
and knives. Imagine that pedestrians sometimes kicked and
spat at you and your friends when you played on the sidewalk,
and cars sometimes tried to run you down when you played in
the street. Imagine that someone from the rich people's world
came to talk with you and asked you, "What is your favorite
place?"

This essay is based on a report, *Growing Up in Canaansland:
Children's Recommendations on Improving a Squatter Camp
Environment,* that was compiled and edited by Jill Swart
Kruger, director of this South African site of the Growing Up in
Cities project, which I coordinate for the MOST Programme of
UNESCO.[1] I have collaborated with her and her research team
since their project's first conception through its different stages
of realization, observed their presentations, and visited the
camp; yet in writing this essay, I am merely giving a new form
to this work whose substance comes from Jill, Peter Rich, who
directed the architectural phase of the project, Melinda Swift
and Greg Jacobs, who served as research trainers, and Jill and

215

Peter's assistants in anthropology, architecture, and planning—
Lineo Lerotholi, Maurice Mogane, Moeketsi Langeni, Nondumiso Mabuza, and Zenzile Choko. Not least of all, this essay
and the report on which it is based owe their substance to the
fifteen 10- to 14-year-old boys and girls from the Canaansland
community of Johannesburg who shared their lives with the researchers through drawings, interviews, walking tours through
their neighborhood, and many other activities.

This essay owes its occasion and spirit to a memorial lecture
that I delivered in honor of Sharon Stephens, late Assistant
Professor with joint appointments in the Department of Anthropology, School of Social Work, and the International Institute at the University of Michigan. Given Sharon's leadership
in child research, the lecture was presented at the University's
symposium on "Secret Spaces of Childhood."[2] Sharon died from
melanoma in June, 1998—only two months from the date of diagnosis. Everyone who knew Sharon understands that, when I
relate this, I do not say a small thing.

I knew Sharon when I worked closely with her in the Children and Environment Program of the Norwegian Centre for
Child Research at the University of Trondheim from 1994
through 1995, and later when she remained a friend and advisor for the Growing Up in Cities project, which includes the Johannesburg site. The Children and Environment Program
which Sharon directed provided a base for the revival of this
project, which was first conceived by the urban planner Kevin
Lynch in 1970, but which gained new relevance after the
United Nations' adoption of the Convention on the Rights of the
Child in 1989. According to Article 12 of the Convention, children have a right to express their views freely in all matters
that affect them. *Agenda 21* of the United Nations Conference
on Environment and Development (1992) and the *Habitat
Agenda* of the Second United Nations Conference on Human
Settlements (1996) have affirmed that this includes a right to
express their views and participate in decisions that affect their
cities, towns, and larger environment. Growing Up in Cities implements these principles through research to understand how
young adolescents use and value their local environments, and
through programs that apply young people's priorities to the
improvement of local places and urban policies. Sharon was a

passionate analyst of the Convention, particularly with reference to its application to the quality of children's environments.

Sharon also believed that it is urgent that we understand how transformations in our contemporary world alter the "ecology of childhood" in which children's everyday experience is nested within larger circles of influence: migrations, urbanization, mass media, violence, an increasingly interdependent global economy, increasingly fragmented ecosystems, increasing divisions between rich and poor, and on the side of ideas, communication about environmental protection and human rights.[3] Growing Up in Cities responded to her advocacy for research on a global scale that would simultaneously consider the global patterning of environmental changes and the different conditions and experiences of children in particular world regions.[4] With the help of the MOST Programme of UNESCO, the Norwegian Centre for Child Research, Childwatch International of Oslo, and a long list of international and national donors, a global network of project site directors and I managed to re-initiate Growing Up in Cities in eight locations in 1995: Buenos Aires, Argentina; Melbourne, Australia; Northampton, England; Bangalore, India; Trondheim, Norway; Warsaw, Poland; Johannesburg, South Africa; and Oakland, California in the United States. In all cases, we focused on low income areas where young people are most dependent on the resources of their immediate environment.

Canaansland was the most deprived project site. Yet it is not unrepresentative of the conditions that many urban children face. According to a 1996 estimate, 13.5% of all South African households live in informal settlements, which have become a permanent feature of the urban landscape.[5] According to an estimate of the International Institute of Environment and Development and the World Commission on Health and Environment, more than 600 million people live in life- and health-threatening circumstances, such as squatter camps—many of them children.[6] The children who live in these circumstances are the type of children who attracted Sharon's special interest and concern: those who fall outside dominant categories of the cultural construction of childhood.[7] They endure a precocious burden of hardship and suffering that violates what "childhood" is supposed to mean, and dwell on streets or in shacks built of scavenged scrap material, on land that is often illegally occupied, that violate what "home" should mean. Yet they are children, the most precious resource of humanity's future, who merit the care of their society, of the world's society, all the same. This essay will examine the paradox of these children's position and their promise within the context of the question: What, for them, is the meaning of a special place?

Home as Refuge

Canaansland, the promised land, is a popular name for squatter camps in South Africa.[8] People driving by on their way to their apartments or houses in the suburbs may see just a jumble of ramshackle huts, but to the people who have managed to occupy the land, find building material, and construct homes, these sites are already a step up from life on the pavement. Like the Israelites in the desert, squatter residents follow the dream of a fair and free life. Perhaps they may be able to negotiate secure tenure and commit themselves to the process of a progressive upgrading of their property. Perhaps their government may meet them halfway in their efforts and provide basic utilities like sewerage, piped water, and electricity. Perhaps, given their visible presence in the city, the government will permanently resettle them on another site where they will be close to city jobs and services. In a country like South Africa that faces an acute housing shortage, squatter camps represent people's own resourceful effort to address this crisis.[9]

In the Zulu and Xhosa languages, the name for Johannesburg is *Egoli,* the place of "gold." For people without access to rural land and livelihoods, cities beckon with promise. No matter how intense the competition, in a city one may be lucky enough to find a job to feed oneself and one's family through the formal or informal economy. Through migration and the natural increase of urban populations, squatter camps and shanty towns continue to grow in cities across the Southern Hemisphere.[10]

In Johannesburg, there are jobs for black men in the gold mines that run across the city's southern edge, but until the end of apartheid in 1994 it was illegal for black families to live in the city. They were consigned to black townships south of the mine dumps and tailings, threatened with eviction if they tried to "invade" the white-owned city, or forced to inhabit the city invisibly. With the election of the African National Congress in 1994 and the end of these restrictions, families from the overcrowded townships, impoverished countryside, and neighboring countries moved into Johannesburg and illegal residents came out into the open, changing the downtown population from white to black in the period of a few years, while white businesses and families just as quickly moved north into the suburbs.

For the families who settled Canaansland across from the Oriental Plaza and nearby shops of the city's Indian community on the edge of the central business district, the location offered a number of advantages. Men collected and sold waste material such as cardboard and used tires. Women found day work as house cleaners and nannies in nearby highrise apartments and suburban homes. Both sexes picked up manual "piece jobs." People could shop for food at competitive prices, some store owners gave the community food products after their sell date expired, and church groups donated food. For children, a great advantage was the New Nation School, a half hour's walk away, which accepted street children, charged no fees, and provided a light mid-morning meal of soup and bread. Nine of the fifteen children in our Canaansland project attended there. Four were not in school or dropped out in the course of the study, and two attended schools with fees. Because the camp had no municipal services, toilets in the nearby Bramfontein Railroad Station, the Bree Street taxi stand, and the Oriental Plaza were important amenities. There was one water tap on the edge of the camp, for more than 1,000 people, irregular rubbish collection from an adjacent vacant lot, and no electricity.

Despite these hardships, when the children in the study drew their homes and talked about their drawings, it was evident that many families had created centers of temporary stability in this place of insecure tenure. Four drew trees outside their homes, although trees were mainly limited to the camp's eastern border. Three drew flowers—although I saw only one poor potted plant, outside the head man's house, on my visit there. Two added grass and two drew sunrises or sunsets. All carefully drew the content of their home interiors.

Consider, for example, the drawing by the boy "C," and part of its description in the South African report:

C's drawing of his home

C said he came to Canaansland in 1996 and helped his father to build the shack for himself, his parents and two sisters. He was proud of his shack's interior with its furnishings and thought it was a safe place although it was miserable in wet weather when everything inside got wet. The cat helped to keep the population of rodents in check. His drawing shows the shack divided into two with two beds for the family to share. C had a bed to himself in the kitchen area; his sister and baby sister shared the large double bed with his mother and father in the "bedroom." Around his bed on the walls were posters of his favorite soccer teams.[11]

Or consider the home of the girl "T": one of the children who included flower, grass, and sun. A later drawing by a student of architecture confirmed her layout, and her family's meticulous neatness and creative use of every nook and cranny.

T's drawing of her home

T's drawing of her home shows it divided into two apartments, one a general living room and kitchenette and the
other a sleeping area. She speaks of her mother having built
the house, therefore calls it "my mother's house." A private
space for personal toilette is to the left of the picture behind
the wardrobe. The family's pet dog sleeps in a kennel outside

the house in the minute area they claim as a garden. Her household interior shows a dining table with cloth at the back right of her picture and a cupboard with crockery and cooking utensils in the right foreground. She sweeps and cleans the house and also enjoys washing dishes.[12]

The South African report concluded that, "Although the children commented that their homes were very cramped and that they spent time indoors mainly when it was wet, cold, or night, they appeared to take pride in their families' attempts to make the available space livable and comfortable."[13]

"Secret Spaces of Childhood" invites readers to imagine worlds away from adult oversight and intrusion: the hollow inside the hedge, the corner under the stairs, the treehouse hidden in the leaves. But what about the many children in the world who have no hedges, no trees, no houses with empty spaces? Where do they find special "spaces of childhood"? The drawings of the children in Canaansland remind us that for children in dangerous worlds, the safe centers that their parents create are special places. When I visited the camp in 1997, Johannesburg had the highest crime rate of any city in the world. The downtown business district was especially dangerous. Criminals often ran into the camp to hide, and adult residents often drank too much and then, not rarely, stabbed or shot each other. Theft was an ever-present threat. For children in these urban areas that James Garbarino has termed "war zones," home is the primary refuge.[14] Children's freedom to create places of their own presumes a safe center to move out from. The children in Canaansland, who saw their parents erect their huts with their own eyes and who sometimes assisted in the construction, knew how special, how necessary, how not to-be-taken-for-granted these shelters are.

Places of Conviviality

The children in Canaansland—like children at other Growing Up in Cities sites around the world—gave detailed accounts of convivial places: places where people were friendly and accepting and there were always interesting activities to observe or join. It was evident from the Canaansland children's drawings, interviews, and neighborhood walks that they rarely ranged beyond walking distance of their homes. Girls and younger children were kept especially close to home, given heavy downtown traffic, a high incidence of child abuse, and fears of kidnapping by medicine men and women who used children's body parts in their brews. Nevertheless, the path home from school offered some irresistible detours, and although a local park was forbidden to some, groups of friends managed to slip away to play there for short periods when their absence would not be noticeable. At their best, these attractions qualify as a favorite place.

In drawing exercises, two girls drew a garage that they visited on their way home from school (admittedly, not directly on the way). Here is the account of "B," who drew the garage when she was asked to draw "the area where you live."

B's drawing of her favorite place in her area

This local garage a few blocks away from the school that most children attended was found to be one of the girl's favorite places to visit, especially on Friday afternoons. B said she had a friend who lived next door to the garage, who attended the same school, and that this was how the children at Canaansland had learned that it provided a friendly and interesting environment for children. In this drawing B showed the main attractions of the garage—lots of room to play, a large clock which helped you keep track of time, lots of customers coming and going, cars being repaired, television sets scattered about and which constantly screened commercials, current sports events or the afternoon "soapies," and clean, cold water to drink from a refrigerated water dispenser.[15]

When the children took the project team on walks to share their regular routes and places of importance, they showed local shops where they bought groceries or drinks or played video games, the local cinema, the garage, a grassed area where they played ball, and Phineas McIntosh Park, which had trees, a sports ground, and playground. The garage and park were shown as favorite places to stop on the way home from school—although they were in the neighborhood of Fietas, several blocks west of the school, whereas home was several blocks to the east.

All of these were busy public or commercial places, not at all "secret spaces" away from the eyes of adults. They resonated with similar places described by other project participants in Argentina, India, Poland, and Norway. For children who live in densely populated urban areas, few places are truly secret in the sense of "for children only." But frequently, engaging multigenerational places with accepting adults offer compensations of their own.

And in their own way, they may be secret. After the first Saturday walk when Canaansland children led the research team to places of significance, the researchers showed up again on the following Saturday and asked the children, with their mothers standing around, to show them other places that they used in the area of Fietas west of the camp. "What?" said the children . . . and they staunchly denied that they *ever* visited Fietas. It is probably no coincidence that B's drawing of the garage in Fietas includes a conspicuous clock for keeping track of the time before she would be missed at home.

Encounters with City Government

What is remarkable is that, in the midst of the severe poverty and harsh conditions of the squatter camp, these children and their families managed to create lives approximating normality: homes of refuge and order; daily routines of chores, school, and play; a fabric of nearby city resources. Yet when the project team led the children through exercises to envision "the best place to live" and changes that would improve Canaansland, the children had a clear sense of what their community needed.

The best place to live, they agreed, would have electricity, piped water, and toilets, and nearby in easy walking distance there would be facilities like ball fields, a park with a playground, a swimming pool, shops, and a school. When the girls and boys divided into separate groups to draw short-term improvements that would make Canaansland a better place, they concurred on most points: public toilets, more water taps, more refuse collection sites, a safe play space on the vacant lot opposite the camp, and a security fence. The boys also wanted a few shops in the camp and the girls wanted the tree-lined side street between the camp and the vacant lot closed to traffic.

This was a reasonable and feasible list. During this initial research phase of the project, Jill Kruger, the project director, had been busy networking to ensure that it would be possible to move from research to action. When she approached Isaac Mogase, the Mayor of Greater Johannesburg, to ask him to hear the children's priorities, he agreed to host a workshop which would include the four district mayors, urban planners, and policy makers from the Greater Johannesburg Metropolitan Council and the four local councils, non-profit organizations and other institutions concerned with children, and privileged young people from the city's Junior and Mini Councils. He agreed to Jill's proposal that they would hear the children's presentations and form groups, on the same day, to make concrete plans to address the needs of the children in Canaansland in particular and squatter families in Greater Johannesburg in general. A workshop date was set for May 17, 1997.

The children in Canaansland were given invitations notifying them about the workshop and asking them to come to a preliminary meeting to prepare their presentations. At this meeting, the children agreed that two girls and two boys should speak on behalf of their group. When the researchers asked whether they knew what "democracy" meant, some said no and others said that it meant freedom to do what you want. After the researchers explained that it meant not just doing what you want but also taking responsibility and doing the job properly if you agree to speak for other people, the children put the names of four boys and four girls on the wall, and voted by each putting a green sticker for a girl and a red sticker for a boy under their chosen names. They then summarized their concerns under four categories that each elected representative would present in turn: improved housing, sanitation, the need for a quiet place where they could gather and do homework, and the need to be treated with respect by people in settled homes. The research leaders later took the four representatives to show them the Metropolitan Council room where they would speak and to rehearse their roles.

The goal of Growing Up in Cities is to use work with children as a catalyst to initiate inclusive community planning that will integrate all ages and both sexes. With the research with the children completed and a groundwork laid for implementation, it was time to broaden the process to include all interested community members. Therefore a meeting for Canaansland adults was called, the work with the children was reviewed, and the purpose of the mayor's workshop was explained. The adults who attended elected four representatives of their own—two men and two women—and identified their own priorities to better their children's lives. Most of their priorities overlapped with the children's, but they also wanted a crèche for the younger children, and the men recommended activities such as soccer and karate for the boys and netball and tennis for the girls, whereas the women also wanted a library and lessons in first aid. Over time, the process that started at this meeting culminated in a formally organized resident-based Canaansland Development Committee, which continues to operate to this day. Its membership of men and women, with child representatives invited to speak on issues related to children, is a leap forward from the initial meeting when the research leaders first introduced Growing Up in Cities to the community, when only men sat in the council and the head man sat at a distance, within earshot but conspicuously removed from this meeting on the topic of children, which he considered beneath his dignity as a man.[16]

The mayor's workshop went successfully. The mayor, who had suffered as a township child himself under apartheid, led the children into the lecture theater with a rousing marching song and opened the proceedings. The Chairman of the Executive Committee of the Greater Johannesburg Metropolitan Council and a doctor from the provincial Department of Health spoke next, followed by the children, the researchers, and the Executive Officer for the city's Department of Urban Policy and Strategy. The officials and guests then divided into five groups to draft a program of action related to the needs of Canaansland, general policies for squatter settlements, and a strategy to make Johannesburg a "child friendly city."

When the children in Canaansland were first asked to make drawings of their homes and the area where they lived, they hesitated and expressed fear that "people will laugh at our drawings"; and as the project began to attract attention, they begged the researchers not to disclose their names for fear that people would discover that they were squatters and tease them cruelly. By the time of the Mayor's workshop, each child in the group wanted a drawing posted on the workshop wall, name attached. When the children were later asked to evaluate the research process and the workshop, several of them mentioned the pleasure of drawing, and a boy noted that one of the best moments for him was in the middle of the workshop, when Nondumiso, a member of the research team, showed their drawings on the overhead projector. "Then," he said, "I felt so proud for all of us."

The resulting recommendations for Canaansland were divided among those that the community could do for itself, those that were the responsibility of the local government, and those that would require external donor funding. The city agreed to make short-term improvements in the camp until resettlement to a permanent location could be negotiated. Canaansland adults made clear that they considered it crucial to stay close to the downtown, where they had opportunities to earn small amounts of cash and where they received food donations.

Planning moved slowly forward, and donors committed funds to build a playground and a children's center that could double as a crèche for the younger children in the mornings and a homework center for older children in the afternoons (courtesy of the Dutch Embassy and a children's fund of the Norwegian Broadcasting Corporation). Then six months after the workshop, when Mayor Mogase was out of town and following a questionable three days' notice, the community was violently evicted and resettled on empty veld 44 kilometers outside of Johannesburg in a region known as Thula Mntwana, Zulu for "hush my child." City workers and private contractors wielding batons and sjamboks (a rawhide whip) and armed with police dogs and guns rounded the people into trucks and tore down their homes for a city contract fee of 1000 Rand per hut (when 1800 Rand was the median monthly income for families in South Africa). Some of the building equipment and belongings were loaded on the trucks, but when people tried to protect their other belongings, gasoline was poured on this "refuse" and it was set on fire. The Canaansland families were dropped on empty land with lots marked out and chemical toilets provided, but otherwise without food, water, or protection from heavy rain at first, and distant from transportation, jobs, shops, and other services. The nearest, distant primary school charged fees that were prohibitive for most of the families. The eviction was carried out the weekend before the children were to have taken their end-of-the-year exams.[17]

Places of Solidarity

For sixteen months following the eviction, the former camp site sprouted weeds. Then large notice boards appeared that proclaimed that a social housing project for persons earning less than 3500 Rand per month was to be built there. Thus the government is responding to the need for affordable housing . . . although this solution is not, unfortunately, affordable for residents with monthly incomes below 800 Rand per month, like the site's former residents. The company that owns the private security firm that tore down the squatters' huts has doubly profited from the eviction, as it also owns the water trucks that now deliver water irregularly to Thula Mntwana, where residents of nine other downtown camps were also dropped on adjacent land.

For people who consider squatters a scourge, these poorest of the poor have been put out of sight and out of mind. Those people have benefited from the evictions at the expense of the squatters. In Thula Mntwana, adults have lost access to income. The children have lost their affordable and accommodating school and the network of places where they found pleasure. There is no neighboring community to give food donations. There is no public transportation, and taxi fares to the city are exorbitant. Families have had to begin rebuilding from the bottom again, without access to all the opportune materials, bargains, income options, and services which downtown districts harbor.

Community organizers who advocate principles of people-centered development often quote the words of Lao Tzu:

> Go to the people.
> Live with them.
> Learn from them.
> Love them.
> Start with what they know.
> Build with what they have.[18]

In the Programmes of Action signed at the Earth Summit and the World Summit for Social Development, world governments committed themselves to a participatory philosophy of development that builds on human dignity. Instead, as one man in Canaansland said, he felt as if he and his community had just been "thrown away."

Distant and difficult to reach as the children now were, members of Growing Up in Cities continued to work with them. They arranged for leadership training for adults from the Canaansland community and neighboring communities, to empower them to negotiate with the local government for recognition of their rights and needs. They lobbied on their behalf for garden allotments, as space was now plentiful and the community's already marginal nutritional status had been further weakened, and they insisted on secure tenure for the housing lots, children's center, and playground. After months of obstructions, the government agreed. In the beginning, when there was no food or resources of any kind, they obtained emergency donations of food and other necessities from the Nelson Mandela Children's Fund and arranged for their storage in the metal shipping container that had already been purchased through Norwegian Broadcasting Corporation aid to serve as a shell for the construction of the children's center.

When the children drew their new location, every drawing gave a prominent place to the shipping container. In the midst of the barren veld, it served not only the practical function of storing necessities, but also as a focal point for the community. As the highest point, it cast some shade from the burning summer sun, and therefore its shade made a place for women and children to gather. It also stood as a testament to the fact that the community was not completely abandoned: not by the project team and the many organizations that now stood behind them.[19] To someone who may justifiably feel thrown away by society, concrete expressions of support of this kind form places of solidarity that demonstrate that other people in the world recognize one's existence and affirm one's rights and needs.

Therefore one may still believe in oneself. Lineo Lerotholi, a student of architecture in the Growing Up in Cities team, went to visit the Canaansland children in Thula Mntwana after a few months' absence. She said that she was struck by the children's self-assurance and social competence as they enthusiastically welcomed her, so different from their shame and fear at the beginning of the project, despite the trauma of the eviction.

The irony is that the participatory, people-centered development process that Growing Up in Cities exemplifies is the most practical, proven means to reduce poverty and set communities on a course of cumulative improvement.[20] Yet few international aid agencies are prepared to implement such a decentralized process. Although one of the goals of post-World War II aid programs has been to strengthen human rights, including the right to self-determination, this goal has been overshadowed by that of helping developing countries contribute to the world economy by exporting commodities and low-cost manufactures and importing the products of the developed world, regardless of how inequitably the gains from this exchange may be distributed. For these purposes, large loans have been given to build highways, airports, factories, processing plants, and military arsenals, leaving many countries bent now under the burden of overwhelming debts.[21] Correspondingly, most aid agencies are evaluated by their "efficiency" in passing large sums of money through minimal numbers of staff. The kind of small scale grants and loans needed by communities like Canaansland, combined with support from facilitators, trainers, and other resource people, represents an alternative development path that has yet to gain dominance, despite evidence of its efficacy. Yet it is on this grassroots level that places of solidarity are constructed that demonstrate to people in need that there are other people who have acknowledged their value and invested in their well-being. The prominence of the container in every Canaansland child's drawing suggests that concrete expressions of support of this kind create a well-noticed form of special and sustaining places.

Places of Possibility

Children's special places are not just in the present. They may also exist in the imagination as possibilities for the future. In the new location in the veld, the children again drew where they lived and their ideas for its improvement. The boy "S" combined the different themes of this essay in one drawing.

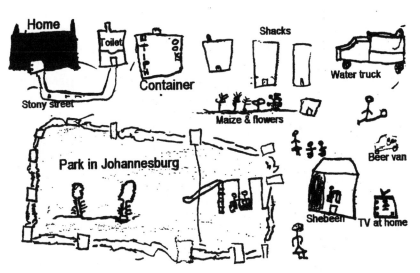

S's drawing of the new settlement site

In the upper left corner, colored in red, he drew his house as his castle, with a road from the front door to the very important next-door amenity, a toilet. Next to the toilet stands the storage container. In front of a row of shacks, a small garden of maize and flowers has begun to grow. The water truck and a beer van are arriving, and a woman is preparing home-made beer in a shebeen. S's battery-operated TV has pride of place in the bottom right corner. More than a third of the area is covered by a park with trees, grassy lawn, and a playground with a slide and swings. But there is no park like this in the veld, so what has he done? Did he misunderstand the directions? No, S explained that it is the Phineas McIntosh Park—one of the children's favorite places that they "never" visited in Fietas. Now it is more than forty kilometers away, at the old location, but S has carried its image with him and superimposed it on the new site, where it now serves simultaneously as a memorial to a special place of the past and as a model for the creation of a better future. His picture demonstrates that happy memories of former places can serve as possibilities for reinventions.

The work with the community has continued. After someone opened a shop, the container was freed for conversion into the children's center. A class of students from the Department of Architecture at the University of Witwatersrand came to do a *charrette* where nineteen children contributed drawings of their ideas for the study center and crèche, including a playground, trees, and gardens which will one day form necessary food sources. Applying the children's and students' suggestions, Peter Rich created a design with an earth berm along one side of the container for cooling (which the children can climb to sit and play on the roof), a wide overhanging roof for shade, openings for ventilation, and the playground in front.[22] A nursery donated trees and the Rand Water Board demonstrated how to plant them in the most water-conserving way. In May 1999— two years after the initial meeting with the mayor—Mayor Mogase returned for the center opening and tree planting ceremony, and Joe Mafela, a popular comedian, volunteered to serve as master of ceremonies, to the delight of the crowd. The children named the center *Ubuhle Buyeza:* "good things are about to happen."

The Canaansland Development Committee remains intact, composed of men and women, including women who defend the children's right to speak about issues that concern them. The Local Council has promised that all of Thula Mntwana will be upgraded over the next five years . . . spurred on, most likely, by the national and international visibility that Growing Up in Cities has brought to the situation. With patient commitment from all sides, good things may happen. Yet the hard fact remains that rather than building on the accomplishments and opportunities in the city center, Canaansland and the other communities like it have been consigned to beginning again, in a barren setting without means of income, services, or affordable schooling. Unless the government of South Africa and international donors act quickly to address the problems of homelessness and squatter communities more wisely, these people, with all their hope and potential, will indeed be thrown away. But problems do not go away in this way. Just as racial apartheid failed under the old regime, leaving behind disastrous legacies of violence, an apartheid based on the geographic segregation of rich and poor will not serve the hopes for peace of the new world order.

This essay has focused on these children who are culturally and literally "out of place" in their society as a reminder that the special places of childhood need not necessarily be secret and apart from adults. Although it is true that children need places where they can create worlds of their own making, just as importantly they need opportunities to work together with adults to create better shared worlds. For those like the children in Canaansland, they need opportunities to work cooperatively with people of all ages in order to create better conditions for themselves, their families, and their communities. Otherwise, if adults do not engage with children to understand what they have, what they need, and what they can do, the fragile resources that they and their families have assembled—the shelters of home, convivial places, and networks of local resources—become indeed invisible and secret spaces that can be abruptly and unapologetically destroyed.

As this essay was written in honor of Sharon Stephens, it will close with her words. In her introduction to a special issue of the journal *Childhood* on "Children and the Environment," Sharon made a case for the need for interdisciplinary research teams to understand "the ecologies of childhood, where global forces are played out in the worlds of children's local experience."[23] This focus on children's environmental experience, she noted, would expose the problems of top-down, centralized state and international agency programs that fail to recognize local needs, experiences, and forms of knowledge, at the same time as it would show the insufficiency of community-based programs to solve problems without external help. She concluded by quoting the Chilean poet, Gabriela Mistral, and then added words that could be applied, equally well, to this essay's general theme:

> Many of the things we need
> Can wait. The child cannot.
> Right now is the time
> his bones are being formed, his
> blood is being made, and
> his senses are being developed.
> To him we cannot answer
> "Tomorrow."

Children are here, now. In order to address profound, wide-ranging effects of environmental changes on children's lives, we are forced to act, on the basis of limited and partial understandings that we continually seek to push beyond their present limitations. A focus on children and environment presents theoretical, methodological and political challenges of the most fundamental and wide-ranging kinds, in connection with the highest stakes: the health and quality of life of the world's children and their children to come.[24]

NOTES

[1]Jill Swart Kruger, ed., *Growing Up in Canaansland: Children's Recommendations on Improving a Squatter Camp Environment* (Pretoria: Human Sciences Research Council/UNESCO, 1999). The MOST Programme (Management of Social Transformations) is the social research branch of UNESCO that tackles issues of social development and environmental management. Updated information on the Canaansland project is available on the website http://home.global.co.za/~sjk/guic.htm.

[2]This lecture was made possible through the generosity of the Center for European Studies.

[3]Sharon Stephens, "Children and environment: local worlds and global connections," *Childhood* 1994, 2 (1/2), 1–21. Sharon borrowed the term "ecologies of childhood" from Cindy Katz, "Textures of global change: eroding ecologies of childhood in New York and Sudan," *Childhood* 1994, 2 (1/2), 103–10.

[4]Sharon Stephens, "Notes on NOSEB Children and Environment Program," unpublished report for a board meeting of the Norwegian Centre for Child Research, 24 November 1995.

[5]D. Van Tonder, "The road to Egoli: historical roots of urban squatting on the Witwatersrand," *MUNIVRO* 1997, 13 (2), 6–7, as cited in Jill Swart Kruger, *Growing Up in Canaansland*, 6.

[6]Jorge Hardoy, Sandy Cairncross and David Satterthwaite, eds., *The Poor Die Young* (London: Earthscan Publications, 1990); World Commission on

Health and Environment, *Our Planet, Our Health* (Geneva: World Health Organization, 1992).

[7]Sharon Stephens, "Children and the politics of culture in 'late capitalism'," in S. Stephens, ed., *Children and the Politics of Culture* (Princeton: Princeton University Press, 1995), 3–48.

[8]The following account draws heavily on the report *Growing Up in Canaansland*, edited by Jill Swart Kruger, except for a few incidents drawn from my e-mail and conversations with Jill and other project members.

[9]Jorge Hardoy and David Satterthwaite, *Squatter Citizen: Life in the Urban Third World* (London: Earthscan Publications, 1989).

[10]David Satterthwaite, *The Scale and Nature of Urban Change in the South* (London: International Institute for Environment and Development, 1996).

[11]Jill Swart Kruger, ed., *Growing Up in Canaansland,* 23.

[12]Ibid., 24.

[13]Ibid., 26.

[14]James Garbarino, *No Place to be a Child: Growing Up in a War Zone* (Lexington: Jossey-Bass, 1991).

[15]Jill Swart Kruger, ed., *Growing Up in Canaansland,* 27.

[16]Jill Swart Kruger, "Children in a South African squatter camp gain a voice," in Louise Chawla, ed., *Growing Up in an Urbanizing World* (London: Earthscan Publications, 2000).

[17]This report on the eviction is taken from the South African project web site at http://home.global.co.za/~sjk/guic.htm.

[18]As quoted by Chris Maser, Russ Beaton, and Kevin Smith, *Setting the Stage for Sustainability* (Boca Raton: Lewis Publishers, 1998), v.

[19]In addition to organizations that have already been named—the MOST Programme of UNESCO, the Children's Hour Helping Fund of the Norwegian Broadcasting Corporation, the Dutch Embassy, and the Nelson Mandela Children's Fund—allied organizations included the Programme for Human Needs, Resources and the Environment of the Human Sciences Research Council of South Africa, which helped cover the costs of research and the report publication, UNICEF, which helped finance research assistants, the Adult Based Education and Training Unit of the University of South Africa, which provided the empowerment training, the Law Department of the University of South Africa, which gave legal advice, the Methodist Church, which gave food donations, and Street-Wise, a non-profit organization for street boys whose staff and board of directors gave invaluable practical assistance throughout the project.

[20]For discussions of this approach to development on the urban front, see Akhtar A. Badshah, *Our Urban Future* (London: Zed Books, 1996), Sheridan Bartlett et al., *Cities for Children* (London: Earthscan Publications, 1999), and Chapter 13 of *An Urbanizing World* by the United Nations Centre for Human Settlements (Oxford: Oxford University Press, 1996).

[21]G. A. Cornia, R. Jolly and F. Stewart, eds., *Adjustment with a Human Face,* Vol. 1: *Protecting the Vulnerable and Promoting Growth* (Oxford: Oxford University Press, 1987); Susan George, *A Fate Worse than Debt* (New York: Grove Press, 1988).

[22]Peter Rich, "Design for a children's center in a squatter camp," *South African Architect,* April 1999, 30–1.

[23] Sharon Stephens, "Children and environment: local worlds and global connections," *Childhood,* 1994, 2 (1/2), 1–21.

[24]Ibid., 17.

JOAN W. BLOS

PRIVAT (SIC) KEEP OUT:
THE DIARY AS SECRET SPACE

So far as I know I never wrote in it, not a single entry. Yet I dearly loved the diary I was given at the age of nine or ten. I recall with affection its green leather cover, the charm of its tiny lock, with its matching, minuscule key. Looking back, I think it was the lock that intrigued me most of all—the lock whose presence signaled the expectation that one might write in the diary what no one else would read.

I already knew about seeing my words in print. The school I attended was in the vanguard of experimental, progressive education. It was in keeping with the school's philosophy to instruct eleven-year-olds in typesetting and the safe operation of small presses, and then to give them the school magazine to edit and to print; it was part of the school's ethos to foster the view that if writing was something one happened to do well, its value was not as a source of personal gratification but rather insofar as it enabled contributions to the school as microcosm. From the time I was seven-years-old, my poems had been appearing in the school magazine. So, as I have noted above, I already knew about seeing my words in print. The lock, with its implicit recommendation that writing might be done *for one's self, for the sake of writing*, must have intrigued me. But I doubt that I saw its presence as an invitation.

Subsequently, which is to say by the time I entered college, I became interested in physiology and then psychology with a special interest in child development. It was by this unlikely route that I became interested in children's books.

It is important to state that I do not offer these memories of the diary not used—the road not taken—with a sense of deprivation or of opportunity missed. My satisfaction in having *be-*

come a writer has more to do with being able to say things that I care about to others—especially if they are children—than with joy in the writing itself. If this is in a direct, developmental line from early school experiences, so is my fascination with words per se. Thus, at age eleven, I and my classmates learned to set type and all the rest of it. At twelve, we moved from concrete involvement with language elements (the type) to abstract engagement with language through the study of words, their origin and history. This brought a fascination that has never left. I love to tell students that our word *umbrella* shares its etymological past with *umber*, the color, and *umbrage,* to take offense, and that all have to do with making or taking shade.

Other influences and circumstances were certainly of importance. Suffice it to say that it interests me that those aspects of early schooling are congenial, still, with the ways in which I think about my self, my work, my interests, and my values— and that I retain such a clear impression of that small, green leather book.

In 1980, to everyone's astonishment including my own, I received the John Newbery Medal, the American Book Award, and several other honors equally valued but less well known, for *A Gathering of Days: A New England Girl's Journal 1830–32.* As the title implies it was, and is, a work of historical fiction for children. At the time of the award I had been a teacher of graduate and undergraduate courses in language arts and children's literature for more than twenty years and was secure in that identity. The book began in an avocational mode and I had researched and written it slowly—mostly between semesters and during summer vacations.

Initially I had no intention to publish. I just wanted to see if I could so fully identify with the nineteenth century that I would be able to write from its perspective. This was part of the motivation for choosing the journal form. Another part was relief: if I cast my story as a *diary*, I wouldn't be required to know about details such as the floors of rural dwellings. Would they have been left bare, or decorated? And if so, how?

It seemed to me that this was the exactly the sort of thing that a truly omniscient (from the Latin *omni* = all, plus *scientia* = knowing) author would be required to know and describe but which, on the other hand, a diarist would not be expected to report. Eventually I changed my mind about not publishing the *faux* diary I had created. I did so even though I knew that it would require compromise on my part, for example the inclusion of dialogue and "opening up" the text in other ways as well. In its final form the manuscript bore less resemblance to a true diary than did earlier versions.

A Gathering of Days was well but quietly received. However, a much livelier flurry of interest followed the awarding of the Newbery Medal. And that was when I began to be asked if, like the book's central figure, I'd been a writer of journals. It didn't take long for me to discover that my honest answer was a disappointment. People *wanted* me to have kept a journal, to be a type that conformed to type, to have been a child for whom a diary's pages offered welcome solitude.

I could not satisfy them then. And now, having come on the idea that writing in a diary may be akin to inhabiting a secret space—to creating and furnishing it—I am again obliged to acknowledge that I do not and cannot speak from my own experience: no diary, no play house, no secret space; not even the longing for one.

But Clare Costello, who was then the children's book editor at Scribner's (a division which no longer exists, having been "folded into" Atheneum as a Simon & Schuster imprint), and the Newbery Committee for the 1980 award, and readers young and old seem to have found *A Gathering of Days* convincing as a diary, albeit a fictional one. In this connection I recall with special fondness a visit to a fifth grade classroom. I had talked about the process of writing the book and emphasized the preparatory phase—the reading, the field trips, the study of documents and artifacts in libraries and museums. For the benefit of these fifth graders and to dramatize my comments I showed and interpreted two nineteenth-century items—a shopkeeper's ledger and a doll-sized quilt. Then it was time for questions. A girl raised her hand at the far back of the room. "Where did you find the journal?" she asked. "Did you have to change it much?"

I should also note that although my personal experience may be limited to the creation of a fictional journal, I have certainly heard about the real ones! I know how important it is that they not be invaded and that unauthorized readings by parents, siblings, and others may lead to tantrums and tears. I understand that young diarists whose journals are not equipped with locks often protect them with fierce notices: DO NOT READ (twice underlined), PRIVAT (*sic*) KEEP OUT.[1]

It appears that although there is a long tradition of diary-keeping by girls, the privacy part is new. Perhaps this is because at one time maintaining a journal was not about expressing the personal. Rather it appears to have been regarded as a genteel means for improving one's language skills, including penmanship. Maybe, when nineteenth-century girls submitted their journals to their mothers for review, it didn't feel very different from presenting their compositions to their teachers for correction. I have recently had occasion to read excerpts from diaries kept by Louisa May Alcott as a young woman and by "young ladies" (girls) who sailed on whalers and merchant ships captained by their fathers, and the "journal letters" kept by their mothers. In an excellent article on the remarkable diary kept from 1810-11 by seven-year-old Marjory Fleming, Alexandra Johnson speaks of the diary as "so long the approved forum for a girl's creativity."[2] But that doesn't answer the question about when it became a personal record *not to be seen by others.* Nor can I.

I am going to make the guess that young (female) diarists began to guard their words at about the same time that their mothers got the vote, entered the workplace, shortened their dresses and bobbed their hair. But I am not going to make a case of it because what matters here is that today the expectation of privacy is characteristic and important: girls who keep diaries expect them not to be read by others and are outraged if they are invaded.

As to why diary-keeping typically begins for third and fourth graders, having sufficient skills to make it possible must be one factor. Also, retiring to write *of* one's self and *for* one's self may be the reciprocal of reading's escapist value. This, too, is a reward reserved for the reasonably proficient and again the age at which it is typically attained suggests third and fourth graders.

It must be wonderful to come newly upon the idea that stories take place in *places,* and that you go there when you read! I am reminded of Emily Dickinson who celebrated the book as a "bequest of wings" and put into words the thought that:

> There is no frigate like a book,
> To take us miles away. . . .

And I have always felt indebted to Nancy Mitford for the story she tells of a conversation she once had with an old fellow up in Maine:

> . . . he chuckled and said, "I used to be a great reader in my day, but I don't want to wear you out with my stories." When I didn't say anything, he continued, "My wife, bless her, could never understand it. She'd say, 'Now, Bert, there you are sitting with your nose in a book again. What'll it get you?' And I'd say, 'It'll get me everywhere I haven't been, Alice.'"[3]

But I have to admit that a part of me objects. "Yes, of course," I want to say, "but the *really* best thing about reading is how books let you understand what's right in front of you, including your own self!" Alice may not have put it very nicely but pragmatism as well as romanticism has its place in this world.

Paul Klee once said something to the effect that the function of art is not to reproduce the visible, e.g., reality, but to render it visible. Do young readers sense this? A young Abraham Lincoln is said to have chosen as a flyleaf inscription:

> My Book and Heart
> Shall never part.

Taken from the anonymous, block-printed alphabet that appeared in edition after edition of *The New England Primer*, the lines suggest that there is privacy and closeness in the relationship to a book. Connection. Possession. Permanence. Love. And if this can be true of feelings related to the books one reads, what transpires when one writes, when one returns to the same, bound set of pages to set down observations, thoughts, feelings?

For readers and writers alike, some possibility of "re-entry" is certainly and enjoyably there. But the writer's role, being the creative one, is necessarily more active. I suggest that what happens when one *writes* is more like play than reading, and that when a diarist—young or old but typically female—quietly and privately returns to her diary's pages, it is very like returning to one of childhood's special, secret places—well loved and well guarded. And I think that that kind of writing, as is true also of play, provides rather more than distraction and more, also, than escape.

So let us tiptoe away from the youthful diarists I've conjured up, leaving them to their writing. I want to turn, if briefly, to an actual diary which for reasons intrinsic and otherwise, has probably become the best-known diary of the twentieth century. It was composed as secret writing in a secret place. It was made public by excruciating circumstances, its pages exposed, scattered on the floor from which they were rescued—a saving denied the writer. I am, of course, talking about *The Diary of a Young Girl* and of Anne Frank.

Until the writing of this essay called her diary to mind as a most fitting example, I had not reread it in a good many years. An element I had forgotten is that each entry is addressed to Kitty, to "Dear Kitty" in fact, and each one closes as a letter does, "Yours, Anne." It is as if Anne, in the enclosed society of "the secret annex," and lacking a confidante, has taken a fictional character as a friend.[4]

Having established this epistolary premise, Anne's tone, as she examines feelings and reports events, is absolutely consistent. She describes things as if continuing to hold up her end of an ongoing correspondence. On the other hand, if one disregards the formulaic salutations and closings, one can hear Anne's words as a conversation that has only one side and which can be relied upon to be held in confidence. Even more salient is the very real and significant way in which the engagement, however unilateral and fictional, enhances her self-awareness.[5]

Sunday, 2 January, 1944

Dear Kitty,

This morning when I had nothing to do I turned over some of the pages of my diary and several times I came across letters dealing with the subject "Mummy" in such a hotheaded way that I was quite shocked, and asked myself, "Anne, is it really you who mentioned hate? Oh, Anne, how could you!" I remained sitting . . . and thought about it. . . .

Wednesday, 5 January, 1944

Dear Kitty,

I have two things to confess to you today. . . . The first is about Mummy. You know that I've grumbled a lot about

> Mummy, yet still tried to be nice to her again. Now it is sud-
> denly clear to me what she lacks. . . .[6]

While not knowing what to make of it, I find it interesting that the reality of the diary is recognized by Anne ("I turned over some pages of my diary") within the conceit of the letter which itself contains reference to prior letters which were, of course, diary entries.

In quite a different connection, the editors of Louisa May Alcott's journals note that their publication complements the prior publication of her letters because:

> . . . letters are designed for the single individual to whom they are addressed. Letters answer immediate questions, concern themselves with current problems, sometimes probe the inner self of the writer, often describe the outside side. . . . [B]ut unlike the letters the journals (with the exception of some early entries that invited parental perusal) were private records. As such they reflected perhaps more closely than the letters Alcott's emotional life and the recurring problems of her days. . . . If the letters were addressed to individuals, the journals, for the most part, were addressed to herself.[7]

With regard to Anne's juxtaposed use of the two forms, one senses that some very complex thinking and fantasizing (the fictional Kitty as personal friend and exterior *persona*) are going on here and that they seem interdependent.

But what *is it* about diaries? Not just Anne Frank's diary, written as it was under extraordinary circumstances by a gifted adolescent (who might, or might not, have become an outstanding adult writer). If any life is "ordinary" in the usual sense of the word once one begins to examine it, what is the meaning and importance of diaries written by ordinary girls in ordinary circumstances?

Somewhat presumptuously but not, I hope, preposterously, I turn to *A Gathering of Days*, the book I wrote entirely as a thirteen-year-old's journal. One of the glories of writing about fiction is that no one—not even a ghost—can complain, "That's not how it was at all." All the better if the fiction exampled is one's own, for who can better the authority of the one who wrote it?[8] It must be acknowledged, however, that this alters the situation so that the questions posed above (What is it about diaries, etc.) now ask something else: What, if anything, did I learn from the writing of this book (including the extended research phase) that might shed light on the subject of youthful diaries?

I cite first of all the realization that the documents which were the most compelling, and which gave the greatest impression of intimacy, were made of the most mundane statements: so many rows planted today (spring); so many jars put up today (fall). So-and-so to visit. Where the references are to events as familiar as the passing of seasons, domestic activities, or social exchanges, it doesn't take sophisticated writing to create (imply) the whole.

Another insight: an important element in finding and maintaining a literal secret space (which then becomes the location of individual or peer group play) is being able to return to it so that it is possible to pick up and go on from wherever one left off. The same is true of diaries—cf., Anne's turning over "some pages" of hers.

Are there other commonalties? I think so. When groups of children form clubs, one of the first things they do is invent a sign or password. *Then* they find a space to which only those who know the sign (or password) are to be admitted. Whether by lock or notice, diaries, too, are guarded.

It further strikes me as pertinent that the diarist chooses what will be included; only that which she *wants* to include *will be included* in the record she is creating. The same is true when a child, or children, play. *They* decide what will happen, who will/will not be present. This is not to say that all will be bright. That is a different matter. Just that consciously or otherwise the content as written or played out has been *selected* as a fitting element of an ongoing narrative. Its very ongoingness affords opportunity for reflection, examination, and trial (imagined) correction—the interior processes that may enable actual coming to terms. In the fragment quoted above Anne reveals that her writing helped her in her struggles with her mother. Catherine, the diary-keeping protagonist of *A Gathering of Days*, notes that, "This year, more than others, has been a lengthy gathering of days wherein we lived, we loved, were moved; learned how to accept."[9]

Are diaries "secret spaces" in the sense intended by the editors of this collection? Does the writing of them constitute withdrawal to a somewhere that is wholly one's own, that no one else can enter? Is withdrawal, which has a rather melancholy ring, the right word to use? Presumably, for some, diary writing is joyous.

It seems to me that there is good basis for thinking that the diary is (or can be) a secret (Keep Out) space. And I would like to suggest that for those who can make it so, it is not necessary to live in a house with an attic, have a yard with a tree big enough to support a tree house or, as an urban dweller, be born into a family sufficiently affluent to have extra residential space even if only the bottom part of a closet. A diary takes up very little room. Once secluded within the process of writing, what can happen on those pages is truly without limit.

NOTES

[1]Statement, complete with misspelling, reported by a friend.

[2] Alexandra Johnson, "The Drama of Imagination: Marjory Fleming and her Diaries," *Infant Tongues: The Voice of the Child in Literature*, Elizabeth Goodenough, Mark A. Heberle & Naomi Sokoloff, eds. (Detroit: Wayne State University Press, 1994), 81.

[3]Nancy Mitford, "De Memoria," *The Writer and Her Works*, Janet Sternberg, ed. (New York: Norton, 1980), 37.

[4]In a personal communication from Dr. Heiman van Dam I recently learned that Kitty is the name of one of the characters in a series of books written for girls that was extremely popular in the Netherlands at the time of Anne's childhood. And was, in fact, her favorite reading. The series is still read there today. The author was Cissy van Marxveldt. The series is named after the protagonist Joop ter Heul. I understand that van Dam plans to include a summary of pertinent aspects of this series in his forthcoming book *Anne Frank's Diaries: A Developmental Study*, to be published by International Universities Press.

[5]The thought that this very much resembles the patient's side of psychotherapy is inescapable.

[6] Anne Frank, *The Diary of a Young Girl* (New York: Doubleday, 1967), 167.

[7]Joel Meyerson, Daniel Shealy & Madeleine B. Stern, eds., *The Journals of Louisa May Alcott* (New York: Little, Brown, 1989), 38.

[8]This is an attractive but specious remark. Others have commented on elements of my books of which I was not aware.

[9]Joan W. Blos, *A Gathering of Days: A New England Girl's Journal, 1830–32* (New York: Scribner, 1979), 140.

MARY GALBRAITH

PRIMAL POSTCARDS: *MADELINE* AS A SECRET SPACE OF LUDWIG BEMELMANS'S CHILDHOOD

> If you know the artist, you will see him always in his pictures, even if they be landscapes.
> Ludwig Bemelmans, quoted in Marciano 110

> I think in pictures, because I see everything in pictures, and then translate them into English. I tried to write in German; I can't.
> Ludwig Bemelmans, quoted in Marciano 56

> Everything goes back to the reproduction of scenes.
> Sigmund Freud, in Masson 234

Picture books offer serious artists a space to return to and depict the dramas of their own childhoods. However, picture-book editorial mandates for a light tone and for content suitable for young children serve as an external censor that drives intense feelings—grief, terror, unbearable pain, and even ecstasy—underground. In addition, picture-book creators' own defenses customarily keep them from fully realizing what they are depicting in their work. The expectations and defenses of readers similarly keep disturbing content at a safe distance or out of awareness. Paradoxically, then, under the protective cover of a children's storybook, primal scenes that would otherwise stay buried can surface without being consciously recognized.

From encountering several classic picture books that fit this pattern,[1] I hypothesize that a necessary ingredient to make a picture book a classic—that is, a book of great and enduring literary value and appeal that meets the conventional criteria of a picture book for a manifestly light tone and happy ending—is that the book be motivated throughout by a creator's restaging of early trauma (primarily through allegorical narrative and line drawing). One or more pictures stand out as the book's primal *raison d'etre*; that is, there is at least one picture which activates a "flashbulb memory" from the creator's childhood and which the story explains in an ambiguous way. The manifest storybook explanation for this primal scene is benign and reassuring while the latent and historical interpretation is traumatic and unbearable. Thus, the classic picture book can be seen as a secret space of childhood whose deepest significance is hidden in plain sight.

A masterful and amply supported example of such an *auteur* picture book is Ludwig Bemelmans's *Madeline*, originally published in 1939. This storybook's 44 pages of seemingly light entertainment feature one child's story of primal loss, death, war, and a bittersweet survival, and range in scope from intensely private scenes to evocations of world history, all against a backdrop of joyful immersion in color and form. In order to convey a sense of these riches, I will first sketch events from Ludwig Bemelmans's "Swan Country" period from birth to six, and his *Lausbub* period from six to sixteen.

Ludwig Bemelmans was born in 1898 in Austria during the last days of Empire, the child of a failed marriage between an eccentric Belgian artist and a German brewer's daughter. The boy spent his earliest years on the grounds of his father's Austrian hotel in Gmunden, cared for by a Frenchwoman whom he called Gazelle (his pronunciation of *Mademoiselle*). Reliving his earliest memories in an essay called "Swan Country," Bemelmans recalled that "I was her little blue fish, her little treasure, her small green duckling, her dear sweet cabbage, her amour" (Bemelmans 1985, 7). Gazelle may well have suckled Ludwig, since putting a child out to nurse was the custom among well-off Germans at that period. According to Doris Drucker, who was a young child in Cologne and Mainz during the prewar and wartime years between 1910 and 1918,

> A wet nurse was usually a village girl who had gotten herself "into trouble." As soon as her baby was born, it was given away to an "angel maker" (a woman who starved to

death the babies in her care), and the young mother was hired out as a wet nurse. (77)

In any case, Gazelle nurtured the boy on "long hours [. . .] with postal cards of Paris, the Album of Paris, the children's stories of France, the songs written for French children" (Bemelmans 1985, 10), even as he imbibed through her the rhythms, colors, and weather of Gmunden. In the picture accompanying, a portrait of himself and Gazelle drawn from memory, note how Ludwig's head overlaps her body in the shelter of a small gazebo covered with vines—the vines that will reappear as an organizing motif in *Madeline*.

Bemelmans's father's sexual liaisons apparently included not only Ludwig's mother and Gazelle, but Ludwig's maternal grandmother. When Ludwig was six-years-old, Lampert ran off with yet another woman, leaving both Ludwig and Gazelle, who was pregnant with Lampert's child. In despair, Gazelle committed suicide by drinking sulfured water. If she indeed had given birth out of wedlock before becoming Ludwig's nurse, with the results as described by Drucker, the prospect of repeating this scenario may well have been unbearable. Without making clear what story he was told about these events as a child, Bemelmans later summarized his childhood feelings thus:

> And then one autumn the leaves in the park were not raked, the swan stood there forlorn and it was all over—all had come to an end. Papa was gone and so was my governess, and I wished so much that he had run away with Mama and left me Gazelle. (Bemelmans 1985, 10)

In the aftermath of this devastation, Ludwig's mother—a virtual stranger to him and also pregnant—came and took him to live with her parents in Regensburg, Germany. At that time, he did not speak German (Miller and Field, 264–5).

> In the beginning Mama tried to replace Gazelle: mostly in tears, she dressed and undressed me. [. . .] [S]he would tell me stories about her own childhood—of how alone she had been as a little girl and how she was shipped off to a convent school. . . . She was much happier there than at home, for her parents had never had any time for her. This made me sad. She cried, and I cried. She lifted me up; I looked at her closely, and a dreadful fear came over me. I saw how beautiful she was, and I thought how terrible it would be if ever she got old and ugly. (Bemelmans 1985, 10–11)

After this beginning, his mother became hardened in her care of Ludwig and "was determined to erase all traces of the past from me." Thus began Bemelmans's *Lausbub* years, in which German relatives tried to make a German out of him: "The golden curls came off my head, I was shorn and put into new clothes, high-laced shoes with hobnails." The effect on the boy was to make him intentionally defiant. "I said to myself they can kill me, but I won't give in. I will not change, never never never" (quoted in Marciano 6). When he was a young adolescent, the lyceums he was sent to tried to cow him into submission, but he persisted in behaving with Gallic fatalistic flair, and he was sent home from them all in disgrace.

Again he was sent away, this time for a stint in the family hotel business in Tyrol, and again he skirted Teutonic authority. Then in 1914 he did something more serious. In an interview with the *New York Times* in 1941, Bemelmans described this serious offense: while working in one of his uncle's hotels as a busboy, a "vicious" headwaiter threatened him with a whip. "I told him that if he hit me I would shoot him. He hit me and I shot him in the abdomen. For some time it seemed he would die. He didn't. But the police advised my family that

I must be sent either to a reform school or to America" (Van Gellens 2). Whether or not this "abdominal wound" story is factually correct—Bemelmans treated the distinction between fact and fiction as something to play with—something else stands out about the time of his exile to America: it came four months after the beginning of all-out European war. Because of his "serious offense," Bemelmans sailed to America in December 1914, escaping service as a "potato-head" in the Central Army and death in the trenches of World War I. His escape recalls the widespread use of self-wounding, and the less common but well-known practice later in the war of shooting superiors as a means to escape the inexorable march to the front. Bemelmans was not opposed to military service per se— he later enlisted in the Allied Army and served in a mental hospital in New York—but to the brutal and oppressive militarism he associated with Germany.

Madeline's story centers on four primal breaks in the life of Ludwig Bemelmans: first, the suicide of Gazelle when he was six; second, his immediately subsequent introduction into German discipline; third, his "disgrace" and evacuation to America in 1914 at the beginning of World War I when he was sixteen; and fourth, the wholesale wartime slaughter of his European agemates (his only brother also died an untimely death).

In addition to the disguised presentation of these events, Bemelmans portrays his own perceived relation to and response to these traumas—crying out for help from his bed, resisting regimentation through defiant behavior, escaping from mobilization in the Central Army by means of a "self-inflicted" abdominal wound, and grieving the loss of his peers.

Specific uncolored pictures in the book capture Bemelmans's traumatic experiences as fused and condensed tableaux: the last picture in the book combines a flashbulb memory of his last sight of his beloved Gazelle ("there wasn't any more") with a complex portrayal of Europe's response to its traumatized youth in World War I; the picture of an elevated but isolated Madeline standing on her bed exhibiting her abdominal scar memorializes both the triumph and the trauma of his escape from the *Lausbub* life at age sixteen; and the repeated pictures of two rows of "soldiers" divided by a "trench," culminating in the picture of the eleven remaining children wailing in their beds too late to escape their fate, register regimented school life as well as the slaughter of millions in World War I.

In addition to objectified figures representing himself as child and artist—Madeline and a mysterious unmentioned figure in a fez who haunts the pictures—the background atmospherics of tone, color, weather, and landscape evoke the sensory and emotional preverbal experience of Ludwig Bemelmans with Gazelle in his "Swan Country" period, when she was for him a place as well as a person. Among these atmospheric elements are the postcard landmarks of Paris which Gazelle used to pore over with him in the wintertime, and the sensuality and emotional significance of the light and weather—rain (which Gazelle referred to as the tears of *le bon Dieu*), snow, and darkness predominate, and the sun is a glorious face shining upon Madeline after her return to consciousness in the hospital. In the color pictures early in the book, even the air is a palpable and womb-like presence, saturated with the personal relationship to form and color Bemelmans describes elsewhere from his earliest memories. Significantly, the early pages of his "Swan Country" memoirs contain no "I," since the "I" is still completely immersed in its experience. Similarly, the landscape and weather in the early pages of *Madeline* evoke an immersed time before the "I" is objectified.

The placement of the uncolored pictures also carries meaning. After the narrative switches focus from Madeline to the other eleven girls, there are no more color pictures—enacting both the change in Bemelmans's life after Gazelle's death when he was six, and the situation of his agemates as they approached the age of being mobilized. The pictorial narrative here is carried by Bemelmans's expressive cartoons only. Most notably momentous are the line drawings of Miss Clavel as she runs fast and faster in fear of a disaster—her figure, always missile-like, assumes the energy and drive of a launched artillery shell that penetrates the room where the doomed eleven are crying out.

Madeline's story captures Bemelmans's survival strategy for coping with abandonment in his early childhood and for responding to the threat to his life from authoritarian adults from age six to sixteen. When Madeline emerges as an individual separate from her eleven compatriots, she exhibits the defiant attitude by which Bemelmans survived after he moved to Germany with his mother. In the narrative of the book, a scenario opening "In the middle of one night" and then "In the middle of the night" is played out twice, first for Madeline and then for the other eleven: being trapped in a room with disaster looming and without access to a comforting or rescuing body, a child cries out for help. Madeline's cry works, at least well enough to save her life: she gets cradled, carried away, and saved, but now she is separated not only from her family but from her peers. Everyone else's cry is summarily dismissed; the door closes on them and "there isn't any more."

The attachment dynamics of *Madeline*, and of Bemelmans's primal scenario, are centered on access through doorways. Miss Clavel is seen ambiguously in a protective or blocking position over and over in doorways throughout the picture book. When Madeline reaches the hospital (an event resonating with Bemelmans reaching the United States), Miss Clavel (a fusion of the loving but finally abandoning Gazelle, European nun-teachers, and the madonna of wartime death) no longer controls the doorway, but both her presence and her loss cut both ways in Bemelmans's life:

> In the middle of the night, I often wake up—and stare at the open doors through which I cannot walk and at the closed ones that I can't open—and the children's books that keep me from blowing out my brains are created in this hour [. . .] . (Bemelmans letter, quoted in Collins 130)

Seen through this lens, the child Madeline crying in bed in the first "middle of the night" and the eleven other children in the bed in the second "middle of the night" all express premonitions of or reactions to the unbearable loss of Miss Clavel and to the unbearable horrors of war. Finally, they express the "traumatic awakening" (Caruth 91) that is Bemelmans's personal legacy, and his survival through an artistic expression that honors and is made possible by his earliest experiences of love and vibrant beauty:

> Like the pages of a children's book, the days were turned and looked at, and the most important objects in this book were the sun, the moon and the stars; people, flowers and trees. Large trees, whose leaves throbbed with color and

which reached up to the sky—black tree trunks, sometimes brownish-black and shining in the rain, young in spring, and yellow in the autumn, when each leaf in the light of afternoon was like a lamp lit up. [. . .] The sky is blue, the gardener's apron is greener than spinach. The eyes of Gazelle are large and brown and kind. ("Swan Country," Bemelmans 1985, 3–4)

NOTES

[1]A partial list: *Millions of Cats, The Story of Babar, And to Think That I Saw It on Mulberry Street, Goodnight Moon, Moon Man,* and *Where the Wild Things Are.* Other picture books clearly motivated throughout by childhood trauma experiences are *The Lonely Doll* and *Curious George,* but I see these as being in such thrall to a punishing parental position that their emancipatory force, and thus their artistic stature, is compromised, though both books exercise a continuing fascination. On the other hand, *The Snowman* is a masterpiece, but too mournful even in its manifest content to qualify for the limited genre I'm considering here.

BIBLIOGRAPHY

I. Works by Bemelmans (for a complete list, see Eastman or Marciano, below):
Madeline. New York: Simon & Schuster, 1939.
Tell Them It Was Wonderful. Ed. Madeleine Bemelmans. New York: Viking, 1985.

II. On Ludwig Bemelmans's life and work:
Collins, Amy Fine. "Madeline's Papa." *Vanity Fair* 455, July 1998: 116–30.
Drucker, Doris. "Invent Radium or I'll Pull Your Hair." *The Atlantic Monthly,* August 1998: 73–91.
Eastman, Jacqueline. *Ludwig Bemelmans.* New York: Twayne, 1996.
Marciano, John Bemelmans. *The Life and Art of Madeline's Creator.* New York: Viking, 1999.
Van Gelder, Robert. "An Interview with Ludwig Bemelmans." *New York Times Book Review,* 26 January 1941, 2+.

III. On creativity and primal experience:
Barrett, William. "Writers and Madness." *Literature and Psychoanalysis.* Eds. Edith Kurzweil and William Phillips. New York: Columbia University Press, 1983.
Freud, Sigmund. *Writings on Art and Literature.* Stanford, CA: Stanford University Press, 1997.
Miller, Alice. *Thou Shalt Not Be Aware.* Trans. Hildegarde and Hunter Hannum. New York: Meridian, 1984.

_____ *Pictures of a Childhood*. Trans. Hildegard Hannum. New York: Farrar, Straus, & Giroux, 1986.

_____ *The Untouched Key: Tracing Childhood Trauma in Creativity and Destructiveness*. Trans. Hildegarde and Hunter Hannum. New York: Doubleday, 1990.

IV. On picture books and primal experience:
Galbraith, Mary. "'Goodnight Nobody' Revisited: Using an Attachment Perspective to Study Picture Books about Bedtime." *Children's Literature Association Quarterly* 23, No. 4 (1999): 172–80.

_____ "Agony in the Kindergarten: Indelible German Images in American Picture Books." In Jean Webb, ed., *Text, Culture and National Identity in Children's Literature*. Helsinki: NORDINFO Publication 44, 2000.

_____ "What Must I Give Up in Order to Grow Up? World War I and Childhood Survival Schemas in Transatlantic Picture Books." *The Lion & the Unicorn*, forthcoming special issue on "Children and War."

Lanes, Selma. *The Art of Maurice Sendak*. New York: Abrams, 1980.

Lobel, Anita. *No Pretty Pictures: A Child of War*. New York: Greenwillow, 1998.

Nathan, Jean. "The Secret Life of the Lonely Doll." *Tin House* 1, No. 2 (Fall 1999): 32–52.

Ungerer, Tomi. *Tomi: A Childhood under the Nazis*. Niwot, Colorado: TomiCo (Roberts Rinehart), 1998.

V. On early childhood trauma and the production of visual narrative:
Caruth, Cathy. *Unclaimed Experience: Trauma, Narrative, and History*. Baltimore: Johns Hopkins University Press, 1996.

Masson, Jeffrey, ed. *The Complete Letters of Sigmund Freud to Wilhelm Fliess, 1887–1904*. Cambridge: Harvard University Press, 1985.

Share, Lynda. *When Someone Speaks, It Gets Lighter: Dreams and the Reconstruction of Infant Trauma*. Hillsdale, NJ: Analytic Press, 1994.

Terr, Lenore. *Too Scared to Cry: Psychic Trauma in Childhood*. New York: Basic Books, 1990.

Wright, Kenneth. *Vision and Separation: Between Mother and Baby*. Northvale, NJ: Jason Aronson, 1991.

VI. Picture books cited (original editions):
Bemelmans, Ludwig. *Madeline*. New York: Simon & Schuster, 1939.

Briggs, Raymond. *The Snowman*. New York: Random House, 1978.

de Brunhoff, Jean. *Histoire de Babar, le petit elephant*. Paris: *Editions du Jardin des Modes*, 1931.

Gag, Wanda. *Millions of Cats*. New York: Coward-McCann, 1928.

Rey, Hans Augusto. *Curious George*. Boston: Houghton Mifflin, 1941.

Sendak, Maurice. *Where the Wild Things Are*. New York: Harper & Row, 1963.

Seuss, Dr. [Theodor Geisel]. *And to Think That I Saw It on Mulberry Street*. New York: Vanguard, 1937.

Ungerer, Tomi. *Moon Man*. New York: Harper & Row, 1967.

Wright, Dare. *The Lonely Doll*. New York: Doubleday, 1957.

KAREIN K. GOERTZ

WRITING FROM THE SECRET ANNEX: THE CASE OF ANNE FRANK

Ever since the Gestapo entered into the rooms where eight people had been hiding for almost two years, the so-called Secret Annex in the center of Amsterdam has become one of the most famous and visited hiding places of Jews persecuted during the Second World War. Anne Frank's diary, begun in 1942 as a confidential correspondence to an imaginary friend and then revised with an eye to future publication, now counts as the most widely read document of the Holocaust. The diary has appeared in several edited and unedited editions since it was first recovered from the floor of the evacuated Annex.[1] A comparison of these versions reveals how Anne's voice has been shaped, some even say censored, by different editorial hands. This fact was again brought to the fore with the recent discovery of five previously unpublished pages which Anne's father had withdrawn from the manuscript before his death in 1980. By request of the extended Frank family, these were again excluded from the otherwise unedited, critical edition published in 1986. The missing pages have sparked discussion about authorial intention, posthumous control, familial privacy and discretion in the public domain. When the Austrian journalist Melissa Müller published her biography of Anne Frank in 1998, she was allowed to use only paraphrases of these deleted passages while issues of copyright were being fought out in the Swiss courts. A Dutch newspaper, however, did get away with posting them on the Internet and future editions of the diary will include the entries that have caused so much controversy. The question remains whether we should be allowed to read material that was either deliberately excluded by the author herself or that compromises the family involved. Are private hiding places meant to be fully uncovered for the public eye?

It seems ironic that once carefully guarded places of refuge and hiding—the Annex and the diary—have now been exposed to the world many times over. One cannot help but feel like a voyeur, privy to the thoughts of a thirteen-year-old girl who never wanted all of her schoolgirl "musings" to be revealed beyond the version she explicitly edited for posterity. For decades, Anne's diary stood in and spoke for, but perhaps also eclipsed the individual stories of thousands of other Jewish children who were forced into hiding places during the Second World War. Amidst public rhetoric of the postwar years that relegated children to silence by casting them in a paradoxical, no-win situation as either "too young to remember" or "old enough to forget," the success of the diary was a remarkable exception. In fact, for many readers today, it remains the first, sometimes the only, introduction to the Holocaust. This essay explores the various manifestations of hiding in and surrounding Anne Frank's diary. It engages the ongoing dynamic between hiding and exposure, refuge and vulnerability, secret and public personae. Hiding takes on multiple meanings, both literal and metaphoric. Within the confines of the Annex, we observe how Anne carves out a private, secret space for herself through writing. As with most diaries, hers functions as a place of refuge, a safe niche in which to construct and explore her various, but carefully hidden, selves. The marked difference from other adolescent diaries is that Anne writes within a historically specific context that has forced her into hiding. The typical teenager's need to salvage a private space for herself is magnified in this claustrophobic, constantly threatened hiding place. As readers, we are witnesses to the twofold hiding—physical and psychological—of a hidden self in actual hiding. The life of the diary since its first publication in 1947 also exemplifies different forms of hiding, including censored, screened, and missing memories and voices.

The Secret Annex

Faced with the bestial hostility of the storm and the hurricane, the house's virtues of protection and resistance are transposed into human virtues. . . . Come what may, the house helps us to say: I will be an inhabitant of the world, in spite of the world.

—Gaston Bachelard, *The Poetics of Space*

The Annex which Anne first describes resonates with this archetypal, universal image of the house as shelter and fortress that both protects against and resists the world outside. Otto Frank had spent months transforming the rooms, attic, and loft into a comfortable hiding place. With furniture, decor, and supplies from the family's former life, he sought to preserve the illusion of order, normalcy, and continuity. Anne dedicates many pages of her diary to the description of the Annex as both physical and metaphoric place. When the diary was first published in Holland, it was called *Het Achterhuis* (The House Behind) rather than *The Diary of a Young Girl*, foregrounding the spatial over the autobiographical dimension. At first, Anne experiences the Annex in benign terms as part of an adventure or an interlude from reality: "I don't think I'll ever feel at home in this house, but that doesn't mean I hate it. It's more like being on vacation in some strange *pension*." In her writer's imagination, it gets transformed into a "unique facility for the temporary accommodation of Jews and other dispossessed persons" with strict rules and regulations she describes in a characteristically playful manner: "Diet: low-fat. Free-time activities: None allowed outside the house until further notice." Irony functions as the house does: it is a protective screen that blocks off or hides the anxiety associated with matters of life and death. By choosing to laugh about the absurdity of the situation, she resists its power to defeat her. The Annex is a world away from the world, existing in spite of the world.

The resilience of this miniature, hidden world is continuously tested from the inside and the outside. Drawing her metaphor from the restricted view of the external world she has through the attic window, Anne describes the Annex's increasingly uncertain function as shelter:

> [We are] a patch of blue sky surrounded by menacing black clouds. The perfectly round spot on which we're standing is still safe, but the clouds are moving in on us, and the ring between us and the approaching danger is being pulled

tighter and tighter. We're surrounded by darkness and danger, and in our desperate search for a way out we keep bumping into each other. We look at the fighting down below and the peace and beauty up above. In the meantime, we've been cut off by the dark mass of clouds, so that we can go neither up nor down. It looms before us like an impenetrable wall, trying to crush us, but not yet able to.

The encroaching external menace and constant terror of discovery corrode and suffocate life on the inside. The Annex, once seen as a safe haven, an adventure, a self-contained and sheltering world, is transformed into a prison. She feels like a "songbird whose wings have been ripped off and who keeps hurling itself against the bars of its dark cage." Circumscribed by safety measures, the days follow the same monotonous routine with long hours of oppressive silence and sluggish movement. Anne describes how, after more than a year in hiding, everyone has almost forgotten how to laugh and that she takes daily doses of valerian to help combat anxiety and depression.

Secret Selves

Anne transforms the privations of everyday life into amusing anecdotes, fear into an interesting adventure story, longing and loneliness into a romance plot. The narratives allow her to distance herself from the situation at hand through irony or retrospective analysis, rather than being submerged by it. They also allow her to explore alternative, more assertive or honest roles she wished she had played.[2] In the claustrophobic context of the Annex, the diary becomes a world into which Anne retreats. Here she can fully express the feelings she must otherwise contain. One can read the diary in spatial terms as a safe place for her real, but still hidden self. It can also be understood in functional terms as a performative sphere in which Anne tests out different versions of herself, giving them a voice and watching them grow. She secures this private domain for herself in direct response to the relentless scrutiny and evaluation of her character by other members in the Annex. These confined quarters where people's moods, thoughts, and fates are so closely intertwined allow very little room for personal enfolding. The diary, like her own person, is under constant threat of being discovered and must therefore be carefully guarded. "Daddy is grumbling again and threatening to take away my diary. Oh horror of horrors! From now on, I'm going to hide it." To assuage the curiosity of the Annex members and to provide them with much-needed comic relief, Anne occasionally reads passages aloud. These readings also serve the purpose of gathering critical feedback on her success as a writer. For the most part, however, Anne considers the diary her own private business and writes under the assumption that it will remain completely confidential. Those from whom she must protect her diary are not the Annex members alone, but also the outside world. Two months after arriving in the Annex, Anne rereads her first diary entries about this initially "ideal place" and adds that she is terrified that the hiding place will be revealed and its inhabitants shot. This fear explains why she omits the name of the man who supplies the Annex with potatoes. She knows that, if discovered, the diary could potentially be used as incriminating evidence against their helpers. Later, when she begins revising her diary for a future audience, she uses pseudonyms to protect the real identities of the Annex members. This coded language reveals yet another level of hiding.[3]

On one level, the diary offers a classic, almost textbook example of the process of individuation from childhood into adolescence, away from externally imposed definitions and parental expectations. Generations of young girls searching for, slowly discovering, and eventually affirming their "true" selves have found a positive role model in Anne. Critics applaud her feminist qualities and trace her development from a girl who has her "own ideas, plans and ideals, but is unable to articulate them yet" into a young woman who shows a quickly developing talent as a writer.[4] What distinguishes Anne's situation, of course, is that this process of self-discovery and adolescent rebellion takes place within a context that allows very little room to test out this evolving self. While her body and self-image are radically changing and she carries within her a new "sweet secret," others still treat and judge her according to the child she once was. Being this former childish self, however, is no longer possible in the Annex with its long hours of silence and necessity of constant self-control. Anne is also tired of playing the family "clown and mischief maker" and wants to take on a role different from the one others have come to expect of her. She describes the clash between these external and internal perceptions and expectations in terms of an internal split in which her "bad" half turns against and beats down her better half. The "good" Anne cannot survive in this miniature world of "negative opinions, dismayed looks and mocking faces." In self-defense, this Anne retreats into the private, hidden world of the diary: "I end up turning heart inside out, the bad part on the outside and the good part on the inside, and keep trying to find a way to become what I'd like to be and what I could be if . . . if only there were no other people in the world."

Revisions and Omissions

Upon hearing a radio broadcast in the Spring of 1944, in which the exiled Cabinet Minister of Education and Culture announced that the Dutch government would be collecting wartime diaries and letters as testimony of "Holland's struggle for freedom," Anne began revising and writing her diary for future publication. How did this internal assessment of "good" and "bad" selves affect the revision process as Anne was consciously constructing an image of herself and life in the Annex for the outside world and posterity? Were there parts of herself she wanted to keep hidden because she considered them too personal, immature, or shameful? Her decision to cut out a passage (one of the missing pages) that relays her physical attraction to a childhood girlfriend and her "ecstasy" at seeing female nudes in art history books suggests that she considered this revelation inappropriate within this new, public forum. Even before hearing the radio announcement, Anne would read through earlier entries, criticizing her former "childish innocence," her "sentimental" or "embarrassingly indelicate" descriptions. Often she found herself face to face with a stranger whom she barely recognized. These self-evaluations reveal how she used the diary to trace and measure her own maturation process. In preparing her "memory book" for publication, however, she begins to consider what would be most interesting or relevant for the future reader. A few sentences after describing the impact of the radio broadcast, for example, she writes: "Although I tell you a great deal about our lives, you still know very little about us." Here, the direct address to her imaginary friend, Kitty, seems to have shifted to us, her new audience. Anne also suggests that, up to this point in the diary, she may not have been conveying the kind of details about hiding to which historical testimonies should aspire. With its new status as historical and public document comes a prioritization of information that involves editing out certain passages and adding new ones written from memory.

This careful screening of information deemed public and private, relevant and irrelevant, was most pronounced after Anne's death. After returning to Amsterdam from Auschwitz, Otto Frank, Anne's father and the sole survivor of the Annex, began assembling the diary entries into a manuscript to share with family and friends. Upon suggestion that he publish the manuscript, he chose material from Anne's original, unedited diary and her revised version, cutting out sections to meet the page number requirements of the Dutch publisher. These posthumous modifications to Anne's diary were not merely guided by practical considerations. More significantly, they reflect the father's desire for privacy and discretion, as well as the social ethos of the time. Passages that were unflattering toward his wife, that dealt too frankly with Anne's sexuality, or were otherwise considered unimportant were omitted. In this first, highly acclaimed edition, Anne comes across as far more even-tempered and gentle than in the most recent unedited version (1991). With the inclusion of formerly deleted passages, Anne is more complex, lively, self-reproaching, and biting. Comparing these versions, one can see how Otto Frank molded Anne's voice to fit into his idealized, paternal image of her. While his revisions may have been well-intentioned, they ultimately kept part of Anne hidden.

Hidden Voices

Inevitably, people and events described in a diary are introduced to us through the biased perspective of the writer. From reported speech and described actions, we may be able to glean the personalities and motivations of secondary characters, but our understanding of them within the context of the diary is always limited and shaped by the narrator. In her diary, Anne describes the most intimate details of the other seven members of the Annex, yet we never come to know them as complex individuals. At times, they seem to be mere caricatures of qualities Anne either emulates or despises: Margot, ever-patient and selfless; Otto, compassionate and understanding; Mrs. van Daan, nosy and bossy. Recent biographies and documentaries have sought to give a voice to—and bring out of hiding—those Annex members who suffered the "fury of her pen." Edith Frank, whom Anne at one point angrily disavows as her mother, and the middle-aged dentist Fritz Pfeffer, whom Anne nicknamed Dussel (dope), bear the brunt of her criticism. Of the latter, we only see the "old-fashioned disciplinarian and preacher of unbearably long sermons on manners." We never get to know the man who sent clandestine love letters to a woman he was forced to leave because racial laws made it illegal for them to marry. Nor do we learn that he had a son, approximately Anne's age, whom he had put on a children's transport train to London in 1938 so that he would survive the war in safety with an uncle. In Jon Blair's documentary film *Anne Frank Remembered* (1995), Pfeffer's son conveys the bitter imprint Anne's diary has left on his life. Whereas Otto Frank became an icon of the perfect, caring father for generations of young girls, his father, with whom he had lost contact after the outbreak of the war, was harshly and unfairly portrayed. As Melissa Müller reveals in *Anne Frank: The Biography*, the recently recovered pages present a fuller picture of Anne's relationship toward her mother. In the pages Otto Frank removed because he felt the public did not need to know about his marriage, Anne expresses sympathy and understanding for her mother whose passion for her husband was not reciprocated. Without this piece of information that explains why Edith Frank may have become "somewhat defensive and unapproachable," we see her only as a source of deep disappointment and frustration for her daughter.

Screen Memory

Not only does the diary contain silenced or hidden voices within it, one can also observe how for many years Anne

Frank stood in for all children during the Holocaust. Generally speaking, scholarship did not begin to focus on the fate of children until forty years after the war, even though being a Jewish child in Europe meant certain extermination. Only 6–7% of Jewish children survived the Holocaust, compared with a 33% survival rate among adults. Most of these children survived the war in hiding. Some remained "visible," passing as Christians in convents, monasteries, orphanages, or with foster families. They were forced to live double lives with new names and assumed identities. Survival depended upon concealing their emotions, remaining silent, and playing roles. Others remained "invisible" for months, even years, hiding out in attics, woods, barns, and other makeshift places, constantly vulnerable to discovery. Many lost not only their childhood, but also their identity, their families, and their lives. The prolonged public silence about hidden children may have to do with a general inability or reluctance to reconcile ideas of childhood with war. As countries grappled first with the shocking revelations of the death camps in the immediate postwar period and then tried to put the past behind them in the years of reconstruction, no room was given to the fate of children in public discourse. Anne Frank's story—that is, the one that ends *before* her deportation to and death in Bergen-Belsen—was the exception.

As Laurel Holliday argues in her introduction to an anthology of other children's secret wartime diaries: "Maybe it was as much as we could bear to designate Anne Frank as the representative child and to think, then, only of her when we thought about children in World War Two." Hers became the story of a Jewish childhood during the Second World War. Anne's life, not her death, became the "human face" of the Holocaust. Her diary functioned as a bearable, collective screen memory that hid the more widespread experiences of children in ghettos and concentration camps, who went hungry in the streets, witnessed their family members die, suffered disease, physical abuse, abandonment and horrendous deaths. Most readers remained unaware of the particular circumstances of Anne's own death. Willy Lindwer's television documentary *The Last Seven Months of Anne Frank* (1988), along with Jon Blair's aforementioned film and Melissa Müller's biography, have since extended the story to describe how Anne was first deported to the Westerbork detention camp, then to Auschwitz-Birkenau and finally to Bergen-Belsen, where she contracted typhus and died within a few weeks of liberation. Her body was thrown onto a mass grave. Some argue that the lasting power and relevance of the diary lies in its indirect, modulated approach to the Holocaust. Even though the terrors of persecution, physical suffering, and death exist only on the margins of the diary, they over-shadow and determine our reading of it. Our sense of outrage, loss, and despair is enhanced because we know that Anne's optimism, faith in humanity, and future dreams will be bit-terly deceived. Others argue just the opposite; that the diary's "naive idealism" allows us to ignore the genocide taking place beyond the Annex's walls. Rather than feeling horror, despair, and a radical uprooting of conventional frames of reference, we are able to feel sympathy and sadness for Anne, perhaps even a deep sense of identification, within the safe boundaries of familiar feelings.

Identifications and Appropriations

Identification with Anne's story has been particularly strong among adolescent girls who feel alienated from their parents while observing their own rapid internal changes with bewilderment and fascination. The diary mirrors their struggle for independence and search for a genuine voice.[5] For adults, Anne is frequently seen as a universalized victim and "symbol of the oppressed." Her diary stands in defiance of in-justice and serves as a "testament to courage, hope, and the faith in human goodness." In some political situations, Anne has functioned as a role model. Nelson Mandela describes how the diary was smuggled into South African prisons during the years of apartheid, giving inmates the will to endure their suffering. Anne has also been an inspiration for writers who recognize and admire in her their own nascent desire to write. These multiple points of identification explain the ongoing, deep impact of the diary, but can also be problematic. Reading the diary as a classic portrait of adolescence, for example, glosses over the anxieties and all-too-real dangers associated with the particular historical context of the Holocaust. Early

Broadway and Hollywood adaptations of the diary demonstrate how Anne's story was transformed into an "infantilized,
Americanized, homogenized and sentimentalized" story of
general human interest that had little, if anything, to do with
Jewish suffering.[6]

Alvin Rosenfeld is troubled by the cultural trend to apply
the term "Holocaust" to a wide range of contexts (from the
AIDS epidemic to the war in Bosnia) and is skeptical of those
who suggest an affinity with Anne when they speak of her as
a "sister" or a "double." Such appeals to a common suffering,
he argues, "flatten history into the shapes we wish it to have."
The Holocaust is then transformed into a trope that expresses
a "personal and collective sense of 'oppression' and 'victimization,'" thereby losing its historical specificity and meaning.
How are we still appropriating and molding Anne Frank's
voice for our own personal or political ends? Does the Chilean
poet Marjorie Agosin fall into this identification trap when—
as a Jew, a woman, a writer, and an exile—she recognizes in
Anne something of herself? In *Dear Anne Frank: Poems*
(1994), she sees themselves connected through the reciprocal
acts of reading and writing: "I name you and you are alive,
Anne, although I died while reading you." They also share a
history of persecution and of being Jews in predominantly
Christian environments. Agosin's family escaped the Holocaust by settling in Chile before she was born and, in her own
life, she left Chile to flee the violence of Pinochet's military
regime. For her, Anne's abrupt end recalls the fate of thousands of victims in Latin America who were abducted and
murdered during the 1970s. "When Chile's military junta
smashed down the doors of our neighborhood to arrest
women—yanking them off by their hair, which would later be
shaved off—when they 'disappeared' them on dense, foggy
nights, I thought of Anne Frank." Like Anne, these *desapare-
cidos* are people without graves. Their deaths filter into
Agosin's poems in the form of decapitations, mutilations, and
rapes that Anne herself did not suffer, but which evoke the
horror of Anne's death. When Agosin writes "the gentlemen of
the Gestapo listened to Mozart" and then "descended to
ephemeral prison cells to bite into your ears, cut off your delicate breasts, your hands of a little princess, to strip you of
your thirteen lived years," she is no longer recalling Anne's

story alone, but rather, torture in its essence—be it in the Nazi concentration camps or in Argentinian and Chilean prisons. The radical disjunction between Anne's image and her end is reflected in this juxtaposition between high culture and barbarism, delicacy and brutality.

In her poetry Agosin initiates an imaginary dialogue with Anne through direct address and questions. She challenges Anne's optimism (Did you really believe that all men were good?), draws attention to things left unsaid (How did you sleep during those nights riddled by airplanes delivering dread?) and inquires about what happened after the diary's end (Was there light behind that barbed fence?). The questions suggest that, if Anne could speak again, she would be unlike the one so many young girls "carry in their hearts, tucked under their arms, in their illusory gazes." Her answers would reflect a voice hardened by the cruelty that followed. Agosin describes how Anne appears to her "emaciated, transformed, like a demon. . . . You and I watching each other, without recognizing each other, with history's equivocal gaze, and you tinge with blood the room and windows." This passage briefly suggests Agosin's awareness of the pitfalls and illusion inherent in her identification with Anne Frank. In defense of her proclaimed kinship, however, she observes that victims' families try to preserve the humanness of the deceased "by means of remembrance that speak the soul's language, that see from within, that question and exclaim." Her poems seek to perform this kind of personal, familial commemoration.

Conclusion

The present collection of writings has been exploring the real and imagined "secret spaces" children create for themselves in different contexts and for a variety of reasons—from play to outright survival. In Anne Frank's case, finding a hiding place was neither a matter of choice nor a game. Next to exile, hiding was one of the few alternatives Jews had to escape or postpone death. Examining this most extreme, literal form of hiding in conjunction with its other, more metaphoric meanings yields a nuanced understanding of the external and internal conditions that created the diary. With the inclusion of five new pages into future editions of the diary, yet another part of Anne Frank's emotional and fantasy life will have been brought out of hiding into the public sphere. With them, the once intimate hideaway will be fully exposed. Just as the diary and its reception reveal different levels of hiding and uncovering, it has, for better or for worse, invited many kinds of identifications and appropriations. The blank page that follows the final signature "Yours, Anne M. Frank" has been and will continue to be an invitation for writers to fill. Their responses may open up new questions and readings between the lines of the diary. It is this multi-layered quality that lies at the heart of the diary's success both as historical testimony and as literature.

NOTES

[1]The different diary versions include a) Anne's original unedited entries beginning June 12, 1942, b) Anne's second diary which she began to revise after March 29, 1944, upon learning that the Dutch government would be collecting diaries and letters as testimony after the war, 3) Otto Frank's edited version of the diary, *The Diary of a Young Girl* (1947), which excluded passages about Anne's sexuality, as well as the unflattering descriptions of the other Annex inhabitants, 4) the unedited version, *The Diary of Anne Frank: The Critical Edition* (1986), which contains all three versions of the diary, as well as biographical essays, other historical materials, and an analysis of Anne's handwriting, 5) and the expanded diary, *The Diary of a Young Girl: The Definitive Edition* (1991), which adds 30% more material to Otto Frank's original version by including the deleted passages.

[2]This transformation of real events into aspects of an imaginary, surrogate world is a common theme in works by and about hidden children (see, for example, George Perec's *W or the Memory of Childhood*, Louis Begley's *Wartime Lies*, Elisabeth Gille's *Shadows of a Childhood*, or Jurek Becker's "The Wall"). These stories function as an escape, a protective shield, an alternative world in which the protagonists can assume more heroic or active roles denied to them in reality.

[3]In her diary *Behind the Veiled Curtain: A Memoir of a Hidden Childhood During World War Two*, Nelly Toll avoids dangerous, potentially incriminating words such as "ghetto" and "Jews." She understands the danger of revealing her Jewishness and uses coded language to help disguise her true origins. "I reasoned that if the Gestapo ever found my writing, they would not realize that I was Jewish and thus would not destroy it! In the foreword of my diary I wrote, 'If I should be killed, at least my *paiçetnik* (memory book) will stay alive so that the whole world can see the terrible things that happened to us.'" The many cheerful, colorful watercolors she painted while in hiding must also be understood as a cover-up or subli-

mation of her actual feelings. They are the inverted, symbolic expression of real and constant fears of being discovered.

[4]See Berteke Waaldijk's "Rereading Anne Frank as a Woman" in *Anne Frank: Reflections on Her Life and Legacy*, ed. Hyman A. Enzer and Sandra Solotaroff-Enzer (2000); Rahel Feldhay Brenner's *Writing as Resistance* (1997), and Catherine A. Bernhard's "Anne Frank: The Cultivation of an Inspirational Victim," in *Modern Thought and Literature* (Winter 1995).

[5]Alvin Rosenfeld attributes Anne Frank's immense popularity to the fact that her story reflects "common teenage fantasies of desire and dread" and recalls for adults the "longings and apprehensions of their youth." The generalized pathos and melancholia the diary evokes, he argues, has undermined our understanding of real Nazi terror.

[6]Bruno Bettleheim, Meyer Levin, Cynthia Ozick, and Robert Alter are among the strongest critics of the two commercially successful adaptations: Albert Hackett and Frances Goodrich's theater adaptation, *The Diary of Anne Frank*, which opened on Broadway in 1955 and won a Pulitzer Prize in 1956, and George Stevens's 1959 film adaptation, based on the play.

WORKS CITED

Agosin, Marjorie. *Dear Anne Frank: Poems*. Translated by Richard Schaaf. Hanover: Brandeis University Press, 1998.

Alter, Robert. "The View from the Attic." *The New Republic* (December 4, 1995).

Frank, Anne. *The Diary of a Young Girl: The Definitive Edition*. New York: Bantam Books, 1997.

Holliday, Laurel. *Children in the Holocaust and World War Two: Their Secret Diaries*. New York: Simon and Schuster, 1995.

Marks, Jane. *The Hidden Children: The Secret Survivors of the Holocaust*. New York: Fawcett Columbine, 1993.

Müller, Melissa. *Anne Frank: The Biography*. Translated by Rita and Robert Kimber. New York: Metropolitan Books, 1998.

Ozick, Cynthia. "A Critic at Large: Who Owns Anne Frank?" *New Yorker* (October 6, 1997).

Rosenfeld, Alvin. "Anne Frank—and Us: Finding the Right Words. *Anne Frank: Reflections on Her Life and Legacy*. Edited by Hyman A. Enzer and Sandra Solotaroff-Enzer. Urbana: University of Illinois Press, 2000.

Toll, Nelly. *Behind the Secret Window: A Memoir of a Hidden Childhood During World War Two*. New York: Dial Books, 1993.

Memoir

Each day I long for home,
Long for the sight of home. . . .
Homer, *The Odyssey*

The dollhouse is a materialized secret; what we look for is the dollhouse
within the dollhouse and its promise of an infinitely profound interiority.
Sarah Stewart, *On Longing*

Helen Sewell and Mildred Boyle, *The End of the Little House Books.*
Final page of the first edition of *These Happy Golden Years*
(Harper, 1943). Courtesy HarperCollins

DIANE ACKERMAN

IN THE MEMORY MINES

I don't remember being born, but opening my eyes for the first time, yes. Under hypnosis many years later, I wandered through knotted jungles of memory to the lost kingdoms of my childhood, which for some reason I had forgotten, the way one casually misplaces a hat or a glove. Suddenly I could remember waking in a white room, with white walls, and white sheets, and a round white basin on a square white table, and looking up into the face of my mother, whose brown hair, flushed complexion, and dark eyes were the only contrast to the white room and daylight that stung her with its brightness. Lying on my mother's chest, I watched the flesh-colored apparition change its features, as if triangles were being randomly shuffled. Then a row of white teeth flashed out of nowhere, dark eyes widened, and I, unaware there was such a thing as motion, or that I was powerless even to roll over, watched the barrage of colors and shapes, appearing, disappearing, like magic scarves out of hats, and was completely enthralled.

What I couldn't know was how yellow I had been, and covered with a film of silky black hair, which made me look even more monkey-like than newborns usually do, and sent my pediatrician into a well-concealed tizzy. He placed the cud-textured being on its mother's chest, smiled as he said, "You have a baby girl," and, forgetting to remove his gloves or even thank the anesthesiologist as was his habit, he left the hospital room to find a colleague fast. Once he had delivered a deformed baby, which came out rolled up like a volleyball, its organs outside its body, and its brain, mercifully, dead. Once he had delivered premature twins, only one of which survived the benign sham of an incubator, and now was a confused, growing teenager he sometimes saw concealing a cigarette outside the high school. Stillborns he had delivered so many times he no longer could remember how many there were, or whose. But never had he delivered a baby so near normal yet brutally different before. He knew that I was jaundiced (which he could treat easily enough), and presumed the hairy coat was due to a hormonal imbalance of some sort, though he understood neither its cause nor its degree. When he found the staff endocrinologist equally puzzled, he decided the best course was not to worry the mother, who was herself not much more than a young girl, and one with a volatile marriage, from what he'd heard from a mutual friend at the country club. He decided he would tell her that the condition was normal—something the baby would outgrow ("like life," he thought cynically)—and prescribed a drug for the jaundice, lifting the clipboard in the maternity office with one hand and writing the prescription carefully, in an unnecessarily ornate script, which was his only affectation. As he did so, New York State seemed to him suddenly shabby and outmoded, like the hospital on whose cracked linoleum he stood; like the poor practice he conducted on the first floor of his old, street-front, brick house, whose porch slats creaked at the footstep of each patient so that, at table or in his study, or even lying down on the sofa in the den wallpapered with small tearoses, he would hear that indelible creaking and be halfway across the room before his wife knew he hadn't merely taken a yen for a dish of ice cream or gone to fetch a magazine from the waiting room; like the apple-cheeked woman he had married almost 25 years ago, when she was slender and prankish and such a willing chum; like the best clothes of most of his patients, who had made it through the Depression by doing with less until less was all they wanted; like the shabby future of this hairy little baby, on whom fate had played an as-yet unspecified trick. It was that compound malaise that my mother saw on Dr. Petersen's face as she glanced over the clean, well-used crib at her bedside and out of the hospital window just as Dr. Petersen was walking to his car to drive home for lunch and a short nap before his afternoon hours.

My mother let her eyes drowse over the crib, where her baby, a summoned life, was lying on its stomach, knees out like a tiny gymnast, still faintly yellow, and still covered with a delicate down. If anything, she found me more vulnerable, a plaintive little soul whose face looked rumpled as an unmade bed when it cried, and whose eyes could be more eloquent than a burst of sudden speech. She sang softly as she held my tiny life in her arms, my every whim and need encapsulated in a body small as a trinket, something she could carry in the crook of her arm. How could there be a grownup in so frail and pupal a creature, one so easily frightened, so easily animated, so utterly dependent on her for everything but breath? If only her husband could be there to see her, she thought, as she watched my hand move like a wayward crab across the sheet, if only he could have gotten leave to be with her. There was no telling how long it would take the Red Cross to get word to him that he had a baby girl. And what would he make of such news, anyway, in a foxhole somewhere in the middle of France, with civilians and soldiers dying all around him, at his hands even, what would he make of bringing this new civilian into the world? Though nearly over, the war seemed endless. The radio had run out of see-you-when-the-war-is-over songs. His letters were infrequent and jaggedly expressed, not that they'd talked much or even politely before he'd left. Marrying him had been like walking into a typhoon. But once in it, her pride had prevented her from returning to her parents' house in Detroit. They had warned her about marrying a man as "difficult" as he was, and, anyway, they still had so many children at home to feed and clothe on her dad's poor salary. She had always been a trouble to them, wanting to go to the fairyland of "college," when there were six other children to give minimum schooling, then running off with him when life on the South Side became suffocating. If she couldn't be a good daughter, or a good wife it would seem (no matter how pliable she tried to be), she could at least be a good mother to this odd little being. When would he return? In shameful moments, she almost wished he wouldn't; it would mean a reprieve, a chance to start life over with someone who shared more of her interests and barked at her less over trivial matters like his fried potatoes not being as crisp as he wished when he walked in the door at 7 p.m. and wanted nothing from the world but a perfect, ready dinner. His mother had always managed it for the menfolk in her family, for whom she'd baked and cooked and tended all afternoon, until they walked in hungry and demanding at nightfall, and he demanded it from his wife, period. It was the least she could do while he was out working hard to earn money for the bread she ate, etc. etc. No, he would probably return from war, and life would go on, though perhaps the experience would mellow him. If not. . .well, she could always have another baby. She looked at me. Just imagine, the baby was alive and didn't even know that. What a helpless, lovable bundle she had created! She spent the rest of the afternoon watching me and fantasizing about my limitless future.

My infant years might have happened in an aquarium, so silent and full of mixing shapes were they. How strange that a time filled with my own endless wailings, gurglings, and the soothing coos and baby-talk of my mother should remain in my memory as a thick, silent dream in which clearer than any sound was the blond varnish on my crib, whose pale streaky gloss I knew like a birthmark, as it was for so many months of my life. At one, six months is half of a lifetime, and for half my lifetime I'd lain in my crib watching how the blond wood bars seemed to stretch from floor to ceiling, my mother's hands coming over them, though it seemed nothing could be higher. My mother's hands always appeared with a smile on her face, which I knew only as a semicircle that amazed me with its calm delight which each day renewed. It would rise over my crib like one of those devastating moons you can't take your eyes off of. I would knit my forehead, perplexed for a moment, and then smile without thinking about it, and my mother's soft hand would stretch over the bars to touch me, though the touch I couldn't remember in later years, nor any sound. It was a time of shapes and colors, and the puzzling changes in the air as the day moved and I could see the sunlight on a thousand flecks of milling dust, watch the sky turn blue as a bead, then strange, vapory colors ghost through the dark and frighten me before night fell. It was a time of complete passivity and ignorance. Odd things happened to me which I could neither explain nor predict. Life was like that, full of caretakers appearing over my crib wall, sometimes carrying things with shapes and colors so vibrant they startled me, things that would ring or chatter or huff. Long, ribboned, shiny things I found especially monstrous, and sometimes a shocking blue or yellow would be so intense it made my ribs shiver and my eyes scrunch closed. When that happened, the caretaker's face would change like a Kabuki mask, and through my wet, twitching eyes, I would see the moon-mask waiting, watching, filled with delight. The moon shone on me daily. Often, in the black ether I sometimes woke in, when the blond crib varnish was nowhere to be found, I could sense the moon's presence standing nearby and watching me, feel its warm breath and know it was close, transfixed by my every stirring. Sometimes the moon would vanish for long spells and my ribs would shake. Sometimes the moon would appear, all angles like a piece of broken glass, though usually that happened only when another face, shattery and florid, was there, too. To see their faces shuffle and twist scared me, though I didn't know what "scared" was exactly, only that my bones felt too large for my body, my eyes seemed to draw closer together, and I forgot everything but the grating noise, the awful, scraping barks. My thoughts, such as they were, were like a dog's or an ape's. Things happened, but what a thing was I didn't know, nor could I fathom the idea of happen. Not thoughts, but images paraded through my days, and feelings I couldn't associate with anything special like a part of my body or a soft blanket. I was like a plastic doll, except that I was, and, if death had taken me, I would not have known it. There was no confusion, no thought, no sentiment, no want. But, for some reason, the blond crib wood pleased me. I touched it with my eyes, I drank it, I smelled its glossy shimmer. When I watched it, I was not with my body but with the wood. I explored its details for long, blond hours; then I explored the sunlight catching dust in the air. Each time I explored them, or a fluffy being put next to me, or a twirling color-flock above me, it was as if I had stepped onto another planet where nothing was but that sight, nothing mattered, nothing gave me deeper pleasure, nothing came to mind.

At two, most of my excess body hair had fallen off like scales, except for a triangular swathe above my fanny, and a single silky stripe from my ribs to my pudendum. My skin softened to the buttery translucence of a two-year-old's, and my black hair made me look like an Inca. Things had names. All animals were "dog," all people were "mommy" or "daddy," but my voice could follow my pointing finger, and when it did it was almost like touching. I was enchanted equally by oddly shaped animals and kitchen utensils, and the maple jungle of recoiling legs below the dining room table. My world stopped at the shadowy heights of the closet, but some things were close to me that were lost to my mother—the clawed plastic brackets holding the bottom of the long mirror in my parents' bedroom, the heavy ruffles along the sofa that tickled my knees when I climbed up to straddle the armrest and play horsey, the sheet of glass on top of the low coffee table, into whose edge I would peer each day for long, dizzying spells, transfixed by the bright, rippling green waves I saw there.

Some parts of the house had no mystery, and consequently I never visited them. For example, the two closets facing each other in the tiny foyer. Long ago, I'd discovered nothing of any interest was in them, just overcoats, scarves, boots, and drab clothes in cellophane cleaning bags. Toys for Christmas or birthdays were hidden in the bathroom closet upstairs, the one I could just reach at three years old by standing on the toilet, leaning forward until I could brace one foot on the windowsill, and then leaping onto the lowest plywood shelf while grabbing hold of an upper bracket with one hand. I could swiftly explore with the other before I fell onto the bathmat. Only once had I actually touched a box, but I could see them up high, brightly colored and covered with unfamiliar words that soon enough I would know by heart. Games I had tired of were kept there, as well, forgotten so completely I thought they were brand new. Sometimes, while I was banging down the long flight of carpeted stairs on my fanny, as I loved to do and always did when my mother wasn't around to scold me for it, it would occur to me that I had played with such and such a toy before, long ago, almost beyond remembering. Early one morning, I walked into my parents' bedroom, and stood by my mother's side of the bed. Slowly my mother opened her eyes and, seeing me standing so close to her, smiled a spontaneous full-hearted smile. She held my tiny hand for a moment, enraptured by her child's presence. Then, reassured by the rightness of all things, I scampered out of the room, walked down the hallway whose boards creaked even when my slight weight strained them, jumped into the carpeted stairwell as if it were a lifeboat, and gleefully bumped down the stairs on my fanny.

It was a lonely world for me, my mother knew, what with my father on the road selling until late at night, and my mother herself making ends meet by canvassing for long hours on the telephone. Half the money she made she put in an account my father didn't know about, just in case she one day had the courage to bundle me up and leave him. I had turtles and fish and dolls to play with, but no children who lived close enough to be casual with. And, often, I would come to her mopey in the middle of the day, complaining pathetically that I was "bored." How could a three-year-old be bored, she wondered, and where could I even have learned such a word? Then she would feel sorry for me and devise some games with empty egg-cartons or paper bags and crayons I could play at her feet while she continued telephoning anonymous users of unnecessary products to ask them intrusive questions about their laundry or eating habits or television viewing. Oddest of all was my father's response to me. Perhaps it was because he was away when I was born, or because he feared being vulnerable and weak, or because he had not been raised in a demonstrative home himself, but whatever tenderness I sought upset him. He recoiled at the thought of brushing my hair or bathing me. My lidless appetite for love and attention suffocated him. My zest made him nervous, perhaps because it seemed faintly erotic, and that aroused in him feelings that disgusted and frightened him. And whenever I ran to him, as I did mainly on Sundays, since I rarely saw him during the week, he would always find ways and reasons for not holding me, turning his head when I tried to kiss him, keeping me just out of reach when I wanted to snuggle. My mother wondered how such a revulsion could be, and, if she dared to broach the subject with him, he would yell and storm out of the room, muttering "Women! Always some nagging, pea-brained nonsense!" and other irate things, until, finally, she thought the scenes worse for me than the withheld affection.

At four, I had a tower of gaily colored, plastic records, and I knew how to make them sing on the toy record player. But for long hours I would listen to a slow, plaintive song, "Farewell to the Mountains," which I played over and over, as I sat on the living room rug and grew more and more withdrawn. What would a four-year-old dream about? My mother often wondered when she saw me like that, and wondered too if it was normal for a child to be so subdued. But to find out she would have had to have spoken to someone—a friend, a doctor, or, most horrifying of all, perhaps even a psychiatrist, which was a shame only whispered about in nice families. In fact, it was no longer possible for such a family to be "nice" at all, if one of its members admitted to insanity by seeking a psychiatrist. My mother shuddered at the thought, as she fed stray wisps of hair back into her pageboy, and checked her list for the next household to call about their consumption of presweetened cereal. She could hear "Farewell to the Mountains" softly wailing in the next room, and knew I would be sitting inertly by the speaker, dreaming of whatever things a four-year-old dreamt of. A new doll, perhaps, or a dog . . . my experience was so limited, thank goodness; how could the daydreams hurt me? She lifted a pencil with which to dial the next number, so as not to callus her index finger. In less than a year, I would be going to kindergarten, with play-mates and things to do, and life would be smoother.

In the living room, while my lugubrious record repeated, I dreamt of escape, of life beyond the windowpanes, of gigantic trees that led into magic kingdoms, of strange, cacophonous an-imals, and endless kisses and hugs, and a giant dollhouse in which I could live, and flowers so big and perfumed I could crawl into them to sleep, and, most of all, I dreamt of a sleek black horse which I had seen on television and had been utterly thrilled by. How it had reared and flailed when people tried to get near it. How it arched its tail and shone in the dazzling sunlight, when it ran up the side of a mountain. How it lath-ered and whinnied and looked ready to explode. I dreamt of playing with the frantic black horse which would scare and ex-cite me and, sometimes, if I were very good, let me get close enough to stroke and ride. Together we would run out to those flat, funny-bushed prairies that stretched forever and we would make the sound of rain falling as we galloped. On her way to bed, my mother would peek in on me, and most days she would find me wide awake at midnight, lying quietly in my bed like a tiny Prince of Darkness, my brain raw as henna, just pacing, pacing. If insomnia was unusual for a child, it was normal for me. There was a switch in my cells that wouldn't turn off at night, which is not to say that I was one of those rare few who could get by with little sleep and wake to conquer the world. If I slept badly, I was tired the next day, and, since most days I slept badly, I was mostly tired. Dark circles formed under my eyes, and I looked oddly debauched for a four-year-old girl. Once, my mother gave me a quarter of one of her sleeping pills, and out of that cruel prankishness of which children seem the liveliest masters, I had pretended not to be able to wake up the next morning, even though my mother shook and shook me. When I finally deigned to open my eyes and fake a spontaneous

yawn, I found my mother in a cold sweat and the most attentive and adoring spirit, which lasted all day. After that, she just
let me grope for sleep by myself, but insisted on a ritual "going
to bed" at 8 p.m., since at the very least I would then get some
rest from lying still.

It was hard to say who looked forward most to my going to
school. Six times my mother practiced the route with me, holding my hand as we walked though the vest-pocket-sized plum
orchard that separated my street from Victory Park Elementary School. There was a more conventional way of getting
there, of course, full of sidewalks and rigid corners and car-in-
fested streets, but it was twice as long and meant crossing
three intersections. My mother preferred to lead me across the
street my house sat on and watch me as I walked down the
well-worn shortcut leading almost unswervingly through the
orchard. Only one part of the path, twenty yards or so, dipped
behind a stand of bushes and out of view. But at that point I
would be able to see the crosswalk guard clearly, since she was
always there, to-ing and fro-ing in her yellow jacket and bright
red sash. Perhaps another mother in another city would have
been frightened to let her five-year-old walk into an orchard
alone each day, but in my hometown crime was not a problem.
As I had discovered, boredom was. And the orchard was full of
such extravagant smells and sights: low, scuffly hunchbacked
things with long tails, chaplinesque squirrels that looked like
grey mittens when they climbed trees, mump-cheeked chip-
munks, insects that looked like tiny buttons or tanks, feathered
shudders in high nests, chattery seedpods, and tall, silky flowers with long red tongues hanging out. Best of all I liked to see
the ripe plums, huddled like bats high above me. With my Roy
Rogers tablet in one hand, and a brown bag lunch in the other,
I would go to school each day in a fine mood because I knew I
had the orchard to look forward to. Then, too, I liked this new
business of dressing up: purple corduroy pinafore, grey check
with a lace collar, red and white jumper striped like a candy-
cane. White ankle socks, black patent leather shoes, matching
ribbon. I would take my seat in the classroom and do the
lessons and play the game and sing the songs, and in the afternoon I would come home again, through the orchard alive with
buzzing and twittering, at the other side of which would be my

mother, dependable as sunlight, waiting in a pale shirtwaist dress, her hair curled into a long pageboy roll.

The novelty of school lasted only a few months. The lessons were dull, the games were always the same, the other children were so distant and alien. They seemed to share a secret I alone didn't know. What they said was different, what they laughed at was different, what they saw was different. When I drew the plum bats curled high in the trees, or used six crayons to draw a rock, which everybody knows is grey, *airhead*, they teased me mercilessly, or, worse, ignored me for hours. Most of all, I liked running games in which I ran until I dropped in an exhausted heap, or spun around in circles until I got dizzy. Next to that, I liked looking at the butterfly and rock collections in the science locker, and sometimes I would spend all of recess playing with the kaleidoscope. The other children played jacks, or marbles, or house, or cowboys. I liked cowboys, but wanted to be the horse, not a man shooting nonstop and pretending to die. In time, I discovered the knack of talking like the others, but it was hard to sustain, and though I dearly wanted the friendship of the other children, nothing I could do seemed to endear me to them. I was different; it was as if I had spots or a tail. I hovered on the edge of elementary social life, making a friend here, a friend there, mainly among the boys, who didn't mind including me in their running and jumping games, where more bodies made little difference. At home, my father had begun taking photographs with a Kodak box camera he had bought at a flea-market, snapshots of the family and neighbors on special days like Fourth of July or Christmas. The first time I saw a photograph it was as if a bucketful of light had been poured over me. In the picture people were always smiling, frozen happy forever. I pestered my father to take more and more pictures, and pleaded until he let me keep a few from each roll, to line up on my pink, Humpty-Dumpty decaled dresser next to the bed. With my dolls sitting rigid in a semicircle on the bed, and all the smiling faces in the photographs, I had quite a large gathering for mock tea-parties and classrooms and cowboys and family fights, in one of which a doll's pudgy plastic arm snapped off.

Though I knew the orchard well, and loved to play in its chin-high weeds, bopping the teasel heads with a bat, or hunting for "British Soldiers," red-capped fungi, among the blankets of

green moss, my sense of geography was very poor. Getting anywhere was a blur. The world seemed without boundary,
unimaginable and infinite. Even though, on most days, I had no
desire to go farther than my neighborhood, I sensed the world
dropped off at a perilous angle just beyond it. I was frightened
at the literal perimeter of what I knew. Had I been a grownup, I
might have been reminded of the Duke Ellington song, "There's
Nothing on the Brink of What You Think." What did I fear? I
didn't know. It was not a rational fear. Just as wailing for my
mother if we became separated in a supermarket was not a rational act. I just feared. But the fear fled when I was with a
gang of children strolling the neighborhood as we did each Halloween when, often, we would go as far afield as three or four
streets away, bags laden, ready to perform the simple acrobatics it took to con strangers out of sweet booty. Spreading my
loot on the living room floor afterwards, I would go through it
with my mother, who adored sifting the haul and always got all
of the Mary Janes, which I loathed the taste of.

One day, as if a typhoon had just ended, my father died of an
ailment that sounded to me like "pullman throbs," and thus disappeared from my life the same stranger he had always been, a
lodger who directed my life with his shouts, who had absolute
control over my fate, and could not be appealed to by tears or
reason. He had been an omnipotent, mysterious stranger who
left the house before I got up each morning and came home
after I went to sleep each night, and on weekends was sullen
and tired. He only ever seemed to read the paper or watch television or sleep or yell at my mother or slam the door to their
bedroom, after which I would sometimes hear my mother crying. For some reason he never had time for me. In my heart, I
knew it must be my fault, that I must be somehow unworthy of
his love, his attention even, the way the newspaper or television at least had his attention. I understood deep down in my
soul that something serious must be wrong with me, that I
lacked something—I wasn't pretty enough, or smart enough, or
funny enough. . . . I didn't know what quality exactly—whatever that alchemical thing was, I lacked it. Otherwise he would
surely have loved me. I had tried in prismatically different
ways to delight him, to please him, ultimately to win him. Some
mornings I would spend fifteen minutes choosing the right ribbon—checked versus striped, plain edged or lace, flat cotton or

broad glossy satin—and then tug on my embroidered ankle socks, and deliberate over the dresses in my closet as if I were a floosie primping for the man who brought my chocolates and cheap jewelry on Sundays. I was like a war-bride with a shell-shocked husband at home, attentive to his every whim, trying hard to reconstruct their tender armistices. After so many silent, private years, I seemed suddenly to be an extrovert, and my mother delighted in the long-awaited change toward what she saw as a normal, if hyperactive, childhood. Without understanding why exactly, I would play the clown whenever my father was around, dancing little jigs, doing impressions of TV characters, pretending to be a dog by fetching his slippers in my mouth and then sitting up in front of him as he read the newspaper in the enormous, rose-colored armchair by the picture window, my tiny hands lifted and loosely flapping like paws. Sometimes I would bake him ginger cookies, his favorite, which my mother would let me cut with bright red plastic cookie cutters shaped like men and women, clowns, and Christmas trees, into which I would press candy buttons and eyes. When he was around, I would follow him like a tropic flower the sun, needy, riveted, always open for warmth. Sometimes he would take me on his knees, or pat my head lightly, and, when he did, I would feel happy and even-hearted all day. But most days he simply ignored me, or yelled at me for pestering him, and, when he did, I would try extra hard to please him. I would eat my food without playing with it first, though I loved taking dollops of mashed potatoes in my hands and rolling them into balls for a snowman, which I would stand on the rim of my plate while I ate. Once, for Sunday lunch, mother and I concocted a "Happy Jack" out of a tomato, tunafish salad, and a hard-boiled egg, scooping out the tomato, filling it with tunafish, and toothpicking the egg upright in the middle. I painted paprika eyes and mouth onto the egg with a wet finger, stuck in a whole clove for a nose, and then attached the cut-away tomato lid with a toothpick to make a beret. Then I dressed up in my Halloween clown suit, and presented it to my father on a dinner plate. He laughed out loud, and hugged my shoulders by wrapping one of his enormous arms around them, and that pleased me so much I was contented for days. But nothing less extreme seemed to waylay his thoughts, which were always galloping away from me. Then he died, and it was as if a door had slammed shut. There was no warning, no reassurance; he just left. Though I had not gone to the funeral, I understood that dead meant being broken beyond repair, as my mother had explained it, and could see that, when it happened, grownups cried torrentially and then walked around gloomy and snuffling for days, as if they shared a secret cold. I understood that he was gone now on weekends, too, and that he had left without saying goodbye to me, though perhaps, surely, he had said goodbye to my mother. While he lived, he would at least wave when he left. Now there was not even that. Now I could no longer even try to please him. Without meaning to, I reverted to my sullen, dreamy ways. My mother shook her head and, without going into details, told friends that his death had come "at the worst possible time for everyone."

The last instruction I received as each hypnotic session came to a close was that I would remember only what I felt comfortable with. It was a relative fiat, and it worked, letting just enough of my subterranean past seep through to give me a sense of origin, of development, without reminding me of any war-crimes that might alarm me. And so it was no surprise that in my waking life I remembered little of my recaptured childhood: its sensory delights, a few events, and its tense, poignant moods. Whether or not a crucial drama lay salted away in my memory, I never knew. Once, coming out of the well of a trance, I noticed my eyes were sore and my nose blocked from crying. Where had I gone? Toward a sexual event? A violent one? I didn't know. At first, the childhood I began discovering mystified me, its iceberg fragments were so high-focus and yet remote. And what was there between the fragments I didn't wish to remember? But gradually, as slants of my past surfaced, I felt like I had adopted a child on the installment plan, a child that was myself, and it felt good suddenly to be part of a community, even if it was only a community of previous selves.

THYLIAS MOSS

THE GENEROSITY OF
ARPEGGIOS AND RAVENS

Please note: The following is an arpeggio.

It was possible to leap from world to world using the sturdiest balloons I'd ever seen. They didn't move despite what should have been the effect of so much unified breathing; they didn't move, but they moved the congregation to song. Such worlds. Such balloons. They had short black tails and were solid black themselves, resting on parallel thin black lines of number seventeen, "How Great Thou Art," some of them arpeggios for the right hand of the organist alone. And in each world, I was there, a guest inside the notes, one of which was High-C# in which a cathedral was guest also—I sensed its height, breadth, and depth even though it was pitch black, all the atmosphere, all estimates, every window pitch black, and there were thousands of windows on both sides of which a thousand birds sang all the dark day, there was only day, and I was never able to touch the ceiling of the cathedral, and the cathedral never touched the ceiling of the note, and the note never reached its own ceiling, for it was a sound reverberating blackly, for everything there was black and in that unity, endless also. Endless unseen dark presences felt. The note echoed only because there were ceilings and walls around which the sound bounced all the dark day, syncopating the choruses of birds whose wings may have been the ceilings and walls. O blessed density and magnitude of cooperation. This was the generosity of arpeggios and ravens. This for a six-year-old who otherwise had to contend with monstrosity.

I enjoyed the volleying of praises in High-C#, a world every hymn didn't contain, a world I didn't want every hymn to contain, so when there, it was an occasion. The exceptional easily persuaded me, even exceptional cruelty when I found it while in the care of a young sadist who tended a fecund garden of despair; how she hurt with bruises and the possibility of knives the outside of the edifice, the only part of me that she knew existed, the part that became the least of me as the most explored the geographies of Elsewhere, some of which existed in pages, the sound of them turning in the library (that was to me a convent for books) such a relaxed unrushed motor it could not have existed on Lytta's earth. When I riffled pages to allow books to breathe, sometimes words and parts of words flew out, High-C#s of alphabet. There was and there remains Lytta's influence, active (though not controlling) in what I've chosen so far to say, but despite the fuller effect of her when she was a literal operative most weekdays, I built cathedrals, perhaps unlit, perhaps the usual incandescence bypassed because of her (for she was limited to obvious arenas), but cathedrals they indeed were—of arpeggios and ravens she has never seen. Such materials.

There was a time that I hoped the stained glass of the Masonic Temple was really just windows cut from massive blocks of obsidian or agate—for nature delights in manufacturing extraordinary blemish, magnificent defect. Beauty most unbearable must be unplanned, unrehearsed; nothing could bear its schemed production. So cut thin, no—thinner obsidian and agate slices reminiscent of a time of rationing or a time of disdain for excess. This world may not abide this presence always. So cut them so thin the windows are always on the verge of breaking. And every moment that they don't break is to be understood as miracle. Why not? I lived and hoped in such a world in which my only assigned role was architect. The world that contained this obsidian world was one where others could and did act against me, but the High-C# world of obsidian windows was known to no one other than me. Nothing in the worlds of notes spoke, but sometimes the birds on either side of the obsidian windows were vaulting and flying words, and I plucked some of their feathers for poems, even wrote some of the poems with some of the plucked feathers. Nothing inhabiting the worlds could speak to betray the worlds—how great are those strung-up worlds to be so closed to violation; how impossible to get by the treble and bass clef gates except as hymn. Don't ask me what the preacher was saying in the world I left behind.

In church I listened most closely to the prayers, the richest ones in baritone and alto, but somewhere in all of them, even in Sis. Ester's over-stretched soprano in which some noted syllables were so high, no one could hear them; even in the soundless fractures of her prayers at altar call were requests that followed gratitude, favors that only had to be asked for to have them granted. I never tried the beseeching, did not want to ask for things because I had them all, tyranny in a baby-sitter and delight in the world my parents made, the world in which I provided all the gravity, all the radiance. They elevated me in ways that most children of my generation (perhaps of any generation) were not. They both solicited and followed my advice, and lived with me in a world within another, a world only we could enter, only we could locate. The geography of that world's stunning splendor I laid out in a recent memoir, so will leave the details to those pages, but with or without the details, it was paradise that saved me, the one I knew was real, our part of the duplex that Lytta's family owned. My address was sanctuary. Sanctuary was arpeggio. Our part of the duplex was one of the arpeggio's notes—and so was my mind—and so was the library—and so was Louis Pasteur elementary school—and so was the lined paper on which I wrote so many arpeggios of words. But to access those places it was necessary to navigate the tyranny, to see and try to comprehend the unbearable beauty of a world in which I saw how few were exempt from the tyranny, not the boy killed on his bike when I watched a truck hit him in the street between the library and a hospital; not the boy whose death came slowly after nails were hammered into his head by boys whom I liked to think didn't know the hammered one was in the box that was their trampoline, but I knew, from a few feet away in the sanctity (in the world) of a thorny bush that produced inedible berries, that the box was occupied, that for some it was an emergency toilet, and that for all who used it, it was some sort of convenience; and not the girl who learned to fly in every world except the one in which she jumped from a balcony fleeing either a rapist or a burning building—sometimes I confuse the worlds, especially worlds visited just once, for in no other did a girl jump from a balcony, and in no other did I fail to catch something falling toward me.

There was no light in the hallway leading to downstairs and Lytta's kitchen door, so the hallway became a tunnel dug only halfway to China and the paradise on the other side of the world. Halfway was the basement where the furnace stood rigid as a tree, its pipes and ducts metallic branches suffering an enchantment with the Tinman. The last steel tree of his forest. The coolness down there fascinated me, the constant coolness despite the source of the house's heat. As if the sun would not have to burn me if, grateful, I approached it. Also the basement was retreat when thunderstorms exercised their necessary rages during which some spawned tornadoes to put icing on what the thunderstorm's gale force winds had already stirred up. Cool and dull-dark, not the perfect darkness of the arpeggio's cathedral. The underground was gray, outlines remained apparent in the basement's always twilight; even after midnight twilight was maintained by the light of a street lamp whose yellowish glow filtered muted through the window from which the Contact paper was peeling, and from which the paint under the Contact paper had been scraped. My birthday parties were celebrated down there as well, the candles on every cake (usually three cakes) providing the only light, and it seemed that Roman candles sparked every February. But this region was also Lytta's, and to claim it she marked it with violations of my body, her cousin's body, and my life-size doll that actually felt the knife. I felt flesh, every form of its weakness; the cousin felt both a heated soleplate and my five nails that were trying not to draw a music staff on a fresh Indianapolis cheek, but what dark chalk can exert its will even if it has will? Lytta was composing on a cousin, manipulating five pens at once, and I was placing arpeggios on the bleeding staff under my obedient five fingers. Arpeggios of cathedrals. Cathedrals of obsidian feathers and beaks. Read my stories from when I was six, seven, eight; read of events all of which are impossible in this world, but that in my architecture of words still stand unchanged. The house Lytta built is gone. She did not exist in a single arpeggio, and when I was singing I couldn't pronounce her name; it wasn't part of the language of song. Thoroughly untranslatable despite an ascending sonic beauty if the name names someone, something else.

Only in a few things did I want permanence, consistency, predictability; mine was seldom a yearning for universals. I wanted worlds ever confounding to prophets and fortune-tellers; so many worlds within worlds, prophets and fortune-tellers had no way of knowing how many, no hope of visiting them all, for hope was denied prophets and fortune-tellers whose gift instead was foreknowing. I could look, you must understand, into things and know something, such as into my hand where I could see how narrow the roads of escape were (one needed to be as small as I was to navigate them) and how they led to falling off the edge of a flat palm; all worlds weren't round. Long ago, scholars, theologians, and cartographers weren't aware (after finally lifting roundness from heresy) that they had merely misidentified which world was the flat world. I could look into my father's morning coffee and in the way the cream swirled into it see promises practically disappear; all that persisted was their influence, their ability to lighten the burden of being unadulterated, being pure and certain. It was influence that made the difference, influence such as how slush and dirty sidewalk pools of rain shined my father's shoes so that by the time he walked from the bus stop to home, his feet arrived in gleaming Stacy Adams vehicles; his wet tracks glowed on the pavement, on the kitchen's linoleum, the braided rug. O that we hadn't cleaned away the shine, my mother and I; O that we hadn't stripped the floor of a kind of flat crown blessed by the soles of his feet. So dusty now are the shoes, and so narrow that only one person in the family has any hope of ever wearing those shoes (my feet are narrow enough, not long enough), but he is too small at the moment, and who knows all that can stunt growth? There are cracks in the shoes that are right now in my mother's attic in their original box, cracks across the vamps and across the perforated toe caps so that the shoes have taken on the design of his hands, his hands I know because our hands gripped identical maps, heralding from the same place, heading to the same places not mapped on any other map; and the tongues of the shoes are patterned also, like, well, tongues, but none of his survivors (none of whom are fortune-tellers) know whose taste is being modeled.

Of course, there's more about obsidian, but only this bit of the more must be said: We walked, my father and I, from world to world, and in one of them I found a piece of obsidian, smoky toned; held up and looked through in light, it still suggests a dark, rudimentary amber and prompts a search for insects, preferably at least one with outspread wings so thin it's necessary to believe that the wings are made of old honey, first honey. What beautiful windows could be cut from it, miniature windows of outspread wings whose designs, whose lines that hold the honey seem nets, honey traps; it should be wings that eventually ensnare me. The obsidian sits on my desk. My sons thought I had a piece of glass bottle, maybe I do; maybe it's a shank of one of my father's Mr. Boston bottles; maybe it's a piece of what I could find after the neighborhood declined and something volcanic seemed to have happened; lots of glass, obsidian scattered like heavy persistent rain, but what windows I still see in it and through it because I opened such windows when I was six—and didn't close them. There was no secret; the cathedral was too vast, the arpeggio too resonant. There was just the need to use my other eyes, the eyes I designed to see it. I think of these eyes—there are as many pairs of eyes as there are arpeggios—as somewhat like masses of roe, glistening, so delicious after one has a taste for it, a reason for it, an appropriate occasion.

One appropriate day, the cathedral took the form of a man. Everything he said was arpeggio. Everything he did was raven. I married him in every world.

CAROLYN GAGE

MY LIFE AMONG THE DOLLS; OR HOW I BECAME A RADICAL FEMINIST PLAYWRIGHT

My career in theatre began at an early age, when I realized that reality was going to kill me.

Raised in an environment of terror where my father had license to act on his irrational and sadistic impulses without fear of reprisals, I learned that it was possible to create another world, one where justice could prevail. Even more miraculously, I found that I could inhabit this world at will. It was, of course, a trick done with mirrors—or, more accurately, a trick done with those brilliant, refractory shards of a shattered identity, but it did enable me to survive the horrors of my childhood.

Everything in my universe as a child was sentient and animate, except for other human beings—especially adults. Like the images of Godzilla or King Kong in the old movies, grownups lumbered mechanically across the enchanted landscape of my childhood, obviously inorganic and superimposed—their outsize scale rendering their atrocities fantastical.

My world was a subtle one, not visible to them. It was a world of spirits, of fairies, of dragons, of pixies, of sorcerers, of fairy godmothers. It was a world I created wherever a stand of trees offered an umbrella of shelter to a little girl, wherever rainwater had pooled itself inside a rotten tree stump, wherever the roots of a large tree twisted themselves over the mossy ground. Nature was my great companion, and my co-conspirator.

It required more inventiveness to accommodate the fairy world indoors, but the stakes being high, I managed. Wherever I went, I carved out little toeholds for magic, crafting habitats for miniature beings in the dark corners of my desk at school, on the top shelf of my locker, in the corner of my closet behind the clothes, on the soap ledge of the bathtub, among the ridges and valleys of the blankets of my bed.

More often than not, these spaces were peopled by my dolls. I had a set of plastic dolls three inches high that I could transport with me like a kind of emergency first aid kit for the imagination. At school, I crafted fragile dolls for my desk out of Kleenex, rubber bands, clay, and pencils. But my *real* family, my primary collection of dolls, was housed at the ground zero of my abuse, in the bedroom.

My dollhouse was enormous, occupying an entire wall of my room. It was four feet high and six feet wide, made up of eight rooms and a garden patio. It had a ballroom, a throne room, and a treasure vault, and I called it "The Palace." Built for me by my cousins, it consisted of three tiers of rough plywood boxes and a moveable flight of stairs. I papered the rooms with sticky-backed vinyl paper, and covered the patio with floral fabric. I built a throne out of small cardboard boxes and tinfoil, and furnished the rooms of the palace with other articles of my own invention. I was never concerned with how others might view the dollhouse, because its function was to stand in for my imagination.

During my childhood, Queen Victoria's dollhouse was touring the country, and I remember how excited I was when I read about this, the most famous dollhouse in the world. I expected it to be a gateway into a realm of utter enchantment, a dollhouse that would raise my pleasure of fantasy to unimaginable heights.

To my disgust, Queen Victoria's dollhouse did nothing of the kind. It was the opposite of everything I thought a dollhouse should do, leaving nothing at all to the imagination. In fact, it forbade it entrance. It was as if there were a red velvet cord in front of every room of the dollhouse, with a placard reading, "Do not imagine." It was apparent even at a glance that the dollhouse had been built by adults, for adults. Everything in it was a meticulously crafted, miniature reproduction, an immaculate replica of furniture and fixtures from the adult world. Exactitude, not inventiveness, had become the index of cleverness. Money was everywhere apparent. Scavenging, the ethical core of my interactions with the adult world, was nowhere in evidence. Everything was *accessible* to adults—completely. What had been the point of the dollhouse? How was it that this child Victoria had allowed this appropriation of her only native territory? Had she embraced her oppression, self-colonized her own childhood? And was the massive colonial hegemony of Great Britain during the Victorian era the revenge of a thwarted child, the result of a misidentification with her perpetrators and their need to strip away all that was native, taboo, mystical, inaccessible to western eyes, and replace it with the sterile replicas of British so-called civilization?

My later orientation toward the stage would reflect this early experience. The bare stage has always been, in my opinion, the best setting for a play, because it permits the audience to conspire with the playwright. Whenever I enter a theatre with a "Queen Victoria's dollhouse" set, I see a red velvet cord stretched across the fourth wall, inviting me to admire but not participate.

The dolls were the focus of my life for almost ten years. There were more than fifty of them, acquired as gifts or as hand-me-downs, and occasionally as found persons. They each had names and specific personalities, and they each had their own place in the palace hierarchy. The queen of the dollhouse was Ginny, my first doll—who, coincidentally, resembled my first girlfriend, the golden-haired and blue-eyed, six-year-old Mary Warren. Mary Warren had been a sunny, simple girl who accepted as her due the fact that she was cherished by her family. Where my world was multilayered and treacherous, requiring vast amounts of energy to reconcile or repress the overwhelming incoherence of atrocity, hers was a garden of delights from which anything unpleasant or harmful had already been banished.

Mary Warren was an angel to me, and in her company I had a taste of heaven. And on those glorious occasions when Mary Warren would agree to spend the night with me, I would create elaborate scenarios based on the fairy tales I consumed so voraciously, in which the bedroom would be transformed into an enchanted forest where we would build shelters for ourselves by draping bedspreads and blankets over the bureau and the desk—or else we would be stowaways escaping from our evil captors in a wagon that bore more than passing resemblance to my bed. And always there would come the point in the story where I would hold Mary Warren, or where she would hold me, and we would comfort each other. And in those moments, I understood on a cellular level that whatever this other adult world might be, so filled with pain and contempt, it was not and never could be real.

Mary Warren never returned the passion I had for her, because she could not comprehend the complexity and torment of my life. Paradoxically, it was her ignorance that had inspired my passion. She transferred to a different school after fourth grade and our friendship did not survive the move, but, by that time, Ginny was already ensconced as the goddess of my alternative world. Ginny was the queen. She was always wise, always compassionate, and her power was absolute—but not in the ways of human dictatorship. Unlike the sadistic patriarchal god who sets his misbegotten world into motion for the thrill of watching it career toward certain destruction, Ginny was one with her universe. She was the embodiment of it. It was not a question of will, but of rhythm.

When I say that I "played with the dolls," I don't mean the dress parade that passed for "playing with dolls" among my peers, and which has caused generations of feminists to privilege the dump trucks and toolkits of male children over the dolls given to little girls.

No, when I "played with dolls," I was involved in sacred ritual; I was recreating the world. I was in my laboratory testing out systems of ethics. I was making detailed observations about the intricacies of human personality. I was healing myself, and I was conjuring. Literally entranced, I could stay present in the world of the dolls for six and eight hours at a time, enacting epic confrontations between the manifestations of patriarchal evil and the incontrovertible power of an overriding matriarchal consciousness.

Ginny presided over these dramas like the *deus ex machina* of the Greek plays, or like Louis XIV at the court dramas of Molière. She rarely participated actively, but the enactments were all performed in her honor and to her greater glory. The heroine of my dramas was a different doll, equally beloved, but much more human. This doll was named Pat, and she had a history as complicated as my own. She had been abused and then rejected by my neighbors, the Whitbys. Pat's hair had been ruthlessly pulled out or cut off, and her body had been stained by various ballpoint pen markings. When I found her, she was naked. Pat, a predecessor to Barbie, was not a child doll, nor was she an adult. She had the beginnings of breasts, but she did not have the exaggerated small waist designed to compensate for the waistband layers of fabric that could not be woven to scale. It is ironic to think that this solution to a purely technical problem has been misinterpreted by generations of girls as a mandate for self-starvation.

I rescued Pat, and introduced her into the royal family of the dolls. Her background was unknown, but she possessed an unmistakable nobility of spirit that put most of the members of the court to shame. She had obviously survived some terrible personal tragedy, which, for some reason, was never discussed by either me or by the other dolls. She had no family, and I made no effort to create one for her.

Pat was, of course, a dyke and a survivor of sexual trauma. This was the late 1950s, and it would be two more decades before I would claim those identities as my own. But I had created her, obviously, in my own image. No matter what evils befell her (and these were many), she always emerged triumphant, vindicated, restored to her rightful position. She was never angry, never jealous, but her protection lay in her absolute integrity, her innate sweetness, a kind of fierce innocence. And, of course, she had access to magic. The fairies and other supernatural beings of Ginny's realm favored her above all the other dolls, and, although this favoritism did not spare her from the trials that constituted my major plot device, these magical helpers made sure that the harsh experiences brought on by the jealousy and intrigues of the other dolls would only cause Pat's qualities to shine all the brighter.

I did not realize that, in creating this myth, I was sowing the dragons' teeth of denial that would rise up as an army of demons in my adult years. My innocence did not protect me. My magic, which was the ability to dissociate, only rendered me invisible to myself, not to my assailants. And my harm was real, deep, and permanent.

When I turned thirteen, my mother told me that it was time to put away the dolls for good, and, in my first step toward becoming an adult, I believed her. We began to pack the dollhouse together, but almost immediately I became overwhelmed with the horror of what I was doing. Sobbing hysterically, I fled from the room, leaving my mother to disassemble my childhood.

Why did I run away? Why hadn't I challenged her? Why hadn't I put up the fight of my life for these dearest of friends, these boon companions with whom I had gone on so many adventures? I knew that what was happening that afternoon was nothing less than a massacre. We were killing off the dolls. Why didn't I fight? I suspect it had something to do with "normalcy."

I was entering puberty. For the first time, there was a possibility that I might have the power to determine the course of my life, to affect my own reality. Perhaps I would be able to live my adventures, my romances, my fairy tales in the *real* world. I believe it was this hope, this promise of a normal life—maybe it was not too late to become Mary Warren!—that seduced me into the abandonment of my dolls.

I had abandoned them, but I had not participated in the putting-away of them. The coward who flees may live to find the courage to return, but the woman or girl who turns her hand against her own dreams—she is more dead than her victims.

My mother had murdered her own dolls. I was sure of it. They would never have allowed her to live with the man I called my father. They would never have allowed her to settle for such unhappy endings, over and over. The woman who can betray her own daughter must have betrayed herself first. Sadly, in the silence and stilling of the imagination that followed the massacre of the dolls, I turned to my mother for solace. She, and not Ginny, became my goddess, and my indoctrination into heterosexuality began in earnest.

And in kindness to myself, I draw a curtain over the next twenty years—years of confusion, chaos, and dissociation. I adopted serial personas, as do many women with backgrounds like mine. I lived on the streets for a while; I hitchhiked around the country, attempting to exorcise my demons by exposing myself to scenarios as terrifying as those of my childhood; I escaped into a religious cult. I retreated into a heterosexual marriage. In the words of Mary Daly, I sought safety in the "presence of absence," in the "absence of presence."

In 1986, Sleeping Beauty—she who had been pricked so young and who had been asleep for so many years—began to awake. I came out as a lesbian, and I came out as an incest survivor, and I came out as an artist. These three identities were not separate, and it would have been impossible for me to have claimed any one of them without the others. My first action upon awakening was to estrange myself from my mother. And then I began to tell my story with my art.

The patriarchal world is not receptive to the story of the incest survivor, because incest is the paradigm of patriarchy. The incest survivor who takes her observations to their natural conclusions will find herself, like Cassandra, blessed with prescience and cursed with lack of credibility. It will drive a woman mad, unless she can find some place of justice, some place where she can reconcile the contradictions.

I have returned to the world of the dolls—you might say with a vengeance—and I redeem my betrayal of them by telling the story of that betrayal. I stand now with the dolls, among them, advocating for the girl who is never believed. I have starved with her, and I have been humiliated with her, and I have raged with her. I have an enemy and I know his identity and I name it. Over and over again. This time around, I understand the difference between magic and superstition. This time around my spells are binding. This time I am working with truth.

U. C. KNOEPFLMACHER

SPACES WITHIN: THE PORTABLE INTERIORS OF CHILDHOOD

> *The White Rabbit put on his spectacles. "Where shall*
> *I begin, please your Majesty?" he asked.*
> *"Begin at the beginning," the King said very gravely.*
> —Lewis Carroll, *Alice in Wonderland*

> *No retrospect will take us to the true beginning.*
> —George Eliot, *Daniel Deronda*

Some years ago a friend gave me a wooden stacking doll of Lewis Carroll's Wonderland Alice. When pried apart, each figurine yielded a smaller shape that snugly fitted, and yet also jarred with, the contours of its host: thus, a blonde Alice housed the red-faced Queen of Hearts; the angry Queen contained a smiling Cheshire Cat; the Cat carried an earless White Rabbit within it; and the Rabbit itself yielded a bean-shaped creature that looked more like a tiny foetus than the playing card it was supposed to represent.

The incongruity of these forms-within-forms strikes me as an apt symbolic starting point for certain questions I should like to explore. If our older selves are composed of layers of former selves, is it possible for us to make our way back into some originary childhood space? Or are all attempts to enter such remembered nooks conditioned by the pressure of later memories of other, related, spaces? Since any notion of a unified "childhood" is fashioned by hindsight, can we ever peel away the impact of later occurrences when trying to bestow meaning on some primary "spots of time" (as Wordsworth called them)? Is not the shape of that bean-shaped creature at the innermost core of my Alice doll necessarily determined by the configurations of all the outward husks I must remove before I can expect to reach it?

I want to test these questions by aligning events that transpired in four vividly remembered childhood spaces. I shall begin with the earliest, yet hardly the simplest, of these memories and then move forward in time in order to reconstruct, as best I can, the perceptions and meanings that each event might have held for the child—and, finally, for the adolescent—who experienced them. Still, by placing my four "spots of time" into a chronological sequence, I am necessarily distorting the significance each event may originally have held. Indeed, had I reversed their order by starting with the last of these four memories rather than with an arbitrary beginning, I might have more fully acknowledged the revisionary operations of a hindsight that inevitably blurs the topographies of early childhood.

I had just turned five when my mother took me to a crowded public swimming pool on an extremely hot summer day. A section for smaller children had been roped off at the pool's shallow end; having satisfied herself that the water was barely high enough to reach my chest, my mother reclaimed her armchair and magazine at the other end of the pool's deck. Children were jumping and jostling all around me. But I was fixated on a new plastic swimming doll that had been specially purchased for this occasion. I carefully wound her up and watched, delighted, as she slithered rhythmically, arms and legs akimbo, through the water. Suddenly, a hard shove from someone nearby made me lose my footing. I slipped and fell. And as I lay on the green tiles, I noticed that I had landed on something—my delicate swimmer-doll had been smashed, flattened. Lying at the bottom of the pool, I retrieved her and stared disconsolately at her deformed shape. Her eyes, seemingly sad and accusing, were on the same plane as mine.

I could easily have stood up again. Instead, I maintained my prone position on the green tiles, firmly clutching the mutilated swimmer-doll. Water began to enter my nostrils and half-open mouth. I kept returning the doll's gaze; she was clearly beyond repair, lost forever. But the pain of losing her now seemed to be replaced by a strange and new feeling of well-being. It was rather comfortable to lie there, I discovered, hardly unpleasant to breathe in some more water. I could no longer hear the shouts of the children around me. It was quiet here. And in my deaf and dreamy acquiescence, I suddenly felt myself being forcefully lifted into the air by familiar strong arms, shaken, carried out of the pool and propped back into a vertical position. My mother, having vigilantly noticed my failure to resurface, had knocked bathers aside in order to reach me. After coughing up all the water I had swallowed, I mutely held up my battered swimming doll as if to explain the logic of my failure to get up on my own two legs.

In trying to come to terms with this vivid personal memory, I am reminded of Trelawney's dubious anecdote about the near-drowning of Percy Shelley: fished out from the bottom of a tide-pool in which he had been passively lying, the poet putatively rebuked his rescuer for having deprived him of an opportunity to unveil the curtain separating life from death. But there are other Romantic and Victorian analogues. Tennyson's youthful poem "The Kraken"—much ridiculed by reviewers who chided the poet for the presumed puerility of his imagination—may better capture a primordial childhood than Wordsworth's allegory, in his famous Immortality Ode, of mythical cherubs sporting at the edge of some eternal sea. Tennyson depicts the "uninvaded sleep" of a sea-monster who blissfully battens on organisms while lying on the ocean floor. Forced to rise up and come in contact with "men and angels," Tennyson's abruptly wakened sleeper experiences the pain of Milton's fallen angels when they, too, had to give up their horizontal position in the torpid, mind-erasing waters of an underground Lethean lake.

The nineteenth-century imagination frequently associated childhood spaces with the oblivion of a death-by-drowning. Wordsworth's Lucy Gray, whose tiny footsteps vanish at the edge of the snow-covered bridge from which she fell, reaches a limbo in which she can forever freely move; George Eliot's Maggie Tulliver, seen first as a little girl dangerously poised at the edge of the waters that will eventually claim her, can be preserved in her childhood habitats by the remembering narrator of *The Mill on the Floss*. These and other such coordinates may capture a relation between endings and beginnings: a death-wish, after all, involves regression, a return to an unconsciousness of external barriers that these writers associate with the small child as much as with the extinction of self.

But literary coordinates can only go so far in answering the specific questions that still puzzle me now as I try to reconstruct what may have gone through the mind of the five-year-old who had failed to rise. Why did I revert to the recumbent position of an infant? Would I have immediately stood up again if my swimmer-doll had not been crushed? I remain convinced that the death of the toy I had fetishized must somehow have licensed my own refusal to return to air and life. But, if so, why did the experience of drowning, of breathing and tasting water, not only seem unfrightening but also curiously empowering?

An answer to these questions may emerge by considering the drowning boy's contrasting relation to the two female figures in my story. The boy's attachment to the swimmer-doll intensified after his mother detached herself from him by going to the opposite end of the pool. Before being knocked down, the boy had rejoiced in the doll's controlled mobility on the water's surface. But as soon as the doll became immobile, unable to rise from the bottom of the pool, he adopted its own inertness. I seem to recall that the damaged doll had to be dislodged from a position under my chest or abdomen. But even if this memory should be unreliable, the product of some later elaboration, it could still be argued that the boy regarded the motionless doll not only as a version of himself but also as his own child, or, more likely, as the equivalent of a more primitive attachment he had accidentally managed to recapture and was now reluctant to shed.

For the doll's paralysis offered the boy an opportunity to recover a symbiosis with the mother who, rather than joining him in the wading area, had positioned herself among grownups on the deck at the pool's opposite end. The boy's memory of that early union would have been reactivated by the mere stimulus of water: even much later in his life, as we shall presently see, his mother figured in weekly rituals of joyous bathings, scrubbings, and towelings. Water thus continued to act as a highly pleasurable reminder of an elementary bond between parent and child. (The intensity of that bond would also have survived, of course, through the boy's familiarity with countless baby photographs of himself being safely pressed against his mother's body or being placed by her, just as safely, within the soft swaddling of his favorite perambulator). The boy's refusal to rise from his watery cove thus suggests more than his passive retrogression into a maternal space. By allowing himself to be smothered in that makeshift womb with his destroyed doll-self, he could bring about his mother's return. She had not joined him in the water. She had preferred to immerse herself in her magazine. He would compel her to come to him, even at the risk of swallowing more water. There was a potency in his paralysis.

Dry land, rather than a watery underground, dominates the landscape in the second of my four reminiscences: declivities of brown Andean earth baked by the sun have replaced the earlier setting. At ten, I am far more aware of explicit social and historical pressures. I have undergone ordeals of separation that the five-year-old at the pool could hardly have foreseen. Only a year after that earlier experience, my mother and I would have been barred from a pool hereafter reserved for Aryans. We were in Austria then; I am now in Bolivia, and I have lately become aware of my difference, even in this far more hospitable setting, that as Jew and gringo I remain unassimilable, foreign. My school is nestled against a huge mountain; behind the paved playground and the flat basketball court is a rising canyon, full of unexplored hollows and furrows that can act as hiding places. During our long afternoon recess, I wander away from the other children into the canyon. I find a child-size crater that perfectly suits my needs. I crouch into it, take a toy revolver out of my pocket, remove my glasses, and, then, in a moment of intense exultation, replace them with a dark green leather mask.

The mask has been fashioned by my mother out of a discarded remnant she carefully measured and fitted to the contours of my face. It is soft, pliable, textured, with an elastic band at the back, as snug as the warm adobe concave into which I have pressed myself. Perched at a considerable height, I cautiously watch the running children in the playground below. I fondle my cap pistol. Yes, I *am* none other than the masked Phantom, the "Fantomás" of my comic books. I am happy in my solitude, secure because unknown and invisible. I feel empowered by the protective mask and by my safe and aloof position. I do not want to descend. There is plenty of time before the school bell will ring again.

My reverie is sharply interrupted. "Who are you?," someone behind me asks. I spin around in disbelief that anyone could have snuck around my vantage point. My classmate Willie Visbeek, the Dutch girl I adore, whose disdain has been so painful, repeats her question. I remain silent, aware that my voice would give me away. "Are you Carlos? or Tommy?," Willie ventures. I now wonder whether she might be teasing me: surely she can tell who I am by simply looking at my attire; the coveralls and that plaid flannel shirt should readily give away my identity as the bespectacled boy who loves her from afar. But Willie seems genuinely puzzled. Like the young woman who fails to guess Rumpelstilskin's name, she tries out some more names, and yet omits my own. Frustrated, she finally decides to return to the playground. I resume my former posture. I cannot believe this confirmation of my impenetrability. The mask—and with it my private fantasy of omnipotence—has been successfully tested. It is a magical moment.

This incident, too, can be embroidered by literary analogues at an English professor's fingertips. My green mask and the caul that covered the head of David Copperfield the Younger appear to bear some resemblance as special, but dubious, marks of maternal favor. But the emotions I felt when Willie Visbeek failed to uncover my identity now strike me as coming close to those dramatized by Christina Rossetti in her wonderful poem, "Winter: My Secret." There it is a female speaker who masks her identity from a male intruder. Her defensive strategies are sexual: her impenetrability is teasing, a sign of her strength, her desirability. Yet beneath what can be read as adult banter lies the coy speaker's ability to tap the inviolability of childhood spaces that are at odds with the drafty corridors and passages of adult life. It is no coincidence that, in her later *Sing-Song* Rossetti should have produced the best child lyrics since Blake's *Songs of Innocence*. This poet for grownups never deserted the secret spaces of her remembered childhood.

But I want to make sense of the green-mask incident by relating it to its earlier counterpart at the swimming pool. For the two narratives seem pendants to each other; they contain similarities within their differences, and differences within these similarities.

What they have in common is, first of all, the same trio of protagonists: a boy, the mother to whom he is strongly attached, and a female figure through whom he tries to rework his powerful primal attachment to the maternal other. Willie Visbeek, a healthy, red-cheeked, real-life girl, has replaced the fragile plastic swimming-doll. She cannot be molded by desire, reincorporated and appropriated as an extension of a regressive child. Instead, it is her distance, her inaccessibility, that has to be reckoned with. That inaccessibility has, in fact, prompted the boy's defensive posture. He must distance himself by masking his vulnerability. Like his earlier incarnation at the pool, the masked boy needs to protect himself against separation. He must devise a strategy that will allow him to deal with the painful recognition that he is no more connected to Willie than he is to a mother who has ceased to act as his prime prop. He therefore welcomes the mask as a maternal token, a token, however, which—like David Copperfield's caul—cannot really protect him from rejection, sexual difference, the approaching vicissitudes of puberty. His play-acting—pistol and all—depends on male bravado, on a displacement of the feminine.

Yet if the earlier story involved three figures—boy, doll, and mother—the second story really features four. The doll's equivalent, after all, is not only the live Willie, as I have suggested, but also the mask itself, which easily adapts itself to the contours of its wearer's face and thus provides him with a more satisfactory screen than did the enveloping water for his counterpart in the pool. The water, though transparent, had blocked out sight, muffled all sound, and, potentially, snuffed out the breath of life. The opaque mask, however, only dulls the boy's eyesight: by replacing his glasses, it removes him from a world of signs, from reading and being read. The silence of the drowning boy might have resulted in his death; the silence of the masked boy allows him to evade the sophistications of a boy-girl dialogue he has not yet mastered. The mask thus protects the boy as much as the hollow into which he had crawled. It is a maternal guerdon that serves him better than the doll who has turned into Willie, herself a replacement for the mother on whom he still depends and yet whom he also recognizes as a source of his vulnerability. (The brandished toy gun marks a contrary wish—but still barely acknowledged—not to be fully identified with the maternal.)

Did the boy in my narrative ever wear his green mask again after he had trudged down from his eminence in those hillocks behind the schoolyard? I cannot really remember. Did it serve him as an adaptive tool by allowing him to develop new and better guises in the sexualized worlds that lay before him, to turn to new substitutes, to other Eves in other Edens? Such a happy ending, as wishful as the boy's feelings of omnipotence during that recess, is belied by my next two "spots of time." For,

in each, the dubious memories of empowering childhood landscapes are subverted by analogues that only yield the painfully
sharp confusions of adolescence.

The sunny outdoor scenes of pool and canyon refuge are now
replaced by two dimly lit interiors. They are rooms in the same
house—a house whose elaborate floor-plan surprisingly still
seems more sharply edged in my mind than those of our later
Bolivian residences, perhaps because in it I moved from childhood to puberty. The first scene takes place in a primitive bathroom that, together with an adjoining storage room that is totally dark, occupies a detached little building which opens on
the L-shaped inner courtyard around which all the other rooms
of the house are assembled. The second scene takes place, less
than two years later, in another dark room, adjacent to our
huge kitchen; it, too, is used for storage, but formerly contained
smelly rabbit hutches taken away from my mother while she
and I vacationed in a warmer, sub-Andean summer resort.

Bathing, as I have already hinted, had by then become a precious restoration of an earlier childhood bond, a drawn out ritual that culminated in my being enveloped in a huge towel
wielded by my mother. The antiquated water heater required
hours of careful manual fueling; it had to be teased with the
dry sagebrush sprigs we used for kindling and be artfully fed by
successive heaps of llama pellets before it produced enough
steaming water to fill the huge, four-footed, cast-iron tub. The
bath itself went through lengthy phases of latherings and
rinses administered by my mother. I especially looked forward
to her brisk scrubbings as a reinstatement of a communion that
had—or so I felt—been severely undermined by two outside
events. My mother had given in to a prolonged period of excessive melancholia after her own mother's death; she wore black
to signify her mourning, and, to my mind, lavished more affection on her ever-increasing hordes of rabbits than on my father
and myself. Perhaps as an attempt at compensation, or, as it
was presented to me, as an effort to help socialize an overly
sheltered only child, my parents had decided to take in two of
my school-fellows as boarders. I deeply resented this intrusion.
Although slightly younger than myself, now almost twelve
years old, Edgar and Kai were, I soon discovered, far more sexually knowing than I. I stood by, affronted but powerless, as

they smirkingly looked up my mother's skirts whenever she bent over in the courtyard garden. And I was more puzzled than shocked when I surprised them in sexual play one Sunday morning: I had no idea why the more placid of the two was willing to expose his bared buttocks to his aggressive and excited partner.

The existence of these two intruders made my weekly bath more precious than ever before. I could be a child again, revel in games I had delighted in as a tiny tot. Such regressive games somehow assured me that my mother and I still shared a private universe. The warm bathroom was poorly lit; the totally dark storage room next to it was screened off by a burlap curtain. I welcomed this reentry into the penumbra of a maternal space. As the naked and shameless recipient of my mother's scrubbings, I harbored none of the deep misgivings that would certainly beset me today, as a father, if I were to find my wife seductively lathering our pre-adolescent son.

One evening, after cavorting in the foamy water, I eagerly stood up to be enveloped in the huge bath-towel my mother had extended toward me. Suddenly, I heard a distinct titter in the adjoining storage room. As I swung around, squinting my eyes, I recognized the grinning faces of Kai and Edgar, peeking out from the burlap curtain. I screamed. In a frenzy, I scooped up and furiously splashed waves of tub-water against the curtain, again and again. It was in vain. Kai and Edgar had ducked and disappeared; I could hear their retreating laughter. But my intense hatred of these two voyeurs quickly gave way to even more painful feelings. I turned on my mother. Had she known that the two boys were in the adjacent storage room? "Yes," she admitted. Why, then, had she issued no warning, why had she allowed me to assume that we were as safely alone as always? How long had the boys watched our private ritual? Her replies were unconvincing. I felt betrayed, embarrassed by my nakedness. Like Adam after the Fall, I covered myself. There would be no more returns to innocent childhood play. Innocence itself seemed polluted, in doubt.

A year must have passed between this scene and what I now recognize as its indirect, though logical, sequel. Kai and Edgar no longer lived in our house. And my mother had divested herself of her mourning attire. Her black silken blouse was now proudly worn by Elena, a buxom and coquettish housemaid in her early twenties. The room which once housed my mother's rabbits had been turned into a storage room in which Elena lingered each evening before leaving. The rabbit hutches in the back had been replaced by heaps of burlap sacks. But Elena had converted the front of the room into a small boudoir.

On a shelf, there was a flask of the potent perfume (also cast off by my mother) that Elena always over-applied before leaving the house. Creeping into a faraway corner of the dark room, well before Elena had finished her work in the kitchen, I covered myself with burlap sacks and waited in eager anticipation. It was all a game, I assured myself. But I had become the disciple of Kai and Edgar, a voyeur.

My expectations were quickly rewarded. The room was feebly lit as Elena turned on the single light-bulb and approached a shelf on which she kept trinkets and ointments. She took a flask and lavishly started to spread its contents over her bared arms and legs. The smell of perfume was overpowering. Suddenly, to my chagrin, Elena lurched directly toward the corner in which I was hiding. Convinced that she had spotted me, I jumped up, roaring, shedding my protective cover of burlap sacks. But I had been mistaken. The shrieking young woman had obviously been totally unaware of my presence. She staggered back in fright, stumbled, and fell on the floor. Highly agitated, she protested that she would tell my father, in his study at the other end of the house, of his son's latest dereliction. I desperately tried to detain her. And, in a moment, as she was getting up, I had pinioned her arms. While I was pleading, babbling excuses, telling her that I had just tried to play a boyish game by pretending to be a wild monster, my eyes rested on my mother's black blouse. I could not let Elena go. I wanted her to stay in this space with me. I wanted to caress that silky blouse, to become totally enveloped in the perfume she was exuding. Yet I remained immobile, conscious only of my strength. A minute passed. And then erotics gave way to prudence. I relaxed my grip and allowed Elena to free herself. And, after she had been allowed to air her indignant accusations, I meekly abided by my father's judgment.

The two scenes I have just described are inseparable from the earlier episodes of the swimming pool and the green mask. Paralysis or immobility seems pervasive in all of these memories: the aggressive adolescent who may be strong enough to overpower Elena nonetheless remains as frozen and supine as the little boy who yearned for his mother's return while lying at the bottom of the pool; indeed, by inducing his mother's return, this passive tot might well be considered to have been the stronger of the two. Seen as a sequence, the four scenes thus dramatize a progressive weakening. Standing in his tub, the raging boy who vainly splashes water on the enemies who have surprised him in his nakedness is far more impotent than the masked boy who warded off Willie while fingering his toy gun. The mask which allowed that boy to feel so secure in his anonymity has been replaced by unreliable cloth coverings: the curtain left unguarded by his mother and the bath towel that can no longer screen him now cruelly mock his wish for an extension of the secure swaddlings of childhood.

There is, however, a special relationship between the first and third episodes, in which the maternal is associated with water, and between the second and fourth episodes, in which the maternal mask the boy wears in order to hide from Willie has turned into an article of clothing now worn by her substitute. In each case, the later experience subverts its childhood antecedent. Let me therefore briefly consider both pairings, before reiterating the questions about hindsight that I raised at the outset of my narrative.

The boy who lingered at the bottom of the pool, I want to believe, anticipated his mother's intervention. Would he have stood up as soon as his breathing became totally impaired? We shall never know. But his willingness to risk drowning stemmed, I like to think, less from a sense of loss than of security. I compared the horizontal boy, earlier, to Tennyson's protected Kraken, secure and invisible at the bottom of the ocean. That marine creature, however, expired when it was forced to rise from heated waters in order to be seen by beings who lacked its childlike unselfconsciousness. I cannot help associating the painful roaring of the boy who rose from the tub with that of Tennyson's sea-monster. Exposed to the gaze of strangers, the boy experiences the shattering of his desire to remain in an infantile state of symbiosis. But what smarts most is his mother's seeming complicity in bringing about his exposure. The rescuer of the little boy at the wading pool has ceased to be his protector. Her hurtful indifference must now be acknowledged.

A similar reversal is evident in the apposition of the second and fourth episodes. I called the green mask a maternal token, a guerdon, that allowed the boy in the crevice to fend off Willie's attractions. But no such easy displacement is possible when it is Elena who wears such a token—the mother's silky blouse—and, to boot, also exudes the mother's perfume. The aroused voyeur must confront a sexuality he can no longer mask through boyish games. He cannot reassure himself by impersonating the aloof Phantom. When he protests that he was merely playing a prank on Elena, he knows the futility of such pretending; he cannot disguise lust as a game. And his exposure is now complete. When Willie failed to fathom the boy's identity, his privacy remained intact; when Elena, however, hauls the culprit to be judged by a father who sees more than this pseudo-prankster, privacy gives way to public scrutiny.

Given such reversals, it is possible to question the accounts of my earlier two "spots of time." Might they not reveal an adult's search for childhood antidotes to the stumblings of his adolescence? Could it be that the little boy who failed to stand up in shallow water was, far from the successful orchestrator of his mother's return, little more than an over-dependent, rather unresourceful, child? I do not know. But whenever I dismantle or put together the various segments of my wooden stacking doll, I have to acknowledge that the outer shapes inevitably determine the deformities of those increasingly distorted inner figures.

CHILDREN AS OBSERVING
CRITICS AND SKEPTICS

Before I started learning how to understand children psychologically as a resident in child psychiatry, I had taken training in pediatrics at the Children's Hospital in Boston. During that time (a two-year spell of constant clinical work with sick, often quite vulnerable boys and girls) a polio epidemic hit the northeastern states of our country (1956–1958) and, unfortunately, we doctors had no Salk vaccine to summon—a far cry from what now prevents such an outbreak of that dangerous and debilitating disease from striking down young people or those who care for them. Much of my days and nights, back then, kept me in a constant whirl of activity (doing examinations, setting up transfusions, infusions, writing medical reports on charts, filling out prescriptions, attending conferences, going on rounds), and often enough, alas, we doctors and nurses had to stand by helpless, hoping to arrest the consequences of a powerfully insistent, potentially destructive and debilitating viral illness— even as we often knew that a particular patient might spend the rest of his or her life crippled, or, God forbid, in an iron lung that breathed for him or her.

No wonder I heard so many of those children spell out their sadness or their apprehensions, worries; and no wonder, too, I heard their parents, or their grandparents, or their brothers and sisters, cry in response to what was happening (or threatened to happen); and no wonder, often enough, I was so busy, so driven to do all I could, that I had little time to stop and let myself catch a breath or two. One late morning, as I was preparing to leave the bedside of a ten-year-old girl, Marjorie, whose beleaguered Mom and Dad stood nearby, down the hall, ready to be there for her as soon as I stepped away, I heard my name spoken, following a question: "Are you alright?" I was surprised, puzzled, literally stopped in my tracks. Quickly (reflexively, I realized later) I said "yes"—my one-word response a fair exchange, seemingly, for Marjorie's three-word inquiry. But she wasn't going to settle for my terse assertion of confidence, of well-being. She told me that she wanted to tell me something, and she asked me if I minded that she do so. I don't have her every word at that moment in my head, but I certainly do remember being confused by Marjorie's apparent concern for me, and I also remember (will never forget) what she said to focus her thoughts, her intent with respect to my condition, as she began to address me: "I told my Mom and my Dad that you're trying hard, but you're wearing down."

Silence followed on her part—as, wide-eyed, she kept looking right at me. I was almost ready to say something, thank her for her evident concern, tell her that I was feeling fine, that I really appreciated her attentive regard for me—but nothing came to me, out of my mouth, until I heard myself saying what I hadn't thought to remark: "I wish it would be better—that you and all the other kids could go home. That will be great."

At that expression of desire, that prediction of progress, Marjorie smiled, but in an instant she took up another matter, giving me considerable pause, if not knocking me for a loop: "Even if us kids go, there will be others to come here, so you'll still be rushing and working hard, so you could get tired, and you'd have to get some rest."

I can recall that scene quite well, its visual and auditory aspects: her wry look, her softly stated, yet explicitly convinced declaration—at once a prognostication and an analysis grounded in careful, knowing observation. I can also recall my judgment that a truth had been stated, that I'd best move on with a quick, off-putting bit of reassurance—for Marjorie's sake, of course. Yet, she had gotten to me, and there I was, trying to figure out what to say that would work to get us both out of a seeming impasse. In no time I was thanking young Marjorie, attempting a certain casual demeanor, readying myself to speak words meant to indicate that I was quite able to take care of myself, that I could manage my responsibilities, however substantial the stress put my way by boys and girls like her. But I had to wait for my voice to work, because this youngster, sick and paralyzed and not with the greatest medical prospects, was watching me so steadily and earnestly that I felt (maybe even half-concluded) that she knew enough about me and my kind (us busy doctors, working long hours, sometimes with desperation) that anything I offered in defensive or apologetic explanation would be unsurprising, to say the least.

But I tried my best; and I told my patient that she was "coming along fine"—I'd learned that phrase as a medical student from a quite distinguished pediatrician, Rustin McIntosh, who kept on telling that to child after child under his care, even as some of us callow, if curious, future doctors couldn't help but notice how ailing some of those youngsters were. Their faces often registered doubt, outright disbelief, when their important, assured doctor spoke of their distinct progress, and we, observers of those affecting, worrisome scenes, were more the worriedly apprehensive onlookers than the quickly obliging assenters. Indeed, sometimes a child would look at one of us, a fixed stare meant to be imploring: do you go along with this bigshot, believe him, in the face of all the evident distress, even danger, you are witnessing? So I thought some of those "lads and lassies" thought (as Dr. McIntosh once in a while called them, thereby signaling his time spent in England, a source of obvious pride to him)—and only later, in retrospective renunciation, did I realize that what I attributed to those young ones was, really, what I had in mind but feared to acknowledge as an aspect of what I was seeing: my eyes were looking around, transmitting messages of unmistakable misery to individuals being told, nevertheless, that all was well, that ahead were healthy days, for sure.

At once, I was brought up short by "Miss Marjorie," as her folks with great respect sometimes called her: "Who's coming with me—if I get to meet our God, I'll be there alone, my mummy says, and the priest." Now I was once again silenced, surprised, stunned even. This sixth-grader, scarcely a decade old, had adroitly, pointedly, picked up on my use of that word "coming"—had taken a doctor's estimate of what was happening, what would happen (that she was "coming along fine"), quite literally, and in her own manner, calling upon a religious tradition quite familiar to her, had turned my words right around, stood them on their nakedly confident, imperturbable head. It was as if a big hint was being made: you want to bring up the matter of where I'm headed, how I'm doing, and the nature of my progress, then I'll take you seriously, I'll take us both further, move us from medicine to theology, a big leap, you might think (when you stop and ponder, rather than pontificate, about what's going to be happening)—so she was suggesting by metaphoric implication: after death another possibility arrives, a meeting with someone who matters, so it's best to have a perspective about time, and to be more blunt, to uphold a view of what's ahead that considers not only temporal healing but a certain Healer of yore.

To this day that moment with young Marjorie figures in my mind—a child who wanted assistance, waited for it, wondered about it, but a child who knew how to move from immediate need to the longest distance ahead, to a consideration that makes my self-assured clinical comfort seem shallow, glib, trite (characterizations that aren't always unmerited by my ilk as we make our remarks in front of patients, among them children). I go back now and then to that hospital exchange, to my comment and Marjorie's responsive inquiry: an elementary school child had shown me how observant she could be, and too, how skeptical she was also capable of being—unwilling to accept unreservedly my offhand predictions, based on my sure sense of professional purpose, capability. It didn't take long for me, alas, to put that girl in her place, to think of her anxieties and fears, her continuing worries, that prompted her reaction to my medical hopefulness. I had not yet "come along" myself, taken the residency in child psychiatry that would later have me zeroing in, fast and long, on the Marjories of this world, unmasking their motives and remarks with my psychological penetrations of their inner thinking. But even then I'd learned to take hold of the "psychology of everyday life," as one Viennese doctor and writer had put it: the way we mask our intentions or our felt desperation with declarations or deeds. Marjorie, her then-young pediatrician had recognized, was not "up" to telling me (knowing directly) how uncertain and vulnerable she felt, lying on that hospital bed, her limbs unable to move, her breath, even, a bit labored—and so, instead, she had become a concerned observer of her doctor, a skeptical listener to his words.

Meanwhile, I fear, that doctor was not quite the observer he thought he was—or put differently, he was taking careful notice of "signs and symptoms," as the oft-used medical phrase goes, physical ones, of course, and even psychological ones, but he wasn't understanding how a child who belonged to a devoutly religious family was trying to regard her bout of illness; and ironically he wasn't observing her observational attentiveness, her inclination to take in the world, sort out those who figure in it: all of us characters in a human scene to which she herself belonged, and in which she was now both a central person and a personality. Nor was this doctor (able to see right through the self-deceptions of others, the ways they tried so hard, so humanly, to resist realizing their considerable jeopardy) himself willing to take a sharp look inward, and glimpse what he had learned to find important, revealing, but also what he tended to overlook, to miss entirely, and at moments, to misconstrue— that last happening, in its own way, something done at the expense of others: their nature, their manner of talk, of being and thinking, resolutely subordinated to his mind's experiences, some of them called "training" and "education."

Years later that doctor would be living through another chapter in his life, would have finished an immersion in a discipline that aims to address the emotions of children, their psychological stumbling blocks, their social waywardness, and would have, finally, gotten to know "children of crisis," as he was wont to call them, and before that, needless to say, think of them: the South's African-American boys and girls who initiated school desegregation against the fearful odds of mob violence; that region's white youth, who all of a sudden were also participants in a historical drama of singular significance; and too, Dixie's other threatened population—young people whose parents are migrant farmworkers or tenants (sometimes called sharecroppers) on large plantations. During those years, on occasion, Marjorie entered her one-time doctor's thoughts indirectly, even surprisingly—especially so when he would be hearing yet another child make clear his or her capacity to take accurate stock of things, of classmates and teachers, of people become street hecklers, shouting their heads off, lest a much-dreaded "integration" occur. "They look tired to me," little Ruby Bridges, six years old, fighting her way through hostile mobs every school day in order to go to school with white children, once told me, as she tried to convey her overall comprehension of dozens of so-called American adults. I asked her, promptly, what she was getting at, by repeating that word "tired"—the questioning lilt in my voice a reflexive (tiring!) aspect of my clinical manner. But Ruby, in New Orleans, like Marjorie in Boston a half-decade earlier, had a quick response (if not retort) to my own probing response that was directed at her use of a particular word: "They be so busy hating me, they forget everything." Yes, I saw her point, but I wanted more—I wanted her to spell out what she had in mind about "everything," and so I asked her what she supposed was forgotten, and right away, heard this: "They don't have much but their being white, and if that's all you've got, then you must be tired of saying the same old words."

I wasn't convinced by her analysis; her hecklers seemed to me almost exhilarated by their daily outbursts—as if, sadly and oddly, their lives had found a purpose through their daily opposition to her school attendance. In time, as we talked further, I shared my thoughts, my take on those she observed daily while going in or out of a school building, and she nodded, as if she followed my line of reasoning, and then shook her head: "When they go home all they've got is themselves, so they must get down in the dumps, my momma says." Her mother's shrewd psychological analysis, become Ruby's, so earnestly and vigorously declared in the face of my explorative curiosity, finally turned my head, helped me think more clearly about people whose lives I had no reason to feel I knew well at all. As if Ruby felt I needed further persuasion, she offered me a detail, an observation that came her way one morning: "I saw one of those women, she was sweating and wiping her face with a [hand]kerchief, and I thought, she was going to fall asleep, because her eyes were almost closed, and I felt sorry for her—I wished she could go and get herself a nap, some rest."

So it goes: a girl hospitalized with polio spots her doctor's exhaustion, and a girl harassed by a hostile street crowd spots a sign of their vulnerability, even as she knows of her own. In each instance a child has taken careful, discerning notice of what is happening to a grown-up and in each instance, as well, the child has challenged the easy explanations, and instead has shown skeptical awareness. In the latter case that skepticism became quite something else: an observer's canny ability to fathom (and render in words) the melancholy side (an almost inexpressible discontent) of visible, audible power, all too solidly backed, then, by the whole city of New Orleans.

For me, these past years, young ones such as Marjorie and Ruby have been in their various ways constant witnesses— their observations from secret sources of intuition an ongoing education I have only slowly learned to appreciate for what it has taught me about myself and others, not to mention about children, their capabilities and possibilities as alert, revelatory observers.

Fiction

Let play be play and nothing else.
Isaac Taylor, *Home Education*, 1838

Ellen Wilt and Larry Cressman, *Tent-Cave,* 1998

ABDON UBIDIA

TELEPATHY AND OTHER IMITATIONS

I had a girlfriend when I was a kid. Her name was Susi. She was skinny and had freckles. I won her over with the only skill I had: imitating animals. It was during summer vacation, in a dry little town. Calling Susi my girlfriend is just a manner of speaking. Neither of us knew anything. She and I were just always together. Sometimes we were by ourselves. Sometimes we joined the gangs of kids that roamed the white sand paths, the streams with their banks of red clay, and the eucalyptus woods, or got together in the morning to go down to the swimming pool, or in the night to sing around a bonfire, catch fireflies and gaze at the starry sky.

There was a boy who played the accordion. Another recited poetry. Another was famous for his traps to catch three different species of doves. Another boy could swim like a fish. I couldn't do any of these things. When I jumped off the board, they had to pull me from the water half-dead.

My animal impressions impressed almost no one. My mother and father got really mad at me one day. My aunt was asking me questions and I answered her with whinnies.

"What grade are you in?"

I whinnied.

"When did you learn to whinny?"

I whinnied.

"You really like horses, huh?"

I whinnied.

"That's enough, boy! Don't be an idiot," my parents said at once. But, though I nearly burst into tears, I didn't stop whinnying.

Other times I would bark or meow. I felt, though, that my masterwork was to baa. I could even confuse the sheep themselves.

Did I say that my poor little talent attracted Susi? She was also different from the rest. Instead of playing marbles or hopscotch, she preferred to climb trees with me.

Hidden in the bushes on the other side of the chain link fence, I would call to her with three quacks.

"Go on, Susi, the duck is looking for you," said her mother one day. I was mortified at being discovered.

In the luminous afternoons of that dusty summer, I would meet Susi at the gate of her family's little summer house and we would go walking into town. Tiny, identical homes. Streets of parched earth. Steely blue-green agaves, some thrusting up a single shoot laden with capers. Jagged-leafed higuerillas. Ovens for calcining limestone. Ovens for baking bread. The dry park. The church with its miraculous Christ. The villagers, a barefoot child, a bundle of firewood, a cow, a donkey laden with sacks of quicklime.

I think that was happiness: the blue sky, the wind that shook the trees, and Susi walking beside me. She would tell me about her parents, her friends, her life in the country's interior in a city that I would only come to know much later.

Always seated on a porch was the Professor, as everyone called him. Paraplegic, old, wrinkled like parchment and dry as the land itself. Forever repeating his eternal discourse to anyone who came near: the climate here, excellent for rheumatism; the "healthful waters," rich in iron and other minerals; the limestone quarries; the likely deposits of coal, et cetera. Such an expenditure of hot air seemed an attempt by the old man to convince himself that he had not spent his life in vain here at the edge of the world.

The pool lay underneath a tremendous pipe, next to the river. In the fantastic cliffs and outcroppings above, you could see all the ages of the earth. Layers of limestone, sandstone, sandy clay, blue clay, and red dirt. High above, at the top of the mountain's wall, appeared thin, solitary algarrobo trees stretched by the wind. Along the river, green proliferated. And, in the middle of the river, among the round stones, barely covered by the yellow waters, there were, every so often, enormous black chunks of lignite, corroded by time. According to the Professor, these were irrefutable proof that there were coal deposits in the area, which would, in the "promissory future," transform the destiny of the nation.

"Healthful" and "promissory" were his key words—among others even stranger.

One day, Susi told him of my skills as an imitator.

"Let's see, boy. Begin your act," he said without smiling (he never smiled). I strove to excel at my imitations. Susi approved each grunt, whistle, or meow with a nervous laugh, while the Professor, grave and attentive, listened in silence.

When I concluded my repertoire, he commented:

"I congratulate you, boy. You have a brilliant future as an animal imitator."

He fell silent, pursing his lips. He focused his eyes on an imaginary point and meditated.

"But there is one bird whose song you won't be able to imitate."

"He can imitate anything that was on Noah's ark," Susi protested.

The Professor spoke a name I've since forgotten. "It's a bird that lives in caves and only goes out at night," he added. "Its song isn't like other birds'. It has no voice. It sings with its mind. Its song is telepathic. A Frenchman who came here thirty years ago told me about it. He took a few pairs back to his country to study. He told me he would write and tell me what he found out, but he never did."

The Professor's voice sounded tired and hesitant, as if he were trying to remember something in the distant past.

"The people of this village," he murmured, "say that only people who are in love can hear that song. If that's true, I think I've heard it only once. But that was centuries ago. Never again. Never again."

He made a gesture that could have served to brush away a fly or a bad memory. Then he resumed his explanation.

"I think it's left over from before the great flood. This is a land where dinosaurs used to roam. Some time ago the intact skeleton of a mammoth was found nearby. Anyone can see that the universe must have begun here. The volcanoes, the mineral waters, the iron, the coal, the limestone, the whole landscape proves it. Even the starry nights, so pure you can see the whole sky gathered together here. That's why I say it's from before the flood. Because some of those animals had no voices. They had a gland in their brains for calling to each other telepathically. We have it too, but it's atrophied and we can use it only very rarely. The scientists should figure out how to reactivate it, instead of making atom bombs."

When we left the Professor, Susi and I went to the pool and told the other kids about the strange bird.

The next morning, the expedition to the caves was ready. Somebody carried a Petromax lamp, somebody else had a flashlight, another an air rifle, another a butterfly net.

It was a fiasco. The caves we entered either weren't very deep, or they narrowed quickly. We found nothing but some bats and a few ferns. Two boys caught a bat and carried it back to the changing rooms at the pool. They crucified it on a wooden door and stuck a lit cigarette in its mouth.

The other kids laughed and joked, and, in passing, made fun of Susi and me. And a chubby little girl, her eyes brimming with tears, said to us, "There's your telepathic bird, you bastards."

The episode brought us even closer. At twilight, Susi and I went back to the caves. That's when we saw, flying out of a cave, a flock of strange, silent birds, large, fast and black against the orange sky.

"The Professor never lies," said Susi. "But we can't tell anyone about this."

That's how the secrets began.

Another secret involved us climbing to the tops of a pair of trees that had grown up together in isolation in the middle of a dry plain. They were very tall and they rocked back and forth slowly. Their crowns moved apart and came together with the sudden changes of wind. We pretended we were riding on the backs of those giant reptiles from the Professor's discourses. We would take eucalyptus and capuli nuts up there with us, and pebbles from the river, and let them fall, to watch them shrink and disappear out of sight.

We would converse in those heights, with fragments of phrases half-lost amid the noise of the wind in the leaves, while the crowns of our trees moved together and apart.

Up there, I told her that I had come to that town completely by chance. First because the climate had been recommended to my grandmother for her rheumatism, and then because my mother was in hospital in our city, very sick, and my father couldn't leave her alone. Otherwise we would have gone to the beach like always.

And up there, Susi asked me, one day:

"Do you know the big secret?"

"What one?"

"The secret of life."

"I never heard there was one."

"This afternoon I'll show you," she said.

We met after lunch and went to the river. We walked along the bank, gathering ferns and little white flowers. Sometimes I would pick up a pebble to give her, and she would tuck it in the pink purse she always carried. At one point, we came to a shallow area where the river curved. There was a lot of oily oxidation on the rocks. Susi said it was good for mosquito bites, and added that we were almost there. The path was getting narrower. There wasn't much space between the river and the moist cliff wall covered with ferns. We had to take our shoes off and wade. I rolled up my pant legs as much as I could and she gathered up her skirt in back and tied it up in front like a washerwoman.

Her calves were much more tanned than her feet and thighs. I told her so. She laughed and said it had happened to both of us because we didn't go to the pool more often. The water was up to our knees and sometimes deeper. I felt the sand and the pebbles move under my feet among the whirling currents. Then the river turned abruptly. A little beach appeared, surrounded by bushes and grasses. At the other end was a small waterfall.

"This is the place," said Susi. "Now we have to hide and wait."

He was perhaps a bit younger than she. After kissing, they took their clothes off and bathed in the waterfall. Then they went on the grass and started to do something I had never seen or had any idea that people did.

"OK, let's go," said Susi.

I told her that I, personally, had no wish to move from my hiding place.

Then Susi couldn't keep from laughing. The couple scrambled away in one direction and we in another.

Back in town, seated on a stone bench in the park, Susi explained to me what her older sister had explained to her.

"But don't say a word about what we saw to anyone. It's a big secret," she warned.

I listened to her, half-intrigued, half-annoyed. She was ten years old, like me, and going into fifth grade. But she knew a lot more things, and in light of them, my imitations seemed useless and stupid.

"I'm never going to imitate animals again," I told her.

"Why not?" she asked, and I thought I saw a flicker of complaint cross her freckled face.

I didn't know what to respond, and she dropped the subject.

"Tomorrow let's go on bikes to the Inca ruins," she said. "And the day after tomorrow, we'll ride horses to the volcano crater."

But there were no Inca ruins or volcano craters. That night, my father came in from the city. My mother had gotten worse and they were going to operate. She had asked him to take me to her. We would leave at dawn.

I had never seen a face as sad as my father's was, that night. It was the face of desolation itself. My grandmother tried to console him, speaking of God and Christ and the miracles and the saints in heaven. But she looked as sad as he did.

It was very late at night, but we weren't sleepy. My father suggested we take a walk around town. At that hour, everyone was asleep. The only light came from the stars, a silvery splendor that barely sketched the outlines of paths and houses.

As we walked, my father talked to me about the stars and the constellations. Their infinite number and infinite distances. Light years, and our insignificance. He pointed out Orion and Ursa Major, Venus and Mercury.

"Among these millions and millions of stars, there must be a planet like ours. But its inhabitants are probably more advanced—they've probably discovered immortality."

He fell silent with a sigh. And we walked quietly for a long time, listening to the wind whispering in the trees and, from time to time, the hoot of an owl.

"Mars," he said suddenly, "is identified by its red color. And Venus by its brightness."

But I couldn't see either of them. Nor the Milky Way, nor the other, more distant galaxies, nor the deep, black, infinite sky constellated with ancient stars that perhaps didn't exist any more except as waves of light.

My eyes were full of tears and I could barely see the path.

I wasn't crying for my mother. I was sure the operation would do its job, as turned out to be the case, because it wasn't right that anything bad should happen to her. I was crying for Susi. I was never going to see her again. I was sure about that, too. And I had no way to tell her so, or even say goodbye.

I don't know how I calmed down and got my father to follow me along the path I always took. I had an idea. We approached Susi's house. And I began to call her with my mind, trying to imitate the echo I thought I'd made out when the strange birds were flying out of their cave that evening by the river.

When we passed in front of her house, I found that Susi had heard the sound of my thought. I could see her at her window, barely illuminated by starlight and waving goodbye with that gesture I'll never forget.

I never went back to imitating animals out loud. And despite the years that passed, and the wanderings of my capricious heart, I was only able to imitate that telepathic song a couple of times more, just twice more, in all my life.

Translated from the Spanish by Nathan Horowitz

KAREN HEULER

SATAN IN ALL HIS GLORY

Clarice Jackson wasn't half as upset by the devil's visits as she was by the fact that everybody thought it was her own fault.

Her little sister had nightmares after hearing about it, her mother shook her head in that fed-up way she had, and there was quite simply hell to pay when her classmate Josephine, that nun-in-waiting, reported Clarice's visitor to Sister Blood of Christ, who in turn told the principal, Sister Three Temptations, who in turn called in the chaplain, Father Reese.

These three people were now assembled in the principal's office—all of them looking very serious and all with their eyes speared straight on Clarice as she entered the room.

"This is Clarice Jackson," Sister Blood said, leaning over to Sister Three.

"Come forward, Clarice." Sister Three had a stern face, flushing red and then draining back to white as her emotions waxed and waned. "You've been telling lies, Clarice."

"No, sister." Clarice tried to keep her voice steady. Her knees were jerking in nervousness and she tried to lock them together so it wouldn't show. She hated being in trouble; she had never been in this kind of trouble before—never a principal's office, never!—and she couldn't imagine what would happen to her.

"What made you tell the girls that you saw the devil?" Sister Blood asked, trying to steer the talk into specifics first.

"Because I did," Clarice said, straining with the effort to be reasonable and confident—which was hard because she could tell they were not going to believe her. "He comes to my room every night and sits in the chair in the corner. I've seen him every night. And he's always gone by morning."

"Nonsense," Sister Three said. "The devil doesn't visit schoolgirls, does he, Father Reese?"

"Not that I've heard," Father Reese said quietly. He sat with his hands in his lap like a star pupil.

"What would he want with a schoolgirl?" Sister Three continued.

Clarice was ready with the answer she'd been preparing ever since she'd caught sight of Josephine—that traitor!—telling Sister Blood about Clarice's devil. "But the saints, sister—didn't he visit the saints and even some people who weren't good enough to be saints, and isn't that how we sin, anyway, from the devil's suggestions?" She gasped it all out, stumbling over her own sincerity.

"Have they been reading the lives of the saints?" Sister Three asked Sister Blood, who answered, "No more than usual."

"Has the devil been making suggestions, then?" Father Reese asked gently.

Clarice took a breath. "He never says anything."

"Then how do you know he's there?"

"Well, . . . I can see him."

"Can you?" Father Reese murmured. "Can you describe him?" Father Reese's eyes were genuinely interested. Sister Three leaned back against her chair and Sister Blood folded her hands into the sleeves of her habit.

"He has a long tail with a barb on it, and he's a reddish-brown color. He's very thin and his eyes are red with white, like a cat's eyes, you know, vertical. And he has a sort of cap with pointy ears."

"A cap," Sister Three scoffed angrily.

"Well, he *does*," Clarice said earnestly. "I can't help it. He does."

"And what is he doing?"

"He sits in the chair by my desk and he watches me. It's dark, so I can't always see what he's doing. He just seems to sit and think. Like he's resting. That's what I think it is, really, he's tired and he just wants to take it easy. Sometimes he taps his finger on the desk, sort of absent-mindedly. But mostly all I hear is breathing."

"He breathes a lot?" Sister Blood asked.

"A sort of hiss-hiss sound. He breathes very slowly."

"Why would the devil breathe at all?" Sister Three asked. "Surely he wouldn't need lungs."

"No, the devil isn't human, Clarice," Father Reese agreed. "The devil is a fallen angel. They don't need lungs."

"Maybe he *took on* a body," Clarice said earnestly, bending in the Father's direction, as if she had a good explanation.

"Clarice," Sister Blood warned.

"You're not suggesting an Incarnation, are you?" Father Reese asked sternly.

Clarice's heart pounded and she flinched; she could tell she'd made an error.

"And what are you doing all this time?" Sister Three demanded.

Clarice heard suspicion in that voice. She had no doubt that there was sex in the principal's mind. Lately they'd been getting sex talks and lectures at unpredictable times. The previous month the entire seventh grade had been summoned to the auditorium without explanation. As soon as everyone was seated, all the nuns rose without a sound or signal and filed out, their hands hidden in their habits, their eyes riding far away. A doctor walked onstage with diagrams and slides, and the lights were discreetly dimmed. So Clarice knew the principal suspected sex—perhaps all of them did, even Father Reese. This was new; she had never been suspected of sex, and she almost groaned. "I'm just looking at him," she assured them. "Waiting to see what he'll do."

The two nuns looked at the priest, who sighed and asked, "What do you expect him to do?"

"I don't have any idea. That's why I watch him." A note of defensiveness had crept into her voice; she saw them noticing it.

"All right, all right," Father Reese said soothingly. "So you don't have any idea. And yet you're sure it's the devil."

"I swear I see him. I see him every night."

"And you're not frightened?"

"I was at first. I said my prayers and he was still there. But he didn't do anything, nothing at all—so I got kind of used to it. But I thought someone should know. That's why I told my mother."

"And what did she say?" Sister Blood asked.

"She said I had too much imagination and that I could sleep with the lights on if I was afraid."

"And did you?"

"I'm not a child. I'm not afraid of the dark. And besides"—her

eyes flickered quickly past the sisters to rest on Father Reese—
"there must be a reason he comes to see me. Having a light on
wouldn't change that."

"Do you think of yourself as an ordinary girl, Clarice?" Father Reese asked.

Her mouth dropped open. The question embarrassed her; she
could think of no way to answer it.

"She's a very good student," Sister Blood said hastily.

"Have you experienced—oh," he considered carefully, "—levi-
tation, the stigmata? Do you spend all your time in acts of char-
ity, religious devotions? Do you start each day by dedicating it
to Our Lord?"

"No," Clarice said, shamefaced. "I'm not that good."

"Well then—do you lie, steal, commit fornication, refuse the
sacraments, act cruelly, wish evil on people?"

"No. Not that either."

"Then you're an ordinary girl, Clarice. And why would the
devil visit an ordinary girl?"

"I don't know." Clarice stared at the floor; her voice had gotten lower.

"Consider it from *his* point of view. You're not planning on becoming a saint, are you?"

"No, Father."

"Then there wouldn't be any great triumph in winning you
over. As a matter of fact, we don't come across saints very much
anymore. Just people who think they can distress themselves
into martyrdom." He smiled apologetically. "These are ordinary
times, Clarice, and you're an ordinary girl. If the devil went
around visiting people—sitting in their chairs—don't you think
we would have heard about it? Whatever the reason, it just
doesn't happen."

Clarice looked sullen. "Just because it doesn't happen to
other people doesn't mean it can't happen to me. I'm not lying,
and I did see him. Besides," she said, sticking her chin up,
"maybe I'm not ordinary. Maybe I'm not." Her voice cracked on
the last word.

Father Reese shook his head. "I'm sorry. I wasn't trying to be-
little you. I meant that you're ordinary in your religious life—
that's all. And before you think I may be dismissing your faith,
let me just warn you. Most people have religious moments,
some of them quite powerful moments. They may feel an over-

whelming presence of God; they may feel called to God. For most people, the moment passes. For others, they do indeed find they have a vocation, and they dedicate their lives to the service of God. But some people, even some of the spiritual ones, fall into the error of thinking they have sanctified themselves, that they are safe with the Lord. That's the sin of presumption."

"That's not me," Clarice protested.

"No; no, it isn't. In a way, it would be better or at least simpler if it were. You see, you're not talking about visits from Christ or the Virgin—you're claiming to see the devil. An apparently harmless devil, too. That's a problem. If he were tempting you—if he were making lewd suggestions—if he were encouraging you to do something wrong or if you were doing something wrong. . . ." He let the sentence trail out, waiting.

"No, no, I'm not doing anything wrong."

"Well, if you *were*, I would think maybe a guilty conscience, sexual hysteria—very real concerns, things that are troubling but can be dealt with." Sister Three nodded in confirmation. "But you don't give me any indication of that. You stand there calmly, saying the devil has taken to visiting you—you, of all people, Clarice Jackson—and it doesn't seem to bother you, you haven't asked how to make it *stop*, you just want us to accept this on faith, so to speak."

"But what can I *do*?" she cried out. "I've tried to think out what it could mean, but I couldn't think of anything. You keep saying the devil comes to people—"

"Who keeps saying?" Sister Blood interrupted.

"Why everyone—the Bible and the lessons and the sermons on Sunday—why, everyone says it. I thought they meant it."

"Oh, they mean it," Sister Three said quickly. "The devil is sin and temptation, and no one can get through life without finding that out."

"The sister is speaking metaphorically," Father Reese said. "In a sense, when we talk of Satan, we're talking metaphorically. We're not saying that everything spiritual exists literally in the mortal world—how could it? the spirit is evident but not material—we're training you to identify the source of your inclinations. And here you're saying you've met the most powerful manifestation of evil ever known, without any ill effects, and we have no choice, no choice at all, but to ask you why you want to see the devil." He paused to look at her. "What do you get out of it?"

Clarice was agitated; she held her hands tightly together, then wrapped her arms across her chest. Her mouth twisted itself tightly together. She shivered. "I could say I haven't seen him," she said finally, lowering her eyes.

"Could you?" Father Reese was encouraging.

She raised her eyes directly to him. "But then I would be lying," she said. "And that's a sin."

Father Reese plucked absently at his cuff before looking at Sister Three. He smiled wanly. "Well, sisters, under the circumstances I think it's best to let the matter rest for the moment."

"This may be heresy, Clarice," Sister Three said with a threatening edge to her voice. "But I leave that up to Father Reese to decide. You are dismissed."

"Yes, sister," Clarice said bleakly. She cast a pleading glance at Father Reese and left the room. As soon as the door shut she heard the principal's voice complaining harshly. She knew no one was going to say anything in her favor, and it was a shock. She wasn't the best girl in the world—she knew that—but to be called ordinary, a liar, and a possible heretic; these things shook her. And to top it all, the most amazing thing was happening and no one believed her.

Because it was all true, it really was, and why would she make it up? She couldn't figure out why it was happening, she couldn't explain it or ignore it, but she didn't have doubts. She trusted herself, she knew her steadiness and she trusted her intelligence.

Except that she would expect people to *know* she was not the kind of girl who made things up. She was not trying to get attention; she was not scaring herself for the thrill of it—she knew girls who did both these things and she was not like them in the least.

And yet no one believed her.

The bells rang for lunch. She retrieved her books from the last classroom and went to her assigned table in the cafeteria. She had brought lunch with her, so she sat down at her table immediately. She was quivering with annoyance and fear.

"Ooo hoo," her best friend Rosemary said. "I didn't think I'd ever see you again. Clarice in the principal's office! Were you talking about me?"

"No one even mentioned you." Rosemary was a simmering type of girl—she had very long wavy hair and a heart-shaped face with eyes that seemed about to wink. She did forbidden things and what's worse, had a tendency to do them in the wrong places. She'd been caught smoking right outside the school, had botched her father's signature on a report card, had told far too many people about cutting school and going to a rock concert (she had been threatened with suspension for that). She was a good-hearted girl who loved her own impulses. She and Clarice were convinced they were the only girls in school who had never once considered becoming nuns. They were friends for life.

"I'm in trouble because I told the truth," Clarice complained, putting her lunch down and wiping her palms dry with a napkin. Now that it was over, she felt terrible—a mixture of fear, repentance (even though she'd done nothing wrong, she was sorry for doing it), self-defense, and—this was odd—triumph. They hadn't proved anything, after all.

"Tell me everything," Rosemary said, her eyes expectant, "and I'll tell you what they'll do about it."

So Clarice told her all about the devil and about telling Josephine. Rosemary frowned at that. "Why in the world did you tell *her*?" she asked. It was obvious that she thought she should have been the first to know.

"She said she'd had a dream where she saw St. Therese wearing her hat."

Rosemary nodded. "She's always having religious dreams. But tell me, Clarice—you're not joking, right? It really was the devil?"

"I thought you of all people would believe me!" Clarice cried.

"Just making sure. So tell me—how tall is he?"

Clarice blinked. "He's sitting down."

"Still—is he very tall?"

"I guess about average, or I would have noticed. Why?"

"They've figured out that Christ was 5'5" tall. See if you can get his height."

Clarice laughed. "You're crazy."

"You see? You're laughing. You're not really in trouble, I bet."

"They had Father Reese in."

"Then it's a religious problem," Rosemary said. "They don't give you detention for that."

"No?"

"No. They have hell for that."

After talking to Rosemary, the devil seemed merely a practical problem. Rosemary had a way of doing that—perhaps because her world was almost entirely directed by cause and effect. At any rate, by the time she went home Clarice was determined to get some kind of proof of the devil's existence. Rosemary had offered to spend the night with her, as a witness, but Clarice had refused. She wasn't sure the devil would appear to anyone else—and Rosemary was not the kind of witness to persuade anyone in authority.

The two girls decided that the first thing to do was to get a camera, preferably a Polaroid so Clarice wouldn't have to wait to see it developed. Rosemary had one—a cast-off from her parents—and promised to bring it the next day. She called Clarice that night to say there was film but no flashbulbs.

The idea of flashbulbs bothered Clarice; what would the devil do if he was suddenly exposed like that?

So she decided to test the devil in a small way. She had been told, in school, that God and the angels knew all, saw all. She supposed it was true for the devil as well, though she couldn't remember any discussions about the limits of the devil's power and authority. Wasn't he also eternal, omnipotent, omnipresent, and omniscient? She supposed so; she supposed there was as little hope of surprising the devil as there was of surprising God. They knew her thoughts. When she remembered that, her thoughts seemed silly. She decided resolutely not to think about her thoughts.

She checked the kitchen until she found a box of matches, which she took to her own room and placed under her pillow. She decided to do it; she decided not to do it. The devil might see it as a challenge—and what protection did she have against the devil?

But he never does anything, she thought, nothing at all. She was counting on that, that he would stay there, watching her, whatever she did. She hoped that she was already protected, was in fact immune. It seemed likely—if the devil sat down comfortably with her, then she was safe.

And maybe there was sainthood in that—or at the very least, lack of ordinariness. Because the truth of it was (she had to approach this sideways, she saw the possible sin), the charge of being an ordinary girl rankled horribly. Was she ordinary? How could that be—she didn't feel ordinary, she didn't put herself in the same group as Margaret, Linda, Barbara—those withdrawn, timid, tucked-in girls who hid in their seats and never had brave thoughts, she could tell. *She* had brave thoughts, she was willing to think of large, uncommon possibilities, she could see herself, someday in the future, facing threats and overcoming them. She was not ordinary.

So that night she said her prayers—perhaps too rapidly to be truly fervent—checked for the matchbox under the pillow, and turned out the light. Her plan was to strike a wooden match after the devil sat down in her chair. She wanted to make sure he would stay, that he was hers and trusted her, that his selection of her was not random but deliberate. In some way, she must be important to him.

She turned out the overhead light and went to bed. She was prepared. She closed her eyes, as she always did, to get them used to the dark. When she opened them, he was there. Seated as usual on her chair, leaning toward the wall, his face turned to her, the red eyes dim but visible.

She watched him for a moment. She heard the hiss-hiss of his breath and felt a twinge of victory. He *was* there; he *did* breathe. She reached slowly under her pillow and took out the box of matches. She did it all by touch; her eyes were locked on him.

She had to move in order to light the match; she had to lean propped up on one elbow; but the movement didn't startle him; he watched her.

She struck the match. The flash blinded her for a second.

He was gone.

She heard herself yelp a muted, protesting "No!" She sat bolt upright, holding the match before her, and then swept it wide to illuminate the room. Nothing. She shook the match out.

She sat, the spent match still in her hand, dismayed by the disappearance. Could he be frightened by light? No—that was vampires. Was there something in his appearance he wanted to keep hidden from her—something that would give her a clue as to why he was there at all, why he'd chosen her? It was impossible, impossible to figure out, and totally unfair. The unfairness of it made her grit her teeth. Who would believe her now,

now that he had fled before her match like it was a crucifix or holy water?

She shut her eyes tight in despair. The hand that held the matchstick flailed out, dropping it. She was in misery, and it was only the sudden consciousness of the hiss-hiss of his breath that brought her out of herself again. She raised her head; her eyes darted into the shadows; he was back, sitting there as always, casual in her chair.

Her hand reached out for the matches, but this time, instead of flaring and holding the match out, she held it cupped in her hand, shielding the devil from sudden exposure.

Then a terrible thing happened. The flame in her hand shed an uneven, thin, flickering light through the fingers of her hand, and as the radiance faltered and flared, so too did the devil appear and disappear. She lit another match after that one burned out, and the same thing happened. It took four matches before she could admit what she saw—and she flushed in the shadows, felt the heat creep into her face and flood her neck, felt a shame so deep and so basic that she wished she could disappear herself on the spot, as the devil did, without effort or explanation.

But there *was* an explanation. He was no more than the image of a tree cast through her window, his cap and pointed ears the pattern of leaves, his forked tail a broken branch. The eyes—the last thing she could figure out as one by one she matched each piece of the devil to something familiar and specific in her own world—the eyes were reflections of a small red light in a window across the street. She matched them up, over and over, faster and faster, confirming her own error with something like fervor: *this* was how wrong she was, and *this*, and *this*.

There was no more need for matches. She lay in the dark, her eyes open. Once she realized what the devil was, there was no further need to confirm, to verify—or even to consider whether the devil was playing a trick on her. He could do that if he wanted to, play a trick on her, disguise himself as a shadow, convince her that he wasn't there when he was. But Clarice knew there was no devil, she was sure of it. Not only was she wrong, but she was publicly wrong. She had told people. Why had she told people? Why couldn't she have kept it to herself? Why?

She lay in bed awake, wondering if she really had to admit it, if she really had to say she was wrong. Couldn't she simply say he stopped showing up, no longer occupied the chair, no longer tapped his finger or hissed his breath—was there any real need to say a branch rubbed up against the wall, or leaves whistled outside her window? How committed to her own humiliation was she?

Because here was the sore spot: they were right about her, and she was wrong. They knew what kind of girl she was. She was excitable, given to fits of imagination. She was the kind of girl who shrieked at bugs, who ran away from snakes, who made things up out of excess of self, of ordinary self. Those three black-clad figures in the principal's office had told her what she was—simply not the kind of girl who was special. She belonged with the crowd of girls, with the tittering, clustering groups of girls. She was not destined for anything but ordinary mistakes, common misunderstandings. They had seen it, and she had not.

The next morning she was called out of home room, right after prayers. This time it was just the principal and Father Reese. She stood in front of Sister Three Temptation's desk, her head lowered, her hands held together in front of her.

"Did you see the devil last night?" Sister Three demanded.

Clarice lifted her eyes to lock on Sister Three's eyes. "I was wrong," she said faintly. "It was the shadow of a tree. I believed it was the devil, and I was wrong."

Sister Three relaxed back in her chair. "We have a recantation, Father."

"I'm glad to hear it."

"Ah, these girls," the principal said. "These emotional girls."

"It's imagination, a wonderful thing in itself."

"When not abused."

"Yes, yes, certainly."

Clarice watched them stonily. They had relaxed, they were amused, now, relieved by her statements, glad to be rid of the puzzle. She had the feeling that at that moment, they liked her. They liked her error and her confession; she was no longer being difficult. Now, at the moment of her deepest humiliation, she had their approval, and she found that a small part of her responded to it. But she caught herself at it and rebelled. When the principal asked, "And what have you learned from this?"

she felt a little demon of defiance jump into her throat. She said, "To keep my mouth shut when I'm wrong."

Sister Three frowned. Father Reese glanced sideways at the principal. He said, "Well, I guess we all learn that one sooner or later. But I think what happened here was that you didn't know you were wrong. Maybe you'll keep that in mind—the possibility—next time."

Clarice said "Yes, Father" very politely, and was excused. She got to the hallway just as the bell rang for end of class, and the halls were filled suddenly with girls rushing and talking. Clarice made her way through them. She assumed they had all heard by now about her devil; they would hear later, by some alchemical process, how the devil was a tree. Even the ones who didn't ask her about it would hear and draw a conclusion. Girls all around her would click that into their definition of Clarice, would use it to classify her or merely confirm something they may have thought they knew.

Clarice lowered her head, already burdened by all the conclusions that would be drawn by ordinary girls all around her. She didn't look forward to seeing Rosemary, either. Rosemary was used to being wrong and reveled in it. She wouldn't understand that this hurt Clarice so much because it caught her where she was most off-guard: in the utter conviction that she knew herself and could trust herself, and from that could see, and judge, and recognize. Now she would have to become the girl they all knew she was, and stop being the girl she thought she was. She had to, because it had been proven to her, like the solution to a math problem.

The girls massed and parted around her. A holy statue cast its shadow in the corridor; she stepped across it, aware of its brief touch on her face, and then the crowd behind her pushed forward, laughing, and she rushed with it down the hall.

CATHERINE RYAN HYDE

BLUE DOG IN THE CRAZY TRUCK

I have to tell you this story so I can tell you the real one.

When Pippin and I were both seven, my father and I were taking her for a walk. We were passing in front of that little store on the next block, which had been boarded up for years, only on that day some new business was moving in. Three big guys were wheeling stuff on dollies, stuff like refrigerator cases and big metal shelves. They had their T-shirt sleeves rolled high, all three of them, sweating in the heat. They all looked a little bit alike, wheeling stuff from a moving van at the curb, passing each other on the sidewalk. Just as we crossed in front of their shop, Pippin stopped and squatted down, and I prayed all she would do was pee. Two of the guys just stopped, and a minute later the third came out and he stood and stared at us, too, with his hands on his hips. Staring at this smelly little pile on their pavement.

Well, I should make this a shorter story, since it's not even the really important one.

The guys said, "Clean it up." And my father said, "Come on. Give me a break. With what? My hands?" And the guys said, "Clean it up, or we're going to call the police," and that's when I noticed they were all a lot bigger than him. That my father wasn't as big as I always thought he was. "Okay," he said, "no need for that." They brought him a skimpy little paper napkin from inside the shop.

When we got home, he told the story to my mother. Only when he got to the part about them calling the police, he claimed to have said, "Oh, come on, you're not going to call the police." Right in front of me he told it like that. Like I wasn't right there when it happened.

That's when I learned about shame, which always feels more painful on someone else's behalf.

338

Less than a year later my mother divorced us, and I didn't see much of her after that. I always figured she must have seen it, too, somehow. Seen some little glimpse of what I'd seen. So now we both knew he wasn't quite as big as we thought. And I was his son, so I must have been what he was, and not been what he was not, which I think is why she divorced me, too. That was always my theory, anyway. You need to be able to explain a thing like that in your head, or you'll never get to sleep. Even an explanation that basically means you suck is better than no explanation at all.

Okay. I had to tell you that story so I could tell you this one.

Pippin and I were thirteen and a half. We didn't live in western New York near that little store anymore. We lived in Echo Park in Los Angeles with Alvie. My father and I were taking Pippin for a walk down Alvarado Street. It was late in the evening, maybe eight-thirty, but still—I swear—eighty-five degrees. September, that weird kind of L.A. Indian summer where the smog and the buildings trap the heat and you can't see the sky but you know it's hot, wherever it is.

It's hard for me to say what happened first, how it started, because I was looking at Pippin. She was rooting around at the edge of a vacant lot, looking for a place to pee. Pippin was a Welsh corgi, with legs about four inches long, so when you looked at her, you were looking at the ground, and you didn't see much else, because nothing much goes on at that level.

When I looked up I saw the man. He had greasy dark blond hair, and a tattoo on his jaw. A long vertical cross with a snake crawling along it. Right on his face. Where someone else would have a sideburn, he had this. It was dark where we stood, nowhere near a streetlight, but just for a minute somebody's car lights lit us up. I expected the man's knife to look shiny. I thought that was part of the dangerousness of the knife. How light was supposed to glint off it into my eyes. But it looked rusty, or just filthy, maybe. Or both. I wanted the person who owned the car lights to stop and help. Things were being said. I guess they must have been. I could hear them, in a way. I remember the sound of voices, but not what was said. My father took off his watch and handed it over.

I got that feeling again. That same feeling like watching him pick up dog shit with this tiny little skimpy napkin that barely covered his hand, with all those big guys watching. I know it's not fair that I felt that. Believe me, I know. I'm just telling you what I felt. I'm not saying it's fair.

At a moment like that you think things, and you feel things, and they happen fast. They don't ask permission. They're not always even important thoughts, and they don't always make good sense.

Like, I thought, Jesus Christ, guy, at least take care of your knife. I mean, you're a robber, a mugger, whatever. This is a tool of your trade.

And I thought it was good he was a white guy like me and my father, because it would be really hard to go home and tell Alvie a black guy mugged my father and sliced him up with a rusty blade and left him bleeding onto Alvarado Street. It would've hurt me to tell Alvie that, because it would've hurt her to hear it, in one of those funny little places where things get in and you can't get in after them to take away the sting.

I make it sound like I had lots of time to think about things, but really it all happened fast.

When my father took his watch off to hand it over, he dropped Pippin's leash. And Pippin took off running. And I ran after her. I wondered later if I ran after her because I was afraid for her, which I'm sure was part of it, or if running after something—*to* something—made it a less obvious example of running away. While I was chasing her I wondered if she was scared. If she was running away, too. But I knew probably not. Pippin would always run if you dropped the leash, as long as I'd known her, which was always. I didn't figure she knew enough about this to run scared. Pippin was always scared of the wrong things. Always trying to defend us from things that didn't matter—like the crazy dog in the blue truck, which I'll tell you about later—and then going off on a romp while some guy sliced up my father. I'd been trying to teach her but she just didn't get it because she was only a dog.

She ran across the street and almost got hit by a car. But the guy squealed on his brakes and stopped in time, and I ran after her, ran by in front of him, with one hand up, like waving. Like, thanks for not killing her, because I've never lived a day she wasn't around. Then a car going the other way actually hit me. Not all that hard, but it did. The guy tried to stop, and maybe another six inches he would have. But the headlight hit my right hip and knocked me down. I didn't even break his headlight, though, and it didn't break me, because I got up and kept running. Pippin started to wear down after awhile, and I caught her leash and we ran home together. I never once looked over my shoulder. After a while I had to pick her up, because she couldn't run that fast anymore. Being thirteen and those little short legs. Still she weighed over twenty pounds, and I was running straight uphill. Seven blocks straight uphill from Alvarado Street, that's where we lived with Alvie. I could feel sweat running on my face; my face felt hot, radiating hot, like my skin was letting off heat. My chest burned, but I think I could have run to the top of that hill if I had to, because I had to. Because I had to get home to Alvie. If I could just get home and tell Alvie, somehow this night could be over.

We lived in a court apartment, one of the ones all the way at the top, up the steep stairs. I put Pippin down on her short legs again. Grabbed the handrail, which was a long welded pipe right up the center of the stairs. And all the way up I screamed for her. Alvie. Alvie. Alvie.

When I got to our door she threw it open, and we stood face to face. Just stood like that under the porch light, two mirror faces, and in hers I could see what she saw in mine. She had fine, dark black skin, Alvie. Shiny black, and hair in a river of tiny, neat, perfect braids. Each braid had beads at the end, and I loved the sound they made, the clattering, like a wind chime. It always made Alvie sound more alive than everybody else. But as we stood looking at each other, her hair was perfectly silent. I could see the whites all the way around the chestnut of her eyes.

I waited in Alvie's car while she made the call. Alvie had a big old-fashioned boat of a car, an old Chevy with no hubcaps, but it ran fine. She took good care of the parts that counted, and it always ran. When she got in, I didn't even look over at the side of her face. I didn't want her to look at mine. I was afraid of what she'd see. Afraid she'd look at me and feel shame, like she was watching me clean up dog crap while a bunch of big guys watched.

I didn't use my voice to show her where to drive, I just pointed.

When we got to the corner there was nothing there. Nobody.

Like nothing had ever happened. Just a black puddle, like somebody drove their car up on the sidewalk and then spilled their dirty crankcase oil. Alvie always carried a flashlight under her seat. She had a knack for practical things like that, very organized, which is one reason my father and I needed her so much.

We got out and stood on the corner together, and Alvie shined her flashlight on that puddle, and it turned red. The black had only been a trick of the light.

Alvie spoke three words under her breath. But I don't know what they were. Maybe because of that sweet, thick accent, or just the way she hushed them. Maybe she wasn't even speaking English just then. I think they had something to do with praying to God but that's only a gut impression. Really I had no way to know.

At the hospital I told everyone Alvie was my stepmother. It should have been the other way around. She was practically his wife, and she should have been telling them I was his son, and defending my right to be there. But she wasn't his wife, not really, and they were more interested in blood. Blood relations. Which made Alvie a poor relation, standing behind me while I tried to explain.

I told one nurse Alvie was my mother, just to see the look on the nurse's face. Just to see her do what I knew she would, look from Alvie's exotic blackness to my own towhead and freckles and back again. I wanted to say, "Fuck you," to her, but I knew I'd regret it later, because it wasn't her fault my father got cut.

"The boy exaggerates," Alvie said, drawing it out song-like and thick, her accent still more proof that I was a liar.

The nurse shook her head as if she could shake us away for the night.

While we sat in the waiting room, while my father lay on that operating table, I confessed a sin to Alvie. It was the first either of us had spoken in nearly an hour, and it startled us both to hear the sound of my voice. "Alvie," I said. "I told my friends from school that you were from Jamaica." What this had to do with the moment I could not have explained. But now I see it was something about that nurse. How she took something away from Alvie—something that rightly belonged to her—by knowing at a glance we were not blood relatives. And then, sitting waiting for my father to make it through surgery or die on the table, it dawned on me that I had stolen from Alvie, too. I had stolen her heritage for selfish gains. For stupid reasons, like the word Haiti sounding like the word hate. And Jamaica being a place you go for a vacation, to lie on white sand and drink rum. And Haiti being a place where Papa Doc and Baby strung innocent people from trees and wouldn't allow their neighbors to cut them down and put their bodies to rest in the ground.

"Why would you say that, Neal? You know where I'm from."

"Yes," I said. "I know. I'm sorry."

She looked at me for a moment. It seemed like a long moment. I prayed I wouldn't look too small to her. Then she set her mouth strangely and shook her head. I knew she would ask no more about it. It had flown away from her mind. "Why didn't you do something, Neal?"

My stomach chilled strangely, and for the first time I realized my hip hurt. It wasn't injured exactly, but it was pretty bruised up, and the sensation broke through, for the first time, and I noticed that. "Like what?" I said.

"Scream, or run out and stop traffic."

"I don't know."

My eyes were squeezed shut, so it startled me when she grabbed me. We were sitting on a vinyl couch together, and she threw her arms around me, and pulled me in against her, and pulled my head to her shoulder. Then my eyes opened, and stayed that way, like they might never close again. I could see the clock on the waiting room wall, and hear Alvie's hair clattering loud against my ear.

"Oh, Nealy," she said. "Please forget I said that. Please?"

I nodded. But of course I would not forget it. How could I? What a gift for words, to be able to take all that free-floating guilt, all those questions, all that hindsight, and force it to the ground in five simple words. The five words I'd been searching for myself. And Alvie found them for me. Why didn't I do something?

"It wasn't your fault, Nealy. It wasn't." Nobody had called me Nealy for years. At any other time I might have objected. Then she found five more words, and I wouldn't forget these, either. "You're only a little boy. You couldn't have done anything, Nealy. You're only a little boy."

Alvie stood behind me, one hand on each of my shoulders, while I talked to the police. I was good, too. For the first time all night, I did something right. They loved the part about the tattoo, because once you know that, who cares if he was five-ten or six feet and who cares what he was wearing because he can change his clothes, anyway. I liked it too because I knew I wouldn't have to go in to look at a lineup unless they really got him, because if it wasn't him they'd know, without my help. I even told them things I didn't know I'd seen until I told them. The way the guy smiled like a dog showing his teeth, and how when the car's lights lit us up I saw a chip broken off his front tooth. I hadn't even known I'd seen that until later. I felt Alvie squeeze my shoulders and I knew she was proud of me.

"Can you officers give the boy a ride home?" she asked.

I'd been telling her, before the cops showed up, that Pippin had never done her business on that walk and somebody should be home with her now. I know Alvie would have cleaned it up. But the hospital was bright and loud and I wanted to go home and sit with Pippin and be nearly alone.

The cops asked if she thought I'd be okay home by myself. She said she'd be home before the night was over, and after all I was not a child, I was nearly fourteen years old. You see, I'd grown older in just those few minutes, and Alvie knew it and vouched for it. I liked that about Alvie. She wasn't afraid to allow for change.

Just before we all three left together, the two cops and me, Alvie pulled me around by my elbow and whispered in my ear. "Don't let them come in," she said, and I remembered that Alvie and my father had been smoking Alvie's bong just before we went out for that walk.

When I got inside by myself, the apartment was dark. Just the glow of the corner streetlight shining through the contact-papered windows, patterned to look like stained glass. Alvie liked them that way because she could leave the bong and the bag out on the table and no one could see in. Alvie's orange-and-white cat was sitting on the back of the couch, looking like a saint in that stained glass glow. The way he looked at me felt like a blessing. I hid everything illegal in my father's dresser drawer, for no real reason I could pin down.

I took a shower because I stank, because all that dried sweat felt uncomfortable, because it was all part of the man with the cross and the snake and the chipped tooth. All his fault, all his doing. I stood in the hot water until it turned cold, and then I put on just pajama bottoms. Eased them over my bruised hip, and then pulled them down again to look at the bruise in the mirror.

I took Pippin out to the very closest patch of dirt, and the whole time she was circling around I kept looking behind me.

Then I sat on the window seat in my room, and Pippin sat up there with me, but I had to lift her up there because her legs were too short. My window was the only one with no contact paper. I liked to see out.

Pippin growled low in her throat and then a minute later I heard him. Pippin always heard him first. The barking, and the low pop of that truck engine. The blue truck was a big, old thing with rust primer spots, and a beefy engine, and not much muffler. It came by every night in the middle of the night, then back up the hill in the early, still-dark morning. The downhill run made the valves pop, a little explosion like a backfire on every cylinder, and I think that dog was crazy, because he barked the whole time. Everywhere that truck went, he ran back and forth in the bed and barked. Pippin hated him. Pippin wanted to save me from him. That's why I started calling him "just the crazy dog in the blue truck." It made him sound less important. I was trying to teach Pippin what was important.

But that night my voice sounded like somebody else's, small and far away. Tinny. Unfamiliar. "It's okay, Pippin," I said, "it's just the blue dog in the crazy truck." It wasn't until I heard myself say it that I noticed I'd screwed it up, and then it didn't seem to matter.

When Alvie came in the front door I didn't get up. I just waited for her to find me.

She came into my room and stood near the window seat. She put one of her hands on my bare shoulder. Alvie's long fingernails were gone. Those gorgeous, perfectly manicured nails with the peach-colored polish; she'd bitten them off. I was so used to her fingers ending that beautiful way. It was a shock to me, like seeing her with the ends of her fingers cut off, or with her eyelashes and eyebrows shaved, or with no teeth. Things that had always been there, missing.

"He's out of surgery," she said.

"How do they think it looks?"

"Touch and go, Nealy. Touch and go. The doctor is worried about infection. Because his intestine was cut."

"Peritonitis," I said. I had a friend at summer camp who almost died of peritonitis when his appendix burst. Almost died. But he didn't die. He lived to tell me the story.

"Come on, Nealy," she said. "You need to get some sleep."

She took me by the hand and led me over to my bed, and I lay down on top of the covers. It was still too hot to cover up. Then she left the room for a while, and I could hear her moving around the house, but I have no idea what all she did.

A few minutes later she came back into my room and lay down on the bed behind me. Not exactly touching me, but close enough that I knew by feel how close she was. I felt her fingers on my scalp, front to back, stroking my hair the way you might stroke a worry stone. Over and over. Immediately I got an erection, and I lay there thinking about my father lying in the hospital, but that didn't make it go away. I thought, Jesus Christ, Neal, what kind of monster are you? But I couldn't do a damn thing about it, except to stay faced away and not make a statement on whether I was awake or not. She kept that rhythm in my hair, but never really touched me beyond that, except that she set her head right behind mine on the pillow, and part of her face rested on my neck. When she breathed through that fine, wide nose, I could feel the light brush of her breath across my collarbone, like a cool touch. I don't know how long we stayed like that but it must have been near morning, because Blue Dog came back up the hill. I heard Pippin growl in her throat. That's the first I let on I was awake.

"It's okay, Pippin," I said. "It's only the blue dog in the crazy truck."

"What on earth are you talking about?" Alvie said, with no real reproach or judgment.

"Nothing. It's just a private joke with me and Pippin. I'm trying to teach her what's dangerous and what's not."

"She's only a dog, Nealy."

"I know that."

"She's an old dog. If she doesn't know by now, I think she won't learn."

"I know," I said. "It's just a game."

The side window in my room was open for the breeze, and I lay still and thought about the man with the book and the razor. He'd visited five women in Echo Park the previous summer, and the police never caught him. He came in hot weather, cut their screens with a razor blade. Stood over their beds and exposed himself, with a book in front of his face so they could never identify him.

Now that's dangerous, Pippin.

And I was home alone with Alvie. What would I do if something bad happened to Alvie and my father wasn't around? How much good would I be?

I lay there, still hard, thinking about that man, wondering if I was any better than him, any safer to be around. I tried to send silent signals to Pippin to be extra watchful, but then I could hear her snoring in the corner. I decided I'd have to stay awake to keep everybody safe.

Alvie woke me with a kiss on the temple. She was standing over my bed, fully dressed. Her hair clattered as she straightened up again. I usually woke up with a hard-on anyway, so I went to pull the covers up, but they were up already. Alvie must have covered me in my sleep.

She was wearing jeans and her "I am your witness" T-shirt—the one she bought as a fund-raiser for all the women victims of the rape camps in Bosnia—and one of my father's denim shirts open over it, like a jacket, so you couldn't read all of what it said. But I knew it by heart, except the parts that weren't in English.

"Are you going to school?" she asked.

"No."

"Okay. You can come to the hospital, but you'll have to move very fast."

But I couldn't get up right then in front of her, so I said,

"You go on, Alvie. I'll take the bus down in a little while." I knew she wanted to leave right then, anyway.

"Do you have bus fare?"

"Yes."

She wasn't thinking clearly. I had a bus pass to go to school. It cost no more to go to the hospital. She kissed me again, this time on the forehead, and swept out of the room. And I wondered if she'd sleep in my bed again that night.

Then it hit me, really hit me for maybe the first time, that he might die. And then Alvie would sleep in my bed every night. We'd have to be very quiet about it at first, but after a few years I'd be eighteen, and we could move somewhere nobody knew us, and if they had a problem with the difference in our ages or our colors, they could go fuck themselves. It was none of their concern. But then my father would have died. I lay there with my perpetual erection thinking, Jesus Christ, Neal. What kind of monster are you?

But he wasn't going to die, anyway. He was going to pull through. And Alvie was going to go back to sleeping in bed with him like she always had. Like last night had never happened.

It was like the lady or the tiger except in that story one of the guy's possibilities is good.

That night I came home from the hospital in a cab, and I waited three hours for Alvie to join me. I showered, and wore only pajama bottoms like the night before, and covered myself with a sheet in spite of the heat, all because I expected her.

If I'm remembering correctly, I was hard before she ever arrived. And I don't know what kind of monster I was. I don't know. Things just are sometimes.

When she got home she changed into one of my father's long shirts, and lifted up the sheet and got underneath with me. Instead of stroking her fingers through my hair she placed one smooth, light-caramel palm across my forehead, like she was checking me for fever, and just held it there, unchanging. She kissed the back of my hair lightly.

"What did they say, Alvie?"

"Same thing they were saying before you left."

"Still not awake."

"No. Doctor says the next twenty-four hours will tell."

"He said that before I left."

"What did I just tell you?"

What I'd meant was, shouldn't it be twenty-one hours by now? It seemed wrong to keep pointing to twenty-four hours that never got shorter, like waiting for a school bell that's always three hours away.

We lay quietly for a long time, and she was close enough I could feel her breasts through my father's shirt, feel them up against my back.

"I called your grandparents," she said. "They'd be very happy to have you. If . . . You know. If. If it should come to that. But they also said you're a big boy, you can decide for yourself who you want to live with."

"I want to stay with you, Alvie."

"Hush!" She barked the word at my ear, tugged at my forehead in a sharp gesture that felt almost like a slap. I stopped breathing briefly. "It's not time to claim such things. You don't make that choice yet. Because maybe there will be no choice to make."

"Right. You're right, Alvie. Probably not."

We both breathed again, and I felt her thumb move on my forehead, stroking me just the tiniest bit. "I would take care of you, though." She breathed it against my ear, so small, like if she said it quietly enough, God couldn't hear it and act on it.

I knew then that what I thought I'd felt the night before I really had felt, even though nothing had happened on the outside. Someone could have been there watching and never seen it, but I knew then it was real. I wanted to say, We'd take care of each other, Alvie, but I didn't want her to bark at me again.

Speaking of barking, a few minutes later he came down the hill, valves popping, and Pippin growled at him.

"Blue dog in the crazy truck," Alvie said.

"Blue dog," I said, feeling we had the beginnings of a language now. Knowing if my father were here, he wouldn't know what we meant.

Just before I fell sleep she said, "Neal."

And I said, "What, Alvie?"

"Do you know what he would have said to do, if there had been time? If he hadn't had the knife to watch, if it hadn't all happened so fast? Do you know what he would have told you?"

"No, Alvie. What?"

"He would have said, 'Run, Nealy. Run away.' And when you got away safe he would have been so happy."

I closed my eyes again and later I had a dream, and in the dream I was running away, and I could hear my father yelling to me, and sure enough, that's what he was saying. "Run, Nealy. Get away." So I was only doing what he wanted me to do, and I was making him happy. Only in the dream Pippin got hit by a car. So, once something like that happens in your life, almost no matter how it turns out, it seems like something will be lost.

The phone woke us. Alvie reached over me to pick up my extension, her body pressing against my back, pushing me forward.

"Yes, this is she," she said. And then, "Thank you so much. I'll be right down."

She hung up the phone and got out of bed, taking the crush of her body away.

"He woke up," she said. "They've upgraded him to stable."

I sat up and blinked. Watched her walk out of my room without saying more, without looking back, without saying goodbye. Something had blown out of her when this new information blew in, like there was only just so much room inside her to feel.

In the same way I understood the realness of what we'd felt, I just as clearly understood that what we'd felt was now over.

My father came home three days later. I wasn't there when he arrived; I was out walking Pippin. We'd been walking two, three, sometimes four miles a day, because I knew if I let myself I could lose the habit of ever walking down a street again. It was like overkill.

And, actually, it was not a surprise to me. I'd gone out walking that day knowing damn well she'd gone to the hospital to bring him home.

I walked into their bedroom. He was lying on his back in bed, with a sheet pulled up to his armpits. Alvie was lying beside him, stroking her fingers through his hair. Just for a minute that stopped me, literally. I just stopped in my tracks and looked at both of them, and none of us said a word. With his eyes my father said, You come over here and sit down with me, and with her eyes Alvie said, It was between us; you never say a word about it.

And I never did.

I sat down beside my father and he grabbed my hand too hard. I expected him to say something coherent and meaningful but he was still doped up on painkillers. I expected him to look small like he'd been doing lately, but instead he just looked so damn much bigger than me.

I let him squeeze my hand too hard. I purposely didn't look at Alvie because if I had I couldn't have said what I said next, even though I didn't say it out loud.

But what I said to him, in the privacy of my own gut, was this: She's the most important thing I ever had in my life, but I'm giving her back to you, because I'm that happy you're alive.

Of course I knew in my head she wasn't mine to keep or give back, but I told you already, this was my gut.

Also, guts don't give up neatly, so after that not a day went by I didn't regret the gift, wrestle with it, resent it, long to change my mind. But just at that moment I said it to him, silently, and believed I meant it, and that felt like enough.

WANDA COLEMAN

BUTTERFLY MEAT

They lived not far from the coast. In that summer afternoon's blessed sweet sunshine, the two children followed the heavy-breasted, shapely sepia woman across the backyard. Blithely, their mother sang nursery rhymes as she marched ahead. The six-year-old loved to help her mother with the laundry, was eager to impress adults, and therefore was content to carry the basket and clothespin bag. The boy followed, but begrudged the chore. Barely five, he frowned as he dragged his basket, under the spell of his father's notions of manhood.

The trio rounded the garage and stopped before a fenceless square chain of land triangulated by three bountiful fruit trees, peach, fig, and lemon. Defined by two hollow iron T-poles, strung with heavy wire lines, the core area was hung with the dazzling rectangular array of the morning's wash flagged briskly by the ocean breeze.

The mother instructed them to study her actions and do their best to do likewise. The children stood against one another, dark spindly arms slack, baskets lowered to knees. They watched as their mother carefully placed her basket in the dried grass before a stiff line of diapers clamped end-to-end by clothespins. She stood behind her basket, at the extreme end of the line, nearest where the yard ended off an alley. Then she reached up and tugged the line. Expertly, right hand gliding along, she plucked the pins, gathering as many as one hand could hold before dropping them into the clothespin bag strapped across her shoulder. As she did this, she simultaneously dropped the garments into the basket with her left hand. Feet synchronized to match flying hands, she stepped sideways to the left and tapped the basket with the instep of her right foot, inching it along. Within seconds she

352

had methodically cleared that line and stood at the end of it, ready to go on to the next.

Appointed two lines each, the children began to pull the garments off the line, after their mother lifted the pins, working to the music made up of their mother's rhythmic snatches and hummings, the buzzings of flies, and the chirpings of birds. Work suddenly turned to fun as they giggled at the underwear, occasionally dropped a washcloth or hand towel then rushed to shake off any clinging dirt or dried grass. When through, they dashed for the fig tree, scaled it victoriously, and watched their mother below. She soon finished everything except the sheets and called the children down to help fold them.

Giddy with play, the boy and girl ran toward her but were stopped short by the unexpected. Several giant orange monarch butterflies, with listless antennae and wings, dotted the sheets and blankets, clinging drunkenly as though trapped in the fibers. Fascinated, the children watched.

"Whoo-ooo! Whoosh!" The mother crept up behind the sheets and shook them.

Startled, the children jumped and screamed as the limp butterflies showered around them to the ground. Amused, the mother admonished them for being silly. She snatched the sheets and blankets from the line and ordered them about the proper way to fold the bedding.

Glumly, the children followed their sniggering mother inside, arms aching with the heavy baskets. They set the wash on the dining room table and began to separate items to put them neatly away.

Without warning, the mother's shriek pierced their ears and flipped their stomachs. She held up the sheet in arms that trembled. The children stared at the giant orange butterfly, uncertain. Why was mother screaming? What was there to fear? Yet her hand trembled.

Before they could decipher her apparent terror, their mother ran toward them with a "yoooowwwww," as if she were being devoured by the thing trapped in the sheet. The children turned tail and ran. The mother chased them around the table, the boy in the lead, the girl on his heels. The children cried, snotted, and shouted "Mammmma!," suffering an imagined loss of the mother they loved, devoured by giant butterflies, yet running to keep from being likewise devoured, running as she chased them under the table and through the kitchen. The mother laughed as she yowled.

The children managed to put some distance between themselves and their mother, who prolonged the ordeal by pretending to lose ground. The boy and girl tiptoed into their bedroom and hid quietly in the closet, behind the door. Above their pounding hearts they could sense their mother's stealth. Suddenly, she was at the door, trying to get inside. Mother and the giant butterflies eating her alive.

Together, the children clung to the doorknob with all their might, elbows taut, knees bent with the strain, shoes braced to the pine. Their thin brown bodies knocked together in the dark as they struggled to hold the door shut against their mother's powerful pull, their terrified shrieks accompanied by their mother's laughs and taunts, her melodic voice a witch's growl.

"The butterflies are gonna getcha! The butterflies are gonna getcha!"